PRAISE FOR *HAPPY IS THE ONE*

'Gentle, poignant and often witty – a love story that's also about loyalty, friendship, betrayal and forgiveness ... A beautifully written and intelligent novel about working out who and what really matters' Susan Elliot Wright

'Katie Allen raises the bar once more with a novel so full of heart it will pull on your heartstrings and nestle itself into your soul. A truly accomplished and sparkling second novel' Emma Claire Wilson

'Katie Allen's complex, relatable central character responds to tough emotional challenges –a sick elderly parent, a relationship breakup, and job loss – with chaotic indecision. Her storytelling is compassionate and insightful, and the whole novel is imbued with warmth and humour. I raced through it' Gill Paul

'Funny as well as heartbreaking, sharp as well as kind. Katie Allen has somehow created a supremely entertaining novel about the surprises and cruelties life can have in store, peopled with characters who – with all their quirks and particularities – feel never less than real' Polis Loizou

'Heartfelt, heartbreaking but also joyful, this novel should be required reading for our generation. Deftly plotted and populated with memorable characters, I didn't want to say goodbye to it at all. Katie Allen is a master storyteller' Awais Khan

'A moving and emotional story told with warmth and humour. The concept is original, but the challenges the characters face are so relatable ... a book to curl up with and forget about the world' Eleanor Ray

'A funny, heartwarming and unpredictable story of old friendships, new connections and fresh perspectives. I laughed, cried, and loved every minute of the ride with Robin' Penny Haw

'Beautifully written, funny, touching and unpredictable, *Happy is the One* is a whip-smart novel about facing the truth, learning to let go, and the importance of old friendships and new perspectives. I loved Robin and his friends, and their story' Penny Haw

'Truly one of the most moving books I have ever read. I defy all who read it not to laugh out loud and shed a few tears' Sally Boocock

PRAISE FOR KATIE ALLEN

'A heart-wrenching, warm and funny debut' Guardian

'Emotionally engaging, witty, clever and wonderfully satisfying' *Daily Express*

'Simultaneously devastating and hilarious' Clare Allan

'A moving, bittersweet, yet ultimately uplifting and most enjoyable novel' Christina Banach

'A heartbreaking, deeply moving and wonderfully witty tale, which celebrates all it means to be human' Isabelle Broom

'This beautifully written debut is sad, quirky and funny' Madeleine Black

'So affecting. Profoundly sad. Funny. I just loved it' Louise Beech

'Darkly funny, yet poignant and moving ... Rachel's quest to find out if everything happens for a reason is both heartbreaking and heartwarming' Anna Bell

'A triumph ... a book of hope and ambition and making sense of the world, a tale of acting spontaneously, living in the moment and throwing caution to the wind' Isabella May

'A heart-wrenching, soul-lifting read about loss and redemption in unlikely places' Eve Smith

'Read it and weep but also, incredibly, find moments to laugh and to know there is life after death' Julia Hobsbawm

'A memorable, poetic read ... The writing reminded me of Eleanor Oliphant' Becky Fleetwood

Happy is the One

ABOUT THE AUTHOR

Katie Allen was a journalist and columnist at *Guardian* and *Observer*, starting her career as a Reuters correspondent in Berlin and London. Her warmly funny, immensely moving literary debut novel, *Everything Happens for a Reason*, was based on her own devastating experience of stillbirth and was a number-one digital bestseller, with wide critical acclaim. Katie grew up in Warwickshire and now lives in South London with her family.

Follow Katie on Instagram and Threads @monkey_and_miko, on Bluesky @katieallenauthor.bsky.social and her website katieallenauthor.com.

Happy is the One

KATIE ALLEN

ORENDA
BOOKS

Orenda Books
16 Carson Road
West Dulwich
London SE21 8HU
www.orendabooks.co.uk

First published in the United Kingdom by Orenda Books, 2025
Copyright © Katie Allen, 2025

A catalogue record for this book is available from the British Library.

ISBN 978-1-916788-11-4
eISBN 978-1-916788-12-1

Typeset in Garamond by www.typesetter.org.uk

Printed and bound by Clays Ltd, Elcograf S.p.A

For sales and distribution, please contact info@orendabooks.co.uk
or visit *www.orendabooks.co.uk*.

To Ralf,

with thanks for the time passed, and the time yet to come.

And to Naomi,

with thanks for your belief, laughter and wisdom.

1.
Halfway

Here's something I've always known: I will die on a Friday. Just like everyone knows their birthday, I know my last day. It's Friday 29th July, 2061 and I'm almost halfway there. Thirty-seven years behind me, thirty-eight more to go. It's great for planning.

2.
Toffee-free

Nothing, down to the tiniest detail of my angry, empty mouth, is going to plan.

I am eight miles from Eastgate, ten minutes to go, and my toffees have run out. I'm paid to count for a living but I didn't count on this. Shrinkflation: a lazy word for a nefarious practice. Companies keep their prices the same and shrink their products. There's been more of it these last few months. Half a centimetre off my favourite white chocolate, five grams less in a tuna can. And now the toffees. I thought I'd spaced them to last the whole way, but there were two fewer in the bag.

I need something in my mouth. I check every compartment. No chewing gum, no cough drops, no toffee. The final miles of my final journey to my childhood home will be made without toffee.

At the T-junction on Badger Hill, I break into a wistful tongue twister. 'Toffee-free, toffee-free, toffee-free.'

Anything not to think about what awaits me.

3.
Is it always like this?

I'm here by accident. More precisely: accident, spinelessness and a
social worker named Carol Coombs.

It started on Dad's seventy-sixth birthday – a Sunday six weeks
ago.

Gemma bought a cake from the expensive bakery by her
nursery. I told her not to, that neither of us had bothered with
birthday cakes since Mum.

'But this could be his last chance,' she replied.

We sat in Dad's bungalow, windows open to let in the sea air
and to let out the wafts of urine and pine air freshener. It's the
smells that assault me first when I walk in. Then the inescapable
signs of his disease: grab rails around the doors, soiled bedding by
the washing machine, the remains of pureed meals on the side,
packets of tablets that do nothing more than make us feel we're
trying. The full sensory experience is completed by Dad's laboured
breathing, his sudden gasps and the constant noise of daytime TV.

But the birthday boy was on relatively good form that day. As
Gemma opened the cake box, he managed a smile and even said,
'Haaaa ssss.'

'He means "Have some",' I said to Gemma. 'Look how happy
he is you bought a cake.' I don't mean to talk about Dad like he's
not there, but I do.

Gemma served thin slices, and I made the teas. As I stirred
thickener into Dad's, I pondered, as I always do, the mystery of
why food is too lumpy but drinks are too thin. The cake was moist,
an Armagnac-soaked chocolate sponge. I fed him tiny lumps from
the tip of a teaspoon. But it sparked a coughing fit so violent that
Gemma fled to the kitchen. She stayed there for the rest of the
afternoon, 'getting ahead on reports'. She filled pale-yellow sheets
with neat turquoise handwriting and pictures of other people's

paint-splattered children while Dad and I watched an old black-and-white film. I finished his slice of cake and mine.

When the teatime carer arrived, Gemma and I set off back to London, kidding ourselves we'd make something of what remained of the summer evening.

We were minutes from home, crawling over Tower Bridge, when a paramedic called. Dad had banged his head climbing out of bed. He'd pressed his red button and they were taking him in.

'He's not supposed to climb out of bed. He's not supposed to move anywhere without help,' I told the paramedic.

'I get it,' he said.

I dropped Gemma, packed clothes and my laptop and drove back down the motorway.

I was intercepted at the geriatric ward by a nurse I'd met before. They'd checked Dad over, she said, nothing broken 'this time'.

Dad is a repeat offender and I'm his feckless parole officer.

'Sorry,' I mumbled.

He was asleep. A thick dressing covered his cheekbone. I squeezed his hand and got nothing back, and so I crept away to sleep among piles of unwanted things in the bungalow's spare room.

Early the next morning, I was back at the hospital, where a very young doctor told me he had 'great news'. A year or so ago, that would have raised my hopes. 'We've managed to get you a social-worker visit for this afternoon,' the doctor continued.

'That is great news,' I said.

Exhausted from the effort of getting Dad out to the car and into the bungalow, we were asleep when Carol Coombs, the social worker, arrived. 'Robin?' she asked as I opened the door. 'I knocked three times. You should fix the bell.'

'We turn it off,' I explained.

Louder than necessary, she called into the room behind me, 'Hello Kenneth.'

'He prefers Ken,' I said, and she looked at the binder in her arms as if fact-checking me.

She declined a cup of tea, asked for an 'upright chair' and took three pens from her bag. 'Is it always like this?' she asked, rotating her head like an owl.

Her gaze fixed on the kitchen, where chocolate-smeared plates cluttered the table, and underpants and tea towels were heaped on top of the washing machine. Yes, it had mostly – if not always – been like this, I thought. It was Dad's way of living. Disability had nothing to do with it.

Carol ran through a form in her binder, updating and amending answers from the last time someone took an interest in Dad's condition, over a year ago. Was he still on solid foods? Was he still using a wheelchair? Were carers still coming twice a day?

'Four times, now,' I said.

'Dad is seventy-five?'

'Seventy-six,' I said.

'Still widowed?'

'No, there was a resurrection.'

Carol Coombs looked up, clicked her pen and read on. 'Incontinence issues?'

Then came the questions about funds for more carers, what did I know about homes, and did I really understand Dad's condition?

'Does anyone?' I said. It seems to me they do not.

'Because it's only going to get trickier,' said Carol Coombs.

Wrong word. Trickier is the zip on the jeans Gemma bought me. Dad will lose control over every bodily function until he can no longer breathe.

'Harder,' I said. 'You mean harder.'

'OK. Harder. And you need to face up to it. It's dangerous for Dad to live here alone. I'm a bit surprised, if I'm honest.'

I was grasping for words to defend myself with, when Dad made a whining sound he'd never made before. It was a whine that would have been a scream if we could only unmuffle his voice. His good arm jolted forwards, the other remained clasped against his body. The whine faded, and his head slumped, defeated. I looked at him, so trapped already. There was no way we were shoving him in a home.

'I'll move back,' I said. 'We'll move down. I'll do it.'

4.
Turning

And here I am, toffee-freely on my way to Eastgate

I touch the brake as I near The Anchor. No resistance. Brake pedals do that, a few loose millimetres before they get to work. It's a safety feature, to nudge us to act sooner rather than later.

Before the bend, I press the pedal again, too hard this time. The car behind beeps.

I could have gone the long way round. But I need to make the bend ordinary. That's the idea now I live here, to drive this way all the time. And one day, I'll drive this way and won't notice it. And I'll say to Dad, 'I went past Mum's bend today without noticing.' If he could talk, he'd say you can't notice what you didn't notice, but he'll get it.

Gemma says that coming back will do the opposite of what I hope, and that I should 'find someone to talk to.'

'When we're settled,' I told her.

The plan has many steps before 'settled'. First, I'll sort out the spare room in the bungalow. Gemma will join me in four weeks when she's handed over to the new head, packed up our last bits and put our bigger items in storage. Selling my London flat – even after paying off the mortgage – will leave us with a good budget for Eastgate's housing market, and Gemma will look for somewhere to spend it: a place near the bungalow and the beach, and within the catchment area of Eastgate's *outstanding* infants' school. Maybe there'll be something left over for a wedding, if she changes her mind.

She's setting herself a deadline of next summer to find a new job but if all 'goes to plan', she'll be in no position to take it.

She's adapted to this better than I expected – better than me. She tells all our friends it makes sense to move here. What's a few months living with my dad and a couple years more popping by the bungalow in exchange for a family, she says. No one, including me, asks why procreation is geo-specific for her.

My own task is clear and pressing: to find a live-in carer for Dad. The women from the agency now come every few hours, but the cost is unsustainable. And the nights are a problem. Dad has coughing fits; he panics and presses his alarm. Carol Coombs the social worker says a live-in carer will solve all that, 'If you're lucky enough to afford one.'

I asked her to help me find one. 'Not allowed,' she said. 'You'll have to ask around.'

I have no one to ask. I've lost touch with everyone from school, I don't know Dad's neighbours, and the current carers say neither they nor anyone they know would want to live in.

Gemma says I should ask my colleagues for advice. But they're all too young to have sick, widower parents. So am I.

My adverts online and in local newspapers have been a waste of money. The only people who respond won't work weekends. As I've said to them, Dad is also disabled on Saturdays and Sundays. In the meantime, the live-in carer will be me, backed up by visits from agency carers. I'll fit my work around Dad somehow. I've negotiated a remote-working trial with Fiona. Toffee misjudgements aside, they know they can't afford to lose me.

I turn into Cherry Grove and my tyres quieten on the conspicuously smooth road. The estate is the first new development in Eastgate for decades. Dad's is one of its ten or so bungalows, all with wraparound gardens too small for lawnmowers. There's also a care home and an empty plot whose hoarding promises another care home is *Coming Soon*. The roads are named after trees – Dad's is Sycamore Lane – but there are no actual trees. There was an article about it in the *Eastgate Newsletter*. Tree roots, it said, would buckle the pavements and 'impede rising wheelchair use'. The future is single-storeyed, tarmacked and best enjoyed seated.

Now I wish I'd never read about the trees. The air is getting thinner the closer I come to the bungalow. I turn the car around. I need to go to the sea first, look out, breathe in.

It's a Monday in September; there should be loads of parking. But since my last visit to the seafront, Beachway has been painted with double yellow lines. The locals have finally won their battle. One of them has tied a triumphalist cardboard sign to a lamppost:

THE LINES MEAN YOU CAN'T PARK HERE NOW

I park a few streets away and walk back to the beach and along the damp sand as far as the rocks. People here say they protect Eastgate. They use postcard words like 'cove' and 'haven'. In reality, the rocks are black and sharp and enrage the sea. I touch one, turn and walk back the other way to where a river feeds the sea and hems in the other side of this tiny town.

The beach is empty except for a woman and a boy at the water's edge, their trousers rolled up. The boy is almost as tall as her but so skinny it's as if he's only ever grown upwards and not out. He's in school uniform; she is wearing an unnecessary sunhat. Short hair, a bright dyed red, shows under the rim. Gemma will start wearing unnecessary sunhats now we're coastal people. She suits hats, but it will go on into October and then November, and I will have to decide whether to tell her it looks silly.

The red-haired woman turns round. She's waving. She's mistaken me for someone else, probably her husband. She isn't that far away. Can't she see I look nothing like her husband? He'll be taller, most likely blonde and as slim as I used to be. Attractive people here stay so for longer – more time outdoors.

She's waving again. I call to her, 'Sorry! It's not him. I'm not him.' I walk closer.

'Geoff?' She uses her hand to shield her eyes from a sun that is behind her. Finally, she comes close enough. The boy stays back, drawing in the sand with a stick. 'Oh,' she says. 'We were meeting someone.'

'An optician?'

'What?' She un-scrunches her eyes. They're a satisfying green, the kind that goes well with red hair.

'It's not me,' I say. 'I'm not meeting anyone. Just me and the sea.'

'It's on its way out,' she says.

I hesitate. I hate correcting women, but tides are tides. 'Actually, it's on its way in.'

'Oh, turning then. OK,' she says, long *O* sounds.

I catch myself before I say, *You're not from here?* I've been in Eastgate ten minutes and the xenophobia has already set in. Instead, I say, 'Not yet. Not until five thirty-six.'

She looks past me and says, 'There's my appointment coming now.' And she calls to the stocky man in shorts making his way down the steps. 'Geoff, over here.'

Appointment's a funny word, but otherwise her English was flawless. I can't place her accent and after my near slip, it feels wrong to even think about where in Europe she might be from. If only there'd been a good way to ask, a way that told her I'm also an outsider. I should have started by telling her that on a clear day you can see all the way to France from this spot. She definitely wasn't French, but she would have liked to know that.

5.
Start however you can

A small Kia is parked on the drive outside the bungalow. I'll go in and introduce myself in a minute. Or maybe it's a carer I already know. I need to catch the five o'clock news first. Someone's been setting fire to celebrities' cars and the police have promised an update.

The carer emerges as I'm getting out the car. She puts the front door key into the little safe box on the wall and only as she turns around does she notice me. She waves and I wave back.

'Hi, I'm Robin. The son.'

'Hi,' she says. 'Can you move back?'

'Sorry?'

'Your car. I won't get round you.'

'Sorry. Yes.' I get back in, reverse, and she speeds off.

Not the best start, but not my fault. From what I can work out, the carers' shifts are six hours' pay for eight calls of forty-five minutes each. All travel is done on their own time. What's even more sickening about the Staying Put agency is that it's run by my old classmate Paul Rogers, a rugby player who never showed any flair for business studies nor understanding of demographics. Now he's getting rich off the sweet cocktail of ageing homeowners and cheap labour.

'I'm here, Dad,' I announce from the front door. I knock my heels together and sand drops onto the mat.

The TV is playing to itself, quiet but not muted. Dad is in his chair. He's thinner again. The flaps of skin around his neck are like the tree roots Gemma photographed from every angle at Angkor Wat.

'There you are. Journey down was hard work. Need to unload
the car, but let's have a cup of tea first. Have you had the news on?
He burned another one – Porsche, the guy off that morning show,
on his drive, behind a locked gate, down the road from here.' I
babble and worry how much more there is to relay about the car
arsonist. I need more topics. Time spent with Dad is time that
needs scripting. 'Anyway, good to see you, Dad. Exciting new
chapter. And boys' night every night, until Gemma gets here. I was
thinking Chinese later, something with lots of sauce, or put yours
in the blender.' A liquefied version of normal.

The corners of his mouth twitch and I squeeze his hand. It's the
best his face will let him do. I watch him watch the TV and
imagine what he's saying in his head. It'll be about the perfume
advert that's on, something that'd make us both laugh.

His speech has been eroding for years. First, the ends of words
dissolved, then he tripped over the beginnings. Phone calls became
impossible. Talking in person still worked, so I drove down more
often. Then one Sunday, all words were gone. All we had left were
sounds: a hiss for 'yes', a moan for 'no'. Now he has a laminated
card with the alphabet on a grid, and the words YES, NO and
STOP. On good days, he points to the first letter of what he wants.
C for chocolate mousse, L for lemon. Most days he manages a
couple of yes or no questions. But stupidly, the YES and NO boxes
are side by side and when the trembling is bad it's impossible to
know which he means. I'll ask Gemma to bring her laminator and
we'll make a new card, but it'll probably be too late. We're always
one step behind. The grab rails around the back door went in the
week he could no longer stand. The phone with bigger buttons
came when he could no longer talk. The adjustable chair arrived
when he could no longer press buttons.

I go through to the kitchen, turn on the kettle and check my
phone. Gemma must be busy; maybe she's popped to her sister's,
or the shops. She didn't mention anything.

I text her. *Got here safely. Xx* Then another message. *Weird without you.* And finally, a picture of the sea from earlier, edited to bring out the sunshine.

I wash, change and tuck in Dad then go to bed myself. I've set up a baby monitor between his room and mine to listen for coughing and calls for help. I don't trust myself to wake so I've turned the volume to full. I lie still and listen to his uneven breathing and the rumble of his hospital bed. It's designed to pump air around the mattress, shifting his weight to stop him getting sores. How frail we are that we can't even lie still without disintegrating. I roll over.

There's something unsafe about this room – *my* room, I suppose. Cardboard boxes of junk line the walls and bulging bin bags are piled on top of them. In the dark, the bags look like an audience of dirty snowmen waiting for me to fall asleep. I will banish them in the morning. The bungalow has a small loft, and Eastgate has two charity shops, where they'll be grateful for Mum's little china and glass animals. Or maybe I should keep those. Her pupils used to buy them for her at Christmas and the end of summer term. What if they saw them for sale? Probably safe after two and a half decades.

I turn off the monitor when the early carer arrives. When I wake properly an hour or so later, the sun has defied the forecast and it calls me outside. The bags and boxes can wait.

The sunshine and my arrival are having a similar effect on Dad. He's upright in his chair and more alert than he's been for months. The carer has put him in a bright-blue shirt, fresh out the packaging with folds down the front.

'All dressed up, Dad! We need to find you somewhere to go,' I say. 'How about a walk?' I throw my arms out wide and realise again that the more his speech goes, the more inflated my gestures become. I'm turning into a kids' TV presenter. 'Ready to roll?' I nod to the wheelchair.

On any other face, Dad's look – mouth ajar, eyes scanning side to side – would be one of apprehension. But I'm getting better at reading him.

'Great. Let's go.'

I line up the wheelchair and lift him to standing. He's lighter than the last time I tried. But he's less cooperative. My requests – for him to swivel, shuffle, lean back – are all ignored and I have to twist him and place him in the wheelchair. Freezing, the specialist nurse called it, not Dad's fault. I call it buffering, like old web pages.

We set off on a loop around the estate's smooth pavements. It's going well, so we venture onto the bumpier road, towards the sea.

'We should write to the council, Dad,' I say and push faster. 'No point having big paths on the estate, then no pavements here. Makes you feel trapped.' A car swerves past and the wheelchair shakes. 'Madness. Someone's going to get killed on this road.' I stop my monologue. 'Sorry, Dad. Not thinking. Anyway, they need a pavement. We'll write to them.'

He makes a wet puff through his lips to join in, and I squeeze his shoulder.

All the usual ice-cream places on Beachway are closed.

'The sun's out, we've made it this far,' I say. 'What the hell, let's go to the fancy bakers. They do ice-creams, don't they?'

The woman behind the counter watches us struggle backwards through the door.

'We're here for ice-cream,' I say.

'Too early,' she says.

I lean over the counter and whisper, 'He hasn't had one all summer, been housebound.'

She appears unmoved.

'And we need a couple of loaves of sourdough,' I add. That works.

With two ice-cream cones in one hand, I manoeuvre back out the door and across the road. I park the wheelchair looking out to the sea.

The breeze is warm and the beach is empty, except for a man with a large dog. I watch their tug of war with a ball on a rope and wonder if Gemma will change her mind on pets once we have more space.

The ice-cream cone is ideal for Dad. He holds it in his working hand, level with his mouth. I take a photo on my phone, wipe his chin and take another. As I look up, I see the woman from the bakery watching us through the glass door. I wave and she raises one hand.

That night in bed, I stare at the photo. My closing eyes blur away the wheelchair until Dad is floating on the seafront, ice-cream in his hand. The trick to caring is positivity and low expectations. We'll be alright.

On day three, I find the leaflet from Carol the social worker and call the helpline.

A woman called Tanya answers. In a stab at anonymity, I tell her I'm called Rob. I explain that I've moved in with my dad, who was diagnosed six years ago. 'It's pretty advanced,' I say.

'That's tough,' says Tanya. 'How's it going?'

'The practicalities are fine. He's in a bungalow, and it's well adapted, with a wet room, a hospital bed. We have some help from agency carers.'

'Oh Rob, it sounds like you've got him a great set-up,' she says, and I wish I'd used my real name.

'It's just the silence,' I continue. 'I run out of things to say, and he obviously can't say anything. So we go for hours in silence and then we put on the TV, and that's just a noisier silence.'

'That's poetic,' says Tanya, and I wonder if this is a premium-rate call.

'Thanks. It's probably a stupid thing to call about – you're probably there for feeding tubes and grab rails – but I wondered if you have any tips.'

'It comes up a lot, actually. Have you tried reminiscence?' says Tanya.

'Read about it.' It's a lie but I can't ruin things now.

'Well, it works for lots of families. You find an object, maybe a family album, a photo, a nice mug. Then you use that to reminisce. Stories it brings up, shared memories.'

'Show and tell?'

'Show and recall,' says Tanya. 'And don't knock it until you've tried it. You don't know where objects will take you. It's good for you too. Practice at holding onto memories.' I suppose in Tanya's line of work they expect everyone to succumb to dementia.

'Does it have to be about the past?' I ask. 'Can you talk about the object itself? You know, describe the mug?'

'Oh. Is your dad blind?'

'Err. No.'

'I suppose you start however you can. Some people like to make some notes first,' she says.

'Notes. Got it.' There's a pause. 'And thank you. I'll make another donation online.'

'It's free,' says Tanya, and then as if returning to a script, 'but we do rely on donations.'

OBJECT: *Baby book*
DATE: *April 1986*
NOTES: *'Show and recall.' I'm sceptical. A memory cannot be shared. But speaking notes are apparently helpful.*

Mum put this together the year I was born. Why is the cover navy blue and not standard baby blue? So few photos, they were expensive then. Mum is permed and smiling, Dad is not. But he's young, 39. Me in two years.

Mum glued in cards, many with storks. Auntie Joanna (who?), said, 'Hope he's behaving.' And there's my wrist label: Baby Blake, born 7.05am, 11 April 1986, male, 8lb 7oz. 'Larger than average.'

On the next page, she wrote, 'Welcome, Robin Edmund Blake. This was the world when you arrived...' There are newspaper clippings and music charts. ('Spirit in the Sky'. 'The Final Countdown'!)

It was a year of disasters: Space Shuttle Challenger. Chernobyl. Cliff Richard re-releasing 'Living Doll'.

Mum made two double pages on 'Halley's Comet Returns', articles from all the papers, including this, of course:

A MATTER OF LIFE AND DEATH

The return of Halley's Comet calls to mind one of the quirkiest tales of American literary history: the birth and death of the great writer Mark Twain.

Born as Samuel Langhorne Clements as the comet appeared in 1835, Twain predicted he would die when it returned in 1910.

The Huckleberry Finn writer said in 1909: 'I came in with Halley's Comet in 1835. It is coming again next year, and I expect to go out with it. It will be the greatest disappointment of my life if I don't go out with Halley's Comet.'

Twain was spared the disappointment and departed this life as the comet passed in April 1910.

I'll show Dad the picture of Twain, he'll like that. I dressed as him for Book Day once. Mum made a wig of wild white hair from wool. I had a glued-on moustache, a borrowed bow tie and a bit of hosepipe as a cigar.

'Twain, Born with the Comet', says the newspaper caption.

'Like you!' Mum wrote underneath.

Like me.

Notes for Dad: *Maradona's Hand of God. Prince Andrew marries Fergie. Plans for a channel tunnel.*

6.
Face to face

Gemma is a texter. Only a talker if you catch her walking somewhere. But mainly a texter, of messages she says she *didn't mean like that*. I've learned to text first, then call.

My latest such text is unanswered. I call anyway, as announced. It's Gemma's lunchtime. She'll be on her way out for soup and a smoothie. So much liquid.

I speak into her voicemail, a bulging archive of my ill-timed affection. 'Assume everything's fine. I wasn't really complaining when I called last night. Anyway, Dad's having a good day. Loving that new shaver I ordered. He's tired now, so I'm out exploring the joys of Eastgate. Thought I'd try that antiques shop, pick up something for the new place. Our new place. Can you even believe it? Try you later.' I read somewhere that if you smile while leaving messages, they're more effective. A woman coming towards me with a pushchair seems to think the smile is for her. She hurries away from me to the other pavement.

A bitter wind is coming off the sea, carrying wafts of Eastgate's two kinds of fish: rotten and battered. A pink crisp bag stop-starts down the middle of the road like neon tumbleweed. The mother with the pushchair has stopped to talk on her phone, and her toddler is watching the bag's dance, mirroring its movements with his little head. His arms join in and as he lifts them, the toy in his hand drops to the ground. He seems to call to his mother but she talks on then sets off. I call after her, 'Excuse me!' and I run across the road. She speeds up. I grab the toy, a grubby rabbit, and rush after her. 'You dropped your rabbit,' I say when I'm closer. She turns around. From her face, it seems I've gone from predator to hero.

'Oh my God. Thank you so much. He can't sleep without it,' she says.

I hand her the rabbit. 'It's nothing.'

She presses it into her son's hands. 'Say "thank you" to the man for saving Wallaby.'

The toddler stares at me. As far as he's concerned, I'm a stranger who was caught holding Wallaby and then called him Rabbit.

'It's nothing,' I say again, rush back over the road and keep going.

The antiques shop is signposted by a giant wooden hand pointing to behind the cheaper fish shop. The hand's fingers look swollen. They make me think of Danny. He had slim fingers but he was expert at drawing hands. He was in charge of all the hands in our comic books, most of the pictures really. My job was setting out the boxes with a ruler and writing the words into Danny's speech bubbles. Sometimes there would be more boxes on the last page than we had story for, so we'd fill them with adverts for things we made up, like mail-order goldfish and re-usable bubble gum. 'What if that happens to a person,' Danny said once. 'More boxes than story, years with nothing to do?'

'It can't happen to us,' I remember saying. 'Born with the comet, out with the comet.'

Funny what a person remembers, and what they don't. Like how Danny and I lost touch. It was my twenty-third birthday when I realised it had happened, that from one birthday to the next we hadn't been in touch. I don't know why, or who let it happen, but it had been a whole year and the rift was too wide and too shameful to bridge. There've been a couple of times on visits to Eastgate when I thought I saw him from a distance. Each time, I managed to flee unseen. It's only a matter of time before I bump into him now.

The shelves in the antiques shop are full of items that are supposed to look like they've been reclaimed from old railway stations: clocks with quaint names on their faces, posters for seaside trips, mirrors painted with words like *Powder Room*. I pick up a faux iron *Toilets* sign. *Made in China*.

The garden gnomes display is more pleasing. The ones in traditional poses – fishing, hands on hips, gardening – are on the lower shelves. The ones on the higher shelves are mooning, flashing other body parts, or are in pairs, performing what you might call lewd acts. Whatever the gnomes are doing, solo or with a partner, they are all the same price: six pounds each, or two for ten pounds.

I step back for a clearer view and my heel lands on something soft. 'Sorry!' I hold my foot in the air. 'Oh my God, sorry. Are you OK?'

The woman with the red hair wriggles her toes. 'They'll mend.' She smiles and I breathe out too loudly. Slowly, I lower my foot.

Flipflops made sense when I saw her on the beach but now it's almost autumn. Are they her only shoes? Her face shows no signs of serious pain, nor that she remembers me. I notice the tiniest of dents on the side of her nose – a hole for a stud.

'You into little people?' she asks.

'What?'

She points at the lower shelves. 'Garden people, Snow White?'

'Gnomes?'

'Ah, gnomes, yes, couldn't find the word. Gnomes.' She pats one on its pointy hat. 'Are you here for gnomes?'

I reach behind me for something to hold on to. I'm not used to this kind of attention. 'Oh gosh. No. Are *you* into gnomes? I mean, buying a gnome?'

'Here for a gift. Maybe a gnome could work.' She looks up. 'Maybe a naughty gnome.' She winks, and I realise I have been wrong about everything, and that thirty-eight years ahead of schedule, I will die right here.

'Which one would you want?' she asks, eyes locked on the mooning gnome's bum cheeks. I keep my own eyes on her unusually white teeth. She reaches up. If she strokes the varnished bottom, I will definitely die. The gnome is out of her reach. She turns back to me. 'Any favourites?'

'I don't have a garden,' I reply. It's technically true. 'And I better get on.'

'Sure. Nice to see you again.'

'Thanks.' I can feel my face going red.

'And I'll see you again.'

She's undoubtedly right. Eastgate is like a bumper-car ring, with less fun and more road rage.

The sound of her flipflops is uneven as she walks away. My armpits are sticky, things are going on down below and my trousers are all wrong for that. When she pauses, I turn and weave through tables and shelves. Was she flirting? Mocking me? This is why I need a wedding ring. Maybe they sell them here. What was her accent?

I end up in a corner full of things for luring and slaying animals: large hooks with bright feathers, brass gun cartridges, spiked iron contraptions primed to snap on a fox's neck, or a customer's hand. A sign says, *Ladies Hunt Whips*. Another layer of sweat forms over my body. The redhead's voice travels over from the till. She's paying and leaving. Or she's looking for something and they'll send her my way. I edge towards the nearest shelf and hide my face. I'm level with a hunting horn: a dappled copper pipe looped round on itself. Grandad Jim had one like it to call me in from the bottom of the garden. I grab it and take the longest route I can to the till. She's gone. No jokes about feeling horny. I'll live.

In the universe, nothing is ever lost. It merely changes place or state. A guide at a planetarium told me that when I was little.

I think about this cosmic law as I move the bin bags onto my bed and rearrange the boxes along the wall.

My plan was to put the bags in the loft, but the hatch was jammed and I cut my hand going around the edge with a knife.

The next-best option is to flatten as many bags as I can and fit them under my bed. I pile the remaining ones into a tower and wedge them in the corner behind some boxes. It's all just temporary, as is my stay.

When I have more time, I'll open a bag or two and find objects for the reminiscence plan. For now, there's the bottom drawer of my chest. It came from my old bedroom, pre-loaded with memories: cinema tickets, certificates, Mum's napkin ring. Something in there will be suitable for Dad.

It's my third day of home working when an email arrives from Fiona saying she's set up a Zoom call. She'll want to check I'm not overloaded. I'm not. Work is slotting in well with bungalow life. Using observations from my first week with Dad, when I was nominally on leave, I made a schedule that allows for eight hours a day at my screen. I'm getting more done than I ever could in a shared office.

With ten minutes to go to the call, I search for the one shirt I've brought to Eastgate. I find it in my rucksack.

'You have an iron, don't you, Dad?' I call into the lounge.

I go through and Dad points to *NO – YES – NO* on his alphabet grid. Then his finger creeps around the letters to spell something. Maybe 'coffee'. Understandable, we were up twice in the night: once for a coughing fit, once for the loo.

'The carer will be here soon, Dad. Big day at the office for me, call with the boss. You can have these back afterwards.' I place the alphabet grid and his bell on the mantelpiece. 'And we'll have to turn the TV off.'

I give the shirt a good shake and change. I remove three mugs from my bedside table, take the hunting horn from its nail on the wall (Fiona is a vegetarian) and click on her meeting link. I have two minutes left to test out where to sit.

Whichever corner I move to, the bed is in the picture. The only

other people with beds and desks in the same room are students
and convicts. It's a dry day, I could go into our little garden, but
that would be flaunting my beach lifestyle.

I try cross-legged on the bed with the laptop angled upwards
and the window behind me. My face is a dark blob. I'm lying back,
reaching for the curtains when I hear, 'Robin? Robin, what are you
doing?'

I feel for the floor to push myself up to sitting. My head is too
far over the edge of the bed. 'Nothing,' I call towards the laptop
and roll onto my side.

Fiona is leaning towards her screen. 'Are you in bed?'

'Only superficially.' I straighten.

'But you are working today?'

'Of course, of course. Just being silly.'

Fiona frowns. In the box next to her, my own face squirms.

'I can't really see you with the light behind you,' she says.

'Give me a jiffy.' Why is screen me talking like that? I swivel on
the bed. 'Better?'

'I suppose you've heard the rumours,' she says. I haven't but I
nod. 'I'm afraid they're true. We're having to lose ten to fifteen per
cent.'

'Of what?'

'Headcount,' she says.

'OK.'

'We've had to look at costs, what clients are telling us, what they
want, who they want,' she says.

Am I supposed to say something? Make a last-minute plea?

'Robin, I'm afraid you are on our list.' I know which one. 'But
the package we've put together is extremely generous. If you ask
me, things can only get worse, and when they do, the package will
be nothing like as good.'

'Don't you have to do this face to face?'

'This is face to face,' she says.

'In person, I mean.'

'You wanted remote working, Robin.'

I did. I've had two and a half days of it.

7.
Never for how long

Gemma arrives on the last day in September in bright sunshine.

She turned down my offer to drive up to London and collect her, saying she never has the chance to take trains. It gave me more time to clean the bungalow, buy tulips for our bedroom and put on the new sheets I bought. I went for yellow and bought an extra double sheet to cover the wall of boxes. I washed it all in lemon-scented detergent. Orange and red cushions are arriving tomorrow. My newfound capacity for such details is one of the many upsides to losing my job.

We'll start with a picnic. I've bought food from the Marks & Spencer next to the station. It was a two-part job. First, I filled my basket with a mix of indulgent foods like sushi, chopped mango, profiteroles and olives. Then back at the car, squeezing it into the cool bag, I realised she'd think I was showing off, with foods Londoners think they can only get in London. So I went back for scotch eggs and cocktail sausages. Then down one side of the cool bag, I slid the printouts from the estate agent. Four houses, all detached and with gardens, all near the infants' school, three of them within budget.

I'm oddly nervous. As her train pulls in – six minutes late – I check my reflection in a shop window. Four weeks with Dad have rounded my belly and my T-shirt clings where it shouldn't. I'll stay face on when Gemma comes along the platform. This must be the effect of her long absence. Maybe she's feeling the same. Maybe she's wearing a dress.

No dress. No suitcase either. I stretch myself as tall as I can to get her attention. I jab my finger towards the train door, mime carrying heavy cases, mouth, 'Your case, you forgot your case.' Gemma smiles back and pats her shoulder bag. As she crosses the barrier, she says, 'We said I'd get a cab.'

I hold her tight. 'I wanted to see you. And I've got a picnic – for the beach. Start off right.' I squeeze harder. She's finally here.

She pulls away. 'OK.'

I reach to take her bag. 'Are you sure that's everything? Where's your pillow?' She made me take my pillow from London and said she'd bring hers, that we'd invested a lot of money in those memory foam pillows.

'That's everything,' she says.

In the car, I put on the playlist I've prepared. 'I called it *R&G Music*,' I say. 'For—'

'I get it,' says Gemma.

We spread the food on an old raincoat from the boot because I forgot the picnic mat. We sit either side, non-touching distance, Gemma digging her feet into a mound of dry sand. Her toenails are painted cherry red. I'll look online later for cherry-scented foot cream. She finds a clip in her bag and twists her hair into the messy but flattering style that suits her face. She goes back into her bag for sun cream.

'Neither of us likes olives,' she says as she rubs the cream into her neck.

'I do. I'm growing up.' I open the pack, put one in my mouth and leave it whole on my tongue while I reach for a tortilla chip. Mum always had a square of chocolate ready when she gave me medicine. Gemma stares. I bite down. The olive bursts and infuses every one of my tastebuds with bitter poison. I fumble with the lid of the dip, scoop with the tortilla chip and coat my tongue. Gemma smiles. I scoop again. 'These ones taste funny,' I say. 'But the dip's good.'

'What's left of it.'

I know this game. She gives me clues (sentences so short they are barely there, eyes anywhere but on me), I ask what's wrong, she tells me, I apologise and I'm safe again – until my next offence. It's a life on probation, but at least there's a pattern. And twice we've had what her magazines refer to as 'make-up sex'.

Today, I don't feel like apologising. She's clearly hungry, and I've provided a vast picnic.

I throw an olive to a lurking seagull. Its friends arrive and I throw them another. They squawk as they fight over it. I take more olives, tear them into pieces and throw them in different directions until the scrum disentangles.

'This isn't right,' Gemma says over the screeching.

'They eat worse,' I say. 'One time, with my friend Danny, we saw them tear apart a rat. The gulls even picked out—'

'We're eating,' Gemma interrupts, except she isn't.

'Change of subject: there's a cinema opened on the way out of town. Or, I was waiting till later but...' I reach into the cool bag.

'I mean, this isn't right. This.' She holds out her hands over my spread of pomegranate seeds and chocolate almonds, sausages and sushi.

'Do you think you're just too hungry to decide?' I leave the estate-agent printouts in the cool bag.

'I ate on the train,' she says, fiddling with the tiny star on her necklace.

'Why didn't you say?'

'I tried to. You don't listen.'

'I can only listen to the things you say out loud.'

She frowns. 'I was hoping we'd go for a walk.' Her longest sentence yet.

She waits on the beach while I carry the picnic back to the car. I lift it into the boot then I lean against the tailgate and drink a can of flavoured water – I'm a boxer on the ropes, unready to be pinged back into the ring.

We walk along the water's edge, away from the groups with beers, pizzas and illicit barbecues – people celebrating this unusually hot day on the brink of autumn, cramming in pleasures that will soon be out of reach.

Gemma and I did something similar before I left London. We took a day to check off all the things I'd been meaning to do in the nineteen years I'd lived there. We started with oozing raclette sandwiches from Borough Market, eating them in the queue for the Shard's viewing platform. The queue moved fast, we swallowed without chewing and I felt sick in the lift. From seventy-two floors up, London looked bigger, not smaller. Its browns, greens and greys stretched in every direction, like an ugly rug with no edges. I pointed out landmarks with silly names and Gemma second-guessed me. 'She's right,' an older man interrupted. 'That's the Cheesegrater, not the Walkie-Talkie.' Gemma took selfies of us, stopping to wipe my cheek with a tissue. She always carries a full pack of tissues. Every photo had the Thames and its bridges as the backdrop. It was the same for every couple up there, everyone drawn to the water. In the afternoon we continued our homage to the river with a ferry roundtrip to Greenwich. Dinner was seafood on the terrace of a French restaurant that felt distinctly English. The day ended with something that wasn't by Shakespeare at the Globe. All in all, the day met expectations and Eastgate's coastal charm beckoned.

My phone buzzes in my pocket. I struggle one-handed to unwedge it, my shoes in the other hand. An unknown number.

'You should answer,' says Gemma.

It's the estate agent, a slot has opened up to view the place with a double garage, can I and my 'wife' get there in the next half-hour? 'I'll have to let you know,' I say.

'A job?' Gemma asks. I haven't told her I've started the house hunt. She likes surprises.

'On a Saturday?' I reply.

'Depends what sort of job you've been going for. Assuming you've gone for any.'

That's it then. My joblessness, and that I haven't called the man her sister says needs an accountant.

I kick away a breaking wave. 'I told you. I'm taking some time.'

'Why didn't you fight back? You ask for remote to be a carer and they fire you. They can't do that,' she says.

'I'm seeing it as a good thing, a chance to branch out in the time left.'

'And you asked me to give up my job. Have you even done the numbers?'

'Of course I have. We're fine for six months, probably eight. The flat will sell for loads, and life's cheaper here, you'll see.'

'I won't.'

'You will. I'll make you a chart. Supermarkets, eating out, no Tube fares.'

She turns towards the sea. 'I can't live here.'

'This is what you wanted.'

'It's what *you* wanted. You rushed me.'

'But you've quit your job.'

'I couldn't,' she says.

'I don't get it. You're here, aren't you?'

She doesn't answer. She looks down at our feet, now covered by the tide. The whole sandbank we were on is submerged. There are shrieks behind us as a couple rescue flipflops from the water.

Gemma goes to touch my arm but pulls back. 'Quick, we'll get stuck,' she says.

I run behind her, my jeans soaking up the sea. 'Was it something I did wrong? Or didn't do right? What do you need me to do? Tell me. This is where we do things better.'

'It's not an appraisal, Robin,' she shouts back to me.

Out of the water, we slow to a walk. 'Is it the bungalow? The smell?'

Her face contorts as if she might throw up her train sandwich. 'It's no one thing,' she says.

'You can't do this. You said that we'd work at life together. What about halfway? What you said?'

She'd called it my 'urgency'. When I told her about the comet, she said all other men were drifting, but not me. I had 'drive'. We'd just met, our work Christmas parties booked into the same bar and merging as the night went on. Drinks for my party were free, hers were not. We ordered prosecco by the bottle and went home together. It was Christmas 2019; I was forty-five per cent through. I told her that when we met again the next night for dinner.

'Found you just in time,' she said.

And now I'm halfway, and we have a plan together: a family, a house, a life lived fully. All while looking after Dad. In fact, Dad makes it better, or Eastgate does. She said that. The house will be bigger, the family will be happier. Why is she ruining it?

'There's a meteor shower in three weeks,' I say, jogging to catch up with her. 'Orionid. Pieces of the comet. Thought we could bring blankets down here, a flask, a better picnic.'

We're back at the steps up to the road. She sits on the bottom one. Her sandals make a sharp thwack as she slaps them together. 'You know,' she begins. Another thwack. 'I heard someone say that the thing that most draws you to a person, in the end, is the thing that drives you away.' Thwack.

'What does that mean?'

'That some things start out exciting and then…'

'So it *is* one thing. Something's driving you away.'

'Your bloody comet, Robin. I get it, with your mum and everything, but now look what it's done.' She glances back towards the town. 'I can't take it. All this pressure to make all your years perfect. All for you.'

'For both of us. We have to do this together. I'm nothing when you're not here.'

'Oh my God, that's it.' She presses her forehead into her knees.

I sit down next to her and she edges away. Behind us, a shutter clatters. It'll be the chip shop opening for teatime. 'How about some warm food?' I try.

'How many times, Robin? I'm not hungry. I don't want your battered food. I want to go home.'

'OK.' I pull out the car keys.

'*Home* home,' she says. 'I'll get the bus to the station.'

'You said you'd love me forever.'

'I said I loved you. Never for how long.'

She's walking down Beachway before I can get my shoes on.

'Change of plan,' I say to Dad when I return to the bungalow alone.

I unpack what remains of the food. 'Salmon mousse here that might suit you,' I call through to him. 'Bought too—'

A car stops outside. The teatime carer. I can't talk to her. I can't talk to anyone. Why did I tell them Gemma was coming today?

I hide the cool bag under the table and flee through the back door.

I press my back against the wall. If I were a little taller, I'd be able to see up the hill to our old house from here. I climb onto Dad's one garden chair and then onto the tiny table. Still can't see it. I reach up and touch the bungalow's roof. It's flat on this side. I jump off the table, check the carer is nowhere near the kitchen window and lift the chair onto the table. There's a wire running down the wall and I grip it as I climb up from the table onto the chair. My waist is almost level with the edge of the roof. All I have to do is lean forwards. As I do, the chair moves under my feet. I breathe deeply, wait for the shaking to stop. I try again, lunging further, scrambling faster and I'm on the roof.

There it is, the Wallmans Estate. *Going down the Wallmans*, people used to say, even though it was uphill from everywhere else. Grandad Jim said it was named after the builders. A father and two sons. 'The Wallmans. Men who make walls,' he said. 'Now, doesn't that make you happy?' He showed me a local newspaper article to prove it. Much later I learned the term 'nominative determinism' and determined never to get sunburn on my chest.

The estate looks more appealing from the roof. The division of gardens is still nonsensical – some wraparound, some uselessly small – but the houses are all roughly the same shape and size. There's washing on the line at our old house, and in Danny's garden – the one that backs onto ours. His mum's still there, as far as I know. I wonder where he lives now?

A gust of wind nudges me and I sit down, pressing my palms into the roof felt, its texture like sandpaper. I swivel away from the estate and look for the station and the railway tracks towards London. Was I supposed to call her? Find a way to turn her back? My phone's on the side in the kitchen.

OBJECT: *Muffin case*
DATE: *July 2002*
NOTES: *I didn't know I'd kept this. It was in the bottom drawer. A rolled-up paper muffin case. I remember stuffing it in my pocket before I jumped.*

We'd just finished our GCSEs and Danny was going to a party in the dunes. His lower grades and better looks kept him in with the cool kids. He made me go with him.

'I'm not invited,' I said.

'It's not an invitation thing,' he replied. 'And Maddy might be there.'

She was. Maddy from next door. And she'd brought muffins. She got the recipe and the essential ingredient from someone in the sixth form. 'Hash brownies' she called them. When she offered one to me, I said, 'Brownies are square.'

'Like you then,' she said. And that's why I took one, and the first can of cider. And probably why I jumped. That and my 'bloody comet'.

Danny tried to stop me. That I remember too. Or I know because he told me for weeks after. 'You were suicidal,' he'd say.

'I can't have been,' I'd reply.

It started with one of the girls talking about death. We were sitting in a circle. A Nirvana tape was playing. She said, 'Who here will die first?'

'Can't be me,' I said.

'Don't, Robin,' whispered Danny.

'Cocky wanker,' Maddy shouted across the circle.

'You know it can't,' I shouted back. 'Can't die for fifty-nine years. So yeah, not saying it definitely can't be me, but it most probably won't be me.' Danny liked to retell that bit, said I was 'even more Robin' when I drank.

It was his fault things went further. 'Don't tell them, Robin,' he said.

So one of the boys – I think it was Carl, this muscly little bully – said, 'Tell us what?'

And I just kept talking.

'I can't die until the summer of 2061,' I said. 'When Halley's Comet passes again.'

'You're immortal?' said someone brighter than Carl.

'Temporarily immortal,' I said. 'Immortal for another fifty-nine years. And then not.'

'So right now, you can't die?' asked Carl.

'Nope.'

'So you can lie on train tracks, get cut up in pieces and live? Get smashed up in a car crash and walk away?'

'Err, yes. Obviously,' I said.

Carl pointed to the cliffs. 'You can jump off, and nothing?'

'Survived worse. And loads of people jump from there.'

'Not in the dark, Robin,' said Danny. 'You land wrong, you'll kill yourself.'

'Except he can't,' said Carl.

'He gets it,' I said.

Another can of cider and we're there. Me on the rock that juts out over the water, the others behind me.

'Need a push?' says Carl.

Danny shoves him. Carl shoves him back. The others pull them apart.

'For fuck's sake, Robin. Let's go home,' says Danny.

'Yeah, fuck off home,' shouts Carl.

'Nope,' I say and step off the edge.

The fall is fast. Legs straight, I hit the water. Cold stings my skin, salt burns my insides. I feel for the bottom. Nothing. I've shattered my spine, I can't feel anything, never will. That's what I'm thinking: fifty-nine years of paralysis. But I kick my feet and they knock together. And I stretch up my arms and I surface, unscathed. Above me, they're cheering. I pick out Maddy's voice, and then Danny's, swearing and calling my name.

I find a rock and crawl out.

The tide was in. The water was deep. And I can't die.

Notes for Dad: Remember how you used to tell us about you and your friends jumping from those rocks?

8.
Where does it end?

I'm in a maple syrup muddle. I should never have taken the bottle off the shelf. As soon as I did, the other bottles – plastic, slippery and huge – came to life and rearranged themselves. Now they won't yield. I can force my bottle two-thirds of the way in, but no more. I hold it there and take one hand away, then the other. The bottle creeps forwards. If I'm quick, I'll be out of the aisle by the time it hits the ground. But it will split and leave a sticky puddle or crush a passing toddler. There are lots of those in Costco, though it's unclear how they've qualified for membership. I had to bring my certificates to prove I'm part of the select group of professions allowed to join. The toddlers must all be the children of solicitors and doctors.

I place the syrup in my trolley and move on to spreads.

I should be happy. I've always wanted to be in an elite club and now I've found one that gives me access to four-and-a-half-kilo bags of pancake mix. But like every milestone, my Costco membership feels undeserved. I examine a giant jar of Nutella. How is it dentists and accountants deserve access to Nutella at eleven pence a portion, but bus drivers and actors do not?

I leave the Nutella. The maple syrup is already eighteen pence a portion – versus eleven pence per portion of pancakes. A topping that costs 164 per cent of the main food. It's as absurd as when Gemma spent ninety pounds on a dress and 150 pounds on the accompanying 'invisible' underwear.

My target is two pounds a day on food. Part challenge, part necessity until I find a new job. Breakfast alone is coming in at seventy-eight pence, taking into account the pancakes, the frivolous syrup, a tea bag, two tablespoons of long-life milk and a small glass of 'fruit juice drink'. Lunch will have to be pasta or rice, if I can find either in this place that unashamedly calls itself a 'warehouse'.

Hair catches in the hinge as I slide my prescription sunglasses from my head to my nose to read a faraway sign. My normal glasses are missing in the bungalow somewhere.

Between the pasta section and the tills, I pass one of the *Special Offer* piles I promised myself I'd ignore. Ice pops, or *icicles*, as we used to call them. Dad loves them too. His favourites were the orange ones, mine were the blue. If we were lucky, Mum would buy us cola ones. The Costco offer works out at fifteen pence a pop.

I try – and regret – a free sample of lentil chips on the way to the wine section. The selection is surprisingly upmarket and disappointingly pricey, but wine is not in the main food budget.

Before I can succumb to any other 'offers', I head for the tills and choose the one that lines up with the exit. As I heave my sack of basmati rice onto the conveyor belt, I consider telling the checkout lady I'm opening a café, or a foodbank.

But she speaks first. 'Where does it end?'

'Sorry?'

'Where does it end?' She adjusts her facemask with blue fingers, latex gloves tight on her small hands.

'It's ended,' I say and touch my face. 'I stopped wearing one a year ago. We're back to normal.' But she is not. Or maybe it's Costco policy. I look over to the other checkouts, no one else is wearing a mask.

'But where does it end?' Wrinkles fold into more wrinkles as she squints at me, impatient for an answer I can't possibly give. My legs are tired from walking, my shoulders ache from lifting, and I'm getting a headache because of the missing glasses. Now I'm supposed to engage in the politics of public health.

'Who knows?' I try.

'You,' she says, now angry. 'Where's the end?' She gestures to the conveyor belt, my cans and packets. 'Is it all yours?' She shares an eye roll with the customer behind me, a man with a trolley load of sardines and an inflatable paddling pool. A penguin handler, perhaps.

'Oh, there,' I say. 'With the maple syrup. That's mine. But I didn't want it.'

The penguin handler mutters something as he places the *Next Customer* marker behind the syrup. I pack and pay silently.

'Hold on to your receipt,' says the checkout woman and I soon see why. As I try to leave, a man stops me, takes the receipt and counts the contents of my trolley.

'Do you suspect everyone of theft?' I ask him.

'Company policy,' he says, scribbling on the receipt and handing it back to me.

I emerge from strip lights to dusk and drizzle and strain my eyes through my sunglasses to find the car.

I place the maple syrup on the passenger seat, wedge it in with the sack of rice and fasten the seatbelt around them both. Stopping at lights, I look across to my plastic passenger. 'I can't afford you,' I tell it. 'But that's in the past.' Something Gemma says. 'That's in the past.' She uses it on the children at work, after squabbles, tumbles, upsets. She likes those words too. She softens everything for the children.

I switch on the radio for the rest of the drive. The car arsonist has been at it again: one town along the coast, a BMW belonging to someone who was once an antiques expert on TV.

Midlife. Other people indulge in sex in lay-bys or Botox. I have spreadsheets. I started the latest one, *Halfway.xlxs*, a week after Gemma didn't stay. In between laundry cycles, thickening cups of tea and manoeuvring the wheelchair to the bathroom, I predict costs, income and the outlook for my few savings. Late into the night, I run through scenarios. Costs go in, budgets come out. Thirty-eight years left, every day of them accounted for.

Now, perched on the end of my bed, I add a column, *Contingencies*. I list all the ones that come to mind: *Hospital car park*; *Replacement glasses*; *Costco special offers*. I type *Dates* then delete it.

No dates. Were a date to go well, all future budget calculations would be off. Breakfast at seventy-eight pence is bad enough; breakfast at 156 pence a time ruins everything. No night with a woman is worth having just forty-four pence left to spend on lunch and dinner.

I'm working backwards from my TRD: Target Retirement Date. 25th July, 2031, eight years' time. I'll be forty-five and have (ideally *enjoy*) exactly thirty years of retirement, same as everyone else. Of course, *retirement* is an inaccurate description.

Matters are currently complicated by not having a job to retire from. I'm having to run scenarios with varying salaries. It's too soon to say whether the twilight years of my working life will be spent in fintech or a café. Once the spreadsheet is in a suitable state, I'll turn my attention to job applications. And then back to my TRP: Target Retirement Place. Goa tops the list; one website called it 'a place where time slows down'.

The front door opens and closes. I will never get used to people letting themselves in. I fade out the sonata playing on my radio.

Jackie. The loudest of them all. 'Oh Ken, you've slipped right down. Robin not here?'

I close my laptop and sit as still as I can. My bedroom door is ajar and it's too late to close it.

In the next room Jackie continues her one-way conversations with Dad and the TV. 'You're not selling that to anyone with those carpets. You watch, any minute, she'll tell them, illuminate the floors.' (Surely, she means *laminate*.) 'Would you buy that, Ken? Two hundred grand for two rooms, neither of them big enough to swing a rabbit? Who did your lunch call? Why's she put those joggers on you? Robin been shopping?'

Jackie is the loudest but also the best. Part carer, part sniffer dog, she misses nothing.

'Hi Jackie, I didn't hear you.' I pick at a flake of loose paint on my doorframe.

'Really?' Jackie's leaning over Dad, her hips twice the breadth of her patient, the blue tunic of her uniform too short to cover the thinning seat of her jeans. 'You could do these, you know.' She holds up the tiny eye-drop pipette. 'The more he has them, the better.'

'Of course,' I say.

'Want to help give him his dinner?' she asks.

'I'm in the middle of something. A work thing.'

'You're working again? Found something?'

'I work for myself now,' I tell her.

'Your own boss. Lovely. Then you can stop and sit with your dad for his dinner.'

I shuffle into the kitchen hoping I can find somewhere to stash the bigger Costco items I'd left on the side. The cupboards are overrunning with Dad's disease and its symptoms. Plastic beakers and bowls fill the higher shelves. The lower ones are crammed with products from the pharmacy: eye drops and lotions, powders that thicken drinks, liquids that replace foods. The cupboard doors under the sink won't close against the bulging packs of incontinence pants. No space for me.

Jackie walks in as I'm holding the maple syrup. 'Fancy,' she says.

'Not if you buy it in bulk,' I say.

She makes a *pfft* sound like a surfacing whale.

'You haven't seen my glasses, have you?' I ask.

'You keep leaving them on your dad's trolley. Not today, mind.' She scoops dollops of something green from the blender into a bowl and stirs it with a pink plastic spoon she found in Poundland's baby aisle. It came with a matching sippy cup. If Dad could speak, he'd shout at Jackie for choosing the set with cartoon pigs.

'You give him this, while I wash up,' she says and hands me the bowl.

I place the spare chair in front of Dad. 'Let's call this spinach and ricotta coulis. Ready?'

I touch the spoon to his top lip and wait for his mouth to open.

I try brushing the bottom lip, then the top again. Feeding him makes me think of the automatic door on the off licence down the road. You have to come at it from a funny angle, tease it open. We manage four tiny blobs of the green stuff, and I stir the remainder around in the bowl until it looks like less.

'Good work,' I say to Dad and retreat to my room.

I need to work on my spreadsheets. More precisely, I need to find more income. I stare at the savings column until my eyes smart. I lift my gaze to the bright-yellow bedsheet covering the boxes. I jump up and fold it into a neat rectangle. It cost me £19.50 in better times. Thankfully, those better times were within the last twenty-eight days and the sheet has never been used for its intended purpose. Tomorrow, I'll return it.

9.
Not for hunger

I'm in the little Tesco when I see the redhead for the third time. I speak first and wish I hadn't.

'You have shoes,' I say. 'I mean you have nice shoes.'

'Glad you like them,' she says.

She's wearing shiny black brogues with tight jeans turned up to reveal mustard ankle socks and smooth brown skin. I guess she's on the way to work, probably in an office full of graphic designers with flat stomachs and thick hair. I've been sent here by the breakfast carer for paracetamol and cream cheese. They're both things Dad never has but I'm glad of the escape.

'Junk food, I know,' says the redhead, holding up a pack of chocolate-filled pancakes. 'But Teemo loves them.'

'Teemo?' I repeat back.

'T-I-M-O. My son. And I'm Astrid. And...' She's staring at my sunglasses. I push them onto my head.

'Lost my normal ones,' I say. 'I'm not a drug dealer or disgraced celebrity, or disgraced celebrity drug dealer, or…' I can't find my way out of my sentence.

'Or?' she says.

'Or … well none of those.'

'Sure.' She's smiling and still staring. Finally, she asks, 'But you are…?'

'Oh sorry. I'm Robin, like the bird.' I've never said that before.

'You live on that new estate.'

'The one with no trees. Yeah. Sort of. It's my dad's place. I'm looking after him.'

She smiles and tilts her head and it makes me think of a teacher who's pleased with me. 'I know your neighbour, Gwen, pink door,' she says. 'We're in a choir together.'

'Not met her. But I'm not here for long.'

Astrid wriggles her nose. 'I used to say that.'

I step backwards. The little Tesco is not the place for sharing life stories. I need to get to the paracetamol and out.

Astrid nods towards the checkouts. 'Are you paying? I'll walk out with you.'

'I need paracetamol,' I say.

'It's there.' She points to behind me.

I take a pack and will myself to think of more things to buy, but neither my brain nor my budget will allow it. And so I dutifully follow her to the self-checkouts.

We scan and pay side by side. I pace myself so I won't have to work out where to wait for her. Then there's the question of what happens outside. When and how do I get away? I should never have started talking to her.

'I'm going the same way,' she says as we step out onto the pavement.

Are my movements that predictable? 'Cool,' I say, coolly, and we walk.

She rips open the packet of pancakes. 'Tell me your favourite thing about Eastgate and you can have one.'

'Impossible and I'm not hungry.'

'They're not for hunger.' She holds the packet across my chest and I stop.

'The sea, I guess.'

A horn beeps behind us and we turn around. There are shouts between car windows, something about parking like a smackhead. 'And the people, of course,' I say and take a pancake.

We head along the high street and she talks fast, unprompted by me. I wonder if all immigrants have a speech like this one: a summary of where they are from, when they decided to move and why. No one ever wants to know where I'm from or how I've made decisions.

She was born in East Germany but ten years later it was just Germany. In her twenties she did a Masters in Birmingham, something with 'social' in the name, then 'moved around a bit', studied more and 'fell in love in Eastgate'.

'With or in?' I ask.

'Both.'

'I'm not staying,' I say.

'You already said. But you're *from* here, no?'

'Is it obvious?'

'Gwen from choir told me.'

Astrid stops at the corner of Archery Road – Mum and Dad's old road. My old road. She looks over her shoulder. 'This is me. Good to meet you, Robin.'

'Thanks. And thanks for the pancake.'

I speed up for the rest of the walk home. The carer will be waiting for the cream cheese, now warm in my hand. I find myself replaying everything Astrid said, like I snatched an enviable moment with a celebrity or someone in senior management. I've never met anyone like her. She's so direct and unexpected. And she's six years older. If she was ten when Germany reunified, she was born in 1980. I break into a jog. Six years is fourteen per cent of her forty-three years, and sixteen per cent of my thirty-seven. Do I look older to her? Maybe she's selling something. If it's make-up, why wasn't she wearing any? Gemma's magazines have make-up for men, mostly for eye bags. I dab at the spot where Astrid was staring. Puffy, like my middle. If she sold me a diet, I'd do it.

I arrive home a wet, breathless mess. I leave the cream cheese and paracetamol on the kitchen table and slip back outside. I lift the garden chair onto the table and when the wind lulls, I climb up. I stay standing and look across to Archery Road, waiting for my body to remember a time before Astrid.

Dad and I have fallen into a routine that is too meaningless to enjoy and too comfortable to shake off.

If the weather's good, I use the teatime carer's visit to go for a walk. She – it's only once been a man – leaves at 6.00pm and I take over. Dad and I watch TV, interrupted by one or two difficult but manageable bathroom trips, until the bedtime carer comes at 9.00pm. Specifically, we watch old quiz shows on a channel made just for that. I enjoy the idea that whatever is about to happen has already happened. And for Dad, I imagine there's some comfort in going back to an era when he could walk, talk and eat solid food.

While we watch people from the past losing and winning money that has long been spent, I eat toast and drink wine. For Dad, there's ice pops. But he's not happy with any of the flavours I bought.

Tonight, I try orange. Dad pushes it away with his good arm before I can reach his lips.

'They didn't have cola,' I tell him again.

He pushes my arm and rocks his head. He's nodding at my wine glass.

'That can't be safe,' I say.

Dad grunts.

'It's cheap. You'd hate it.'

He bangs his fist on the arm of his chair.

'What about your medicines? Can you even have alcohol?' I ask.

'Sssss,' he hisses for 'yes'.

I read in one of the leaflets that good care is about 'respect and consent'.

'OK.' I take a teaspoon from his trolley and wipe it on a tissue. 'I respect that you want wine.'

I scoop wine from my glass and lift it to his lips. A fraction goes in and the rest drips down his shirt. The bedtime carer will see it. With my luck, it'll be Jackie.

'I'm going to have to get you into a new shirt. Or early pyjamas,' I say.

He bangs his fist again. He moistens his lips with his tongue, a parched animal, pleading for help. I try again with the spoon. More goes in, and more goes down his shirt. His eyes close. The disease is winning again.

'Hang on,' I say. 'There's another way. Your peg.'

That's what the carers call his tube, his *peg*. It's an acronym for something long and medical, but the principle is simple: you fill a syringe with liquid food, or in this case Costco Malbec, and it flows down a thin bendy tube that goes through Dad's skin and into his stomach. The tube's there to supplement the little he takes from a spoon, and one day it will be the only way to feed him. No reason it can't have more than one use.

'What do you think, Dad?' I ask as I come back from the kitchen with a syringe.

'Sssss,' he hisses. Consent.

We give him the equivalent of half a glass and he sleeps through the rest of the shows. I change him into pyjamas before the carer arrives and then help her get him to bed. He doesn't wake me all night.

The next night we do it again. A glass for me, a syringe for him. And the next night. A happiness of sorts for both of us and worth the *Dad* column (£1.47 per day) that I've added to the spreadsheet. I've also had to add eleven pence per day for disappearing slices of bread. I suspect Jackie.

It's been five days since Astrid asked my name and turned off into Archery Road. Since then the weather has been miserable and so has my mood – not helped by a low-level headache brought on by more wine each night.

Today things are clearing. Through the kitchen window, I see shafts of sun pierce the clouds and light up the hilltop behind us. Mum would say that God is 'having a little peek at us'. No doubt He'll regret it.

Not that Dad's my boss, but I ask him for a night off.

'The teatime carer will be here in a minute. She'll set you up with your quizzes,' I say, avoiding his face and any irritation it might be trying to convey. 'I'm going for a late walk. Do me good.' Then in a whisper, 'I'll be back for a nightcap,' and I see his good hand relax.

I take my usual route, with the golf club on my right and badly built little houses on my left, each decorated with signs bearing iterations of the same message: *Don't Park across My Drive.*

Usually, I'd carry on down to the sea, but at the corner of Archery Road, I turn left.

It's my first time here since we moved Dad into the bungalow. As I approach number nineteen, I text Gemma and tell her I'm *confronting things*.

We should talk soon, I add in a second message.

Then I keep my phone in my hand, waiting for her to surprise me.

Little has changed. There are yet more signs for the tourists about parking and litter, a dog that barks through the window of number five and coloured lights in the magnolia tree outside number nine as if the owner died one Christmas and no one has dared nor bothered to remove them.

Just as before, every household on the road has arranged their living the same way. Kitchens at the back, TVs in the front room. More than one is playing *The Simpsons*. I can't imagine Astrid living in any of these houses. How could she, or anyone, let themselves get stuck here? And yet there she is, in the window of number seventeen, Maddy's old house, the house next to our old house, looking out, waiting for something or someone. She waves.

10.
As expected

'Robin! Robin, are you running away?' Astrid's on her doorstep.

I stop. 'It's you.'

'Yep. This is me.' She's all in black. Her face stands out like a floating mask.

'No idea you lived here.' I look around. I'm by the house where the twin girls used to live, the ones who weren't allowed out on weeknights.

'I do … We do,' says Astrid.

She glances down at a cat weaving through her legs. 'Going somewhere?' she asks, maybe of me, maybe the cat. 'Nice evening for it.'

It's hard to know if she has a natural knack for dispelling awkwardness or if it just never occurred to her that someone might stalk her. I move closer and answer her question. 'Round the block.'

She looks puzzled.

'A stroll. A wander,' I add, sounding like someone forty years older. I'm sure that's how she sees me too: an old man walking off his early dinner. Then she holds up one finger on each hand. 'Give me two seconds to find some shoes.'

'Oh, I wasn't…'

She disappears into the house, leaving the front door open enough to see colourless tiles have replaced the dark-red carpet that was there in Maddy's time. It's sixteen years since they moved out. One summer, I came back from university and they'd gone. Dad had known for months and hadn't thought to tell me. Maddy too had been away at university and by then she was irretrievably cool. I texted her to share my surprise and she waited a week to reply, *Times are changin'*. I regret it now but texted back, *A-changin'. Great song though*. I never heard from her again.

Astrid reappears in green trainers and with a large cloth shopping bag. She locks the door and puts the keys under the doormat. 'Timo should be back soon,' she calls to me and any passing criminals.

I wait until she's close and whisper, 'Why don't you just leave the door unlocked if you're going to do that?'

'Because this is better,' she whispers back.

'It's worse,' I say. 'Now someone can take your keys and come back when you least expect it.'

'They'll be disappointed. I don't have anything worth stealing.'

I sense I'm supposed to laugh, so I do. 'You must have something worth stealing. TVs, jewellery, cash?'

'No, no and no,' she says.

'You don't have a TV?'

'Not one worth stealing. Nothing worth much. Conscious choice. That and I've only been there two years.'

Two years. So after we'd moved Dad from Archery Road to the bungalow. 'Autumn 2021?' I ask to be sure.

'The September. Why?'

'Oh, you know, 2021, weird year.'

As we walk, I picture the inside of her house as an empty art gallery with a boxy old TV in one room. I tell her Dad's TV is probably the most expensive thing in the bungalow. She asks what we like to watch, and I worry I'm boring her with my long answer about outdated quiz shows. We follow the road past the primary school and towards the churchyard, where angel heads and crosses poke above the hedge. It's the same walk I used to do with Mum whenever she thought I'd been inside too much.

As we near the main road, I slow to signal to Astrid that the walk's over, that she's released.

'I'll do the loop with you,' she says.

'Oh, don't worry. It'll be dark soon and this road, you know, no pavement, and I'm another ten minutes from here.' Again, I sound like a pensioner, or her dad. Her dad probably is a pensioner. Where is her dad? Where is her son's dad? A light hits me in the eyes.

'We have torches on our phones,' says Astrid, hers aloft.

'Fine,' I say, shielding my face.

'Fine,' she repeats back and bursts out laughing. I do too.

'Sorry, I mean great, not fine. Fine sounded rude, didn't it? Too much time alone with my dad and bad TV.'

Astrid holds up her hand and the torch blinds me again. 'Honestly, it's … fine.' The torch beam dips as she folds over laughing.

'Thanks. But seriously, they should do courses for people like me. Carers. You know, like they do for astronauts when they get back to Earth.'

'They do that?' she asks.

'Yeah. How to walk with gravity, how to eat proper meals, be around people.'

She scans me from top to bottom with the torch. 'You seem OK with gravity.'

'I feel heavier than I should.'

She laughs again, and I sigh, with relief. And suddenly, I'm exhausted. I need to get home. But I'm hungry too.

I do something rash.

'How about fish and chips on the beach?' I ask. 'It *is* Friday.'

She opens her mouth to say something and makes an *aaah* sound. 'It's...' she begins.

'Sorry. Shouldn't have. You don't eat fish. I knew it. Sorry.'

'I love fish. I just need to call Timo, check he's home, can make himself a sandwich.'

Politeness compels me to step away while she calls her son, but then I realise they are speaking German. I learned bad French and even worse Spanish at school. Never thought I'd need German. I hear the word 'sandwich' – with a 'v' sound – and wonder how one would say, 'A man I've barely met is endangering your dinnertime.'

'How old is he?' I ask when she's hung up.

'Thirteen in a couple of months,' she says. 'He's fine. Just angry we're having chips without him. I promised I'd bring some back.'

Astrid leaves me in the chip-shop queue with a ten-pound note and her order while she goes into the little Tesco for what she calls 'weekend things'. I dry my sweating palms on a tissue and give my nose a good blow. The queue is long and we shuffle as one from pavement to shop. Then we stall and I'm stuck holding the door with my foot.

From the front of the queue comes a voice I recognise, ordering four battered sausages and two Diet Cokes. Jackie. As she gathers up her order, I face the door. Her elbow brushes my back as she squeezes past. She's on the phone and I catch the words 'absconds him of all responsibility'.

The fish and chips are warm and reassuringly heavy in my arms as I walk beside Astrid. The setting sun reflects in the little pools left behind by the tides. Out to sea, the fishing boats and even the brutish tankers make neat black silhouettes. The seagulls are fighting over an abandoned burger.

Astrid taps a patch of sand with her foot. 'Dry enough to sit on, wet enough to stay out of the food.' She reaches into her bag, pulls out two more cloth bags and smooths them out on the ground.

I inch my allocated bag away from hers as I sit down.

Astrid rummages again, this time producing two mini bottles of Tesco white wine. She unscrews the top of one, hands it to me, then opens the other. We clink. 'To Fridays,' I say too loud, but she smiles and repeats it back.

I gulp and my throat unclenches. The wine is ice cold and fixes everything it touches: my aching back, my knotted shoulders, the stinging tips of my fingers, raw from being gnawed in front of quiz shows.

The chips are crisper than usual, the batter on the fish is fresher. But the woman behind the counter has yet again skimped on the vinegar.

'Don't have any vinegar in your magic bag, do you?' I ask Astrid.

'I call it my *matryoshka* bag.'

'German for magic?'

'Russian!' she says. 'You know, *matryoshkas*, dolls, with more and more inside them.'

'Oh, Russian dolls! We call them Russian dolls.'

'Who's *we*?'

'Sorry, I mean in English, they're usually called Russian dolls.' I pray the fading light is hiding my flushed cheeks.

'Except they're not an English thing,' says Astrid. 'They're Russian and the Russians call them *matryoshkas*, so do the Germans, *we* Germans.'

There's a pause. It's taken me less than an hour to offend her.

'Sorry. I just wanted to ask about vinegar,' I say.

She laughs. 'You're funny. I thought you might be.'

'What does that mean?'

'You're as expected,' she says.

'I don't get it.'

She tips her head, appraising me. 'I sort of know who you are.'

'What?'

'Well, I heard about you moving here. And you know what it's like here, little Eastgate, big gossips, and there aren't that many people called Robin, are there?'

'True.'

'And my friend Danny, I think you know him, and he's just so awkward about you – about the two of you – and he's in a difficult phase, I thought you could…'

'You know Danny?' I say. 'Danny Thompson?'

'In a sense.' She puts down her chip, wipes her hand and holds it out. 'Meet Mrs Thompson.'

'You're Danny's…' I can't take her hand. I can't touch her. She tricked me. I've been lured to the beach by a siren. I stumble as I stand up. 'If you're married to Danny, what's this?'

'This is dinner on the beach – your idea,' she says.

'But—'

'And we're married but not together. But we're so bad at paperwork, you know? And then there's Timo.' She grins up at me and the scream rising from my stomach lodges in the back of my mouth. Now I'm gagging.

'I can't…' I bend to pick up my food and stumble. My palm lands in the fish batter. I wipe my hand on the wet sand and then on my trousers, and all the time she's watching me. Finally, I'm up again and I'm running.

'Oh, come on,' she calls after me. 'What about dinner?'

At the stretch without pavement I pull out my phone and turn on the torch. God, she acted like she invented the lightbulb. There's a message from Gemma, a reply to my text about confronting my old house:

That's great, Robin. Out with Chloe. Will call in a bit. We do need to talk.

No reply necessary. And she won't be calling 'in a bit'. Nights out with Chloe – Gemma's sexier, sharper doctor friend – always run to Chloe's beat. Dinner in Chinatown, on to several bars, ending in a club around 3.00am. I joined them only once.

'Meet Mrs Thompson.' I say it out loud. I despise dramatic gestures, especially ones set up by women I've met in gnome shops.

I know Danny got married, but Dad never said she was German. I heard about a child too. Can't remember if it was a boy or a girl. I know that's shameful. I hate what's happened, this distance. But I've always supposed it's what he wants. That he grew out of me.

I read Gemma's message again. *We do need to talk*. She's right. There's practical stuff to discuss, like the fact she's living in a flat I own.

Just gone seven. She'll be in the second bar by now, mojito in one hand, the other playing with the silver star on her necklace. 'Oh this?' she'll say. 'It's his star but we're not together.'

I run the rest of the way to the bungalow and arrive aching and desperate for a wee.

'Through in a minute, Dad,' I call from the bathroom.

In the kitchen, I fill a pint glass from the tap, drink half, top it back up.

'Sorry I'm so late, Dad.' I change over to our channel. 'Got carried away on my walk. How about a full glass tonight, make up for it?'

I pour two glasses of wine and fix a clean syringe onto Dad's tube.

'Remind me: I need to try to call Gemma back before we go to bed. Think she's finally sorting a moving date.'

I trickle wine from Dad's glass into the wide, plastic syringe and hold it aloft.

'Remember bathtime, Dad? All those tubes you brought back

from the plant. Loved your bathtimes. I was your apprentice, remember. Bet you're relieved that didn't come to anything – or pissed off.'

Dad's lips try to smile, but so slowly it's impossible to tell which bit amuses him: the memory of bathtimes, the relief I haven't attempted a career in engineering, or how predictable it is that I've gone sweary after downing one glass of red. My 'angry drink', Gemma calls it. Time to build up my tolerance. Dad, on the other hand, is unaffected by a glass of wine straight to the stomach.

The next morning, I shuffle, sore and barely rested, into the kitchen and find an envelope awaiting me. Large writing: *ROBIN*. The usual breakfast carer – Vicky, Nicky or something with icky – is shy, but if she's got a complaint, she seems the type to tell her bosses, not write a letter.

Or maybe it's not a complaint. She does this face whenever I come out of my room, like she's surprised I'm here, maybe even happy. A couple of times, I've noticed her hands shaking when I get near.

I sit at the table and stare at the envelope without touching it. I'm no expert, but it does have the look of a love letter. Thick paper, proper ink, wildly varying character sizes in my name, with the final N bigger than the initial R.

I'm in an impossible position – one not covered in any of the leaflets. I'll have to call Paul 'Rugger' Rogers at the agency, except Paul will flat out refuse to believe it.

Or the envelope could go missing. I slide it under the pile of free newspapers, then take a loaf and the juice carton back to my room.

11.
When the moon has set

'You made it sound like it was urgent,' says Gemma.

I've called her from my Saturday morning walk, out of Eastgate and through the fields.

'You know I have my class,' she continues.

'What about the flat? You ... Ahh—' My foot slides on something and I catch myself on a tree.

'What now?' asks Gemma, and before I can mention the sheep poo, she snaps, 'We're starting,' and she's gone.

By class she means her women-only kickboxing in the park with an Antipodean man. I observed them from afar once. They punch pads while the Antipodean shouts 'harder'. No one kicks anyone. When I asked Gemma about it, she said it was to do with pelvic floors so I left it there.

I wipe the sole of my trainer back and forth on the grass. It's clean but I wipe more. I can't stop. It's maddening being in conflict.

The walk is pleasantly lonely, but the landscape is inadequate.

The hills around Eastgate are hardly hills at all. They are sloping fields, and if you do find the top of one, there is no reward: in one direction, a grey town pressed up against a grey sea; in the other, more little towns dotted between fields that autumn has faded to a patchwork of browns and beige.

Locals talk about wildlife, but sheep aren't wildlife. There is birdsong, of course. One of the first things Jackie ever said to me was, 'Don't get birdsong in London.' Not true, but also not worth arguing about. I stop and tilt my head to the treetops. I hear three or four different calls, and above them all, seagull screeches.

According to Google Maps, if I keep walking north, I'll reach London by 10.00am tomorrow. Twenty-two hours on foot. Nothing compared with what the Norman soldiers would have covered when they started from these same fields. They understood the comet, the change it augured. 'What a word,' I say out loud to the spray-painted sheep that has been watching me for some time. 'Augured.'

Twenty-two hours to London, or an hour back to the bungalow.

The envelope has wriggled free and is back in the middle of the kitchen table.

I call through to the lounge. 'Was it Jackie did the lunch visit, Dad? She say anything? Or the other one?'

No reply, of course.

If it's as I fear, I'll write back to the breakfast carer and tell her about Gemma. I flip over the envelope. She's tucked the flap in – spared me her saliva. Inside is an orange card.

> Robin,
> That went badly. My intention was to help. Can we try again?
> Do something together with Danny?
> You know where I live. Or my number's on the back.
> Welcome (back) to Eastgate,
> Astrid x

'You!' I shout.

I take the card and its envelope to my room and stuff it under the socks in my top drawer. As I slide the drawer shut, it jams. Everything in this damn bungalow jams. I tug the drawer loose, re-angle it, push, and slam. I scream. My fingers are trapped. I grip the tiny knob with my left hand, lean back and I'm on the floor. My fingers are free but it's as if I've cut a tourniquet and the pain is spreading through my whole hand.

I suck my fingers, tasting for blood. I feel for damage with my tongue. If I look at them, I'll vomit or pass out, or both. That's how people choke and die.

My eyes are wet with the pain. That's not true. I'm sobbing. I crawl onto my bed, lie on my side. I press my face into my stupid memory-foam pillow and wrap it around my ears to block out the ringing from Dad's bell in the lounge. He'll have to wait. For once, he'll have to wait. I tug the duvet out from under me and throw it over my head. The crying takes on a rhythm, waves rising and crashing. I let them rock me back and forth.

Eventually, they ebb and leave me shivering and sniffing. Mum used to say a cry does you good, but I've never felt so emptied out.

My fingers are numb. I tighten my teeth around them and the pain returns. Under the bedside light, they are red and puffy – the bruising will show later. It hurts to bend them. I need to run them under cold water.

As I stand up, I hear the front door. I dab at my face with my T-shirt and wait, listening.

It's Jackie. 'Only me, Ken,' she says. 'Was at the pharmacy and they had your formula back in, and I'm not with you until…' Her voice falls away as she goes into the kitchen then it rises again as she calls through to Dad. 'Robin not about? He see that note that came for him?'

With my good hand, I grip my bedroom-door handle.

'Oh Ken, not again.' She's in the lounge now. 'Let's get you changed. Bathroom first, see if there's more before we get the best trousers out.'

That's what the bell was about then. I press my back against the door and slide down it to the floor. I don't know if I can do this. I'm almost certain I can't do this. The bell, the carers, the washing, the toilet trips, the nights. Does Dad not realise I have my own problems? Broken fingers, women who want me, women who don't.

It's going to take Jackie a good twenty minutes to clean and change Dad. Except it's not her job, not this time. She's not on a call. I check the mirror, blink hard until the worst of the red is gone, wipe my cheeks with my sleeve and smile like I'm happy to take over.

We're woken by the teatime carer, Paula. I've stretched out on the sofa and had the sleep I so badly needed. As I straighten up, I relive snatches of dreams invaded by football commentators and Formula 1 cars.

'Sorry, bad night. Catching up,' I say.

I like Paula. She only comes on weekends but she knows Dad's routines as well as the others and always makes an extra cup of tea for me.

'You look washed out,' she says.

I rub my face. My injured fingers are still tender. 'Washed out?' I say. 'Accurate. I like that.'

'I'll get you a tea,' she says.

'That'll fix it.'

She looks hurt.

'Oh God,' I say. 'That wasn't sarcastic. It will fix it. Fixes everything. Especially when someone else makes it.'

'Coming up then,' she says, and hurries into the kitchen, saving herself from me, and me from myself.

I sip my tea and spoon Dad's thickened cup into him while Paula defrosts and warms his puree. When she's ready to feed him, I tell her I need to do a bit of work and I retreat to my room.

I tug open the top drawer with my good hand.

Is it normal to own orange card? That's the difference between us: I live in Dad's spare room; she has a home with accumulated stationery. None of it worth stealing though, apparently. And she's used two types of pen. Her number is written in thick marker.

I don't have to call. I can text. I type slowly:

Thanks for the card. Sorry I had to go.

Then in another message: *This is Robin.*

My phone rings in my hand. I drop it onto the bed. I tap the screen and say 'Hi?', wishing I'd waited a few more rings, or not answered.

'It's Astrid.'

'I know.'

'You're still grumpy?' she says.

I wait for more. It doesn't come. 'I thought I was funny,' I say.

'You can be more than one thing.'

'Kind of you to allow that.'

'So what do you think?' she says, as if someone has fast-forwarded the chunk of the conversation where we apologise to each other.

'About?' I ask.

'What I said.'

'Oh, on the orange card?' I turn over her note.

'Err, yes. The orange card. About meeting up? Something with Danny?'

'I didn't know you meant now,' I say.

'Why not? Unless it's too much for you.'

I fall back onto the bed. 'Why would it be too much? I'd love to see Danny. Been meaning to call him, but you know, moving, my dad, work.'

'Great then,' says Astrid. 'When's good? Where?'

I go to the window and hold my injured fingers against the cold glass. 'I'm not really a pub person.'

'My house then?'

It sounds like a trap. Her house is no longer an empty art gallery. It's a cell without doors. The walls are orange.

'Now I feel like I'm pushing you again,' she says, and sips something.

I lean my forehead against the window. 'There is this one idea I have … Maybe just for Danny.'

'Oh,' she says, finally out of words.

'You said this was to get Danny and me together.'

'What's the thing? Your idea?' she asks.

'It's a bit last minute.'

Astrid sighs. 'Fine, give it a few days. No one's rushing you.'

'It's just they are.'

'Who's *they*?' Astrid asks. 'Who's rushing you?'

'Oh, on this? The calendar, I guess. Time. And place. Or position really.'

'I'm lost,' she says, with the irritation of someone who rarely is.

'Sorry. It's a meteor shower and the best night's tonight. After midnight, when the moon has set.'

'Does the moon set?' she asks.

I explain as best as I can over the phone and then tell her more about the Orionid meteor shower, how our atmosphere collides with the debris left behind when Halley's Comet passed this way. When I name my comet, I try to keep my voice casual, but fail. 'Some people say it the other way round Comet Halley,' I babble on. 'Anyway, I was going to take a picnic blanket up to the fields, out of the light. Maybe a pack of biscuits and a flask.'

'Let me bring the biscuits,' she says.

'What?'

'I'll bring the biscuits. And Danny,' she says.

'But your son? We'd be out past midnight.'

'Timo spends the night with my mother-in-law on Saturday. Granny Bee.'

'That's brilliant,' I say. 'For Timo, I mean.'

'She asked about you,' Astrid says, and my throat tightens. Drifting away from Danny was organic and mutual. But abandoning Bee was callous. After the crash, I spent most weekends at hers. The first summer, she and Danny took me on holiday to the Isle of Wight, where Bee said yes to everything: sleeping outside, picnics for every meal and swimming in the dark.

'Keep meaning to pop by,' I say to Astrid. 'But, you know.'

'So we'll come to you at eleven? Danny should be finished by then. Favourite biscuits?' Astrid asks.

'I'll come to you – it's on the way. If you're sure it's your kind of thing. Could end up being cloudy, forecast's not great, might rain. And Danny might not want—'

'It'll be perfect, when the moon has set. Favourite biscuits?'

'Shortbread,' I reply, which is a lie, but Jammie Dodgers are both childish and expensive.

OBJECT: *KitKat wrapper*
DATE: *1996*
NOTES: *Danny had a KitKat in his lunchbox every day. It was the only biscuit he liked. Fridays, we'd stop at the newsagents on the way home and he'd get an extra KitKat. Double KitKat Day. I'd pick a different thing each week and take ages deciding. It wound Danny up; he always needed the loo on the way home. At some point, we decided I'd work my way along the newsagents' display, row by row. I had variations on the Yorkie bar three weeks running. Danny said I should skip some things, but a system is a system and without it, I'd never have discovered Munchies.*

Danny was passionate about KitKats: the way the logo pressed into the foil wrapper when he ran his fingertip over it, the way the fingers broke apart so perfectly when he snapped them next to his ear, the way the chocolate came away from the wafer with one scrape of his incisors. 'Do you think they study teeth thickness?' he'd say.

There was another reason he ate so many. A story had worked its way through the lunch hall, into the playground and down the year groups to us: a boy in 6A had bitten into a KitKat only to discover it was solid chocolate. Each day, new details reached us. The boy had written to the factory and they'd offered him a lifetime supply of KitKats. His mum was selling the story to a newspaper. His teacher said he should tell Newsround. *His dad knew someone who knew someone at the BBC, and he was going to be awarded a* Blue Peter *badge. After that, every KitKat Danny opened, he'd kiss it first for good luck. 'I need this,' he'd say.*

And then years later we were walking home from our usual Friday newsagents stop, Danny bit into the tip of the first finger, grabbed my arm and held his KitKat up to my eyes.

'They've lined the wafer up wrong,' I said. Danny was always too quick to get excited about things.

He bit into it again. No wafer.

He insisted I take the second finger. He wrapped his bitten one in the foil and I slid my whole one inside the paper wrapper. He called his 'solid chocolate'; I called mine 'waferless'.

We agreed to save them and bring them into school on the Monday. No one cared. Most people had forgotten the legend of the boy with the solid KitKat. Those who did remember said there was nothing special about it happening a second time. He was Neil Armstrong; we were the crew of Apollo 12.

So we ate them. But I kept the wrapper, this wrapper. It's been in my bottom drawer for twenty-seven years.

Notes for Dad: *KitKats used to be bigger.*

12.
Not exactly ejaculation

I choose my opening words on the way over then mess them up.

'Great to meet you again. I mean see you. Again.' I hold out a hand to Danny. He seems to have grown taller still in our years apart. He wipes his palm on his jeans and shakes my hand, holding on for too long.

We're on Astrid's doorstep. Danny arrived seconds ahead of me, on a bike with red and white flashing lights. He sped past on the uphill stretch of Archery Road. I'm out of breath and he's not.

'Oh my God! Look at you like businessmen.' Astrid appears with a bundle of woollen things under one arm and the other outstretched, in mockery of our handshake.

Danny weaves past her and lifts his bike into her hall. He takes off his helmet, revealing a bald patch that starts at the front and spreads to the back. It looks about halfway through its advance, or is it the hair that's in retreat? His face is as perfect as ever. If anything, it suits him better now. 'A face for catalogues,' Mum used to say. She'd touch Danny's cheekbones and I'd flinch on his behalf.

'Anyone need to go before we go?' Astrid asks, and chuckles at her wordplay.

Finally, Danny speaks. 'I will. And I'll grab something to eat. Starving.' His voice has changed. I will him to say more so I can work out how.

Astrid taps her rucksack. 'No need. Packed sandwiches for us. You can eat them on the way if you can't wait.' She reads my face and adds, 'Plenty for you too.'

Gemma has a rule about everyone making their own sandwiches and packing their own bags. It's the Montessori way.

We walk side by side towards the fields. The streetlamps catch the top of Danny's head. He talks and talks, as if scared to stop, recounting my adult life to Astrid like he's giving my eulogy. Either he's read up on LinkedIn for this or Dad relayed various milestones to Danny's mum in the years when he could still speak. He knows about Gemma, about my accountancy exams, my prize, my job.

'Always the cleverest,' he says. 'Making big money in London.' He's angry – I think at everything, but particularly at me. I don't know what I've done other than to have a salary.

'Not that big,' I say.

'You bought a flat right in the centre,' he says, and I wonder again how long it will take to get used to his deeper voice.

We're cutting across playing fields now, the streetlamps far behind us. Astrid stops, takes a head torch from her rucksack, sets off again. We follow behind her like ducklings, me last.

After a while, I say, 'My flat's more north than central and it's really small, like a post box.'

'Ha!' says Danny, tone mean as ever.

'I meant phone box.'

'That why you move back here?' he asks.

We reach the wide metal gate to the fields and there's a thud as Astrid drops her bag. 'My God, Danny. He moved back because of his dad.' She climbs onto the gate and Danny holds it steady for her, the way he used to do for me when we were children and fights would only last a few words.

'Nicely done,' I say to Astrid and hand her bag over the gate. I go next.

'Who's with your dad now?' says Danny, letting go of the gate just as I swing my leg over the top. I grab on with my injured hand and wince out loud.

'Danny!' Astrid reaches for the gate, steadies it. With her other hand she touches my thigh in the dark. Maybe by mistake, maybe for comfort.

'I'm concerned,' says Danny. 'You said his dad was dying.'

'He's not dying, as such,' I say. 'Just won't get better.'

'And he's OK on his own?' Danny jumps from the top of the gate.

'Really, Danny,' says Astrid. 'Why are you being so hostile?'

'How is this hostile? You said you wanted me to talk to him.'

There it is. He thinks this is normal. That I deserve it. I don't know what I've done, but I know I can't take this. I tried and now I can leave, knowing I was right all along, we were supposed to drift apart.

I step back onto the gate. 'Know what? You're right. I shouldn't leave Dad.'

Astrid touches my arm. 'Oh, come on, Robin. I've packed loads of food, and I read up on the meteors, even the moon. This is my first…' she pauses '…celestial event.' And she walks on without waiting for my reply.

'And I bloody rushed back from work,' Danny snaps, and jogs after her.

A gust of wind shakes the gate and I climb off, still on their side. I should go but I stand there holding my throbbing fingers against the cold metal and watching the beam from Astrid's head torch bob up and down. And then something pushes me, like someone telling me I can't let him win.

'Why do you just call it work?' I shout. 'Why are you so weird about it? You a gigolo? Drug dealer? Oh my God, you're back at the chicken farm, aren't you?' I stop. I always go too far. The chicken farm is too far. Danny worked there the summer after our GCSEs. He said it was free-range eggs, back when free-range eggs were only for hippies and rich people. Then it was on the news for animal cruelty. There was hidden camera footage. Danny told everyone he'd worked in the office, that he hadn't seen anything.

'Sorry,' I shout after him.

Maybe he didn't hear any of it. Astrid's torch bobs on as they walk into the distance. 'So I'm going then,' I call, louder. 'You know where to go to watch them? Top field.'

Danny shouts back. 'It's not the fucking egg farm. They shut it down, you idiot.'

Lured in, I walk towards him. 'Well, what do you do?' I try to sound interested, not nasty, but it's hard to modulate over the distance.

'Typical Robin; we're all just a job.' Danny's lit from behind by Astrid's torch. His angry silhouette turns on me. 'Used to be A-levels, you were physics or nothing.' He swings his arms up and down for physics and spins his hands for nothing. 'Then it was all university drinking clubs,' he goes on – drinking gesture, I guess, but looks like blow job. 'Now it's big City jobs.' Swivelling hips like an X-rated shadow puppet. He yells and writhes, and it seems there is still so much pent up inside his lanky frame. I step backwards but know I shouldn't; I'm guessing Astrid is as scared as I am. Only a coward would leave her with him.

'You're so bloody narrow, Robin, always were. Narrow,' Danny continues, palms together, elbows poking out.

He pauses and I move closer. 'I was just asking what you are.'

'I'm a father. Not that you ever bothered to find out. Have been for twelve years.'

'Basically thirteen,' says Astrid, then louder, 'Robin, when are your meteors? We should get to your spot.'

'They're not my meteors,' I say.

'Whoever's then, but these are your sandwiches and they're making my bag weigh a ton, so you have to come along and eat them.'

'I can carry it,' I say.

'Ah, but you can't do that if you abandon us,' says Astrid and she holds the rucksack out towards me. 'And only you know the way.'

'Seriously?' says Danny. 'It's a field and his meteors are in the sky. We lie down and look up.' He drops to the ground as he speaks.

'Actually, there is a best spot,' I say. 'Furthest from the light pollution, less sheep poo.'

'Oh God.' Danny jumps up.

'And shorter grass for the picnic mat,' I continue. 'Ah … Was I supposed to bring the picnic mat?'

'All in here.' Astrid holds out her bag again.

'Fine.' I take it and follow her, leaving Danny patting down his clothes.

My spot is smaller than I remember and the trees and hedgerow are thicker, hemming us in on two sides. When I earmarked this patch of grass this morning, I imagined lying with my head towards the open field with space to spread out, alone. And here I am with Astrid being relentlessly cheerful and Danny being irrationally petulant in a voice that doesn't suit him.

At least the sheep have moved away and settled down for the night, their bleats distant and sporadic. On my advice, Astrid uses her torch to check for droppings before laying out her picnic blanket, also too small.

'I took a chance,' says Astrid, handing me a package wrapped in baking paper. 'I figured you eat most things.' I pull in my stomach.

After two long walks in one day and weeks of cheap white bread, Astrid's sandwich tastes phenomenal. She's filled chunks of baguette with ham, a mature cheese, gherkins, mustard and maybe mayonnaise. I feel churlish for noticing the tomato slices are unsalted.

We eat in silence until Astrid asks with a full mouth, 'So where do we look?'

Danny snorts. 'Up!'

I finish chewing. 'The key is dark. You need to turn off your torch, when you're ready, and Danny needs to stop looking at his phone. It'll take a while for our eyes to adjust. Then, the more sky you can see the better. Shuffle away from the hedge a bit.'

She switches off her torch, lies on her back and wriggles around. 'Is this right?'

'It looks good to me,' I say.

'I need to look for Orion?' she asks. She really has read up.

'Not necessarily,' I say. 'They will be all over the sky, if we're lucky. Orion is the radiant – the place they appear to fly away from.' I brace for Danny to scoff at 'radiant', but he's still on his phone.

'Are we too early?' Astrid asks after a while.

'Maybe.' I want to tell her to be patient. I also want to lie down. But I can't work out where. Astrid is along one edge of the picnic mat. Danny is on the edge opposite her. If I stretch out, I'll be close to both of them.

'In the photos, they were all over the sky at once,' says Astrid.

'Those will have been long exposure,' I say. 'It looks like things are happening at the same time, when really what you're seeing is some meteor trails beginning as others have already ended, and they just all show up on the same photo.'

'Many moments squished into one,' she says.

'In a sense,' I reply.

We're quiet. Danny's breathing is slow and sleepy.

Many moments squished into one. I tip back my head and imagine painting my own long-exposure picture onto the night sky, all the decisions and accidents that have brought me to this tiny picnic mat. Dad's fall, the pushy social worker, Gemma without a suitcase, Astrid and the gnomes.

My neck aches from looking up. I let go of my knees and ease back onto my elbows, stretching my feet out inch by inch until I'm fully lying down, my feet by Astrid's feet and my head by Danny's feet. Together we make a U shape.

'It's not exactly ejaculation.'

Astrid's words startle me. 'What?'

'Ejaculation. Didn't the Romans say the meteor showers were

the gods ejaculating on the fields? Or has it worn off with age, like all ej—'

'That's not these,' I interrupt. 'They said that about the Perseids, in the summer.'

'Are they better?' she asks.

'Anything's better than this,' mumbles Danny.

I take a long breath. 'We need to wait. They haven't…' I can't finish, the word *peaked* now impossible to use. 'Just keep looking up.'

My eyes move from one dark patch to another, willing distant specks of dust to collide with our atmosphere. *Pressure to perform*? I say in my head. It was an advert on the Tube that stalked me for months.

'There's one!' Danny cries out. 'And another, same place. You guys see them?' His sulk is broken.

'Where?' asks Astrid.

'Over to the right – your right,' says Danny.

We wait.

One streak, then another, brighter, wider, longer.

'Yes,' Astrid whispers.

'Me too,' I whisper back.

'Yep,' says Danny.

Then nothing. The sky and the fields fall silent. No breeze, no birdsong.

'Baaaah.'

I scream. Astrid screams.

Another 'Baaaah', right next to us.

'Jesus Christ!' shouts Danny.

Astrid shrieks, snorts, shrieks again. Her laughter sounds painful. Danny is laughing too and saying, 'Sneaky bastard, that sneaky bastard.' I press my face into my hands. I'm still trembling from the *baaaah* and now I can't stop laughing. I'm folded over.

Astrid's trying to talk between the snorts and tears. She takes run-up after run-up, 'Do you think he … Do you think he…' She gasps for air.

'He what?' I manage.

'Do you think he's cross, cross about...' She's crying now. So am I. Danny's casting around with the torch on his phone. '... About being ejaculated on?' Astrid gets out before shrieking again.

Danny's torch lands on the sheep. It stares back. 'That's a yes,' says Danny, the beam shaking with his laughter.

'It's too much,' wails Astrid. 'I need to pee.'

She staggers off towards the trees, head torch on.

Laughter still in his voice, Danny says, 'I'm a driver.'

'A what?'

'A driver. Earlier, you asked what I am. I'm a driver, minicabs. And a rider, on my bike, Deliveroo.'

'Oh.'

'I move stuff and people. Food I can't afford and people who are rude to me.'

We're quiet.

Then I say, 'I lost my job. And my girlfriend left me.'

'Because you lost your job?'

'It's unclear. We fell out, but I don't know what about.'

'Oh, Robin.'

'What's that mean?'

'Nothing. It's ... You're you, like you always were. I like that,' he says.

'Thanks,' I say, not quite ready to believe he means it. 'And you look younger than you should by now. It's like your voice has aged but the rest of you hasn't. Guess it's all the cycling.'

'And the sea air.' Danny takes a big sniff.

'My girlfriend likes the sea air. Said she did.'

'God, Robin, I'm sorry. And I'm sorry I was being a dick. It's...'

'Yeah.'

'You disappeared,' he says. 'When you went to uni, you disappeared, like Eastgate didn't exist anymore, like none of us existed.'

'I got caught up in things.'

'Shit! Drugs? You?'

'What? No. Econometrics. Studying.'

'Right,' he says.

'But I'm sorry. And I'm sorry you hate your job.'

'Don't hate it. OK, I do. But it's only temporary.'

Astrid returns, whistling. 'Did I miss any meteors?' she asks.

'There'll be more,' I say.

We lie down in our previous spots and Astrid passes around a pack of shortbread then a bar of dark chocolate. Every distant bleat from the sheep makes us laugh, Danny the loudest. 'He's coming back for you, A,' he says.

I figure there's no other polite way to shorten Astrid.

There are more meteors. Not many, but enough.

When the cold gets too much, we pack up and walk home, faster, lighter and sipping from the flask of hot chocolate that Astrid has only now remembered in her rucksack.

'Robin, that was exceptional,' she says as we reach her front door.

'All the sky's doing,' I say, and hand back her bag.

As I turn to go, Danny follows her in, to retrieve his bike, I suppose. I glance back as I walk down the hill but don't see him leave again.

At the end of her road, I stop and text her:

Your sandwich was exceptional too.

13.
A girl's name

'Tea?'

'Sorry?' I shout back from the bathroom.

'Making tea. Want one?' says Jackie, voice louder, as if she's moved right up against the door.

I clench. 'No. Thank you.'

I'm out of rhythm, and Jackie is making it worse. Unable to fall asleep after the *exceptional* meteor shower, I turned off my alarm, and when I woke, it was almost ten, time for me to take over with Dad. Now Jackie's here and I can finally have some of my own time in the bathroom.

I unclench and look around for something to read. There's dense text on the moisturiser the carers slather over Dad before bed. I reach it down and learn it's highly flammable. There are long warnings about saturated nightwear, unwashed pillowcases and naked flames. We've turned Dad into a detonator. My insides loosen and my rhythm is restored. Reading always helps in one way or another. In the bathroom in London, I kept a basket of autobiographies. Gemma called them 'unhygienic and unsavoury'. For all her unfinished sentences, she always uses more words than necessary to attack me.

I'm still thinking about the chances of there being naked flames in Dad's bedroom when I see something that shouldn't be there. Or maybe it's a trick of the light. I'm thirty-seven years, six months and eleven days old. I have no data to go off, but it's fair to estimate that what I'm looking at is there at least seven years too early. I tousle the hairs and look again. Still there. Still grey. My first grey pube.

My fingers are oily from the moisturiser tub. I wipe them with toilet paper, grip and tug. The hair stays planted and my skin stings. It's wirier than the others, with a thick root, and unmistakeably grey. Gemma has a thing called hair mascara that I found in our bathroom drawer. I tried it on my sideburns and for the rest of the day my fingers were covered in brown smudges; turns out I have a habit of rubbing my sideburns. It said it covered grey. But I never noticed any grey on Gemma, either before or after finding the hair mascara. Maybe I was looking in the wrong place.

There's a bang on the door.

'You coming out? I need to take your dad before I finish at one,' says Jackie.

'Two minutes!' I reach for the nail scissors and cry out as I nick my skin.

'You OK?' Jackie is still behind the door.

My eyes water. 'Stubbed my toe. Rushing.'

'Not my fault. You've been in there for twenty minutes.'

When I emerge, towel wrapped around my pyjama trousers, Dad is in the wheelchair with Jackie behind, ready to push.

'You don't have to…' I want to say she doesn't have to speak to me like that in my own house. But this isn't my house and she'd tell me so.

'Don't have to what?' she asks.

'You don't have to…' The towel is slipping. 'You don't have to take him. I can do that. You get home. It's Sunday.'

'Go on then.' Jackie squeezes Dad's arm. 'I could click out a couple of minutes early. John's been bad again today.'

John is her husband. What he's ill with, I have yet to discover.

I look over to Mum's cuckoo clock as Jackie closes the back door. Quarter to one. 'A *couple* of minutes early,' I say to Dad.

Dad's mouth tries to smile.

'Played for a fool by a lexically challenged toast thief,' I continue. 'Let me tidy away this towel and we'll get you into the bathroom.' I try not to think about comparing hair colours.

Weaver Close is almost identical to, and runs parallel with, Archery Road. Neither road has a dead end, and yet whoever decides these things has called Weaver Close a close.

It's steeper than I remember and I'm sweating despite the cold. Bee's house is halfway up. Her garden backs on to what was once Mum and Dad's garden. There used to be a hole in the back fence, and Danny and I would roll up our comic-book pages and post them to each other – an editorial gateway of sorts.

Bee's garden was smaller than ours and always tidier. Whenever she was out there watering her tomatoes or mowing the lawn,

Mum would say how hard it was for her without Danny's dad. He left when Danny was tiny and sent money every so often. 'As if that's what they need,' Mum used to say. But as far as I could tell, it was all they needed. There was something so still and easy about Danny's fatherless family.

I knock Bee's lion-head door knocker three times, only really getting loud enough on the third go. Tap, tap, *whack*.

Inside, someone bounds towards the door and shrieks through the frosted glass, 'Papa?'

Has Bee moved?

'Papa?' the voice says again – a girl, or possibly a young boy.

I back away. 'Wrong house. Sorry!'

I keep walking backwards, looking for the number 18 on Bee's wall.

The child's outline is pressed against the frosted glass, their eye level with the spyhole.

I hold up a hand. 'Sorry again!'

At the pavement, I stop. Next door down is 16 and the next one up is 20; there are large stickers saying so on their wheelie bins. So right house, wrong owners. At least I tried. I set off down the hill.

Behind me a door opens. 'Excuse me, did you knock?' Her voice is as it always was, so soft it won't let her shout. 'Robin?'

'Auntie Bee!' I scrunch my eyes closed to start again. 'I mean, Bee. Was worried you'd moved.'

She shrugs. 'Still here.' She's kept the same short, blonde hairstyle, but something is different, more modern. Glasses. She's wearing thick-rimmed glasses. A boy's head pops out from behind her. I know him from the beach. Astrid's boy. And Danny's. Danny has a boy who calls him Papa.

'Who's that?' he says, manoeuvring in front of Bee. He has Danny's long legs and Astrid's wavy hair.

Bee wraps her arms around his shoulders. 'We don't ask like that. We wait to be introduced.' She tickles his sides, and he wriggles free.

'I'm Robin,' I call over from the pavement and start towards Bee's path.

'Gosh, I'm sorry,' says Bee. 'Robin, this is my cheeky grandson, Timo.' She says his name differently to Astrid's *Tee-mo*. Bee's way is a simple Tim with an O. 'And Timo,' she continues, 'this is Robin. Your dad's friend.'

'And Mama's friend,' says Timo.

Bee looks at me quizzingly.

'How…?' is all I can manage.

'She wrote you a note and made me drop it round,' says Timo. He sounds like Astrid, high and lively, but without the accent. 'I thought Robin was a girl's name.'

'Timo!' exclaims Bee.

'It's fair enough,' I say. 'It's both, or neither. More for a bird really. But I'm not a bird, am I?' My elbows flap involuntarily. 'Anyway, stupid name. But you get used to things.'

Timo's smile is a mix of pity and amusement. If only my pretend wings would carry me away to explode against the sun.

Timo brings me back to Earth. 'Is that for now?' He nods towards the Tesco cheesecake that I picked up on my way here.

'Yes, as a matter of fact it is, or could be,' I reply, as if struggling in a foreign language. 'I bought it for your … grandma.' At that word Bee winks at me, and now I see what she's been reminding me of with the smart hair and the new glasses: a newsreader.

'Let's have it now,' says Timo, and Bee shrugs.

I feel the need to explain myself. 'I wanted to come and say hello and didn't want to turn up empty-handed.'

'Well, you could have done. No cheesecakes needed,' says Bee. 'But Timo and I do always have room for second pudding…' She seems about to say more but turns back into the house. Timo follows and, eventually, I do too.

Astrid did say Timo spends Saturday night with his grandma, but now it's Sunday afternoon. I hadn't bargained for a child. I wanted to see just Bee. The grey pube seemed like a message to get on with things. It made me think of something Gemma said last year: 'Always on about bloody time, Robin. Always wasting it.'

As I take my shoes off in Bee's hallway, I feel myself reddening at the thought of texting Gemma that she's right and attaching a picture of the hair. No. That's called a dick pic. And Gemma believes we are currently not together. Not together enough for a dick pic, at least.

'Come on through,' Bee calls softly from the kitchen.

I remove my second trainer without untying the laces. I straighten up and I'm level with a framed picture of Bee and Mum I've never seen before. They are in stocks, hands and heads hanging through the holes, glancing sideways at one another. Mum's saying something; Bee's eyebrows are arching at whatever it is. I touch the glass over Mum's face with my fingertip and hurry through.

In the kitchen, my linguistic struggle continues. 'It's a new recipe,' I say as I hand over the cheesecake. 'Not mine, I mean. Theirs, obviously. It says so on the box. It was on a special offer, introductory.'

'Berries and lavender,' Bee reads off the box. 'So unusual.'

'Wasn't even sure you could eat lavender,' I say, grateful that what the cheesecake lacks in gastronomic appeal, it makes up for in conversational material.

'It's a herb in the same family as sage and rosemary,' says Timo.

'Oh.' I look at Bee.

'Timo likes to bake,' she says.

'I watch other people bake on TV,' he says.

'You made me that amazing birthday cake. Three layers.' Bee points to a photo fixed to her fridge: Astrid and Timo looking at Bee as she blows out candles, Danny's reflection caught in the window behind them.

'Sit down, sit down,' Bee says as she fills the kettle. She slices along the edge of the box with a knife and slides out the cake. It's so small, it fits onto a side plate.

'Sorry,' I say. 'It said five portions on the label. I nearly bought you flowers.'

'Cheesecake is better,' says Timo, reaching for his slice then picking off a speck of lavender. 'And this is cheesecake and flowers.'

I laugh. I can't remember being funny when I was twelve. Danny was funny, but fart jokes and impressions funny. Timo is witty.

I take a spoonful of cheesecake. It's like biting into a bath bomb. 'I was right,' I say. 'You can't eat lavender.'

Bee tastes a tiny piece. 'Different,' she says.

'I'll have yours.' Timo reaches across the table. 'And yours,' he says to me.

'I'll try again with mine. I skipped lunch,' I say. I had no appetite after the grey hair and Dad's bathroom trip.

'Oh, let me make you a sandwich,' says Bee, and slides my plate to Timo. 'You can't eat that.'

She takes ham, a block of cheddar and a jar of pickle from the fridge. 'Still no margarine?'

'Nothing's changed,' I reply.

We're quiet for a while, Timo eating the entire cheesecake, me re-reading the box, Bee slicing cheddar and making tea in a pot. Her kitchen is bright and uncluttered with a familiar smell of bleach and toast. On the windowsill, an orchid and two other plants are in matching white pots. At the end of the worktop is a small television that didn't used to be there. It's off but still draws my gaze.

Bee cuts the sandwiches into triangles. 'Crisps with it?' She lays out three flavours.

'He gets crisps?' says Timo.

Bee takes another pack from the cupboard. 'Why don't you take these up with you, finish that maths?'

'I'm stuck,' he says. 'Stupid double brackets.'

'What do you need to do?' I ask.

'A thousand questions.'

'Tough school,' I say. 'Want me to get you unstuck?'

Timo looks at Bee.

'That's a super idea,' she says.

I stand up. 'Come on then.'

'Alright,' says Timo in a way that suggests he would rather have stayed stuck.

I follow him up the stairs. 'Algebra is a language, you know? One you'll fall in love with once you see how it lets you express anything you want.' I thought about being a maths teacher for a while.

'Don't look at the mess!' Bee calls up after us.

I stop in the doorway, surprised. Timo has his own room here. And it's almost the same as when it was Danny's. Sketches on every wall, the desk covered in paper and pencils, the wardrobe door ajar with a fleece sleeve peeking out, and hair and skin products the length of the windowsill. All that's missing is a bin full of KitKat wrappers. Timo even has Danny's old bunk beds.

I touch the bed frame. Still creaky. One night, when Danny was in the top bunk and I was in the bottom, a screw came loose and the whole thing lurched sideways. After that, we'd take the mattresses off and sleep on the floor.

'This one,' says Timo from his desk.

I move a pair of trainers off the chair next to him and sit down. I ask Timo for paper and a pencil, go back to basic principles, on to brackets and explain the question. I stop short of answering it. Then we complete the rest of the questions together. Timo listens better and learns faster than any adult I've ever worked with.

'All sorted,' I say as I return to Bee and my sandwich. Timo stays upstairs doing something on his laptop.

'Oh, you're brilliant!' says Bee.

'Maths. My one true love.'

I nod towards the hallway and the picture of Mum. 'Why were you in stocks?'

'School trip to a castle somewhere – your mum would remember. They needed extra helpers, so they asked us assistants. Those were in the courtyard and the kids were desperate to put someone in them. Your mum said something like, "I'm not above being pelted with tomatoes. Got to get your veg."'

'Are you sure she didn't say fruit?'

'Maybe. Long time ago now.' Bee glances at her watch. 'Danny's back in a bit.'

'To collect Tee … Timo?' I don't know whose way to say it.

Bee pauses. 'No. At least, I don't think they have plans.'

'So he's just … he's…' I can't use 'hanging out' with someone Bee's age. 'So he's just here?'

'Oh no, sorry. Danny lives here. And Timo at the weekend. His mum's in the week. She…' Bee stops, embarrassed maybe. She cups her hand, rounds up the crumbs on the table. As she tips them into the bin, she says, 'You'd never guess where she lives. House next to your old house.'

'Wow,' I say, the only way I know how to act surprised. 'Handy, I guess.' I twist to see down the hall. 'So Danny's tidy in his old age?'

Bee laughs. 'Those were my terms. Finally house-trained him. Apart from his room.'

'Our place is a mess. Dad's bungalow, I mean.'

Her face saddens. I shouldn't have mentioned Dad.

'How is he?' she asks, in the kind of voice people use to talk to the recently bereaved.

'Not too bad really. He has amazing carers. It's great he can be in his own home, TV on all day. You know Dad. And he still manages his favourite foods.' No need to mention they are puréed. 'We re-vamped his bathroom recently.' To a wet room with a weird toilet. 'And re-did the bedroom.' Adding a hospital bed with bars on the sides.

'Sounds lovely,' says Bee, either reassured or playing along. 'And you're down here for … I mean, you've moved? Or … I imagine with your career…' She stops. In Eastgate, the word 'career' is reserved for people like me, fugitives. But now, as she's correctly surmised, I've thrown mine away.

'I've moved back,' I say. 'Dad had a bad fall, on his birthday actually. So we thought I should be closer. Someone there at night.'

'Oh, Robin.' She reaches across the table. Her hand is smooth and cool. I want to pull away but I don't want to hurt her.

'Ah, it's OK,' I say. But it really isn't. If I'd visited two months earlier, I'd be telling her about work, about the flat in London, about Gemma.

'And what about your job?' She speaks in a whisper, like she's giving me the option to pretend I didn't hear.

'They said I could work from here.'

'Well, that's lovely.' She sips her tea.

I reposition myself on my chair but can't get comfortable. My crotch is prickly, specifically the spot where I cut off the grey hair. I can feel it growing back. I open my thighs under the table.

'And you do it over the phone,' Bee is saying.

'Sorry?'

'Your job,' she says.

'Actually, they let me go. Restructuring.'

'Oh.' She looks into her tea. 'You'll find another one. Always knew you'd do well for yourself.'

I did for a while. 'I'm thinking it's a chance to change direction. And Dad needs me for now.'

'I'm sure he appreciates it,' she says.

'Yeah.' I sigh. What does it mean to 'do well' for oneself?

Bee looks at me. 'Done anything nice since you've been here?'

'Fish and chips, ice-cream. Browsed that big antiques place. But I'm on an economy drive.'

'Of course,' she says.

'I did get redundancy money. And there's my flat in London, if I decide to sell it. But I need a buffer, for later you know…'

There's a key in the door and Bee jumps up. 'There he is!' Her relief is obvious, and I share it.

14.
Our thing

'You've got a special visitor,' Bee calls through to where Danny is leaning his bike against the wall.

I copied her and stood up at the sound of the key and I don't know when to sit again. I rock onto my tiptoes and wave to him.

'Robin,' says Danny. 'Shooting star superstar!' And he points one arm up, the other down.

Bee's eyes move between us.

'We watched a meteor shower last night,' I tell her. 'The Orionids.'

'Still stargazing? Lovely,' she says. Then to Danny: 'Work OK, Presh?' She's always called him that.

'Four from the Chinese, couple of pizzas,' says Danny, taking off his fleece and draping it over the back of a kitchen chair. He goes on, describing customers and their orders. It sounds like he knows most of them. Few of them tip him.

I'm still standing behind my chair. I should go, give them their afternoon to themselves. But I can't leave Danny. All it took was that moment alone on the picnic rug last night and it's like before. I need to know everything about his day. I unclasp my sweating hands and sit down again.

Danny continues, 'Bunch of so and so's too lazy to make it down the hill and get their own chips.'

'It's a trend,' Bee says to me. 'People having takeaway chips with their Sunday roast.'

'This one woman, when I delivered her chips, she asked me to get her gravy granules from the little Tesco,' says Danny.

'Did you?' asks Bee.

'I told her she had to use the app, and she was like, "I could give you a quid, skip the delivery fee."'

'And did you?' asks Bee.

Danny pauses. 'Too risky if a better job came in. She was right at the top of James Street.'

Bee sucks air through her teeth in agreement.

'Your job sounds so exciting,' I say.

'Very funny,' says Danny. He takes off another layer, releasing a waft of sweat and deodorant.

'It wasn't sarcastic,' I say.

There's an unnerving sound of flipflops on stairs as Timo hurtles down to join us. 'Papa! How was work?'

'Exciting, according to Robin,' says Danny, and nods across the table, 'This is Robin.'

'We met,' says Timo. 'And he's kind of right. You get to cycle everywhere and they give you free chips.'

'You didn't tell me about the free chips.' I shift my chair to make room at the table for Timo. From this new position, I catch sight of the apple tree. 'No way – you still have the rope ladder.'

Bee, Danny and Timo turn their heads as one.

'Your dad used to climb it to call over to Robin,' Bee tells Timo. 'He was in the house behind the fence, next to your mum's.'

Timo's smile suggests he's been told this before.

'Cheaper than texting,' says Danny, and Bee laughs but Timo doesn't.

'Is the hole still there, in the fence?' I ask, and stand to look out. A thick holly bush blocks where it used to be.

'Good question,' says Danny. 'Mum?'

'It should be. Unless the new people filled it in, or your dad, of course,' she says, and looks at me.

'Why?' asks Timo.

'Well, it's just Ken, Robin's dad, was never that keen on it,' she says. 'The boys wanted to make it bigger, to fit through it, a secret door. I was happy with that, safer than them walking all the way round the estate. But Ken said no, didn't he?'

'It's because we were going to get a dog,' I say, surprised to be coming to Dad's defence.

'Did you get a dog?' asks Timo.

'No,' Bee answers for me.

I force a laugh.

'Oh well,' says Timo, and again, I wonder how his words are so much older than his face.

'Remember when we used it for that dolphin comic?' I say to Danny.

'You set me deadlines,' he replies.

'I'd love to know if it's still there. Shall we look?' I say, conscious of how hard I'm trying to show Timo that I'm fun.

'I'll grab my shoes,' says Danny. He looks down. 'And yours.'

'You coming, Timo?' I ask. I've settled on the English pronunciation.

'In a minute.'

I follow Danny into the garden and pause to take in the sounds and smells of families getting things done on a Sunday. A house nearby is having a bonfire. Someone else is strimming a hedge. In our old house, the curtains of what was my bedroom are closed. 'What are they like?' I ask Danny.

'Don't know them,' he says. 'Think they have a little one, hear him sometimes.'

'She was pregnant when they bought it,' I say, my forehead clammy at the memory of packing up Dad's house while Danny was the other side of the fence.

Danny taps a football out of our path and it lands in a flowerbed. Bee knocks on the kitchen window and as we turn around, she wags a finger at us, but she's laughing. Timo is still on the back step.

The holly bush is deep and dense. 'What side, do you think?' asks Danny.

I twist to recreate the perspective from our old garden – the sort of pirouette Gemma does when reading a map. 'Your left,' I say.

Danny steps into a gap between bushes, seemingly unbothered by holly prickling his bare arms.

'Can you see it?' I ask.

'Not yet.' He stoops down and goes in deeper.

'Yep,' he says. 'Still there.' He edges back and stands aside for my turn.

I pull my sleeves over my hands. In the darkness behind the bush, the fence looks solid. For a second, I imagine the hole might be magic, coming and going as it pleases. I crawl closer.

'Wow. Still there!' I shout. 'Still there.'

It's about a foot off the ground and no bigger than a ping-pong ball. I remember now how tight we had to roll up our pages. Our names are still there too, where Danny scratched them into the wood and went over them in felt tip. *DANNY L. THOMPSON* and *ROBIN EDMOND BLAKE* with a funny O. We had to turn the U in Edmund into an O when I found out my parents had spelled it wrong. The revelation came from a book Grandad Jim bought me about Halley, first name Edmond with an O, not Edmund with a U. Of course, I could correct the fence graffiti but not my birth certificate. In the end, my physics teacher, Mrs Waites, eased my existential crisis by finding documents where both Edmund and Edmond were used and where Halley himself used the Latin form Edmundus. The idea of being named after someone both inconsistent and grandiose carried new problems, but I forgave my parents.

I run my finger round the O one more time and back out. 'Timo, you need to see this. It's still there,' I call towards the house.

'Really?' says Timo, looking to his dad.

'Come on, Timo,' says Danny. 'It's pretty special.'

'It's a hole in a fence,' says Timo.

'Our hole,' says Danny.

'Fine.' Timo slides into what look like Bee's gardening clogs and shuffles across the lawn. 'Here I am. Where's your portal?'

'Behind there,' says Danny.

Timo is slim enough to fit between the two bushes easily.

'OK. I've seen it,' he says. 'Can I go back in now?'

Danny turns towards me, his lips pressed together, embarrassed or angry, or both. I shrug.

'You know what, Timo?' Danny says into the bush. 'I look at every bloody thing you build on *Minecraft*. And we're showing you one piece of our childhood…'

I touch Danny's arm. 'It's OK, Danny, it's just a stupid hole in a fence.'

'It's not OK. That's ours, we made it. It was our thing.'

'Actually, it was already there. And Timo's seen it now.'

'He's laughing at us. Can't you tell?' says Danny.

Timo's re-emerged. He's blinking hard. He rubs his eyes. 'I'll look, I'll look properly,' he says, his voice small and broken by Danny's sudden rage. 'I get it. And I wasn't laughing at you.'

He kneels in the mud, puts his face right up against the fence, his eye lined up with the hole. 'They have a dog,' he says.

'Is it there?' asks Danny.

'Nope,' says Timo. 'But there's a giant pile of dog poo, right in front of your hole.' He makes a retching sound. 'Wanna see?'

Danny laughs and then Timo. It's a laughter I recognise, the kind that papers over things and can tear at any moment.

Danny walks towards the house without waiting for Timo.

I hang back. 'Sorry,' I say when he's back out. 'About the poo portal. My stupid idea.'

'It's OK,' says Timo, older again now. 'At least someone got a dog.'

OBJECT: *A letter to Miss Clarke*
DATE: *January 1997*
NOTES: *This won me a prize for 'creative writing'. I wasn't being creative.*

Write at least two pages about your Christmas. Write your account as a letter. It can be to a pen pal, a relative, or to me, if you like. Make sure you describe how you felt and use lots of adjectives and good sentence openers from our list. I really want you to make the person receiving the letter feel like they were there.

Address: Robin Blake
19 Archery Road
Eastgate

Date: Monday, 6ᵗʰ January, 1997

Dear Miss Clarke,

I hope you are well. I am writing to tell you about my Christmas disaster.

Firstly, it started well. Before the holidays my mum got me the huge Argos catalogue and asked me to give her exciting ideas for my present. Happily, the catalogue had lots of pages of Lego. Additionally, it had Lego Technic where you can make things move. I showed her the set with a helicopter that can be a car and a boat. She looked sad and said I should pick something that is less than £40 and said maybe my gran would give us some money but she won't promise.

The next Saturday my mum went to the shops and I saw her out my bedroom window when she came back. She had a giant Argos bag. My mum hides everything under their big bed behind fluffy pillows. While she and my dad were watching A Question of Sport I crept into their messy bedroom. I wanted to just check a bit. Lying on the scratchy carpet I reached my arm under the bed and kept my eyes closed. Unbelievably the box was as big as the helicopter one and it made a Lego noise.

On Christmas Eve I was too excited to get to sleep and wanted to make myself dream about the helicopter turning it into a giant version. My mum said I'd have to wait to see what I get but she was stopping herself from smiling.

On Christmas Day I ran downstairs as quick as lightning and I yelled as loud as a siren when I saw the big box. We always have to wait to open things together. 'Get up, get up!' I said and my dad said he needed his cup of tea first so I put the kettle on for my mum. She made the tea and shouted that he has to come down for it. She whispered 'little trick' to me. Then we had to wait while she put the turkey in. It was a big one because my gran, my Auntie Sandra and my cousin Jamie come for Christmas dinner. Next, we had to wait more because we always call my mum's Auntie Mary in New Zealand. Did you know it's summer there?

Finally, we were allowed to open our presents. The box looked even bigger wrapped up but my mum had done the same thing as last year where she puts screwed up newspaper balls inside the paper to change the shape. She didn't do it very well on the Lego box, it was still a rectangle. Yes, Lego! I spoiled it. Sorry. It was the helicopter-car-boat and said ages 11 to 15 but I'm 11 in 13 weeks and 4 days. It's the biggest Lego Technic I have ever had. I felt ecstatic.

My mum said I could get it out on the kitchen table while she did the vegetables but my dad said I had to go with him to get my gran. He promised we'd be quick but we always have to go in and put her necklace on for her, check her windows, feed her fish and turn all the plugs off. She had a washing basket full of presents for us and Auntie Sandra and Jamie. He gets the same as me but he's actually a grown-up. My gran gets us the same every year: chocolate orange, shower gel, socks and a flannel. Additionally, I also get Pokémon cards because I said I liked them when I was little.

You probably want to get to the disaster so I'll just say that dinner was good and Jamie ate more pigs in blankets than turkey. My mum always makes me have a mix on my plate. Auntie Sandra says Jamie is hungry because he's been at university. He eats his chocolate orange in one go.

After lunch we watched Keeping Up Appearances but Jamie said it was old and asked if he could do my Lego in the kitchen. My mum said that was a nice idea but I said I wanted to watch to the end and then do it. But really I wanted to do it with my mum because she finds the pieces fastest.

Suddenly, there's this noise in the kitchen. Jamie just tipped out the biggest bag on the table. He tore the box too. He said he wanted to give me a head start. He was putting different bits together without the instructions, just looking at the helicopter picture on the box. Then he opened another bag, tipped it out and the pieces fell on the floor and some went under the dishwasher. My dad said it was running so we couldn't move it. Then Jamie went to look under it and when he did he kicked another piece under the washing machine. I didn't want to cry but I couldn't stop and Auntie Sandra said I was being silly and my mum said I'd been looking forward to the Lego all year and Auntie Sandra said 'alright for some' and my dad said 'every Christmas' and my Gran shouted 'she's on' and they all went back to the lounge for the queen.

The washing machine is built in. When my dad tried to get the piece out with a ruler he pushed it further back. It's a cog for making the helicopter rotors go round and there's another piece missing we can't find even with a torch. We put the other pieces in the box for until it's all there again. My mum said it's like when my dad taped over the end of Top Gun. I don't want Jamie to ever come to our house again.

I hope this makes you feel like you were there. If you were there I think you would have helped. My mum said we can move the washing machine when my dad is back at work. We might do it today after school.

From,

    Robin

Notes for Dad: When did you last hear from Jamie? We should get the new Top Gun *on streaming.*

15.
Entertain me

'Are you awake?'

I roll over, change ears. 'How did you get my number?'

'From Astrid,' says Danny. 'I was supposed to call you in the week, set something up.'

The red digits on my radio come into focus. 'So you waited until 6.00am on a Sunday?'

'Five, actually. The clocks changed. Catches us out every time, doesn't it?' Danny speaks with the energy of my former colleagues, the ones who run to work then read out heart rates from their smart watches.

'Does it?' I switch ears again, as if Danny might make more sense from a different angle.

He continues, 'Something to do with more light for farming, right? Or the war?'

'Don't you have a hill to swim up?'

'I have a minicab run. Gatwick. Except I messed up the time and now I'm waiting outside. Then I thought, if you're up, you can come with me.'

At last, he pauses.

'I'm not up.'

'Entertain me and I'll give you some of my fare.'

'But it's 5.00am,' I say.

'You know, if you're looking around, this is like work experience. If you get up now, I can grab you and be back here for the client.'

'What are they like?' I switch to speakerphone and open Google Maps.

'No idea. They booked with a surname. Jenkins. Mrs Jenkins. What does it matter?'

'It's one hour and twenty minutes to Gatwick in current traffic,' I say.

'So?'

'What if Mrs Jenkins is difficult? Or talks a lot? Or, I don't know, she thinks I'm your boyfriend?'

'This early, they generally say hello and something about where they're going and we put the radio on,' says Danny.

'And what if Mrs Jenkins doesn't want to get into a car with two men?'

'Then I'll tell her you're my boyfriend.'

'Smart arse,' I say.

'I'll pick you up in ten? There's this thing I wanted to talk to you about.'

'I don't know if I can leave Dad that long.' It's not entirely true. I'd be back as the breakfast carer leaves.

'I know this van on the A21, does sausage sandwiches with chips and gravy. We'll stop on the way back. Super fast. You won't be gone for long.'

'Well,' I say.

'Ten minutes. Look out for me.'

'What car? You don't know where I live.'

'I do. Astrid. Silver BMW.'

'What are you wearing?' Danny asks as I climb in.

'*You* used the word "client".' I'm uncomfortable about everything: my clothes, being here, leaving Dad, this seat so close to the dashboard. I feel around for a lever.

'At least take the tie off,' says Danny. He nods towards my seat. 'Button on the side but leave her some leg room.'

He pulls away without waiting for me to put on my seatbelt. There is more than one button on the side of the seat and they are sliders rather than buttons. I try the first one and the backrest springs forwards so that my head is touching the windscreen. 'Whatever you do, don't brake.'

'Jesus, Robin. We're driving down Sycamore Close at twenty, not a police chase through the streets of Rome.'

'Lane. It's Sycamore Lane. And it's Turin, not Rome.' My fingers finally find the slider again and I tip myself back.

'What's wrong with Rome?' asks Danny.

'It's not where they set it, or filmed it.'

'What?' He slows for a red light.

I feel for another slider. '*The Italian Job*. You meant the Mini car chase – it's in Turin, not Rome.'

'I meant any car chase,' he says.

'Then why say Rome? You said Rome because you were thinking of *The Italian Job*.'

'How do you know what I'm thinking?'

'It's obvious. If you weren't thinking about *The Italian Job*, you'd have said Brighton or London.'

'Always comes back to London. Shiiiit…' We're flung forwards as he brakes for a fox. He accelerates away again, engine roaring. 'I know what I meant.'

Mrs Jenkins lives in one of the detached houses on the way out of Eastgate. Who else would take a minicab all the way to Gatwick?

The gravel drive is a semicircle with a *way in* and a *way out*. A floodlight blinds us as Danny pulls up to the front door. 'Still ten minutes early,' he says.

There are uncarved pumpkins on the steps and a wreath on the door made from fake leaves in autumn colours.

'Bet you five quid she's flying to America,' I say to Danny.

'I already know she is. Chicago via New York. They give you the flight details with the booking.'

'You said you didn't know anything about her.'

'I don't. Just where she's going,' he says.

'Well, that tells you a lot about a person.'

More silence as we both check our phones for messages that are never going to be there at 6.00am. I text Gemma to remind her about the clock change, then I continue the research I started while waiting for Danny earlier.

'How often would you say you have minicab jobs and what do they pay on average?' I ask him.

'Goes up and down, depending.'

'Your outlay is around £2,500 a year, right? Without petrol. That's just your private-hire licence and the licence for the car, taxi insurance, criminal-record check.' I look up and see he's playing something on his phone. 'Danny!'

'Yeah?' Eyes and thumbs still on his phone.

'Do you have an estimate for petrol?'

'Not really. And I don't pay the insurance or any of that stuff. Will does. It's his car.'

'Will from the year above?'

'Different Will. You don't know him.'

'But Will's what then – a friend? Colleague? And you share it? A public cab. Is that even legal?'

'There she is.' Danny opens his door and jumps out.

Mrs Jenkins is almost as I imagined: long coat, short hair, leather gloves but white trainers. A man, presumably Mr Jenkins, follows her out with a large suitcase. Danny takes it and loads it into the boot. The man is also wearing trainers, curiously large ones with thick soles. I imagine they might be sportswear tycoons and Mrs Jenkins is off to negotiate a big deal in Chicago. But tycoons wouldn't live in Eastgate, not even on the edge.

She sits behind me and I tense up. If she says good morning first I'll know it's OK to talk. She fastens her seatbelt, says nothing.

Danny twists around to her. 'This is my colleague, Robin,' he says. 'He's a trainee.'

'I didn't realise driving had trainees,' says Mrs Jenkins. 'My son Stephen's a trainee ... of sorts.' She pauses before the last two words, inserting as much distance as she can between me and her son.

Danny asks if she'd like the radio on and turns up the volume without waiting for an answer.

'Bit early, don't you think?' she says, leaning forwards. Her perfume is floral and invasive.

'Suppose so.' Danny turns off the radio.

'It's Stephen I'm visiting in Chicago,' she continues.

I consider things we could talk about instead of Stephen: customers' rights when returning bedsheets, the wastefulness of decorative pumpkins, the stalling police investigation into celebrity car torchings – there was another one last night, the Land Rover of a reality TV star's ex-girlfriend.

Mrs Jenkins is not letting up. Stephen is over there for two years, she tells us. He's booked to come back for Christmas. He's met someone out there.

'Sorry,' I say, hoping she'll pause. I turn to Danny, 'Know what? If you're going up Beachway, you could drop me at the corner and I'll walk.'

'Walk where?' he asks.

'Home.'

Mrs Jenkins interrupts from the back seat. 'I thought you were a trainee. Trainees can't leave before they've learned anything.'

'Today's training was in pick-ups and greeting the customer,' I say.

'Well, I think you could do with more training in that, if you want an honest opinion,' she says.

I don't want any opinions but if I'm playing a trainee, I might as well do it right. 'I take your point,' I say. 'I'll feed that into tomorrow's sessions. But now I need to go. I've got my dad at home sick.'

'Why didn't you plan for that?' she asks, and I wonder if everyone in the sportswear industry is this heartless.

Danny drives past the turn towards Dad's. I throw my hands up. 'Danny! Were you even listening? You missed it.'

'Mrs Jenkins is right,' he says. 'You need all the training you can get.' He laughs and Mrs Jenkins joins in. I've been kidnapped.

Danny speeds up as we join the main road, and I wonder how the car would need to skid, flip and land to trap him and Mrs Jenkins but not me. The way we're sitting makes it unlikely, but not impossible, and I've been spared before. With my hands, I discreetly mime different rolls and trajectories. I know it's perverse, but it strikes me that I must be doing better if I can contemplate our crash and future crashes so playfully.

'My Stephen is training to be a dentist,' Mrs Jenkins says after a while.

'So he's not one yet?' I ask.

'Very nearly. He changed courses. He has a scholarship.'

'Great,' says Danny.

'He's done so well,' she says.

Is this what parenthood is like in other families? Giving up all inclination to talk about yourself in favour of marketing a distant and unexceptional child. It makes me think about the worst of all the things Gemma has texted me: *You just want a family so you've done something.*

Mrs Jenkins is still talking: 'He has the option to stay there.'

I hope that poor Stephen will take it.

'Danny has a son, too,' I say. 'Don't you, Danny?'

'Yep.' Danny nods.

'Your son's bilingual, isn't he, Danny?'

'Kind of.'

In the wing mirror, I see the glow of Mrs Jenkins' phone screen. She doesn't care about Danny and his son. She doesn't care about anything either of us says. And even if she did, she'll be gone in forty minutes, never to see us again. Suddenly, I envy Danny this job.

'I wouldn't want to be a dentist,' I say.

'Excuse me?' says Mrs Jenkins.

'Robin, don't,' Danny whispers.

'It might be right for Stephen,' I say. 'But it's got to be a very narrow world, people's mouths.'

'Well, you'd need science A-levels anyway,' she says.

'I have science A-levels. And I'm a chartered accountant.'

She makes a noise as if my revelation has caught in her throat. 'Like my husband. Except he's not re-training as a minicab driver.'

'I could afford to try a change, I guess. And I needed a change.' I pause. 'I don't have as much time as everyone else. I have this condition.'

'Oh,' she says.

Danny sighs loudly.

'It's OK,' I say. 'But it does make you look at things differently.'

'I could see how that might be,' says Mrs Jenkins.

'None of us actually know how long we've got,' says Danny, and he taps out a rhythm on the wheel – something he does whenever we slow for traffic. 'We could all die right now if that truck swerves.'

'You know that's not true,' I say. 'I can't.'

'You're not still doing this?' he says.

'I don't understand,' says Mrs Jenkins, her head between us.

I twist towards her. 'What would you do, Mrs Jenkins, if you knew exactly when you were going to die?'

'It would largely depend on when that might be,' she replies.

'OK. So how old are you?'

'You can't—' Danny begins.

'I'm sixty,' she says.

I nod, appreciatively. 'So let's say you have fifteen years left.'

She laughs. 'Not bad. It would divide up nicely. I would spend five volunteering, because we can assume I no longer need all my pension. And then I would spend five travelling … and probably another five volunteering.'

Typical response for a woman from the outskirts of Eastgate. 'But honestly,' I begin. 'Wouldn't you just want to be on holiday for the time you have left? And volunteering as what?'

'I'd find a way to make myself useful,' she says.

'I don't think you're thinking it through, or saying what you'd really want to do.'

She lets out another laugh. 'How would you know what I want?'

'He does that,' says Danny.

Mrs Jenkins leans back into her seat. 'Do you think we might have the radio on now? News, not music.'

Danny and I reach for the button at the same time. 'I'll find it,' I say.

As we approach the drop-off area at Gatwick, I turn to Mrs Jenkins again. 'So you and your husband are in sportswear?'

'Why would you ask that?'

'Your trainers, and his.'

'Comfort. We both have faulty feet!' She laughs at her turn of phrase, undoubtedly as over-used as her feet.

'So what *do* you do?' I ask.

'I'm an anaesthetist.'

'But you said you're Mrs not Doctor.'

'I am today.'

'What the hell was that?' says Danny after he's helped Mrs Jenkins with her case.

'Yep. She was a funny one.'

'Not her. You. All your comet bollocks and being such a bastard about her son.'

'Not like you'll ever see her again.'

'Er, apart from when she's booked for us to pick her up next week,' he says.

'Us?'

'The cab firm. Not you. You're never coming again,' he says.

'You wanted entertainment. And she liked me. We've dropped her to the airport *and* opened her mind.'

I wait for Danny to finish swearing to himself as he tackles a roundabout then I ask, 'What was the thing you wanted to talk to me about?'

'Not important.'

'Oh, don't be like that.'

'But it's really not. Just if you'd seen the Scout huts are up for sale.'

'So?'

He sighs. 'Yeah. Like I said, not important.'

16.
The gateway pickle

There is one carer who always forgets the 2061 code for the key box. Whenever the doorbell rings before nine, it's her.

Today she rings twice in a row. I should say something but I know I won't. Instead, I unlatch the door and turn back into the lounge as I tell her, 'He's on the toilet.'

'Who?'

'Oh God!' I spin round and open the door properly. 'Astrid. Sorry. I thought you were someone else.'

'And who is on the toilet?'

'My dad.'

'Ah, OK. Here.' Astrid hands me one of those glass jars with metal fastenings that ping in your face. 'Lime. The gateway pickle.'

'Gateway pickle?'

'The way in to pickling, before you move to the tougher stuff.'

'Like heroin?' I ask.

'What? No. Like cucumbers. My next pickle is carrots. I'm not ready for cucumbers.' She pats the bag on her shoulder. 'And here:

some portions of vegetable curry to go with it. Two for the fridge, two for the freezer?'

'I'll need to check for space.' I step aside for her to come in.

On her way to the kitchen, she stops and looks through the open door to my room and the bin bags. I was going through them last night, looking for my Scout badges after Danny mentioned the huts. They seemed like objects ripe for reminiscence work; each one took weeks to achieve and even Dad got excited about them. I bet he'd love to see them again, if I can ever find them.

Astrid is still staring at the bags and their contents on my floor. 'Having a sort out. Mum's old things,' I say.

She nods, carries on to the kitchen and drops her bag on the table. 'How do you feel about chickpeas?' she asks, unpacking plastic takeaway boxes.

'Sure. I mean I wasn't expecting any. But sure.'

It's far too early for visitors soliciting views on chickpeas. I'm in my pyjamas and a hoodie. Astrid is wearing yet another pair of ironed jeans – black this time – a dark-green wrap-around coat and a voluminous orange scarf that should clash with her hair but doesn't. She unfurls the scarf, folds it, arms wide, as you do a bedsheet, then drapes it over a chair. She studies my face. 'You look like a rabbit standing in front of a snake.'

'Specific,' I reply.

'It's an expression. German.'

'I'm a rabbit who's not quite with it yet.' I slide onto a chair. My pyjama trousers are thin, have a fly that gapes open and are all there is between her and the newest grey hair I discovered just minutes ago. The web forum was right, you pluck one out and three take its place.

Astrid holds two takeaway boxes in each hand.

'You really didn't have to do this,' I say.

'Well, Sunday is our batch-cooking day, and Danny told me about your…' She pauses as she rearranges the fridge. 'About your constraints. And I'm always helping the foodbank, so I thought, why so anonymous, why not look nearer home?'

'What?' Acid bubbles up to my throat. 'Is this about the sandwich yesterday? Bloody Danny. Bribes me with a sandwich and makes *me* pay for it.'

The sandwich in a layby near Gatwick wasn't even that good. Not five-pounds good. Thin white bread, three chips and two skinny sausages. The much-hyped gravy was so watery it turned the bread into a paste that melded with the paper napkin. I was picking tissue off the roof of my mouth for the rest of the day. And we'd ended up having a row because Danny ordered for both of us but only paid for his own.

'Danny said you've barely got enough money to eat,' says Astrid, now rearranging our freezer.

'What? Only because I'm on a budget. I have money if I want it.'

She holds up a red ice pop. 'So many of these ice sticks … And what's this?'

'I wanted nachos and dips, and those things with four dips are cheaper than buying the guacamole and sour cream on their own.'

Astrid peels back the clingfilm, sniffs and looks at me.

'Salsa and cheese dip. I don't like them,' I explain. 'But I figured I'd find a use for them in the end. Put the salsa in a pasta sauce and maybe someone else would eat the other one.'

She turns back to the freezer. 'Wait, you have two more of these in here.'

'Isn't a man's freezer private?'

She scowls. 'Why? What else have you got in here?'

'The body of the last person who rummaged through my freezer.'

'Funny.'

'My freezer, my dips, my budget,' I say, closing the door.

'So your budget is, like, per day?' she asks.

'Yes. It's quite satisfying.'

'So food poverty is a game to you?'

'Wait, what? No. It's just a budget. Targets,' I say.

'So people are missing meals to feed their kids and you're freezing dips for fun?'

'I'm saving for something – travel. And I don't see how me freezing dips stops them getting meals. And I'm…' I give up. No point telling her about the time I bought two copies of the *Big Issue* in one week, or about my monthly donations to four charities whose people cornered me outside the office. Her smirk says she's already made up her mind about me. So I ask her, 'Why are you being so mean to me?'

'This isn't about you.'

'Feels like it is. Look, if you can't spare the curries, take them home again. We've got plenty.'

'I made them for you. And the pickle,' she says.

'I love pickle.'

She rubs her chin.

'And curries,' I add. 'And Dad does. I can put some in a blender for him. That's what all the pots in the freezer are: purées. He can't chew.'

Astrid drops onto a chair. 'God. I'm sorry, Robin. You're right, I—'

'It's OK,' I interrupt. 'We cope. Having said that, he's been on the toilet a really long time.' I laugh and she hides her face in her hands. I nod towards the bathroom, 'If you don't mind.'

'Of course,' she says. 'I'll…'

I open the back door for her. 'Here, go this way. Avoid walking back through our mess.'

'Hey, don't apologise,' she says.

'Yeah. Sorry.'

I'm asking Dad from the doorway if he's definitely finished, when Jackie arrives.

'Someone looks happy,' she says as she brushes past me.

I check the mirror. 'Not me.'

'You sure?' Jackie's face crumples as she tries to wink. 'You're all twinkling.' She pulls off a long strip of toilet paper and folds it around her hand.

'Don't think so,' I say, retreating. 'I'll let you get on.'

'I should show you how I do this, so you know for next time,' she says.

'I do know. But I knew you were coming any minute. And like you say, you're better at it.'

'I am. And I know the other girls won't tell you this but you're not doing it right. And as unseemly as it is, it's part of your dad's care.'

Dad's head is too slumped to see his eyes. I don't need to.

'I'm his son,' I whisper to Jackie. 'We can't talk about this here.' I nod toward Dad. 'Do you really think he wants me in here with him?'

'He used to do it for you,' says Jackie.

'I don't believe he did actually,' I say.

Dad groans, and I feel ashamed that we've yet again forgotten there's nothing wrong with his hearing.

'Well, it's part of the parcel, if it's him you're here for,' says Jackie.

'Another time,' I say, and leave before she can stop me. I've been attacked enough for one morning.

I lie on my bed, stomach like someone's going at it from the inside with a grater. I'm angry at myself for getting this way. I'm even angrier at Jackie. How dare she question why I'm here? I should tell her everything I've given up: Gemma, my flat, sleep, a job I was great at – I know Fiona would have kept me on if I'd stayed in London. All to become Dad's inadequate carer.

Minutes later she bangs on my bedroom door, and I jump up. She opens it and leans in. 'You can sort those bin bags out while you're in there. You'll get mice, things laying all over the floor, crumbs everywhere, sneaking off to eat in bed…'

'I *am* sorting them. That's what this is,' I gesture to the ornaments and old clothes covering my floor. 'And it's all temporary. It was supposed to be temporary. I wasn't supposed to be in here this long.'

'Mice,' she says, and goes.

I sweep toast crumbs under the bedside table with my foot. Then I get down on the floor, pack everything back into the bin bags and shove them under the bed. I straighten the duvet and pull it down on one side until the bags are hidden. Better. But now the pillow stands out. My London memory-foam pillow, its cover all crinkled and the sides all lumpy around my head crater. I punch it. Then again with the other fist. And again. But it holds its ugly shape, ready to squeeze my head tonight and every night. I throw it at the wall and it hits the hunting horn.

I need to get out of here. I inch open my door and see that Jackie's next to Dad in the lounge, her back to me. The TV's on loud. I creep out, run through to the kitchen and out the back door. Then I feel the cold slabs on my bare feet.

Jackie's voice rises as she goes into the kitchen. I press myself against the wall. I can't go back for shoes. I can't explain myself again, not without screaming that I shouldn't have to.

I wait for Jackie to return to the lounge and quickly lift the garden chair onto the little table.

The sun has warmed the roof's dark cladding. I lie there and watch the clouds, so wispy they might dissolve with the tiniest gust of wind. The sun is a small blessing given Jackie isn't due to leave for another twenty minutes. If I had my phone, I could check where the comet is and line myself up.

Will I still be in Eastgate when it returns in 2061? At least the light pollution is low. I picture it passing overhead, its fiery tail filling me with the same mix of wonder and terror that our ancestors have reported over thousands of years. Of course, I'll actually have a reason for the terror.

I remember Grandad Jim telling me that every time the comet nears the sun, it shrinks a little and that one day it will disappear altogether. I asked him, 'Then why does it go so near?'

'It's the way things have to be,' he said.

Thirsting for my own taste of the sun's malevolence, I look straight at it. I stare until it stings, and when I blink, puddles of pale, creamy custard dance inside my eyelids. I stare again and the puddles turn egg-yolk yellow then darken until they're the rich orange of Astrid's hair.

17.
That's how it goes

Danny's phone goes to voicemail. I dial again, and again.

'What?' he answers on my fifth attempt.

'I don't like leaving voicemails,' I say. 'People ignore them.'

'Then text me.' He's out of breath and there's traffic in the background.

'I needed to talk now.'

'This isn't about grey pubes again?'

'No! And I told you about that, and everything else, in confidence.'

There's a pause. Hopefully, he's contemplating an apology for telling Astrid about my budget. But he simply says, 'What's up?'

'The minicab jobs. I'm in.'

'I didn't ask you,' he says.

'Yeah, but you were thinking about it. And we could split the money, or even do sixty-forty for you.'

'That doesn't make any sense,' he says.

'I need to get out the house. And if I do your cab runs, you can do more Deliveroo.'

'What about your dad?' he asks.

I bristle. 'Does everyone think I'm totally useless? I've worked it all out. This fits between things. Half the time he's just watching TV. Doesn't need me for that.'

Danny's quiet.

'Anyway, when's your next job?' I ask. 'I'll do it.'

'Got one this afternoon and then I'm on till late. But…'

'Then consider yourself free for the afternoon.' My voice has gone posh.

'But…'

'It's outsourcing. Everyone's doing it. Just another form of those lazy buggers who send you out for ketchup.'

'So now I'm the lazy bugger?' he asks.

'Wise bugger.'

'But I need…' He makes a clicking sound. 'OK, how about this for wise? You leave me seventy. Seventy-thirty. And you can't tell anyone.'

The first job is collecting a man from the hospital and driving him to the estate by the caravan park.

I'm using my own car and have stocked up on toffees. Danny offered me the shared BMW with its funny seats and weird smells, but I declined. To give me an air of legitimacy, he's loaned me his ID badge, on which the photo is helpfully small and fuzzy.

The man's waiting on a bench, a small suitcase at his feet, a plastic bag on his lap. He looks about Dad's age.

'Mr Curtis?' I call through the window, and he gives a little wave. I ignore the beeping from the car behind as I get out and take the suitcase. Mr Curtis follows and sits in the front seat.

Neither of us speaks as I navigate my way out of the hospital car park, which has all but eaten up my thirty per cent of the fare. But I'm not doing this for the money. It's research.

He's still quiet as we join the dual carriageway, and I wonder if hospital is like prison – is it rude to ask what someone was in for? Or rude not to ask? In the end, I say, 'Are you comfortable, Mr Curtis?'

'Bill. And all dandy.'

He seems friendly enough, and we only have ten minutes of journey time left so I jump in. 'Can I ask you something?'

'Give it a try,' he says.

'What would you do if you knew exactly when you were going to die?'

He gazes out of the window at a sign advertising a pumpkin farm. He didn't hear me over the engine, I'm guessing. But then he says, 'Not much I can do. I'll need to find someone to take Sal. But the house is sorted, the social worker says they will take care of that. They visited me on the ward, two of them.'

'Oh God. I'm so sorry.' I speed up, letting the hum of the tyres flood my head. 'I'm so sorry,' I repeat. 'I had no … Cancer?'

'Yep,' he says. 'Bowel first, now a full takeover.'

'But there must be something they can do?'

'Nope. Nothing to be done.'

We are racing away from the hospital he should never have left. I slow down. 'Who said that? How many of them? What if I talked to them? We can go back there now.'

Bill's gaze is fixed on the passing fields.

'They just wanted the bed,' I explain to him. 'I won't charge you for the trip. We'll turn off next exit, drive back, go in together.'

Bill is silent. I sigh, more loudly than I mean to. We pass another sign for another pumpkin farm. No one even eats pumpkin.

'How long?' I ask.

'Couple of months.'

'But you seem so well.'

'That's how it goes,' he says.

'Do you have any family, if I'm allowed to ask?'

'Just me and Sal now.'

'Sal is…?'

'My cat. Black and white.'

We drive on in silence. Bill declines my offer of a toffee and only speaks again when we reach his estate. 'Tucked away at the end,' he says.

'I see it. Lovely,' I say, and immediately regret it. Surely, the more lovely a house, the harder it is to leave behind. Dad's bungalow is a better place to die.

'Thanks,' says Bill. 'And thanks for wanting to … do something…'

As he fumbles with the seatbelt, I focus on not saying *see you again*. Instead, I release the belt for him and ask, 'How about I help you in with your case? Make you a cup of tea? Have you got any milk in?'

'Should do,' he says and I follow him inside.

The next job is collecting a woman and her shopping from the out-of-town Sainsbury's. I don't speak and I drive three miles in the wrong direction after missing a turn. My head is full of Bill and black-and-white Sal, and the tidy home they will share for only two more months. I asked if they needed food, lifts to appointments, help with paperwork. There must be so much paperwork at the end. Then again, what repercussions could there be for leaving it unfinished?

'I've got my neighbours,' Bill had said. 'And if I need a lift, I'll call the cab company. Maybe it'll be you again.'

I wonder how I might have made a bigger impression.

The job after the supermarket is a woman in her twenties going to the station. She seems like the right subject on which to resume my research. But cautious after Bill, I begin with small talk. 'Ever had a memory-foam pillow?'

'Memory foam? Big fan,' she replies, her excited tone as wrong as her view.

But the cheeriness is reassuring. I push on. 'A guy I picked up earlier got me thinking about something funny. This thing he said made me wonder what it would do to someone if they knew exactly when they were going to die.'

'Dark,' the woman says without looking up from her phone.

'Maybe. But gets us all. And imagine you knew how much time you had left. What would you do?'

She locks her phone, turns it face down in her lap and her eyes meet mine in the rearview mirror. 'All the people I want to murder, I'd do it the day before.' She grins an unreadable grin. 'Maybe the week before, spread them out, if I had somewhere good to hide.'

'Are there many?' I ask.

'Enough to fill the week. Or when are we talking? If it's a way off, there'd probably be enough to fill the month.'

'What have all these people done to you?' I ask flatly, wary of being added to her list.

'Oh, you know. People lie. And slag me off. A couple have owed me money for years. One friend borrowed my two-grand Stella McCartney bag for a wedding that was four years ago.'

I've picked up a mobster. 'All things deserving murder?'

'Well, if I'm going and they're not, that wouldn't be right.'

'And they say you can't take anything with you.'

'What?' she says.

'Gun or knife? How would you do it?'

'Both. And poison, and a shove off a cliff. Nice to have a mix.'

'Nice,' I repeat back. 'And then you could work out the most effective.'

'You're weird,' she says.

The next passenger is a man going from the station to an office on the loosely named 'Science Park'. It's really an industrial estate where several of the small factories have chosen logos depicting atoms and test tubes in an obvious bid to obtain government grants.

When I ask him about death, the man says he would get the dog he'd always wanted, or possibly two.

'Concurrently?' I ask.

'No. Well, depends on how long we're saying.'

'Let's call it thirty-eight years, rounded up.'

'Then three dogs, one after the other ... No, hang on. How long do you reckon Jack Russells live? I'd wait ten years, get one. Or wait five years, or—'

I interrupt. 'If you want a dog so badly, why not get one now?'

'Because you're telling me I've got time.'

He's no help.

Danny calls when I've stopped to eat my sandwich and write up my notes. He offers to take over but I tell him I can fit in one more job before getting back to Dad. I'm rewarded for my enthusiasm with a woman who thinks before she answers.

'Would they be healthy years, the ones left?' she asks.

'Good question.' I made up my mind on this a while ago. Twain's last years weren't healthy, but his was an era of disease and poor nutrition, and he smoked like it was a religion. 'Yep,' I continue to the woman. 'Good health until the day you drop.'

I watch as she tucks her hair behind her ears in contemplation. She's the same streaky blonde as Gemma but older. She's aged well.

'I would budget,' she says. 'For half the time, I would budget to save, and then for the next half, I would budget to splurge. People forget to budget upwards, to spend what they really can.'

'Wise,' I say, although I've always found the word 'splurge' a little American.

'I'd fly to see my sister in Australia, stay for months.' She looks out of her window as if towards the southern hemisphere.

I point out my side. 'That way.'

'Sorry?'

'Australia. South is that way.' I tap my window.

'Well, Australia for a few months. One of my best friends is in Spain. Another is in Greece. I'd see as much of the people I love as I could. That's all that matters, isn't it?'

She twists a strand of hair around her finger.

'And I would plan a good funeral. I've already started. I keep a playlist in Spotify for my partner to put on at the wake. She's not allowed to look at it before. It's full of little surprises.' She laughs and seems to feel in her pocket for her phone, the keeper of the funeral secrets.

'You've thought a lot about death,' I say.

'Not really. Just the funeral. The playlist. And I've said to bury me in natural fibres. No one thinks about what all our polyester does to the worms.'

'No one thinks about the worms,' I say.

After I've dropped her by a sports field where her son is playing rugby, I pull over and start a new note on my phone. I need a funeral playlist. And a funeral guestlist. It will be shorter than the woman's, I know. Then again, life won't always be this constrained. Plenty of years ahead to expand it.

I'm almost home when I stop, make a three-point turn in five moves and drive back to Bill's with a final offer of help.

OBJECT: *Theatre ticket,* Julius Caesar
DATE: *January 1999*
NOTES: *According to Shakespeare, Caesar divided us into those who fear death: the 'cowards'; and those who simply let death happen when it must: the 'valiant'. He needs a third category for people like Twain and me: the 'enlightened'.*

This was a children's version. Mum had booked it for the Christmas holidays. She'd left the tickets on the fridge. I told Dad we didn't have to go. He hates theatre, or pretty much anything you pay for that isn't edible, or drinkable.

'It'll fill a day,' he said.

'There's a comet in it,' I said.

'You'll be happy then.'

I knew about the comet because Mum bought me comic-strip versions of Shakespeare. I got my Shakespeare from those and my history from Asterix. *The beauty of* Julius Caesar *is the crossover.*

Caesar's wife Calpurnia has the comet line. It seems she's seen one and taken it as a sign her husband is in danger, telling him:

> *'When beggars die, there are no comets seen;*
> *The heavens themselves blaze forth the death of princes.'*

Caesar's reply is clever:

> *'Cowards die many times before their deaths;*
> *The valiant never taste of death but once.*
> *Of all the wonders that I yet have heard,*
> *It seems to me most strange that men should fear,*
> *Seeing that death, a necessary end,*
> *Will come when it will come.'*

Or maybe not so clever. Calpurnia was right, and Caesar was murdered later that day. But his point was, it's exhausting to dwell on our 'necessary end'.

We sat down just in time for those lines. Dad couldn't find anywhere to park.

We went for Chinese afterwards, I got a headache and Dad said something that pretty much sums up the rest of my childhood.

I'd asked him for paracetamol. 'Mum always had some in her bag,' I said.

He slammed a fist onto the table and a glass tipped over. 'Well, it's not like she left me a fucking manual.'

I kept the ticket. Put it with all the Mum ones. The Nutcracker, Peter and the Wolf, more Shakespeare. I'd asked her once why Dad never came with us. 'It's how he is,' she said. 'Like how some people don't eat tomatoes. You don't pester them about it, you just enjoy having more tomatoes.'

Notes for Dad: *Now I'm the one who needs a fucking manual.*

18.
Witty little weirdo

'Come on, Robin! It's as easy as riding a bike,' Danny shouts from far up ahead.

I squeeze my brakes and feel for the ground with my toes. 'Not funny. Also illogical,' I shout back.

We've lowered the saddle on Danny's spare bike as far as it goes, but I still feel like a circus clown on a comically high unicycle. We also tried Timo's old children's bike, with even more clownish results; my knees knocked into the handlebars and my foot caught in the front wheel. At least I'd have been able to climb off.

I call up the hill, 'We should have—' A van roars around the bend and I wobble into the brambles as it passes far too close. 'Oi!' I yell after it.

The van beeps its horn in a mocking rhythm. I pull myself out from under the bike and check over my shoulder for the next assault.

We've ridden north out of Eastgate, past the orchard and the reservoir, and then west, catching glimmers of grey sea through the trees and hedgerows. It's the same route we always took, back when we used to come here in the summer holidays. We're headed for Mingin' Falls. Maddy from next door called it that, the time we let her come with us. She complained from the minute we set off, about flies in her mouth, sun burning her shoulders, too many hills.

When we got to the woods she was even worse. She whined about the brambles scratching her provocatively bare legs, and when we finally reached our secret spot, she said, 'Smells like dead people. Mingin' Falls.'

And this is what I'm thinking about as I push my borrowed bike up this endless hill. And I tot it up. Danny and I made this trip an average of seven times a summer from the ages of eleven to seventeen. Forty-nine times. And my mind, the most persistent of my attackers, chooses to remember the one time Maddy came along and ruined things.

'You alright?' Danny asks as I reach him. 'This was your idea.'

'Stupid idea.' I'm out of breath. My thigh muscles are about to snap and I'm bruised in places I'll need a mirror to check on.

'It's brilliant,' says Danny. 'The old you. The adventurer.'

'Oh.' My skin tingles.

'No need to flinch. I was being nice.'

'Sorry. Gemma says I do that when people talk to me.'

'We've all got our stuff. Are you going to make it?' He nods towards the top of the hill.

'As long as you've got the Auntie Bee picnic safe, I'll manage.'

Danny pats the bag on the back of his bike. 'She put some Halloween chocolates in. Should have seen how many she bought. Like she's expecting the whole cast of *Thriller*.' He laughs then says, 'Let's walk this bit.'

We push our bikes side by side, me nearest the hedge. If I hadn't just been called an 'adventurer', I'd demand we walk single file. I consider asking Danny what he meant about the old me. I've been sensible for as long as I can remember. Life's easier when it's calculable. But when was it last fun? Was that why Gemma didn't stay?

I glance across to Danny and have one of those moments I only ever normally have when drinking, or very occasionally when someone says something I agree with on LinkedIn. 'Thanks for giving me a chance to be your friend again, Danny. It's … I mean, it's special. And you're kinder to me than you should be.'

'God, Robin, stop making yourself into some kind of dick you're not. Please tell me you don't say stuff like that to Gemma.'

'Not anymore.'

'See! You're funny. You've always been funny,' he says.

'Funny weird or funny witty?'
'Both. You're a witty little weirdo.'

The final stretch is mostly flat. The sun is in our eyes, but I ride behind Danny and that helps. Aside from the correct bike, hours of practice and his natural sportiness, Danny also has the advantage of proper clothing. He's wearing shiny black leggings with a padded bottom. I'm in jeans, the only trousers I have at the bungalow aside from a suit. Under the jeans, I'm wearing a pair of thick black tights. They were among the 'emergency' things Gemma once left at the bungalow. They seemed essential given the weather app was predicting a 'feels like' temperature of four degrees. But now my legs are fighting against a combination of stiff denim and sticky nylon.

'Don't remember it being this far,' I call to Danny.

'It's right there.' He waves his arm. 'You can see the gate.'

As it has always been, the gate is padlocked. I climb over first and then Danny passes me the bikes and follows. We lock the bikes out of sight from the road.

Little has altered in twenty years. That's probably the way with woods: change with every season but each full year the same pattern with largely the same results. Much like life as an accountant.

I hear the falls up ahead, and there it is, the familiar tug on my bladder. 'Back in a minute,' I say to Danny.

'Ha! Me too,' he replies.

I wait for Danny to set off one way, and I go the other, stepping over brambles to reach a wide tree. The tights are cutting into my waist and I need a hidden spot to readjust them. Surely, they make tights for men. There's a word I've been looking for all morning. Gusset! That's it. Men's tights would have a roomier gusset.

'You OK over there?' calls Danny.

'Yep. Sorry. Replying to a quick text message.'

'Lucky to get any reception up here.'

As we walk on, I catch myself making a clicking sound. Danny looks at me as if trying to read my thoughts. So I tell him. 'Your cycling leggings, am I right in thinking they have a padded gusset?'

'Why, yes. I'm rather fond of a padded gusset,' he says.

I mimic his airy tone, 'Flatters one, I suppose.'

'Not that one needs it.'

That's enough of gussets. 'So ready for that picnic,' I say, and as the path twists to the left, there are the falls.

The rockface is covered in ivy and ferns. High up, water gushes from two hidden spots and pools on the ground below.

'Remember when we used to put our heads under when it was really hot?' I say.

'Go ahead,' says Danny.

We sit side by side on the fallen tree that has always been here and stare at the waterfalls.

'I'm glad we came,' I say.

'Yeah. Better than your other idea.' Danny laughs.

My other suggestion was just as adventurous: to drive out to where the latest celebrity car was burned, a house near the cliffs by Seaford. The victims are getting more local, the cars cheaper and the term celebrity more stretched. This one was once a golf commentator, his Audi torched in the night behind a closed gate.

'Can't believe you didn't want to see how they did it,' I say now.

'I know how I did it,' Danny replies.

Bee has packed us sandwiches, a packet of chocolate Hobnobs and two apples. She's also filled a large freezer bag with Halloween chocolates wrapped in orange, green and purple foil. We start with those.

'Timo would be fuming if he knew about this. Chocolates in the woods on a school day,' says Danny.

'Has he ever been here?'

'Once or twice when he was little, with Astrid. We all came. She loves it here.'

'Do you miss being with her?' I ask.

'I miss it being the three of us. When it was the three of us it was great. But when it was just her and me, she exhausted me.'

'Exhausted you?'

'Always trying to make me something. She reads all these books and was always saying how they were about me. Stuff like *The Marriage Detox*, or *Life is Short and You're a Twat*, and *The Joy of Overthinking*.'

'Are those real books?' I ask.

'Something like that, anyway. And then one day she comes back from this weekend thing, a retreat, and says she can't love me again until I can love myself.'

'So she might love you again? Does she love you again?'

'That's not the point, Robin. She was basically saying she couldn't stand being with me. All because I didn't read the same books.'

'Did she say that?'

'Pretty much,' says Danny. 'And I found these messages on her phone. She wasn't with him but she was about to be. And then she was for a bit, after we broke up.'

'Shit.' I take a chocolate and hand it to him, then another for me. I flatten the foil wrapper in my palm and fold it into a tiny square.

'How's it going with your dad?' Danny says after a while.

'Maybe good, maybe bad. I don't know how it's supposed to be going.'

'I couldn't do it,' he says.

'It's not that hard when I do what the carers tell me. The worst bit's when we're on our own, that he can't talk. And so I prattle on like those mad people who talk to their pets—'

'You're good at it,' he interrupts.

'Funny. But I'm not. I run out of prattle. I'm supposed to be doing this thing where I use objects from our past to ... "reminisce" with him, they call it. So I find the objects and make loads of notes. But I haven't talked about them to him. I don't know how to start.'

'Astrid says if you're scared of a start, you've made the start too big. Or you're a useless procrastinator.'

'Is that what her job is?' I ask.

'Making me feel shit?'

'Her career. Is she some sort of therapist?'

'Oh my God.' Danny shakes his head and blinks like a concussed cartoon. 'She hasn't told you what she does? Hasn't done her whole "I work at the university".' Danny's Astrid accent is pretty good. '*The* university, like there's only one. She's a lecturer. German literature. Kafka. All about trapped men, I'm told.' Danny's clearly delivered this rant before. He speeds up as he talks, pauses to laugh at his Kafka line. 'But yeah, she also wants to do the therapy stuff. That's what the retreat was about, becoming a life coach. Watch yourself, she's always practising on people.'

'I think she already has.' Two questions are fighting to be answered in my head. If Astrid has a job that serious and impressive, why has she kept it from me? And how have I never asked what job she has? Call it reductive, but it's the first thing I want to know about anyone.

Danny laughs suddenly.

'What?' I ask.

'Was just thinking, God knows what she'd make of your, you know ... thing ... If it's still a thing.' He grimaces.

'The comet? So you haven't told her?' I sound too eager. I stuff a sandwich into my mouth – cheese and coleslaw.

'God no. Thought you'd be past it by now,' he says.

'Why?'

'Seriously? What you said to that woman in the cab about having a time, you can't really still believe it.'

'I can't not,' I say. 'It's a belief. You wouldn't ask the pope if he still believes in Jesus.'

'Nope. Wouldn't compare myself to the pope either.'

'It gives me structure. It's what my budget's for. I'm saving and then I know I have what I need to retire and to stay retired for exactly thirty years – same as everyone else.'

'You don't know how long everyone else will get.'

'But we know averages, and I know that compared with the averages my time isn't fair. Unless I do something about it. And that's what I'm doing.'

'What if you're wrong? And then you're living in a bungalow with your dad in Eastgate for nothing,' says Danny.

'That bit I don't have any choice over. He needs me. But yeah, it works for the budget. And anyway, you're living with your mum in Eastgate.'

'But we live in a house.' He picks up another of Bee's Halloween chocolates.

'You're right. When it comes to working out who is most pathetic, let us not forget you have stairs and an ample supply of confectionery.'

'Then again, I do have a kid and no money,' says Danny.

'Only one of those is a bad thing. And anyway, I lost my job and my girlfriend, I think.'

'I lost my wife and I've never had a proper job to lose. And I have a kid, and you're supposed to have money when you have a kid. But I don't even know what I could do. I look at job adverts and it's "who would want me?" And I've never left Eastgate. And my back is killing me because I spend half my day on a bike, the other half in a car and then I sleep in a bunk bed.' Danny rubs a hand up and down his spine.

'My memory-foam pillow is trying to kill me,' I offer.

He laughs. 'Guess it's a draw then.'

A plane passes overhead, cutting into the sound of the falling water. Danny looks up. I watch it too and try to picture one particular passenger, front row, far left, and imagine where they're going. It's something Grandad Jim started when I was little. This one is a dad with his wife and son, and they're flying to the Italian Alps, where they'll set up a shop selling thermal underwear. But they'll be undercut by cheap supermarkets and in less than two years they'll return to England, bitter and debt-laden.

When the plane's passed, I ask Danny, 'You ever feel like it's not worth it? That it's all too hard?'

'Oof. I guess.' He pauses. 'But then you get these … I don't know, these moments, little good things, like a sunset, a nice sandwich, people saying something funny, things that keep you hanging on.' He holds up another Halloween chocolate. 'You know, titbits.'

My sandwich flies out of my mouth. 'Titbits? Did you just say titbits?'

'Yeah. Titbits. I said titbits and I'm proud of my titbits.' He takes a second chocolate and holds one over each nipple.

'Oh God, stop.' I fold over.

'My titbits too much for you?' He writhes like a table dancer.

'Stop, stop, stop. Oh God, you're right. We keep hanging on for the titbits. Like you saying titbits.'

'See?' he says.

We started our picnic lined up with a low ray of sunshine. Now the clouds have shifted and the air is chillier. I hop from foot to foot and flick my fingers as if it might fill them with warmer blood.

'Shouldn't we watch the light?' I ask Danny.

'Guess so.' He begins tidying things into his bag. 'But first this.' He pulls out a thermos and two plastic mugs. 'Coffee!'

'Oh, I love you!' I shout.

Danny grins.

'Wait! Stay like that,' I tell him, and I fumble with my phone taking photos while he poses.

We balance the mugs on the fallen tree and Danny pours out the coffee. He hands me one mug and holds his own aloft. 'To finding each other!'

'And titbits,' I say.

We touch mugs and then blow on our coffee. Just as we do, the clouds above us move and the sun reappears a little further along the tree trunk. We sit and I make Danny pose for a selfie.

'I think you just need to find the right thing, the right fit,' I say after a few sips.

'You're sounding like Astrid,' says Danny.

I tut. 'I mean, it's hard to find something to be both happy about and good at.'

'Thanks.' He sets his mug on the trunk, finds his drinking bottle and adds some cold water to his coffee. 'I do have this idea for my own thing. And if you didn't have your saving and retirement plan, I was going to ask if you might be interested.'

'Is this the thing you keep not quite bringing up?'

'Well, if you're going to be a dick about it...' He shifts to face away.

'I wasn't. I mean, is it that thing? What is it?'

'OK. It's the Scout huts. You know how they're for sale – an auction, super cheap – and they're right by that inlet. And you know how the water sports place has gone all expensive, exclusive...' He trails off again.

'Yes...' I draw it out as best I can to sound encouraging.

'Well, I've got these saving plans my dad set up. Haven't touched them. And anyway, I had this sea kayak idea. And the huts could be turned into dorms, and kids could come for a week. Or adults. But adults are dickish. And maybe the campsite would want to pair up. Or the holiday village.'

'Kayaks?' I say.

'Sea kayaks.'

'In the sea?'

'No, Robin, in a bathtub. Yes, sea kayaks in the sea. It's perfect there. Nice wide inlet, calm to get the kids started. Then out to the sea for a paddle around.'

'A rental place?' I ask.

'No. Well, yes, maybe. But mainly lessons, courses.'

'Courses by who … whom?'

'Me. I've been paddling for thirty years,' says Danny.

I'm trying not to laugh. 'Paddling' is a normal term for people from Eastgate but it's years since I heard it used like that. What's wrong with 'kayaking'?

'And this is something you want to do with me?' I ask. 'I haven't paddled for years. I've barely ever paddled.'

Danny bites into his knuckle. 'I mean, I'm looking at ways to make it work. With the savings. But yeah, a partner would be great. Pretty cool, no? Us together again.'

'This isn't home-made comics. It's real estate on a flood plain. And again, I know nothing about kayaks.'

'But you're great at money stuff. You'd work out how we run it, fund it, do the website,' says Danny.

'While you're out playing on the water? Paddling?'

'Your bit would be fun too. You love all that. I really think this could be something. I need this. And the Scout huts are just there. Waiting for us.' He stretches his arms over his head. He's gone from embarrassed loser to would-be kayak mogul.

It's all too possible. 'Oh God, I don't know.'

'Come on. If we're not brave now, then when?' says Danny.

This isn't what you do when you have a target retirement date. I need a spreadsheet, but off the top of my head, his idea will lose money for years before it makes any, if at all.

He persists, 'At least come and look at them with me. Just come and give me your opinion.'

'That I can do.'

The sunlight is dying as we unlock our bikes. Danny is unable to say if the batteries in the bike lights are new or old. But he promises the return journey will only take half an hour. 'Downhill most of the way,' he says. I test my bike's brakes.

We cycle in the same formation, with Danny in front to soften the wind. My feet mimic his and we fall into a rhythm, knees folding and stretching, wheels whirring. We're migrating swans, efficient and unshakable. I take one hand off the handlebars and stretch my arm out. I uncurl the fingers on my other hand and as I lift it, in front of me Danny slumps. Crash. He's down. I hit his fallen bike and lurch forwards then back. I catch myself on one foot, my knee buckles and I'm on the ground.

Next to me, Danny lies on the grass verge, legs astride his bike, its front wheel still spinning.

19.
Lucky me

'Danny?' Nothing. 'Danny? You OK?'

I throw my bike at the hedge. Fucking bikes. No reception on my phone. Fucking coast. Danny's pale, and so still. I kneel over him and his stubble scratches my cheek. A deep groan fills my ear. I jolt back. He blinks, groans again. His eyes are frightened.

'You fell,' I say. 'You went floppy and slam!' I gesture with my arm without meaning to. 'It was like someone switched you off. And I couldn't stop—'

Danny shushes me. He shifts on the grass and frees his legs from his bike.

I dislodge the water bottle and offer it to him. 'Did you hurt anything? Lucky you went into the hedge.'

Danny wriggles his fingers, reaches for the water and lets out an 'argh!'

'Your arm?'

'Fucking kills,' he says, and somehow that makes us both smile.

We get him sitting up and with his good arm, the right, he holds the bottle to his lips. He squeezes, sucks and the bottle falls into his lap. His arm flops down and suddenly, his eyes are so empty and his skin so grey that it seems he might slip away again.

I squeeze his thigh and he shudders awake. 'I don't get what happened,' I say.

He takes a loud breath, then another.

'I mean, I didn't see you hit anything,' I say.

He cradles his arm against his belly. 'You can't tell Astrid. Or Mum.'

'What?'

'I passed out.'

'Passed out?'

'Fainted,' he says.

'Just like that?'

Danny sighs.

'Has it happened before? Have you told a doctor? Does it happen a lot?'

Danny lifts his head. 'I'm tall, I get hungry, I get light-headed.'

'We just ate.'

'Fucking leave it,' he snaps.

Danny sends me down the hill to find phone reception and call minicab Will for help. 'Just tell him my wheel got caught,' Danny shouts after me.

I call, return to Danny, and we huddle in the hedgerow. He winces every time I move. As the sky darkens I point out stars, and he tells me to shut up.

Will arrives in a minivan. Danny sits in the front and I go one seat back, the bikes slotted in next to me. We convince Danny to go to hospital and head straight there. As we get closer, both Will and I offer to go in with him, but Danny insists his arm is 'just bruised' and that he wants to go alone.

'But if you did want us to come, I know where we can park for free,' I say. 'As long as you can manage a bit of a walk.'

'Seriously?' says Danny.

'Well, is it just bruised or not?' I ask.

'Drop me outside, will you?' Danny repeats.

'If they put it in a plaster, you won't be driving for a while,' says Will.

'I don't need a plaster,' says Danny.

I lean forwards. 'Are you going to tell them how it happened?'

'That I fell off my bike? Sure.'

'Do you think they'll ask if you've fallen off your bike many times before?'

Danny sniffs. 'I don't know what they'll ask, do I?'

'And would you say you had?'

'Had what, Robin?'

'That you'd fallen off your bike many times.'

'God. Maybe. Who hasn't?'

I lean back into my seat, unlock my phone and add Danny's questionable health and lack of transparency to a growing list of reasons not to join the kayak venture.

I fell asleep reading about the difference between a break and a fracture. Now my phone is buzzing somewhere in my bed.

Danny.

'How is it?' I ask.

'Can you help me?' he asks.

'I waited up for you to text back.'

'How am I supposed to text with a broken arm?' he says.

'So it *is* broken?'

'Yes. And I've got a shift. That's why I'm—'

'Oh God, Deliveroo? I can't do that,' I say.

'Minicab. And I need to Deliveroo tonight, but we can talk about that later.'

'Is Deliveroo its own verb?' I ask.

'What? Anyway, the minicab jobs. I'll text them to you,' he says.

'So you *can* text?'

'I can now. I've worked it out. It's the left that's broken,' he says.

'That's helpful at least.'

'Yes. My helpful broken arm.'

'You're being very arms half broken,' I say and hang up.

'Want me to sit in the front or the back?' asks my first customer. She's holding a gift bag and a large, heart-shaped helium balloon.

'Well, you've already opened the front door, but the back would be more traditional.'

'Suit yourself.' She opens the back door, shoves the balloon in, closes the door and climbs into the front. She places the gift bag at her feet, then moves it onto her lap. 'New baby,' she says. 'My friend. Her first. She called him Eric though.' Her voice is so sickly sweet, it sounds like it's not really hers, or anyone's.

'There are worse names,' I say.

'You can't do anything with Eric. Except maybe Ricky.' She follows my eyes to her seatbelt buckle and fastens herself in.

We've missed a gap in the traffic and I wait sixteen cars for the next one.

'What would you have called the baby?' I ask.

'Not Eric.' She laughs. 'But I wouldn't have a boy anyway.'

'You can't choose these things.'

'God, yes you can. In America they do it all the time. In labs.'

I speed up. Something about a world where women choose not to have boys makes me think of Gemma.

I rehearse a run-up in my head then say it. 'While we're on the topic of life. What would you do if someone told you exactly how long you had left to live?'

The woman makes a sound like a punctured tyre. 'Like a few weeks? A day?'

'Thirty-seven years … or I mean, something like that. Thirty-five, thirty or so.'

'Well, first I'd tell them they're creepy. And then … I don't know … Actually, one of my friends, this fortune-teller did give *her* a date, I remember. And told her loads of stuff that did come true…'

'Was her death date right?' I ask, sucked in.

'Well, I don't know that yet, do I? She's still alive. Anyway, if I was told my death date, and it was, like real, I'd get surgery. Might as well spend my money now and stay young. And sort these out.' She smacks her lips, which have clearly been messed with once already.

'Fair enough,' I say.

It always comes back to money, how to get it, what it can get you. It was the same for Twain. His life lurched between financial fortune and desperation, and he was forced onto exhausting lecture tours by what he called 'pecuniary compulsions'. I doubt anyone wants to hear lectures about inventory accounting.

The next job is another young woman.

When I ask what she'd do if someone told her when she's going to die, she asks to see my badge.

'I don't have it with me,' I say.

'Stop the car. Stop here. Anywhere. I need to get out.'

'Are you ill?' I ask.

'Stop the car.'

'I was just making conversation.' It occurs to me she might photograph my number plate so I speed away.

Danny calls when I'm in the little Tesco car park making notes on the morning's research and eating an over-ripe banana that was reduced to twelve pence.

'One more job. In an hour. Texting you,' says Danny.

'So you've called to tell me you're texting me?' I ask.

'No. Yes. No. I wanted to ask about this evening, if you can take me round some Deliveroo jobs in the car.'

I've never liked driving in the dark. No one does. 'It's a tricky time with Dad.'

'Yeah,' says Danny. 'I can try Astrid or Mum. But I was thinking, if it fitted around when you eat, the chip shop always put in a free portion or two of chips for me.'

'I'll check when the carers are coming and let you know.'

I drop into the bungalow before the next job. Dad is unusually bright and the kitchen is unusually clean. There's a new carer on the roster who seems keener than the others, for now. I ask if it's her for all the calls today, and when she says yes, I text Danny: *All good. Let's Deliveroo.*

He replies with emojis and *Pick me up at 7 latest.*

I text back: *How are you feeling by the way?* I get no reply. I should have used emojis. I bet there's one for fainting without explanation. I Google it and a face with spiral eyes comes up.

It's quickly clear that the next passenger will provide neither useful nor honest answers. He's an estate agent who tells me three times that his own car is at the mechanic. He's meeting the prospective buyers of a house outside town. Like the Chicago-bound doctor's house, it's behind a tall hedge. The buyers, a couple around my age, have already arrived when we pull up and they're standing next to their car, a red Fiat 500.

'I reckon they're wasting your time,' I say to the estate agent.

'That car's worth more than it looks,' he replies.

'What's the point of that, though?'

'For the other people who know it's worth more than it looks. Wait here.'

It's on the hour. I turn on the local radio station in the hope the car arsonist has struck again and maintained the pattern of diminishing prestige. Perhaps the Ford Focus of someone who once cut Jason Donovan's hair.

I switch off. The only news of note is pumpkin farmers complaining of a glut because, as one says, 'health and safety' means no one carves anything anymore. I make a note in my phone to look up pumpkin recipes.

I look over to the house for signs of the estate agent. There's movement in a downstairs room. The couple have their backs to me. The current owners must be keen gardeners, or they pay one. Under the main downstairs window they've created a rockery with a stream and a bridge, and what looks like, no they wouldn't … I wind down my window to see properly. Yes, they have. A gnome.

Leaving the car door open, I go closer. I make it obvious I'm stretching my legs in case the agent looks out.

Not just one gnome, but two more, together, behind a bush. So people do buy the naughty gnomes from the antiques shop. I go back to the car and grab my phone.

The light is tricky and what little can be seen of the gnomes' disturbing expressions is in the shade. I crouch down, shift angles, zoom in and at last capture them properly. A window opens above me.

'You alright?' the agent calls down.

My insides cramp. 'Really beautiful butterfly,' I say without looking up.

'In November?' A woman's voice. The couple have come to the window too.

'Yep. Crazy.' The blood drains from my head as I stand up too fast. I stumble to the car half blind and slam the door.

I write the caption many times over. Finally, I decide to name them.
   Spotted in the wild: Enid and Glenn.
   I send it.

Astrid writes straight back: *Why are you sending me this?*

Oh God. She's forgotten. *The naughty gnomes*, I type. *From the antiques shop.*

She replies. *I knew that! Winding you up. Lucky Enid!*

Oh God. What have I done?

Just thought it was funny someone bought some. Saw them at this place. Made me think of you. I send it and then I see what I've said.

She replies before I can hit delete. *Did it? Lucky me!*

I switch my phone to silent, and then off. Off is safer. My thighs are shaking. The over-ripe banana is making its way back up to my mouth. I turn on the radio for distraction. It's a song I've never heard. The lyrics make no sense. I try Radio 4. They're discussing female chimps on *Woman's Hour*.

Lucky me. It doesn't have to mean what it sounds like. Maybe it's *Lucky me, I look like Enid.* Unlikely. Enid is a bawdy washer woman who's taken her lover to the rockery on a rare day off. She's spilling out of her dress.

The estate agent and the couple reappear on the doorstep. I turn down the radio, lower my window and watch them in the mirror. The agent is promising to *sound out* the seller, *nail down* a price and *touch base* soon. The couple are nodding but without the kind of bounce that imminent buyers have on the property shows I watch with Dad.

Then the woman cuts the agent off. 'Oh my goodness! I've just seen it.' She points to the rockery. She goes closer, pulls out her phone. 'Kath's gonna love this.'

The man turns towards me and raises his eyebrows. I shrug.

The estate agent is saying, 'I'd really rather you didn't.'

'Oh, come on,' says the woman, and she nods towards my car. 'He took some.'

'The artwork in the bedroom makes more sense now,' says the man.

'Really. I don't think you should,' the estate agent goes on.

The woman ignores him and takes another picture. 'Do they come with the house?'

'Come!' says the man. 'Nice one!'

I laugh and wish I hadn't.

'That was unprofessional,' the agent says when he's back in my car.

I flick on the wipers. 'Really? They put them in their front garden, they want people to see them.' Not for the first time, I notice my minicab persona gives fewer fucks than my chartered-accountant persona. The wipers judder in the timid drizzle. 'What are they like, the sellers?' I ask.

'I'm not telling you.' The agent crosses his arms as if that might be enough to zip himself up.

'Oh, go on. Just what they do for a living.'

'OK, OK. But I'm not saying any names. They both work in TV. A big show. Friday nights.'

'Would I know their names?' I ask.

'No.'

'So why won't you say them?'

'They're well known to some people,' he says.

'Aren't we all?'

'Are you?' he asks.

'Suppose not.'

The rain has finally committed to falling when I pull up at the bungalow. I stay in my seat a while longer, sucking a toffee and watching sheets of water wash the autumn mess from my windscreen. 'Detritus,' I say out loud, then another way. Is it *i* like 'shite' or *i* like 'shit'? I'll have to watch my minicab persona. I've never liked what Mum called 'coarse language', as useful as it can sometimes be.

Still in the car, I switch my phone back on. My screen is unusually busy. A message from Danny asking where I am and several from Astrid. I place the phone on the padding next to the handbrake, roll my cramped shoulders back and forth and open her messages first.

Six minutes after *Lucky me!* she wrote, *You still there?*

Two minutes later: *How are Enid and Glenn getting on?*

Then: *Oh well. You're probably busy. You've livened up my morning anyway and for that I thank you. And Enid and Glenn.*

Finally: *Drink later?*

20.
Jesus or something

As suggested in one of Gemma's magazines, I leave myself just five minutes to get ready so that my 'gut' will tell me what to wear. It picks my one shirt, my smarter pair of jeans, a hoodie and my puffer jacket, and then it makes me change into my navy woollen V-neck and my office coat.

'I'll be back for when he goes to bed,' I tell the carer, and run out, later than planned.

I'm on Beachway, jogging the last stretch to The Fish, when Danny messages.

Where are you? We said 7.

My legs tremble and my stomach cramps. But something's different. This isn't fear. It's what brave people feel.

Argh, I write back. *Didn't get a chance to call. Something came up with Dad. Will explain tomorrow but in the middle of it right now. Sorry to let you down.*

It's OK. I get it. Night off then.

I've got money for you from today's cab jobs. And tips.

I wait to catch my breath and for Danny to reply that I should keep the tips. As I picture him, I wonder how much Astrid knows about the broken arm. What if this is a ploy to press me for information on the bike ride? If she asks, I'll say there was oil on the road, that I was lucky I was behind Danny, didn't encounter it first. 'Encounter' sounds rehearsed. I'll say 'hit'. If she asks.

Astrid is already at a table, close to the bar in the non-restaurant section. She's on her phone and doesn't see me come in. I unbutton my coat and thank my gut for choosing the shirt. She's wearing make-up that makes her eyes look even more awake. Her black top is a little translucent. On the table are two glasses, one full, one empty, and a bottle of white wine.

'Hey.' Something other people say. I nudge the table with my thigh, harder than I mean to.

'Oh. Hey. Hi. Sorry.' She slides her phone to one side. 'Love the shirt.'

'You look younger,' I say.

'And you look older.' She nods at the chair opposite then glances at her phone.

'Don't let me stop you,' I say.

'It's this stupid chilli pissing contest,' she says.

I wince. 'What?'

'A chilli pissing contest. A mum at school has invited some of us round for dinner and she's asked the WhatsApp group if they're OK with spicy, and now they're all coming back with *hot as it comes* and *I'm a jalfrezi girl* and *I smear vindaloo on my—*'

I hold up a hand. 'I get it.'

The pub is almost empty. An older man sits alone a few tables along; two men in shirts and ties are at another table; a woman behind the bar is writing on the specials board in uniform handwriting.

'Shall I get us some crisps? What flavour?' I ask.

'Anything but chilli,' says Astrid, and she pours me a glass of wine. 'And get us some ice cubes too.'

'Ice cubes?'

'To go in the wine,' she says.

'Do people do that?'

'What does it matter what people do?'

'Fair enough.'

As I return from the bar with two packs of plain crisps and a glass of ice, a group of men comes in, talking over each other, laughing loudly. One laugh is familiar. As they move towards the bar, I recognise the action-figure shoulders, too broad for the short body. Carl. Carl from the cliff jump.

He's still laughing as he and his three friends make their way to the restaurant section. He stops for a second as he passes me then turns back to his friends.

'You know him?' Astrid asks as I sit down.

'Don't think so,' I say.

'The way you were looking at him.'

'Guess anything and anyone in Eastgate is entertain—' I stop. Astrid is using her fingers to put ice cubes in my wine. 'Thanks.'

She lifts her glass. 'To Enid and Glenn, and their perseverance in all weathers.'

'Your English is amazing,' I say, my glass meeting hers. 'Sorry, should I not have said that?'

She grins and her one dimple reappears. 'Why not? You're right. It is. It's my perseverance.'

She beams, and I take her in. She's so gloriously un-British. She's funny without making anyone small, not me, not even herself. I shuffle the open crisp packet closer to her.

We talk about everything but Danny. When Astrid mentions work, I ask, 'Why didn't you tell me you were a lecturer?'

'I'm sure I told you. Or I thought you knew. Everybody knows.'

'I didn't. It's not like you wear a badge.' I lift my eyes away from her chest.

'If we did wear badges, would the whole truth fit onto them?' she says.

'Mine would. "Robin, thirty-seven, chartered accountant, part-time carer, Costco member."'

She straightens up. '"Astrid, forty-three, mother, wine drinker, pickler, Kafka devotee, apprentice meteor spotter, part-time student, one-time costume maker, future Vespa owner."'

'A big badge.' I feel both relieved and guilty that she hasn't squeezed Danny on there.

I want to ask why she'd leave a university job for something like life coaching, or whatever Danny called it, but it'll give away that we talked about her. Instead, I say, 'Is it always Kafka you teach, one man and his books, all the time?'

'Mainly. I teach the first years about other German writers, or writing in German, if you're being precise. But Kafka is my main man. You remind me of him.'

'Oh.'

I spent the afternoon reading about her 'main man' in preparation for whatever this is. Kafka worked (unhappily) for an insurance company, never married, had a difficult relationship with a domineering father and then starved to death aged forty. I take a handful of crisps.

Astrid moves on. 'Do you think you'll go back to London?'

I swallow. She won't understand the target retirement date, or Goa – or whichever target retirement place works with what's left. 'I doubt it,' I say. 'I have a flat there but I'm selling it.'

'Is it on the market?' She takes out her phone. 'Can we look it up? Sorry, I'm so nosey. I'm trying to imagine your style.' The grin, the dimple.

'Not quite yet. There's someone living in it.'

'A tenant? Shit. In Germany it's a nightmare getting a tenant out. My parents have been stuck with this woman and her geckos for years.' And she goes on, talking about tenancy laws and reptiles.

I should shut up and just listen. But I'm like those alcoholics and porn addicts who want to be called out. 'It's not a tenant,' I interrupt. 'It's my ex, Gemma.'

'Oh. Your ex is your tenant?'

'She just hasn't moved out yet.' I examine her face for signs of jealousy but find disappointment.

'Have you asked her to move out?'

'It's … it's…' I bite off the piece of dead skin next to my thumbnail that's been bugging me all day. 'I just … I shouldn't need to.'

'But you do. Or she'll exploit you. She's living rent-free in London. You need that money.'

'I did tell her we need to talk,' I say.

Astrid makes a face like a praying mantis: bulging eyes and a cannibalistic glare. 'Perfect,' she says.

'God, you're right. You are nosey. But yeah, I'll tell her. Throw her out on the street.'

'Unless you're getting back together with her,' she says.

Five minutes ago, I'd have said that was impossible.

Astrid is motionless. 'Are you?'

'Ha! More wine? By the glass maybe?'

'Sure,' says Astrid, in a tone she almost certainly uses for students who hand in their essays late. 'Small for me.'

The bar is busier and there are two people serving now. I edge into a gap between two women. I smile to convey that I'm not pushing in.

There's a shout from the other end of the bar. 'Oh my God. It *is* him,' says Carl. 'Guys, look. It's comet boy!'

His friends have finished dinner and they're coming over to the bar. They scan around like a gaggle of meerkats. 'There, that guy.' Carl points at me. 'Comet boy. The kid I told you about from school. Knows the exact day he's gonna die. Says a comet told him.'

I pray that Astrid's on her phone, lost in messages about chillies and the dinners people invite her to.

Carl isn't finished. 'Robin, remember – like a bird.' He laughs at his misogyny. 'Said he can't die until some exact day. We dared him to prove it.'

'Come on, Carl. You're shouting,' says a less-drunk member of the group and grips what he can of Carl's bulging shoulders.

The man behind the bar waves in my face. 'What you having?'

I look at the woman next to me, she gestures for me to go ahead. I can't. I need to get out. The barman puffs through his lips and moves on.

I dare to look over to Astrid. She mouths 'white' to me. I wait for the barman to come back my way and I buy two small white wines and ask for more ice, then change my mind. Ice will only eke things out.

My hands are shaking as I place the glasses on our table.

'So you *do* know him,' says Astrid. She's heard it all.

'Fantasist,' I say. 'Didn't recognise him before. He didn't stay on for A-levels, sad to see it shows.'

Another shout from Carl. 'Do you still believe it? When you're gonna die? Oi! Not even a hello?'

I turn towards him. Everyone is staring. I hold up a hand. It's part wave, part plea for him to stop. 'Have a fun night, Carl.' I swivel back to Astrid.

'Fucking bully,' she says. 'Let's down these and get out.'

We drink, and she grabs my hand. Carl shouts after us as we weave through tables and out onto the street.

The rain has stopped and wet-pavement smell mixes with the fish and grease oozing from the pub. The warmth of Astrid's hand lingers on my skin.

'Thank you. And sorry,' I say.

'Don't apologise for being bullied, Robin.'

'Well, I nearly said something. Better not to engage though.' I shiver. I should have worn a scarf. Useless gut. 'Anyway, it's late.'

Astrid flicks out her arm to free her watch from multiple cuffs. 'It's half-eight. What about we walk a long way home?' She has worn a scarf, of course, another of her blanket-like ones that wraps round and round. This one is dark green and gives her the look of an ancient warrior queen.

'I need to get back to Dad,' I say.

'Do you?' She fixes me with a stare, her face now dimpleless. 'Nothing to do with what happened in there?'

Bloody hell. Is she difficultly wonderful, or wonderfully difficult? Either way, I'm exhausted.

'It was just some rubbish from school,' I say.

'So you don't believe you know when you're going to die?'

'Can we start walking?' I cross to where the pavement is wider.

'Oh my God, you think you know when you're going to die.'

'No.' I don't *think* I know. I know.

'So what was that about a comet talking to you?'

'It didn't talk to me. I'm not some lunatic,' I say.

'No, because that would be the moon.' She elbows me, clearly pleased with her etymological knowledge.

'And you said you knew nothing about the moon.'

'What I want to know about is your comet,' she says.

'It's not my comet. Why does everyone call it my comet? If anyone's, it's Edmond Halley's comet—'

'Halley's Comet!' Astrid interrupts. 'I remember that one. OK. His comet. He saw it first.'

'No, he didn't. It had been seen before, over centuries. It's in the Bayeux Tapestry.'

'Oh.' She follows my gaze towards France.

'But Halley saw something no one else dared to see: that all these comets observed through history weren't different comets at all. They were all the same comet, returning to our skies again and again, one and the same, every seventy-six years, sometimes seventy-five. And he predicted its next return and he was right.' I turn to face the sea, loud and close, waves crashing at steady intervals. 'One and the same. Halley.'

Astrid touches my arm. 'You're educational when you're angry.'

I lean away.

'And Halley's Comet tells you things,' she says.

'That a question?'

'Yes. We should talk about this. Everyone believes some crazy shit or another.'

'I wasn't ready to tell you.' I stop. I can't walk and defend myself.

A low wall edges the pavement. I sit on it, and spray from the waves hits the back of my ears. Astrid sits next to me. She leans, her arm touches mine and I surrender.

I talk fast so she can't interrupt. I tell her about Mark Twain coming in and going out with the comet, and about how I too was born with the comet, at the very moment Grandad Jim saw it, and how he said I too will go out with the comet, no earlier and no later. And I tell her about Carl and the cliffs, but not about Mum. 'So yeah, one way or another, it became pretty clear he was right.'

'Hang on.' She pokes a finger into my thigh. 'So you're Jesus or something?'

'When did I say I was Jesus?'

'You said you can't die.'

'For now. Not until the comet returns, in 2061. July 2061.'

Astrid lets out a loud breath. 'And what do you do with this … knowledge?' The pause is mean.

'I plan.'

'Plan what?'

'What I have left – time and money.' I take out my phone. 'I made this counter, so I can always see what's left.'

'You're literally counting down the days until you die.'

'Not literally, numerically.'

She frowns. I continue. 'And it's a counter, not a countdown.'

We stare at my phone, watching the seconds elapse.

Astrid lifts her eyes to the sky. 'Mmm. Happy is the one, I guess.'

'What does that mean?'

'You know, in the Bible. "Happy is the one who reads this

book…" As in, happy is the one who knows what's coming next, does what he's told. People have been selling certainty for millennia.'

'The Bible has nothing to do with it.' I tuck my freezing fingers into my armpits.

'But human nature does,' says Astrid. 'We like to think we can know the unknowable. The alternative is unbearable. I get it.'

'When were you going to tell me you're into the Bible?'

'Not *into* it. I know it. You can't grapple with all those tormented Germans without knowing how it all started.'

'Life?'

'Their existential angst,' she says.

I've never had a conversation like this before in Eastgate. Or anywhere.

'Thought you were a creationist for a second,' I say.

'And for a second, I thought you were ruled by a space rock.'

'Guided not ruled, and you know it's a comet. Mark Twain was right. There've been others too. The astronomer Josef Allen Hynek was born with Halley's Comet in 1910, died with it in 1986. We crossed over by two weeks.' No need to tell her Hynek is best known as a UFO expert.

'Coincidence,' says Astrid.

'Or not. And really, what does it matter to you?'

'Are you telling me to shut up?'

'Seriously, what does it matter to you that I know how long I have and can plan it out? You're not the first person to be envious.'

'My God, Robin. I can't be envious of you confusing feelings with facts, of your desperation for control going to extremes.'

'It's not extremes.'

'So what's the "living off two pounds a day" about? It's part of it, isn't it?'

'Why not? And it's just until I find the right job. I'm saving.' If I had my laptop I could show her. It's clearer on a spreadsheet.

'Saving for what?'

'My target retirement date – end of July 2031, when I'm forty-five. Then I get a fair retirement. Thirty years.'

'And what do you do in your retirement?' she asks.

'Find the right place to live, like Goa, somewhere warm, affordable … peaceful.'

'And then?'

'Then I have another plan, but I can't talk about it yet.'

'Don't then.' She folds her arms.

I fold mine.

'I think…' She waits for a moped to go by. 'I think I get it. You're *finding* the right job, then *finding* the right place, for a plan you don't have, all while starving yourself and counting down to your death.'

I stand up. 'And you're *finding* the most unkind way possible to see this.'

'Bollocks,' she says. 'I'm asking you – what about now? What do you do with now? What do you care about now?'

'Right now? Getting warm.' I stop as I realise she's got to her feet and moved a step away from me. 'Sorry. I don't normally shout.'

She turns away. 'I'll walk home on my own.'

OBJECT: *Order of Service*
DATE: *February 1998*
NOTES: *There it is, my 'space rock', on a map on the back of the order of service for Grandad Jim's funeral – heart attack, aged sixty-five. His friend Ron drew the map for me. We were in the graveyard after the service.*

Ron was with Grandad when he saw the comet in 1986. They'd travelled to Australia – better chance from the southern hemisphere – and they spotted it the day I was born. The same moment. Grandad told the story often. I'd ask him to. He'd 'forked out' to call Mum from his hotel and Dad had picked up, Mum was at the hospital. She'd had a little boy, two weeks early.

'A boy born with the comet,' Grandad would say. 'Now doesn't that make you happy?' and he'd touch the tip of my nose.

I always thought that if I got the chance to be a grandad, I'd be like him. He taught me how to find Venus, Mars and Jupiter. We'd sit on the garden bench with blankets and binoculars. Granny Chris would bring out Ovaltine and retreat to the sofa, Polly following at her heels. He'd tell me the stories of the constellations: bears flung into the sky, Orion running scared from Scorpius. And he'd tell me about Twain. In with the comet, out with the comet.

His was my first funeral. I missed school and wore a black tie. Mum was weird in the graveyard. She said, 'You have to meet Ron,' as if we were at a party, and as if I were an adult.

Ron showed me a picture he kept in his wallet: the comet on the day I was born. Then he took the order of service from his pocket, turned it over and drew the solar system, rings marking the orbits of each planet, including poor old Pluto.

'Right now it's here,' said Ron and he drew the comet between Uranus and Neptune. Then he traced its path with his finger and wrote 1986 and 2061 next to Earth.

'Twice in your lifetime,' he said. 'Lucky chap.'

That night, I wrote that on: 'Twice in my lifetime'

Notes for Dad: Remember Granny's little terrier? Pongy Polly, you called her. You said I came back smelling of her.

'I can't smell it,' Mum would say.

'You grew up with dog pong,' you'd reply. 'Broke your nose.'

And every time, she'd feel for crookedness and laugh.

21.
Choices

If the comet had a bumper sticker, it would read *I'm coming for you*.

Ever since I was born, it's been travelling away from us. But now it's gone about as far as it can go. In a matter of weeks, it will loop around and begin its journey back towards Earth.

My plan was always to spend these critical weeks reviewing spreadsheets and shortlisting retirement destinations. More recently, I tweaked the plan and resolved to apply for three proper jobs before the day of the aphelion itself, when the comet is furthest from the sun.

In short, the comet's turning point was supposed to be galvanising. In reality, it has coincided with an unprecedented gulf between me and the rest of humankind that has left me unable to think, sleep or digest. As a child, I would have lain under my bed telling SuperTed that no one understood me. As a teenager, I would have turned to Radiohead and, as a student, to Mozart's 'Lacrimosa'. As a man and chartered accountant, I lie on the roof of Dad's bungalow and wait for a seagull to defecate on my face and prove that things still happen to me.

I've brought my old camping mat with me. My head hurts from last night's cheap white wine and Astrid's tirade. I was thinking that with the proper padding, I might drift off.

My phone buzzes in the pocket of my inner coat. I'm wearing two over my pyjamas. I'm also wearing ski gloves – a bin-bag find and a relic from my graduate-trainee ski trip, a time of slimmer hands and fatter budgets.

I yank off one glove and extract my phone. A message from Astrid:

All I suggest is you ask what it's costing you. See attachment. A xx

The kisses are reassuring. The attachment is 527 kilobytes and the roof is beyond the reach of the bungalow's Wi-Fi. *It will cost me a data charge*, I write back.

You make no sense, she replies.

I wriggle my fingers back into the glove. The attachment can wait.

A minute later, the door of the morning carer's electric car closes and there are *boing* sounds as she reverses out of the drive. I roll up my mat and go inside.

The attachment is five photocopied pages of tiny print. On the first page, Astrid has written in biro:

> *Franz Kafka*
> *Written in 1922*
> *Edited in 1924 (on his deathbed)*

The title and its hyphen are unsettling: *A Fasting-Artist.* The story itself even more so.

The eponymous artist has made a living, and somewhat of a name for himself, by sitting in a cage on public display and starving himself for forty days at a time. He would fast for longer but his manager always stops the fast at forty days, claiming it's the optimum length to cultivate public interest. When fasting falls out of fashion, the fasting-artist parts ways with his manager and joins a circus, where he is put not inside the main tent, but with the animal cages, for the audience to ogle in the interval. Except no one ogles, they merely rush by his cage on their way to the animals. The ending is particularly odd and sad. As the forgotten fasting-artist lies near death, he is rediscovered by circus people investigating the seemingly unused cage. In his last breath he admits to never having found a food he liked and that therefore fasting had always been easy, that in fact he couldn't help it. His emaciated body is scooped up and buried with the rotten straw on which it lies. In his place, the circus puts a young panther, hungry for food, and for life. The public, predictably, adore the panther.

It's clearly a metaphor. Kafka, an unhappy man who could not help but write and yet feared his writing would find no audience, decided to leave the world with a big *Fuck you! You killed me!*

What's also obvious is how Astrid has twisted the story to fit me. She'll be annoyed I got it so quickly. I look up how to put bold typeface into a message and text her.

*I read it. Others consume life but life consumes me. All **I** suggest is **you** realise how lucky it is to be born a panther.*

I skim the story a second time and Google what others think I'm supposed to make of it, but I get lost in a debate over whether it should be translated as *A Fasting-Artist* or *A Hunger-Artist*. No one mentions the unnecessary hyphen.

I message Astrid again.

Guess Danny never told you he believed it too. For years. The comet was pretty close when he was born. Happy is the one who keeps massive secrets.

It's mean but necessary. Why should I take all her anger and Kafka?

No reply. I leave my phone in my room and sit with Dad, watching a couple on the TV look for a house in Spain. They're shown several and like none. I change channels and we watch another couple trying to move out of London. The husband ruins the whole show by announcing in the final minute that he's not ready to 'leave the capital'.

'Never felt that about London,' I say to Dad. 'Temporary for me. Place to make fast money, and to bloody spend it just as fast...' I pause for Dad to register my insight. 'It sucks people in, London. They can't even imagine anywhere else could ever match it. Everywhere but London is the third world. Are we allowed to say that? And they all go on about the theatres and—'

Dad grunts and I stop. He gestures with his better arm for me to bring him his alphabet card.

I perch on the arm of the sofa and hold the card on his lap. His hand is tensed into the shape of a crab claw, like the ones they sell to tourists at the chip shop. Trembling, the claw slides around the laminated card and I guess at where it's trying to settle. 'Is that G, Dad?' A tiny nod. 'And a D?' Grunt. 'An E?' Nod. 'M?' Nod. 'Are you saying "Gem"?' Nod. '"Gemma"?' Nod. 'Oh Dad. You're asking about Gemma?'

A hiss for 'yes'.

'I told you, didn't I? Remember? She's not moving. One of those bloody Londoners, I guess.' I take the card off Dad's lap. 'It's alright. She was all wrong for me. Bossy.'

Dad snorts and makes a *ha* sound.

'Exactly,' I say. 'You know she wouldn't let me eat on the sofa? And she had this thing about the dishwasher, always—' Dad groans, jerks his arm towards the TV, where a new show about attics is starting. 'I'll leave you to it then,' I say, and return to my room.

Still nothing from Astrid. She'll be on the phone to Danny, dissecting my life plan. Does she even know about the broken arm?

And talk of the Deliverooer. A message.

How's your dad? Can you do Monday at 10 for the Scout huts? Want some minicab runs today?

It's pretty clear he doesn't know about last night's pub trip. I should tell him. But then what is there to tell?

Better. Sure. Yes, I reply.

When questioned, my first minicab passenger says he'd get a divorce and track down an old girlfriend; another says she'd run the Rio marathon; another says she'd have a baby using a donor. (I assume she means sperm donor, not baby donor, but it seems rude to ask, or to say 'sperm'.)

I park behind the little Tesco and note them all down on my phone as I eat a ninety-five-pence cheese twist and a full-price banana. Then I play around with the wording of an additional question, one I'll ask if I'm feeling combative, or *Astridial*, you might say. I repeat *Astridial* to myself in her accent – a scratchy *tri* sound.

Next is a woman about my age going to the station. When I give her thirty years to live, she doesn't pause to think. She'd learn the cello and retrain as a midwife, she says.

I debut the new question. 'What's stopping you from doing that anyway?'

'Mortgage, kids, time,' she says.

'You'd still have a mortgage and kids if you knew you had thirty years to live,' I say.

'You're right. Guess it changes nothing then. Maybe if I had two or three years left, I could be more selfish. But not for thirty years.'

'Makes you wonder if we can ever really change anything. If we all get stuck one way or another,' I say.

'I don't know. We make choices and, sure, we get stuck, but then we can make more choices, and we can make the best of what we're stuck with. Like me. I don't want to do this meeting in London. But I will enjoy the hour on the train on my own.'

'It's an hour and ten minutes,' I say.

'Even better.'

I drive the long way back from the station, past the marshlands and the sheep fields, down the street where every house flies a Union Jack, and out along the coast.

What choices have I made? I've always done whatever came next. I took the A-levels my teachers suggested, studied the subject I'd find easiest at the university they recommended, took a job with the first firm to accept me and followed the well-plotted path of so many accountants before me – my prize for exceptional exam results underscored that it was the right, and only, path for me. As for my time with Gemma, we moved in together because lockdown made it the only way to continue our relationship. No choices, just steps.

I pull into the nearest side road and call Gemma. As hoped, she doesn't pick up. I leave a voicemail: 'I need to sell the flat. Text me to let me know you got this. Don't call, I'm at work.'

She can move in with her sister, or her parents, or a colleague. She can stop buying hair implements and notepads, and pay for her own place. Did she think my politeness would continue indefinitely?

When Gemma hasn't responded by the end of the day, I book a non-peak train ticket for the morning and email three previously untested London estate agents.

22.
What we had

I'm about to sell a flat worth at least nine hundred thousand pounds, so I've flouted the budget and bought myself a Marks & Spencer lunch, including thick crisps, chocolate pretzels and a miniature bottle of white wine. I lay them out on my table, at the non-toilet end of a near-empty carriage. The aspiring cellist was right: the solitude of the train is reinvigorating.

Between my hoisin duck wrap and the pretzels, I message Gemma: *On my way up to meet agents. I have keys. Assume it's tidy.* It will be. Gemma is maniacally tidy.

She replies when I'm buying a £2.55 coffee from the trolley. *God Robin, you could have warned me. Today doesn't work.*

You can't *God Robin* someone you have broken up with. I secure the lid on my coffee and compose a reply:

I told you I'm selling. I need the money for an investment. You'll need to find somewhere else. I won't ask for rent for the last five weeks.

What happened to you? Gemma replies.

I down the last of my wine. *What indeed?*

She messages once more asking when I will arrive and I ignore it.

I spend the rest of the journey looking at sketches from Danny. They are his plans for the Scout huts, detailed and beautiful but also unnerving; he's more serious about this than I ever imagined. Drawing onto floorplans, he's divided each hut into bunk-bed rooms, social rooms, kit rooms, kitchens, bathrooms. There are pages of drawings of how each area will look: pegs for kit on the end of the beds, pictures of dolphins on the walls, herb pots on windowsills. On the last page, he's written, *This one's new. Your office. Ideas. All up to you.* He's drawn in a coffee machine and a biscuit tin, and an armchair facing the window. An arrow points towards the river with the words, *Sunsets/kayak shed/wave to me.* I look away before his fantasy can pull me in any further.

I emerge from the Underground to London's typical assault on my senses. Only, this time it's intensified by my two months away. Traffic roars in the heavy rain, umbrellas and people collide on the pavements, a moped spews out acrid black smoke. I pull my coat collar over my mouth and nose.

Several shops along my walk to the flat have changed hands and purpose. But they uphold the area's commitment to empty promises. I step around a sandwich board that proclaims *New hair, new you.* A bento place offers *Bliss in a box*, and a salad bar declares itself *The way to good health.* More like the way to poverty and afternoon snacking. At least the food shops of Eastgate know what people really want: *Free pie with every large fish 'n' chips. Three battered sausages for the price of two.*

Thoughts of frankness and Eastgate bring me on to Astrid. I haven't heard from her since the *Fasting-Artist.* I tuck myself in a pub doorway and message her:

What Kafka would you recommend next? I like him.

Then another message: *Anyway, in London sorting the flat. Loud and wet.*

And then another: *London, I mean. Not the flat. That's usually dry and quiet.*

I slow down as I near the flat. What will Gemma have rearranged since I left? The sofa is her favourite thing to move. We never watched

TV from the same angle for more than a week. In the kitchen, she likes to switch the glasses and crockery in pursuit of the optimal proximity to the dishwasher. I always helped with that. She'd say something like, 'You know what? It's the small plates we use most.' Or, 'When it's warmer, we get through more glasses.' And we'd rearrange again, usually on a Saturday afternoon. It made her happy, until she wasn't.

I let myself in, wipe my feet and pick up the post: two envelopes addressed to us both. They shake in my unsteady hand. I'm sweating. And I'm saying *hasty* over and over in my head. Am I being too hasty? I love this little entrance, or, really, I love its existence: an airlock between chaotic London and my ordered home. There's the door from the street, the grey tiled floor, a carpeted staircase and a second door to the flat itself, also locked, different key.

I lean against the front door and count the fifteen steps to the landing. I'm here now and two agents will soon be here too. I can't disappoint them and I won't disappoint myself.

Halfway up the stairs, I notice Gemma has left two pairs of new shoes on the landing. I move them to one side, one pair on top of the other.

The mess continues inside: a coffee cup and a packet of gum on the sideboard, a half-open umbrella leaned against the wall, a duffel bag by the wardrobe. Gemma hasn't been coping as well as she makes out.

The kitchen is tidier, but it's unlike her to leave washing up on the draining board.

I fill the kettle. Twenty minutes before the first agent arrives. Perhaps he or she (neither agency gave any names) will have advice on how to empty the place. I won't need all this furniture in Eastgate, nor the collection of kitchenware we amassed over the last three years. Maybe Gemma will want it.

I take two Hobnobs from the biscuit barrel and leave my tea to brew while I go around making a photo inventory of my London possessions. The kitchen appliances and the wall-mounted TV in the lounge can stay. In the bedroom, there's just the chest of drawers, the tulip painting by Gemma's mother and the bed (she's moved her memory-foam pillow to the middle).

I photograph the pictures on the wall as I climb the stairs to my office. I've stressed to the agencies that the flat is over two floors but I fully expect them to use the word 'mezzanine' wrongly.

Gemma's left the blinds down, and my flash goes off automatically as I take a photo of my office. And she's left the sofa bed folded out. I open the door wider and stumble back. There's someone in the bed. Brown hair peeks out the top of the duvet. A foot peeks out the bottom. The toenails are painted green.

My first thought is I should wake her. But how? I switch on the light, switch it off again. Distance. I should wake her from a distance. I creep down the stairs and into the hall. I use my key to turn the lock and close the front door almost silently. I pass the shoes – clearly belonging to the green-toed feet – and again, I use my key to close the door to the road.

Back on the pavement I ring the bell three times. Then another three. Nothing. I press again. A woman walking past gives me a weird look. She's about to say something. I get there first. 'Guess I'll let myself in then,' I say, and hold up my key.

At the top of the entrance-hall stairs, I bang on the door. I wait the time it takes to get out of bed and descend the stairs from my office – *my* office! – and knock again. Finally, there are footsteps, unhurried.

The door opens a crack.

'Chloe?'

First-class Chloe, who always gets what she wants. Obvious now.

'Robin?'

'I rang the bell. Seven times.'

'I switched off the intercom. I'm on nights.' She yawns to make her point. 'Why are you here?'

'It's my flat.'

'Well yeah, but...' She's holding the door with both hands, presumably ready to block my entry.

'I'm meeting some agents to do a valuation,' I say. She doesn't move. 'And why are you here, Chloe?'

She runs her hand through her hair, and that smell that only women have escapes from her armpit: sweat wrapped in washing detergent. There are black make-up splodges in the corners of her eyes. 'Ahhhh,' she begins, but stops. She straightens her T-shirt. 'Guess you want to come in.'

'Yes.' I look at my watch. 'The agent's here in ten minutes. Assume it's tidy.'

'You know Gemma,' says Chloe.

'I did once.'

'Yikes.' She turns towards the kitchen, and I follow, noticing the grey T-shirt she's wearing is mine and the pyjama bottoms are Gemma's. 'Want a cup of tea?' she asks over her shoulder.

'Shit. Sure. I mean sure.' I'm panicking. I slow down. 'But I'll make it. You should get dressed.'

Too late. She's standing over my stewed mug of tea. 'That's weird. Don't remember making this.'

'Probably when you came in,' I say. 'Must have been quite the night shift.'

'No,' she says, reaching for the mug.

'Leave that!' Then I lower my voice. 'Honestly, I'll make you a fresh one.'

'What? It's still hot.' Chloe studies the mug then me.

'Weird.' I bite my lip to hide the smile my face keeps trying to do, like my unravelling amuses it.

'That's fucking messed up.' She sniffs the tea.

'Your professional diagnosis?' I attempt a chuckle.

'You have keys, don't you?' she asks.

My throat closes up.

'You have keys?' she asks again.

'Well…'

'You have keys?' she shouts.

'Well, it is my flat.'

'But you don't live here. You made this, didn't you?' She holds up the mug. 'You were already here. Fuck, Robin. You were sneaking around while I was sleeping.' I think about the photos in my phone, the one of her in bed. She's getting louder. 'Fucking made yourself a cup of tea with me in the next room.'

Hot tea hits my face. The teabag lands on my foot. 'Jesus!' I cry out. I lean over the sink, splash myself with cold water. It's not burning yet. Or I'm in shock and I'm burning and I don't know it. Scalded. Assaulted by a doctor.

When I turn around, she's gone. 'This is not OK,' I shout up to my office.

I dab my cheeks with a damp tea towel. Above me, Chloe stamps around. She thuds down the stairs, passes me without looking up and shouts from the front door. 'You're a fucking weirdo, Robin. You've always been a fucking weirdo.'

'Take your shoes,' I call after her.

The agent is a man, stares without comment at my tea-stained collar and gives a valuation that suggests my Marks & Spencer lunch was ill-judged. More than once, he describes the market as 'wobbly'.

I'm not ready to trust him. I stayed up until 2.00am on property websites and used the area's typical price per square foot to calculate my own valuation. It's twelve per cent higher than his.

The second agent is due in five minutes.

I help myself to the last two Hobnobs and re-read a message from Gemma announcing her imminent and angry arrival *home*. What I want to say doesn't fit in a text message. She set me a trap. She's lucky it ended with my tea scalding and nothing gorier. I could have been stabbed. In America, I'd have been shot.

I wait by the window for the agent. On this one street, in this one moment, there are more people than I'd see in a week in Eastgate. The rain has stopped and two window cleaners are chatting to each other as they abseil down the new office building on the corner. Below them, a traffic warden is taking pictures of a van on double-yellow lines. The *Big Issue* woman is in her usual spot. She shouts as a kid comes too close on an electric scooter. No one else is working. A couple goes into the Greek place. Another couple holds hands as they read the menu outside the Italian. Schoolkids queue for bubble tea. Two of them are vaping. Outside The George, the crowd of pavement drinkers spills onto the road. London is full of people who finish early on a Friday.

The intercom buzzes. I press my forehead against the glass and see a woman in a smart coat. The agent has arrived before Gemma. If we're quick, I have a chance of getting away.

'Lovely,' the agent says as she climbs the stairs to me. 'I'm Daisy.' She hands me her card.

Chloe's shoes are still encumbering the entrance. 'Sorry about the mess,' I say to Daisy.

'That's nothing,' she says.

Inside, she rotates on the spot. 'Lovely,' she says again. 'Don't want to put any horses before any carts, but I have a lovely couple desperate to buy on this road.'

I want to correct her mis-ordering of an idiom about mis-ordering, but I stop myself.

'Sounds perfect. I'm in a hurry,' I say.

She takes notes and talks all the time as we go around. In my office, she seems to appreciate the sofa bed being left out. 'Lovely to have a second bedroom for when you need it,' she says with an odd smile.

She's taking pictures from my office window when there's a key in the front door. 'My partner,' I explain. This doesn't have to be a disaster. The front door slams. It will be a disaster.

I call down to Gemma, 'We're up here, love. Just finishing.' Back
to Daisy, 'She's been manic. Maybe we could tie up the rest over
the phone?' I gesture for Daisy to follow me down the stairs.

'I think I—' Daisy clasps the banister as if the rage in Gemma's
face might knock us both flying.

'What is wrong with you, Robin? What did you do to Chloe?'
Gemma shouts.

I'm distracted by her hair. It's shorter and brushes against her
shoulders as she bellows up at me.

'Wow! New haircut,' I say.

'What? Don't do that, Robin.' Her gaze moves to Daisy, who's
still gripping the banister.

No one speaks. Outside, the chatter on the pub pavement is
growing louder. A taxi door slams, and its arriving passenger is
greeted with a cheer.

Daisy clears her throat.

'Sorry,' I say. 'Daisy, this is Gemma. Gemma, this is Daisy.
Daisy's doing a valuation.' My self-sabotaging brain realises I sound
like a picture book, and again I'm smiling when I shouldn't.

Gemma frowns at me and voice barely softened, she says to
Daisy, 'We're not ready to sell.'

'Come on, love. Daisy has a buyer super keen on this road.'

'Cash,' says Daisy.

Gemma moves closer to the bottom step and I find myself
wishing for a tea towel or taser to shoo her back. I edge down one
step, then another. 'Daisy needs to get to another property.'

'Good,' says Gemma, and finally moves aside.

In my rush down the final stairs, I stumble and Daisy goes into
me.

'Sorry,' she says.

'My fault,' I reply.

At the door to the street, she says, 'If you don't mind, Robin,
this all seems a bit delicate.'

'Too messy after all,' I say.

'Really sorry.' She smooths down her coat.

'But say you did have to do a valuation on the spot, an estimate…'

'Um, gosh, well, based on the area, the size … a few shy of a million.'

'A few…?'

'A few thousand. Or maybe a million, could go over. It's a popular road.' Daisy's smile is back at the thought of her commission.

'Brilliant. I'll call you.' I glance over my shoulder. 'I can sort this out.'

Gemma is at the kitchen table, her back to me. My chance to speak first.

'Why were you like that in front of her?'

She lifts her head. 'Not now, Robin. I've had a shit day. I've had Chloe screaming down the phone. Another parent made a complaint, and I'm starving.'

'Someone nick your lunch again?' I sit down opposite her.

She smiles. 'Yep.'

That happens a lot. They take their lunch breaks in shifts, and if Gemma is last, her food is often gone from the fridge. I once bought a large tub of dog food, emptied it out and cleaned the container so she could take her lunch in that each day. No one would dare to open it, was the thinking. But she wouldn't dare open it either, she said.

'And you couldn't go out to get something else?' I ask. Presumably she has plenty of spare money.

'An incident ate into my break.' 'Incident' is our code for things involving nappies and potties.

'How about a bowl of pasta across the road?' I ask, my mood lifting at the thought of escaping the flat.

She massages her cheeks. 'Actually, that would be lovely. Thank you.'

While Gemma goes to get ready, I make a plan: I'll have the garlic and chicken penne and one beer, be on the train by 7.30pm and home by 9.00pm. Bungalow home. And then it strikes me, when I sell, I won't have my own home. I'm on the brink of homelessness. That's something I must never say in front of Astrid. I check my phone. She's replied. She messaged while Gemma was shouting at me. As usual, it's in many parts.

Great to get these things done

Then a picture of a Kafka book: *Metamorphosis and Other Stories*

Then: Ein Hungerkünstler *is part of four stories. I imagine you'd also find his letters to his father interesting.*

I've barely told her anything about Dad.

Another message appears:

When are you back?

'Ready?' Gemma asks from the bedroom doorway.

I turn my phone face down. 'You look lovely.'

'Who's that?' She nods towards my phone.

'No one.'

'Right.'

She's wearing one of my favourite tops, blue with a V-neck. The shoulders are less puffy than on lots of her other tops.

At the front door, we both pull out our keys. 'Sorry,' I say. 'You go.'

The restaurant is busy but we get my favourite table, tucked in a corner, furthest from the door. Gemma orders her usual and I order mine.

'They've changed the breadsticks,' she says after the waiter has gone. She's been here without me and wants me to know it.

'What's the deal with Chloe?' I ask.

Gemma sighs loudly. 'I didn't want to fight.'

The waiter brings our drinks. My beer, her glass of red. 'And some tap water?' Gemma asks without a 'please'.

'You could have warned me she'd be there,' I say when we're alone again.

'It's just while she's between places.'

'I'm between places,' I say.

'Only because of your dad. Only for now.' She holds a breadstick in mid-air. 'Which is what I wanted to talk to you about.'

'Oh.'

'What if we sell the flat and then we regret it?' She snaps the breadstick.

'We?'

'I mean what if we realise Eastgate was the problem. That we let Eastgate get in the way of what we had here.' She gestures with the remaining breadstick towards the flat.

I take my own breadstick, bite off the end. She's right, they're saltier. I bite again. Hers is still angled at the home we used to share. What did we have there? Safety, I suppose. And maybe passion, certainly at the beginning. One time, we left the curtains open; another, I came home to find her naked in the kitchen. Mind-blowing at the time, then disappointing when I discovered it was recommended in one of her magazines under 'Last-ditch Lovers'. We shared largely the same taste in TV and the same joy at the arrival of a takeaway on a Friday night. We both enjoyed setting and then switching off our alarms on a Sunday morning. Neither of us likes Pilates, gin or jogging.

Gemma touches my hand. 'What are you thinking?'

'About what we had.'

'We had a good pandemic.'

'Gemma!'

It's what we always used to say, but knew we shouldn't, and whoever said it, the other one would reprimand them.

The breadsticks are making me thirsty. I need another beer. But then I'll have another and another, and there'll be no way out. And so while I still can, I say, 'This isn't what I want. I want to live in Eastgate. I have plans in Eastgate.'

Gemma leans away. 'So I'm competing with Eastgate? First a comet and now a shitty seaside town?'

'You're competing with what my life could become in a seaside town,' I say.

'You said you needed me.'

'And you need my flat. You and Chloe.'

She folds her napkin, places it on the table and stands. 'Must be nice having money so you can lord it over the people who love you.'

'You don't love me,' I say.

Our food comes and I'm grateful to the waiter for acting as if Gemma has merely gone to the ladies. After two spoonfuls of my penne and one spoonful of her lasagne, I call the waiter back and ask for the bill and for him to pack up our meals. 'And a plastic fork, please, if you have one.'

The waiter returns with the food in boxes and a metal fork. 'Bring it back whenever,' he says. I know I can't so I add a large tip.

I down Gemma's wine and jog partway to the station. I make it before the drunken Friday-night commuters and enjoy my two boxes of pasta at a table alone. I'll be home earlier than planned and I can update my spreadsheet with the valuation before bed. Tomorrow morning, I'll go round to Danny's and tell him how much I loved his sketches. Maybe I'll check in on Astrid.

23.
You two talk about me?

'Smell my watch,' says Astrid.

I lean away. 'Must I?'

She steps in front of me. 'Go on. One sniff.' Her wrist is in my face. With her other hand, she lifts her watch strap away from her skin. 'In there, that bit.'

I invited her on my Saturday walk to pre-empt us ending up in an intimate setting. And now here we are, alone in the sheep field, her damp wrist touching the point of my nose.

Eventually, I have to breathe in. It's bad and yet I want more.

'Ha! You smell it, don't you?' Astrid takes her own deep sniff. 'Mouldy, right? You smell it?'

'There is no right answer,' I say. 'Let me smell it again.' Her wrist is so slim that my fingers wrap all the way around it. My lips almost touching her, I inhale.

She pulls away. 'See. Mouldy.'

I envy and pity Danny all at once, that he had to navigate her strange and wonderful way of being. 'OK. Yes, I'd describe it as musty,' I say. 'And we're discussing this smell why?'

'Because for ages, I thought I smelled bad. I changed my soap, my deodorant, I read up about the perimenopause…' She narrows her eyes at the face I'm trying not to do. 'All because I kept smelling this smell. And then last night, I take my watch off to go to bed, and I smell it. That's the mouldy smell. It's my watch that smells bad, not me.'

'Apart from your left wrist,' I say, my hand curled into the same shape as when it held her.

'That ever happen to you?' she asks, eyes hopeful.

'I generally find all of me smells when I smell. Or is this another metaphor? Looks like a man in a cage but really, it's a cage around a man.'

'Smells like.'

'Fair enough.'

'And you should read it again,' she says.

'Fair enough.'

We follow my usual path and reach the stile into the woods. As we climb over, she says, 'Lived here fourteen years and didn't know this place.'

I worry that too is a metaphor, maybe about hidden depths, or trees. It would be so much easier if I didn't know she was a Kafka expert. It's like the time I was seated next to a psychiatrist at a wedding. When she asked what I did for a living and I said accountant, she immediately followed up with did I like it? I settled on 'some days' and from those two syllables she dredged up anxiety and self-loathing, raising her eyebrows as she said I didn't sound sure. I retaliated with why did she become a psychiatrist? And she fired back: 'Because I'm excellent at it.' I then spent as long as I could in the toilets and returned to find they'd served a long, cream-filled brandy snap as dessert. I love brandy snaps but whichever way I went at it, she'd have inferred a sex life that was twisted yet unfulfilling. I said I was lactose intolerant.

Astrid's still talking. 'You come here every Saturday?'

'I like routine,' I say. 'And a break from Dad and his carers. I think they hate me.'

'I reckon they probably don't think anything about you.'

'That feels worse. I get in their way and then it's obvious they're thinking, if I'm there, why should they have to come?'

'Would you rather they didn't?'

'God no. I need the breaks. And sometimes the nights are so bad, I just need a chance to catch up. We have this baby monitor and he wakes me if he panics, gets a cough, needs the loo.' I do and I don't want to talk about looking after Dad. No one ever asks me about it. But the topic involves so many bodily functions. I wrap it up. 'I guess I'm still working things out.'

'We all are,' says Astrid.

'Like you changing career?'

She tips her head like an inquisitive beagle.

'Danny told me,' I say.

'You two talk about me?'

'Argh, God, no. Not really. He just said you're becoming a life coach.'

'A what? A life coach?' She spits the words. 'Oh my God, he knows it's psychotherapist. He does this to wind me up. Life coach!'

'Isn't it the same thing?'

'Er, no. Six years' training, deep self-analysis, accreditation, standards…'

'But they sort of give people the same thing?'

Astrid flings her arms up. 'One gives you a huge body of theory and treatments the other gives you T-shirt slogans. One's Sigmund Freud, the other's Taylor Swift.'

'I had a coach at work,' I say. 'He was more Elon Musk than Taylor Swift. Less change the world, more conquer it from space.'

Astrid smiles at last.

'I think it's admirable you're doing something new,' I add.

'Torsus panic,' she says, or something like that.

'Sorry?'

She slows down. '*Torschlusspanik*. Freaking out about time running out, or literally about the gate closing.'

'Tor-schluss-panik,' I repeat back, and she nods. 'Hence your psychotherapist plan.'

She scrunches up her nose. 'It's at the beginning. But yes, I don't want to be one thing forever. Like you – do you want to be an accountant forever?'

'Of course not. I'm retiring in seven and a half years.'

'Oh yes. And until then?'

'Well … This one agent yesterday valued my flat at…' I pause. Gemma has made me ashamed of the little wealth I have. 'She valued it at more than I was expecting. So it changes things.'

Astrid frowns. 'How? You still need something to do all day, a purpose. Or are you denying yourself that too?'

'I'm giving myself a break. And it's a chance to be with Dad.'

She holds up a finger. 'You have the opposite of *Torschlusspanik*. You have *Torschlussunentschlossenheit*. Indecision. The gate's closing and you're standing there weighing up options.'

'Fascinating word, but no. I'm doing research.'

'Research? How?'

We've reached the wide tree stump in the clearing. I lean against it and run my finger over its rings. Astrid stands next to me, then in one smooth movement, hoists herself onto the stump. She sits, legs dangling over the edge.

'Research?' she prompts again.

'Don't think this is weird, but Danny gave me some of his minicab jobs, and I've been asking the passengers what they'd do, you know, if they knew how long they had left.'

'Wow. And what did they say?'

I feel under pressure. People don't generally find me interesting. 'Hang on.' I pull out my phone and open my notes: 'Volunteering, travelling, more volunteering.'

'Done and done,' she says.

'A killing spree.'

'Not yet,' she says.

'Get a dog, go to Australia, plan a "good funeral".' I make quote marks with my fingers.

'No, no and good idea.'

'You don't like dogs?' I ask.

She shrugs. 'Cat person.'

'Oh well. Then we have plastic surgery, divorce, track down a childhood sweetheart.'

'Never. Sort of. I'd consider it.' She winks.

'Right. OK then. And the last few are: run a marathon…'

'Maybe walk one.'

'Have a baby with a donor…'

'That's detailed,' says Astrid.

'Not really. She didn't explain. It was all a bit weird.'

'I sense that.' Astrid squeezes her lips together. Her dimple is fingertip sized.

'Learn the cello and retrain as a midwife. Same person.' I lock my phone.

'That's all?'

'All the ones worth mentioning. I have a separate list for the ones who misunderstood and focussed on the last twenty-four hours and the apparent carte blanche for recklessness – so much recklessness.'

'Ooh. Like?'

I shiver. We shouldn't have stopped walking. 'Another day,' I say, and push off from the tree stump.

She jumps down and follows me. 'And from all this, you take what?'

'So far, no one has come up with anything better than my current plan. I haven't asked you yet, of course.'

'Mmm.' She looks up to the sky as if she might be picturing her distant future. I imagine her at seventy-five: still dying her hair red, still wearing tight jeans.

'Got it!' she says and knocks her fists together. 'I'd pretty much carry on as normal until the last few months, then I'd set up online deliveries for everyone I know. One of those flower subscriptions for Bee. Same for my parents. Chocolate biscuits to my choir for every practice night. A giant grocery delivery for Timo with all his favourite foods, a recurring order ... I guess he'd have kids by then, so things for them too. Do you think people will still read magazines? Or I could pay for their Netflix? What?' She frowns at my smile.

'I'm imagining Timo with a recurring order of pancakes he can't stop, thirty years after he's grown out of them.' I'm also smiling at her delusion that Bee and her parents will outlive her. Somehow, I'm not surprised she believes everyone will live forever.

She nudges my arm. 'You I'd send recurring gnomes. One a week for three years.'

'A hundred and fifty-six gnomes?'

'Mmm,' she says. 'They probably don't do a hundred and fifty-six positions.'

I hide my reddening face and push away thoughts of a gnome *Kama Sutra*.

She nudges me again. 'And you're going to tell me what *your* plan is?'

'I'm not ready.' We're back at the stile to the fields. I gesture for her to go first, but she doesn't move. 'A few more details to sort,' I add.

'Go on. Just the … the essentials? Is it an invention? Something with space, you want to go to space? Or a cure for something? Ooh, a novel? Science fiction?' She hops from foot to foot.

I mime zipping my lips shut.

She mimes unzipping them, and her fingers brush my skin.

'I have a question too.' I touch her cheek with my fingertip. 'What's the German for dimple?'

'*Grübchen*. Little hole.' She climbs over the stile and stops as her scarf catches on a nail. I free it. 'Thanks,' she says. 'So you really won't tell me?'

'Soon,' I say. 'Unless a passenger comes up with something better. Then I plan from the beginning again.'

She watches my unwieldy legs as I climb over and offers me her hand for the small jump down. 'And what if you're wrong?' she asks.

'I go back to my own plan.' Is this what therapy is like?

'Not about their plan,' she says. 'Wrong about what time you have left. What if you're wrong about your comet?'

'I know for a fact I'm not. I know I have a time.'

'You can't *know*.'

I leave her to walk ahead a little. When she turns back, I say, 'I know because I survived something that was supposed to kill me. I survived the crash that killed my mother.'

'Oh.' She looks at the ground. I've found a topic worse than Dad's toilet trips.

'Sorry. I've ruined our walk,' I say, and edge towards her.

She grabs my hand. 'I'm touched you told me.'

'Thanks.' The only thing to do is walk. I pull away, but her grip tightens and now we're moving as one, holding hands.

'I mean, I knew your mum had died. Danny told me,' she says. 'But not really how.'

'So you two talk about me?' I nudge her ribs.

'Hey!' She elbows me back. 'But yeah. You fascinate us.'

Our hands apart, I relax again, and we carry on along the path home. We talk about Mum: how I was around Timo's age when it happened; how I was at a friend's and Mum was picking me up; about how Mum loved these woods; how she'd have loved Astrid's pickling. I tell Astrid how I catch myself thinking it's for the best Mum didn't end up as Dad's carer.

'That's allowed,' she says.

And she talks about Timo: how he never settled at junior school but he loves his secondary school, even though she hates the competitive parents; and how the school means she can't leave Eastgate, plus she loves the sea and being near Bee. 'My husband married someone scarily similar to his mother,' she says, clearly pleased with herself.

'Ex-husband,' I say.

'Not technically.'

We're where a patch of woods encroaches on the field, a clutch of ancient trees on the wrong side of the fence. Astrid loops between them, touching the trunks, inspecting them.

'So you get it then? What the crash means?' I say.

Hands under her scarf, she rubs her shoulders as if they ache from my heavy past. 'Well, do you get it, Robin? What the crash means? If you truly believed it, if you really knew for a *fact*, then you wouldn't be asking me. You wouldn't care what I think. You don't ask me if I think the sky's blue, do you?'

'But I do care what you think. For a start, you *think* more than anyone I've ever met.'

'Well, I *think* this goes back to what it's costing you.' Her elbows jut out as she works on her shoulders. 'You want to believe you know your time, but you worry that if you really commit to it, you'll be alone, a weirdo on the outside.'

'Why does everyone keep calling me a weirdo?'

'I said *you're* worried that's what you'll be to people. And you're worried that's what you'll be to me, a weirdo.' Her hands slide out from her scarf. She clasps my cheeks. 'But you're not.'

Everything about her is warm: her hands, her lips, her tongue. She digs her nails into my scalp. I'm good at this, several women have said so, starting with Maddy. *You're a great snogger, Robin Blake*. Astrid moves down to my neck, holds my skin between her teeth. I push her against a tree, kiss harder.

Telling people about Mum has never ended like this before.

I reach under her coat.

'You naughty gnome,' she whispers.

'Shush. No gnomes.'

I feel my way through her many layers. It's pass-the-parcel and I'm the only kid playing. As my fingers slip under her bra she gasps. Her nails are in my scalp again, and she tugs a strand of hair. No one has ever liked my mousey hair. Oh God, my hair. Hair that Danny doesn't have. I step back.

'We shouldn't,' I say.

'There's no one here.'

'But what about Danny?'

She looks around. 'He's not here either.' She laughs. I turn towards Eastgate and she pulls me back to her, kisses me, vacuum-like.

'Danny,' I say.

'Stop saying "Danny" whenever I kiss you.'

'I need to get back.'

She releases me. I press my palm against the tree trunk and get my balance, then join her back on the path.

After a few steps, our hands touch. 'Did you know Edmond Halley was an expert on magnetism?' I say.

'I did not.'

We walk on in silence but our hands speak in little squeezes.

She does a rhythm and I echo it, same game as I used to play with Mum. 'This is messed up,' I say.

'Will you tell me now?' Astrid asks.

At the top of her road, she speaks first and in detail, and I love her for it.

'I have a thing with Timo now, shopping for a shirt for his school trip to the theatre, then at dinner time, I have the chilli-pissing contest I told you about.'

I cross my legs.

Astrid continues: 'Then in the morning I have some work to catch up on. But I think maybe we can see each other later in the day tomorrow, if you'd like.'

'I'd love to. I mean, if you've survived the dinner.'

'Shall I text you in the morning?' She folds her arms. 'Or is that rubbish? You'll be waiting to know. Shall we plan something more concrete? If you want.'

Is she nervous?

'I see you've picked up that I'm a planner,' I say. 'But no, it's OK. You're busy. Text me in the morning. Let me know how spicy dinner was. I'm free. We could go for a wander along the beach.'

'Perfect.' She reaches up and gives me a hurried hug.

/

OBJECT: *Notebook*
DATE: *1997*
NOTES: *Mum loved note-taking. She had notes on all the kids she helped, notes on craft ideas, notes for recipes, notes on gifts to buy. She always used the same notebooks, narrow with lined pages, same as we had for spellings. She kept them on her bedside table, except for this one. This one stayed hidden in her handbag.* Nathan Bailey's Swear Words. *She was his teaching assistant in year five when I was in year six. One of those children they have meetings about. They told his mum about the swearing and she wouldn't believe them. Mum said she'd keep a list.*

A few days into her dossier, she said at dinner, 'I've never heard so much coarse language from a ten-year-old. Or anyone.'

'What sort of language?' I asked.

'Coarse,' she said.

'For example…'

'Eat your sweetcorn,' she said.

'Yeah, eat your bloody sweetcorn,' said Dad.

Mum liked us to eat together. She sat at the head of the table, nearest the hob, and Dad and I sat either side. After the crash, Dad moved her chair and no one sat at the head.

She'd say the same thing every dinner: 'Tell us one thing you've learned today.' And I'd have to come up with something. Then Dad would tell us about some disaster or row at the plant. And she would say, 'I shouldn't tell you this but…' and recount the antics of Nathan or whoever was her most demanding pupil that year. Dad said our family gained an extra boy every year. They were always boys. Dad gave them nicknames, like Feral Phil, who ate three class tadpoles for a dare.

I never minded that she was at my school. Some days, I'd go to her classroom and wait for her so we could walk home together. She'd give me jobs, like taking books to the library, or asking the secretary to photocopy worksheets, or searching for the elusive pole with a hook that she needed to open and close high windows.

It was the window pole I was bringing back on the day I saw Nathan where he shouldn't be. The kids had gone home, most of the teachers too. Mum must have been in the staff room. But there was Nathan, standing over her handbag, a ten-pound note in his hand.

He saw me, shoved it in his pocket.

Emboldened by my window pole, I blocked the door.

'Put it back,' I said.

'What?' said Nathan, empty hands aloft.

'It's stealing,' I said. 'It's my mum's ... Mrs Blake's.'

'What?' he said again. I was disappointed he didn't swear.

'Nathan?' Mum was behind me.

'He took something,' I said. 'From your handbag.'

'Did you?' she asked Nathan.

'No.'

'He took ten pounds,' I said.

'No,' Nathan said again.

'Did you take money from my bag, Nathan?' Mum asked.

'No.'

'Well, that's OK then. But you should be home by now. Shall we ring your mum?'

'She's out.'

'Can you walk home? Is someone there?' Mum asked.

'But I saw him take it,' I said. 'It's in his pocket.'

'But he says he didn't,' said Mum.

Nathan was in front of us now, hand in his pocket. He pushed past me and swaggered down the corridor.

'He stole from you,' I said to Mum.

'He says he didn't. Let's leave it.' She walked over to her handbag, picked it up.

'Check your wallet,' I said.

'Robin, he says he didn't do it. Let's get home.'

'It's our money,' I said.

'It's OK,' she said, and closed the classroom door.

At dinner, Dad said to me, 'You're odd tonight.'

'He's tired,' Mum jumped in. 'Up too late writing his comics. Making things up.'

'Yeah,' I said, and ate my bloody sweetcorn.

The swear book stayed in her handbag long after Nathan had moved on. I found it in there after the crash, among the tablets, safety pins and cough sweets. Just like I'll never know why she protected Nathan, I'll never know why she protected me from his 'coarse language'. His main offence seemed to be adding 'shit' to everything. For page after page, in her perfect handwriting, Mum noted the date and words like catshit, dogshit, mouseshit, penshit, headshit. Nor will I ever know why she wrote each of them as one word.

Notes for Dad: *Mum's other kids.*

24.
Time and how to fill it

I wake to several messages from Astrid sent Messerschmitt style at 1.00am, none of them about the kiss:

—*I know – it's something dodgy. You're bringing down the government. A government? All governments?*

—*I've been Googling. You are going to find and dig up the Ark of the Covenant.*

—*Or the Holy Grail? Cliché, don't you think?*

—*I'm good at quests. I found the watch smell. Let me come.*

And finally

—*OK. I need to sleep. But tell me soon. 3.00pm, steps to beach?*

Jackie is blocking my way to the front door; she's been growing wider as the weather turns colder. 'Nice to be able to come and go of your own accordance,' she says when she notices me.

'It is my house,' I say. I'm late. I'll have to run to the beach.

'It's your dad's.'

'Only sort of, but the ins and outs are private.'

'When will you be back?' she asks.

'Do you need to know?'

'Nice for your dad to know, don't you think?' It's like she's figured out the new distraction in my life and fears as much as I do that my ineffective care will deteriorate further.

I loop around her. 'Probably an hour and a half, two.'

Astrid is on the steps, looking out to the receding sea. Her hair seems redder than usual and pokes out of a black felt hat that isn't a beret. There was a winter when the girls at school wore berets and not one of them could explain the point of those little stalks. I'm also wearing a hat – a dark-blue beanie that I hope gives me something of an untamed sailor look.

It's cold but not so cold the beach is empty. There are some kids with a football, another with a kite. Dogs and their owners comb the edge of the water.

Astrid turns around and holds up a mini bottle.

'Ah, red,' I say as I come closer.

'You don't like red?'

'It's been called my "angry drink".'

'I was hoping it's your chatty drink.' Astrid raises one eyebrow.

'Uh-oh.' I put my hand in my pocket. 'I also brought you something. For your watch.' I hand her an alcohol wipe I took from Dad's trolley.

Astrid examines the packet. 'I thought you liked my mustiness.'

'I do. But you seemed troubled by it.'

'That and so many things.' The eyebrow again.

We haven't walked far when Astrid suggests we open the wine. She lays a rug on the sand and we sit against a wide boulder, arms not quite touching. We tilt our faces towards the shifting clouds and the emerging sun.

'Don't you wish you could soak up enough to see you through the winter?' Astrid says.

'Let's try,' I reply.

She's brought glass tumblers wrapped in cloth napkins. She fills one and hands it to me.

I slurp the top off. 'I got your texts.' The wine's good. I sip more, and again, like it's hot chocolate and I might drink it all in one go.

Astrid fills her own glass and gives me a nod to keep talking.

'You'll think it's stupid,' I say.

'So you can read the future now?' she says.

'Argh.' I don't want a therapist, I want … I try not to want what I want. 'Fine. You'll think what you think,' I say, and she shifts closer. 'So you know I plan to retire when I'm forty-five, leaving me with thirty years?' She goes to say something and I hold up a hand. 'Rhetorical. Well, I'll use those thirty years to assemble my big plan. My big plan for how to relish life…'

'Relish?' she says.

I shouldn't have paused. 'Relish, enjoy. Not relish, pickle.'

'Got it,' she says. 'Your plan is another plan…'

'Argh. Not a plan. A thing. It's a best-things thing.' I pause again. I'm ill-prepared. 'I mean … it's a quest for best things. No. It's finding the best things.'

'A quest for the best,' she says.

'That sounds like the slogan for washing-up liquid. No, it's this: I listen to all the best music, opera, symphonies, maybe modern stuff. And I watch all the best films and read all the best books, fiction and non-fiction – and I suppose essential as well as best, so you'd have Newton's *Principia* in there and so on. And this is a new addition: I find the best meals at the best restaurants. And I compare, narrow down and end up with the best one hundred in each category. And all the time, I blog about it, and then I turn it into a book. A guide for the time-poor, you know, on getting the best … the ultimate guide to what humanity can offer.'

'If you can afford it,' she says. 'The best meals at the best restaurants.'

'They go last: I use the advertising money from the blog.'

'Sure. But your followers?'

'Well, the books, films and music would be pretty cheap for them. Or they pick the top five meals. At least they know they are spending their money on the best.'

Astrid tucks her knees under her chin.

'I've started on the book – notes for it, ideas,' I say. 'I might add places too, in conjunction with the restaurants.' I stop. She's staring at me like I'm a podgy version of the fasting-artist. I drink.

'So…' she begins. 'It's *Time and How To Fill It?*' She moves her hand through the air as if unfurling a banner.

'I like that,' I say.

'And you're doing this because…?'

'Because someone should. And I'm in the perfect position to.'

'How so?'

'I have plannable time. Four years, on average, per category plus a ten-year buffer.'

Her nose twitches like she's doing the maths. I've never told anyone the details before. With Gemma I always said I planned to write once I retired. She'd loved that at first. She told other people.

I touch toes with Astrid. 'So?'

'It's not stupid. It's…' She looks up to the sky.

'You don't think it's me having a laugh for thirty years?'

'With books about maths and gravity?' Her nose wrinkles again. 'What? … You think you're the only one who knows Newton?'

I touch her hand and wine splashes onto our fingers. 'You're brilliant.' I lean to kiss her and there's a shout behind me. A dog is running at us and a man is calling its name, something like 'Misfit' or 'Little Shit'. I straighten. 'We could go…' My phone buzzes in my back pocket. 'Sorry,' I say and shuffle as I get it out.

It's Jackie. I let it ring out. She rings again. And now I see she's been texting.

—*Your dad had a fall. Can't lift him. You need to come.*

—*Where are you*

—*You need to keep your ring on. Call me.*

'You OK?' Astrid asks.

'Dad,' I say, and we tip our wine onto the sand and fold away the rug.

Dad is heavy, awkward and uninjured. As we change and lift him, Jackie tells me many times over that she's worked an hour past her shift. We both know I should have got back faster, but her nagging only makes me want to stay away more. 'I wasn't going to leave him,' she says, as if it might earn her an OBE for services to the bare minimum.

Once she's gone, I text Astrid and ask what she's doing.

Homework with Timo, she replies.

Another time then, I write back, and take a bottle and my laptop through to Dad.

'A large glass tonight, Dad, after all the upset,' I say. 'Not a word to Jackie.'

He makes his laughing sound.

'I'm not joking.'

It's pretty clear the mystery illness Jackie's husband suffers from is alcoholism. She's said more than once that she never drinks and she raged at me the other morning for 'flaunting the rules' by leaving a bottle on the coffee table. 'Drink in your room,' she said. 'Shared spaces are safe spaces.'

I fill Dad's syringe, hold it aloft and get to work re-reading the terms of my mortgage. Then I put the surprise flat valuation into the spreadsheets. I'm two sheets in when Astrid rings.

'I'm actually away for the week, with work,' she says as soon as I pick up.

'Hang on.' I go into my bedroom and close the door.

'Until Friday,' she says.

'Oh, OK.' I stretch out on the bed and wonder what else I'm supposed to say. What would happen if I told her I've replayed every detail of that moment against the tree, that I've imagined us back in the woods, my hands braver, her layers fewer?

She clears her throat into my ear and repeats, 'So, until Friday.'

'You know where I am,' I say, and want to punch myself in the face. Then I make it worse: 'If you need anything.' I sound like the local cocaine dealer.

'Great,' she says.

She doesn't ask about Dad and she doesn't mention my plan.

25.
It's never just gnomes

The next morning, Danny appears at the bungalow on his bike.

'One broken arm not enough?' I ask.

'It's all good. I never use both hands anyway,' he says, and wheels his bike through the door.

'We said I was picking you up and driving us,' I tell him.

Danny looks around the bungalow, leans to see into the kitchen. 'Where's your dad?' he asks in a whisper.

'In the bathroom with his carer. Why?' I whisper back.

'Is it Susie?'

'Why? What's with Susie?' I ask.

He grins.

'You're seeing one of the carers?'

'Sort of. She's not calling back. Anyway, is it her?'

'I don't know. What does Susie look like?' I say. 'Don't do that face. There's tonnes of them and they never introduce themselves.' Early on, I asked Jackie if they could all wear name badges, for Dad's sake. She told me that would be an 'envision of privacy'.

'Blonde,' says Danny.

'The one with several earrings? Isn't she about twenty years old?' I ask.

'Yes and yes.' He stares at the bathroom door, presumably imagining his beloved the other side, wiping Dad's arse. 'So is it her?'

'No. But I'll ask her to call you next time she's here. And we can check the folder to see what days she normally comes, if you can decipher her signature.'

'You're being weirdly helpful,' says Danny.

'No I'm not. Just happy for you.'

'Don't be. It's not really anything,' he says.

'But you want it to be?'

'Maybe. I thought she liked me.'

I leave him to go through the timesheets while I make tea and wonder if that's all any of us are looking for: someone who likes us back.

The Scout huts are larger than I remember: two long buildings perpendicular to each other, one slightly bigger, both single-storeyed, both coated in bumpy cement full of tiny stones. When Danny and I were Cubs, Mum always dropped us off early, and while we waited to go in, we'd pick at those stones with our nails, hoping to free one and return it to the ground. We never managed.

Now we're early again. We wait in the car, Danny playing something on his phone, me calculating the cost of my inborn need to be early: say almost ten minutes each day, or an hour per week of my life so far. That's a total of eighty-one solid days of waiting around, or 0.3 per cent of my total lifespan.

The estate agent has the opposite problem to me. He's late. He pulls up next to us, parking in an uncontrolled manner that leaves little room for me to open my door. He's wearing sunglasses and has turned up the over-sized collar on his coat.

'Don't let on how interested we are,' says Danny. He wriggles in his seat trying to stow his phone in his jeans one-handed.

'Shouldn't be hard,' I say.

'What's that mean?'

'You said I was just here to look.'

'You said you liked my sketches.'

'I thought it was you,' the agent calls over when we're out of the car. 'Coming to nose around this one too?'

Damn the smallness of Eastgate. Damn the smallness of gnomes.

'What?' Danny says to him.

'Your cab driver. Is he coming with us?' the agent asks.

'Errr…' Danny looks at me.

'Ah, yes! Last week, wasn't it?' I say, and turn to Danny. 'This chap was one of my minicab runs.'

Danny gives me a look that says *you never say 'chap'* and turns back to the agent. 'That's funny. This is Robin, my business partner. And I'm Danny. Thanks for meeting us.' He holds out a hand.

'Freddy,' the agent says, shaking Danny's hand then mine. His gloves have bobbly fingertips for using on phones.

'So you're gonna make it a minicab base?' he asks.

'God, no,' I say.

'Kayak base,' says Danny.

'Ah. Nice,' says Freddy, and Danny beams.

Freddy unlocks the door to the larger building. The smell hasn't changed, only it's stronger from being bottled up: a blend of chemical-washed lino, PVA glue and damp curtains. I breathe it in.

'Remember making that raft?' I say to Danny.

He laughs. 'Disaster.'

'Not much to it,' Freddy is saying. 'But you know, depending what the buyers want to do with it. One guy's looking to turn it into a music venue.'

'That won't work around here,' I say. 'Who's the seller?'

'I'm not supposed to say, but I can tell you he's a farmer,' says Freddy.

'Pumpkin farmer?' I ask.

'I can't go into details,' says Freddy.

Kids must have broken in at some point because there are body parts graffitied over the original mural of rainbows, children and sheep on the back wall. An old sofa and a smashed-in TV have been left behind and the floor is littered with newspaper pages, crisp packets and things that don't belong in a Scout hut. I stop myself from asking Freddy why he hasn't cleaned it up. An interest in used condoms will only compound my gnome misdemeanours.

The space is plenty large enough for the bunk beds Danny sketched, the kitchen is still there, with its hatch into the main room, and the toilets are in a better state than feared, with doors on two of the three cubicles. But most of the windows are cracked, there are mysterious holes in the floor and something large or multiple has defecated all over one corner.

'Pigeon issue,' says Freddy, following my gaze.

'Past or present?' I ask.

'Both,' he replies.

'So present then,' says Danny.

'Not in this building.'

Wings flap as Freddy opens the door to the second hall. Two pigeons swoop to the little stage at the end of the room and disappear into its rafters. From there, they join a whole chorus of cooing sounds, presumably pigeon for *get out*.

'Right,' says Danny. 'So you're basically selling us one hall full of potholes and another full of pigeons.'

'You'd just need pest control. Good news is, they're not protected. Be a right headache if they were bats.'

'Right,' says Danny.

'Or dormice. Or otters,' Freddy continues.

'Otters?' I ask. 'Didn't you say the water was disconnected?'

We zig-zag across the hall between piles of pigeon droppings. I stop to marvel at the regularity of their spacing, then I realise the piles are lined up with the beams above us. There is another sofa in this hut, a broken table propped against it and empty spray-paint cans on the floor. A disco ball hangs from the central beam.

The stage is so covered with chunky black-and-grey lumps of pigeon poo, that it looks like the model of a mountain range. I glance up and make eye contact with one of its creators. The bird tips its head as if it's speaking to me. *Yep, the Himalayas. Everest took six attempts.*

The smell is oddly tolerable.

'They get in through a hole in the soffit, I bet,' says Freddy, looking proud of his architectural vocabulary.

I find it odd that Freddy has allowed us to spend so much time inspecting the faecal Himalayas. Or is he trying to put us off? He sees a man with a broken arm and his pervert minicab friend, and he's decided we're timewasters. That's what I wanted to be, as much as I hate that term. Scout huts, kayaks and strangers' children were never part of the plan. But the stage is in Danny's sketches too. It's where we would give out awards at the end of each course, *and maybe hold talent shows*, Danny wrote in his confidently wild handwriting. And one half of the hut would be more bunk beds, the other half a room with bean bags, table football and a vending machine. We would own and stock a vending machine.

'You had much interest apart from the music man?' I ask Freddy, and Danny's smile widens. 'The pigeons must put people off.'

'Serious buyers don't worry about things like pigeons,' says Freddy. 'Everything's fixable.'

'Dangerous motto,' I say.

'We are serious,' Danny says, seemingly forgetting his own instructions not to show interest.

'Well, I've got more viewings next week, and then it's open season with online auctions, you get people from all over. Whole different ball game to ballroom,' says Freddy.

I picture basketball players tripping over ballgowns.

'Ballroom?' asks Danny.

'Ballroom auctions, when there's people, in a room.' Freddy sniffs. 'Anyway, work out how high you can go. It's gonna smash the guide price, this lot.'

That's rubbish, but I say nothing. I checked last night: the huts were on the market for a year before the seller resorted to this auction. What people like Freddy call 'sea views', lenders call 'flood risk'.

But Danny falls for it. 'You think so?' he asks.

'Course. It's got everything: location, space, potential,' says Freddy.

'You can say that about anything,' I say. 'Anything has a location, space and potential.'

'So we agree then,' says Freddy.

'You're picturing it,' Danny says when we're back in the car. 'Look over there, the shed thing, that's where we'd store the kayaks. And down there is a really good way into the water.'

'What's that next to the shed thing?' I squint at the boxy shape covered in a tarpaulin.

'It's a ride-on mower. And those are the Scouts' old kayaks. They're included. Freddy just told us that. Weren't you listening?'

'I found he's the kind of person where you can only – and should only – take in sixty per cent.' I turn up the heating and wait for Freddy to pull away.

Danny is jiggling in his seat. 'Come on, Robin. What do you think?'

'It doesn't seem bad for the money, if it goes for what they're guiding,' I say. 'But do you really want all your savings gone? And loads of mine? And then you'd need the same again to sort it out, to buy the kayaks, do the kitchen. Have you looked at insurance for something like this? Did you see the windows? And those pigeons.'

'Everything's fixable.' Danny grins. 'Come on, Robin. What if it goes well? What if it's amazing?'

'What if,' I say, and reverse over the boggy ground of what was once the car park.

We are turning into Dad's estate when Danny says, 'What did he mean, Freddy, that thing about, "you coming to nose around this one *too*"?'

'Nothing,' I say. 'I just got out of the car when I dropped him at this big house, to stretch my legs, and he was all weird about it.'

'You're going red.'

'No, I'm not.' I turn off the heating.

'It was weird the way he said it. Sure nothing else happened?'

'Nothing happened. He *is* weird. And he's a smug bastard. He called me unprofessional,' I say.

'*Unprofessional?*'

'Yeah.' I straighten up the car on Dad's drive and switch off the engine. Danny is staring sideways at me. I hate secrets.

'Fine,' I say. 'I got out of the car to take a picture of something – something funny – and he saw me.'

'What the hell, Robin? What were you taking pictures of?'

'Gnomes. In their garden. They had these weird gnomes.'

'And you needed a picture?' Danny drops his head into his hands, melodramatically. 'Only you, Robin. Only you.'

'What's that supposed to mean? It was just a picture. Wasn't even for me. It was for Astrid.' I open my door and swallow the cold air.

'Astrid?' Danny says.

'Because she likes gnomes too.'

'So you both like gnomes?' Danny climbs out and slams the door.

'We both like gnomes,' I say over the top of the car.

'Great,' says Danny. 'That's great.'

I hold up the house keys. 'I'll just grab your bike. We'll put it in the boot and I'll drop you home.'

'I'll ride home,' he says.

'With one arm?'

'Yes!'

'Because we both like gnomes?'

'Because you sent her a picture of gnomes. You send each other stuff and I look like a total fucking idiot.' Danny flicks the fingers on his good hand.

'You OK?' I ask.

'No.' The flicking speeds up.

'She's your ex. And it was just gnomes,' I say.

'It's never just gnomes.'

26.
Cheat it

Danny sulks for twenty-four hours, then calls.

'It's you I'm worried about,' he says.

I puff out my cheeks, gluing my lips together. I've just woken from a nap and yet another dream about my pubic hair. I'm in no state to discuss Astrid. My cheeks deflate.

'Except there is nothing to worry about,' I say. And there isn't for now, with Astrid away and unresponsive. 'But I'm sorry you found out about the gnomes that way.'

Danny makes a spluttering sound down the phone, like a horse on a hot day. 'Anyway…' he begins, then pauses. 'Onto more—'

I cut him off. 'The Scout huts. Yeah. I need more time.'

'Don't take too long,' he says.

I ask how his minicab and Deliveroo jobs are looking and find myself agreeing to an evening as his Deliveroo chauffeur, on the understanding I'll only do until ten, when I take over from the bedtime carer. Luckily, people in Eastgate eat early.

My offer turns out to be a good move. In return for driving Danny between shops, takeaways and lazy people, I receive petrol money, free dinner and the comforting feeling of skipping two glasses of Malbec, thereby leaving me up on the week. Dad didn't react when I explained our temporary break from wine time.

Danny, of course, uses the Deliveroo runs to pester me about the Scout huts. I use them to lay out the costs, the risks and my research into pigeons. Danny is neither aware that pigeons carry salmonella, nor that they are employed by the Chinese military.

I agree to help him the next evening and the one after.

The daytimes with Dad are inescapably harder. Ever since the fall that called me back from the beach, Jackie has been asking me to go to social services for more funding. She's insisting Dad needs two carers to move him.

She's probably right. Dad is slower, stiffer and the little joining in he used to do has gone. The painful truth that neither Jackie nor I will say out loud is that soon no amount of care will make Dad comfortable. I know I should use this knowledge to plan. Instead, overcome by *Torschlusspanik*, I get out while I still can. I get out the minute I've got Dad back from the toilet. I get out as soon as his favourite TV show starts. I get out whenever the carers come. I run to Danny. I run to the little Tesco. I run before it's just Dad, the bungalow and me.

I'm tripped up. On Wednesday afternoon, a woman from the carer agency calls. I'm putting their staff at risk of injury, she says. I can have two carers per visit or none at all. I reason with her, promise to stay in and help as a second carer on the daytime calls and to pay for two of her staff on the bedtime calls when I'm out as Danny's driver.

'That should work,' she says, and takes payment upfront.

Jackie sets out a protocol she calls a 'prototype'. As 'family carer', I must be the one who lifts Dad into the wheelchair, onto the toilet and back. The agency carer is there to 'support' me. Support is a loose word.

On the first day, the early carer – the man who I've only met once before – seems to want to help, and as I heave Dad to standing, he's the other side of him, palms out, knees bent like a cricket fielder. The lunchtime one – a new woman – pretends to help. She rests one hand on Dad's shoulder and the other on his hip. It's impossible to move Dad without us touching fingers. The teatime one, who I now know is called Susie, refuses to help at all. She leans against the nearest available surface and expends what little energy she has brought to work on scrolling up and down her phone. 'You could be changing his bed while I do this,' I say.

'Not in my tasks,' she replies without looking up. My face flushes as I imagine her saying the same to Danny.

When she's gone, I leave Dad in his chair and go into my room to search YouTube. Someone out there somewhere must be able to show me how to lift Dad without chin dribble soaking into my shoulder and without my hip touching his crotch. I find a woman with a soft American voice. The key is explaining the 'process' to the 'patient' so they can 'assist', she says. I try it on the next toilet trip. 'That foot needs to go forwards ten centimetres and then they both need to twist,' I say, and feel like a salsa teacher without the clothes or charisma. If anything, Dad becomes stiffer and heavier.

Between manoeuvres, I'm left with spans of time too short to do anything but watch more TV and check for messages from Astrid, of which there are none. I fear she's forgotten me. She hasn't even told me what city she's in. I Google 'Kafka conferences' and 'Kafka symposia' and nothing comes up.

No Deliveroo tonight, so it's me and Jackie on the bedtime call. She provides more support but shows no sympathy when I tell her about the half-heartedness of the others.

'You're just put out they sent a man,' she says. 'People are so sexist about carers.'

When she's gone, I resume my investigation. 'How to tell if my girlfriend is shagging a randy professor', I type. The pictures are diverting.

Friday morning, I wake from a broken night knowing I can't face a second day as the over-scrutinised and under-helped 'family carer'. I call the agency.

'The change is too sudden,' I tell the woman. 'For me and for my dad. We need to ease in. I'm happy to pay for double carers for all of today.'

'Last minute,' she says. 'You're lucky we're quiet. We can put you on double from lunch.'

I call Danny and ask for minicab jobs, all too aware I'm justifying my escape with something that will pay towards this extra care.

I help the breakfast carer, wait an hour to take Dad for one more toilet visit and then I write a note for whoever's coming on the lunch call: *Out today but Dad doing better.* I scribble over the 'but', kiss Dad on the forehead (an experiment I won't repeat) and run out to the car.

Before the first pick-up, I buy a croissant at the little Tesco and take it to the steps by the beach. The sky is the same grey as the sea and they blend into one dull canvas. Straight ahead, a dog darts in and out of the water, as if chased by the waves. It runs up the beach to its owner, shakes, throws itself down and writhes in the sand. Then it does it all again – water, shake, sand, as if it's trying to cleanse itself of something. I pull back my hood and let the drizzle coat my face. I lift my croissant, hold it against my nose and inhale. Finally, I bite into the pastry. Maybe the titbits are enough to keep us going.

The first job is top-notch escapism: driving two students to the mainline station, a long run that will take me past buildings with more than two storeys and onto a road with more than two lanes.

The students are boys with bad haircuts and good manners. One asks how I am, the other asks if I have a busy day ahead. I return their questions and they tell me they are going back to London after a twenty-first birthday party. The one wearing an orange ski jacket meets my eye in the mirror and adds, 'I know, on a Thursday, right? In the middle of term.'

They are second-year physics students at Imperial and have known each other since school.

'I was at UCL,' I tell them.

'Oh,' they say in unison. Their manners clearly prevent them from asking how I've ended up driving a minicab in Eastgate.

The silence becomes unpleasant.

'Can I ask you something I ask all my passengers?' I say and see them exchange a look. 'Nothing weird,' I add quickly. 'My own sort of scientific pursuit, if you like. I'm not a Jehovah's Witness. Nor am I usually a minicab driver. This is on the side.'

'Sure,' says the ski-jacketed one.

'Go on,' says the other.

'What would you do if you knew the date you were going to die?'

'When is it?' asks Ski Jacket.

'Let's say it's when you're seventy-five, so in 2077, I'm estimating,' I say.

'By that point, seventy-five is a pretty bad outcome,' says Ski Jacket.

'True. But that's your lot,' I say.

'Then I'd do everything I could to cheat it. There've been some really successful trials in mice, swapping out zombie cells. I'd put everything I've got into that.'

'Like a tech billionaire,' says the other one, sounding awestruck rather than insulting.

'Except this isn't just about me,' says Ski Jacket. 'If I made a breakthrough, it would help everyone.'

'But you can't prevent accidents,' I say. 'What if you put billions into zombie cells and you still die in an accident in 2077.'

'Life's getting safer.' Ski Jacket types into his phone as he speaks. 'Listen to this, self-driving cars could eventually cut road crashes to zero.'

'Says General Motors,' his friend adds.

'OK, well this newer study says they'd cut them by a third.'

'Under what circumstances?'

They go on like this for some time, reading out from their phones, disagreeing over human errors and robot malfunctions. It's both embarrassing and flattering how much they seem to care about impressing me.

Finally, Ski Jacket asks me, 'You're the professional driver. What do you think?'

'Well, obviously in my industry – my side industry – we're not massive fans of self-driving cars.' I pause as I overtake a truck. 'What I would say is not all car crashes are caused by human error. You've got to take into account the car itself, weather' – I nod at the wipers going full speed – 'road conditions.' My mind throws up a fuzzy memory of a girl at school asking if Mum had been drinking. Her question had the stink of something her parents must have said. 'She never drinks,' I replied. 'Never drank.'

'But yes, humans are pretty fallible,' I say now.

The students round up the fare by two pounds and wish me luck with my research as they climb out.

'You too,' I say.

As I watch them run through the rain to the station, I wish I'd asked their names for when they one day appear under headlines like 'The Men Who Cheat Death'. Not that any of it will apply to me. I check my phone: thirty-seven years, eight months and nineteen days to go.

In the afternoon, I pick up a man in a suit without a tie. He talks non-stop from the moment he opens the front passenger door. He's going to a school – I wonder if it's Timo's – where he's giving a talk, he says. He's a financial advisor but loves to volunteer. The chatting is unprompted but welcome. It's a contrast to the bungalow and it makes it easier to ask my question.

'This is financially related, if you like,' I begin. 'What would you do if you knew the date you were going to die?'

'Great question,' he says, as if he's being interviewed on the radio. 'What sort of time are we talking? How long?'

I glance across. His age is impossible to guess. 'How about the day you turn seventy-five?'

'I love it,' he says. 'You know exactly? No risk you could live longer?'

'Dead at seventy-five.'

'And your state of health? Care needs?' he asks.

'Good health. No carer needs.' God, that better be true.

'OK. So I'd chop up my savings into lumps and give each risk category a go. But the beauty is, you know when you can afford to run out, so you put a bigger lump in high risk, high return.'

'What if there's a crash?' I ask.

'What if there isn't and you leave it all in cash, eking it out, paranoid about losing it. That's what people do, terrified into inaction by the thought of crashes that come round once a century and never last.'

'They're being … prudent, you call it, don't you?'

'Scared is what they are. But with this, there's no excuse. You work out what you can risk, go for it, make a bomb.'

'A bomb. Sounds dangerous.'

'See it this way: you can do what you want and be certain you can afford it,' he says.

'Is that what you'll be telling the kids today?'

'Someone has to,' he says and I picture them going home to invest their parents' meagre savings in Russian cryptocurrencies.

I drive back to Eastgate with the window open as if the rush of cold air might clear my head. The financial advisor's words won't leave me: *Do what you want and be certain you can afford it*. There's no such thing as certainty. But there are worst-case scenarios. And if you add those together, assume no returns – no financial ones at least – you get a worst-case cost. That's what you work with. You work out if you can afford the worst possible cost.

I almost go into the back of a tractor as I calculate in my head. I need to get to my laptop.

I stop at the end of Sycamore Lane and text Danny that I'm done for the day. Dad's drive is empty but another pair of carers will be here any minute. I park on the next road along, walk to the bungalow, sneak in the back and into my room.

I work from *Windfall*: a spreadsheet I created after the flat valuation. It whimsically maps out a stint as an entrepreneur. I re-save it as *Affordability?*, make generous assumptions about every outlay, then add ten per cent. I create a 'Disasters' column and cost every possibility from 'storm damage' to 'drowning'. Two hours later I'm finished.

Danny doesn't pick up the first time, nor the second. To my third attempt, he responds, 'What happened?'

'Let's do it,' I say. 'We should do it.'

'The Scout huts? You're bloody joking. You're joking? If you're joking, it's not funny. You're a dick. Are you—?'

'I mean it. I'm certain I can afford it and I think it's what I want.'

'Oh my God! This is awesome, Robin. Awesome. You're not a dick. You're the opposite of a dick…'

'So I'm a va—' I can't say it.

'Awesome,' Danny says again. 'I'm registering us for the auction now. I should call Freddy. Should I call Freddy?'

'Maybe. But play things down. And ask about the ride-on mower.'

27.
Cheerleader

We are in Costco, where toothbrushes come in packs of eight.

'Do you need one?' Astrid asks as I take a packet and turn it over.

'Sort of depends,' I say.

When I invited her to come with me to Costco, I expected her to reply with something about being tired after her conference. Instead, she squealed down the phone, said she'd always wanted to go and laid out a plan for us to buy food and cook it at hers. Then when I picked her up, she kissed my cheek and said, 'I haven't stopped thinking about you.' I wanted to ask why, then, was she was so incommunicative all week. Instead, I opted for what I believe they call 'taking the win'. She left her hand on my thigh and it hampered my driving – that and the question of whether I will need a toothbrush. I've got double carers booked all day and Dad's alarm is linked to my phone. I reckon I can stay at Astrid's until after midnight if Dad doesn't want me, and she does.

'They're good value,' Astrid says now, pointing at the price per unit of £1.96.

'Also depends.' Buying a toothbrush this way costs £15.68 and I will be left with £13.72 worth of toothbrushes I will never use because at the bungalow I have an electric toothbrush – itself an expensive choice but one that leaves me better off over time because I don't need a dentist.

Astrid leans against me and puts her head on my shoulder. I add the toothbrushes to our trolley.

We spend another half-hour with Astrid visiting every aisle and asking my opinion on things I have never thought about. No, you probably don't need six hundred cupcake cases, I tell her; no, Timo does not look like he needs chewable multivitamin tablets; but yes, the cat will probably enjoy sleeping in a four-poster doll's bed although he may feel threatened by the depictions of horned llamas.

'Llamacorns,' replies Astrid. 'I have to buy it. Timo will love it.'

My own shopping is quick: the usual breakfast supplies, pasta and wine and two bottles of 'Mabel' syrup for Jackie.

As for our joint dinner, Astrid and I agree on salmon fillets and white wine. She has rice and vegetables at home, she says.

On the drive back, I tell her about the Scout huts, sparingly at first, and when she doesn't interrupt or deride Danny's business sense, I give her more. 'There are four kayaks, a ride-on mower and a disco ball included. And we'll have a vending machine,' I say. 'I'll fill it with things from Costco.'

'You have to let me help,' she says. After a moment, she adds,

'You're great for Danny. He's wanted something like this forever, and he just needed you.'

'Are you always nice to each other?' I ask.

'How do you want us to be? How is it with … with … your ex?'

I laugh. 'She's called Gemma.'

'God, sorry, I went blank.'

'Best approach. But yeah, Gemma. And I want to kill her.'

'You have to let me help,' Astrid says again.

The salmon is raw and the rice is microwaved. Astrid serves them with salad leaves and lime pickle. 'It goes with everything,' she says.

'I've been finding that,' I say.

'Vitamins for when you're in a hurry.'

'Are you in a hurry?'

She gulps her wine and reaches under the table. 'Yes.'

Rice catches in my throat. I cough and she looks straight into my eyes. It's arousing and unnerving all at once. Her hand tightens. I shuffle forwards obligingly. I drain my glass. Her hand loosens and her chair screeches against the tiles as she stands up. 'Come on,' she says.

I pour myself more wine and drink fast, spilling some down my jumper. At the top of the stairs, I catch myself on the banister. The cat is lying across the final step, camouflaged against the carpet and shunning his new llamacorn bed. I try to edge around him but he stretches out even longer. I step over him, and as soon as I'm on the landing, he jumps up and rubs against my legs.

'Not now, Max,' says Astrid, watching from the bedroom door. She's taken off her top and is in jeans and a black bra. 'Quick,' she gestures at the bed behind her. 'Run and jump or he'll follow you in and never leave.'

I do as I'm told. I make it into the room in two strides but my leap turns into a belly flop. Astrid slams the door and falls onto the bed next to me. I dab at my smarting nose.

She strokes my cheek. 'Are you hurt?'

'Not physically,' I say.

Her lovemaking is like her Costco shopping: painstaking yet muddled. She kisses me, moves lower, kisses me again. She undresses me, then herself, all the time returning to kiss me. Then she's beside me, her teeth on my neck, then astride my middle, her hands grasping behind her back for me and missing. She slides off and manoeuvres herself under me. More kissing and just as I lift my head for air, she pulls me into her. Her breath is hot in my ear as she says, 'I thought you wanted this.'

Why do we have to talk?

'Show me you want this,' she says. 'Show me.'

And I do, immediately.

We lie on top of the duvet, big toes touching. I contemplate how an apology might go.

She speaks first. 'I rushed you.'

'Sort of,' I say. 'Or more like the long wait then the rush.'

There's a scratching sound at the door then loud miaows.

'Fuck off, Max!' shouts Astrid. It's somewhere between jokey and frustrated. That's my fault.

'Isn't Max a dog's name?' I slide to the edge of the bed then under the duvet and back.

'It's after Max Brod,' says Astrid. 'Kafka's best friend and biggest cheerleader.'

'Maybe he can come and give me some support.'

'Oh, come on.' She shuffles closer and kisses my forehead.

'I'm sorry that was so rubbish,' I say.

'Don't. We'll get better.' She pulls her T-shirt onto her naked body. 'Wait here,' she says and disappears downstairs.

Her disregard for underwear fills me with hope that a second chance is imminent.

Were Gemma and I this mismatched at the beginning? The

hands-on part of our first time is fuzzy. There was prosecco by the bottle, me telling her to imagine she knew when she was going to die, and a cab. We woke up aching and apologetic in her bed. All I remember is the sequence we settled into: always in the evening, always beginning with my hand on her, rarely with kissing and never on the same day we'd changed the sheets. It was stale and almost certainly sub-standard but the good thing was that neither of us talked about it, either before, during or after.

Glasses clink as Astrid pushes against the bedroom door with a tray. Between her teeth she grips a large bag of posh crisps. She nods at the space next to me and I pull back the duvet for her to set down the tray. She's made a cheeseboard with grapes and crackers, and a different pickle. There's a new bottle of wine and a bowl of cashews. She drops the crisps next to the tray. 'Max ate the rest of your salmon,' she says.

'This is better,' I reply.

She hands me the corkscrew. 'Could you?'

'I feel like I'm hiding something from you,' I say as I fumble with the wine's foil wrapper.

'That you can't open wine?'

'That I grew up in the house next door.' The foil tears and I prick my finger. I suck at it and explain further. 'Ours was the house next door, the one that backs onto Bee's garden. Feels like something I should tell you.'

'I already knew,' says Astrid. 'Not that it matters. Unless you feel haunted?'

'No more than anywhere else.'

I stab the cork and twist. It comes out with a pop.

'My favourite sound,' says Astrid.

We drink, eat and barely talk; I tell her my favourite sound is probably the sea, 'but only at night when the seagulls have buggered off.'

We try again. Astrid is calmer, and I am bolder. I work through my moves like a champion ballroom dancer; it doesn't matter that the routine is old if the audience is new. Astrid screams into the pillow next to my ear, and when we finish, I say, 'I have a new favourite sound.'

'And I have a new favourite celestial event,' she replies.

It's 4.00am when I remember Dad. I check my phone. No alerts.

Astrid is sleeping on her side, facing away from me. I stroke her arm, then squeeze it. I press my lips on the back of her neck and breathe in her hair, all sweat and perfume. She shifts slightly, sleeps on. I dress, stuff the cork from last night's wine into my pocket, go downstairs, wedge her front door open with a shoe and walk out to my car. The toothbrushes are at the bottom of my Costco shopping in the boot. I take out one brush – rather belatedly, I now realise as I swallow the taste of wine, fish and sleep – go back inside and put it on her bathroom sink.

I crouch down, face level with hers, hand in front of my mouth. 'I have to go,' I whisper.

'You don't,' she says, eyes still closed.

'I can't leave Dad.'

'OK.'

'But one day I will,' I say as I close the door. It's a pipe dream not a promise, and I immediately feel terrible. I speed the short journey home and rush straight to Dad's room. He's fast asleep, loud breaths rising and falling in time with the whirring of his hospital bed.

Unable to sleep, at 6.00am I get up and shower. Astrid is an explorer so I take the loofah from Dad's cabinet and use it on every crevice. I soap, scrub and rinse until all the dead skin larvae are gone from my ankles, neck and toes. Inspired by her neat grooming, I give myself a trim with the nail scissors, pluck out four new grey hairs and flush all the evidence. I finish with a sprinkling of Dad's talcum powder and in a moment of haste, get some on my teeth. I attempt to rinse it away with mouthwash and it turns to minty froth and goes down my throat.

As soon as the breakfast carers arrive, I set off, talc flavour still on my tongue. I text Astrid I'm on my way. *Can't wait*, she replies.

When I arrive, Max is in the front garden and runs to join me on the doormat. We wait side by side for Astrid.

'There you are!' she says, I think to the cat, but she grabs my hand and tugs me upstairs.

Afterwards, we lie there silent for a while, her on the duvet, me under it.

'One more time within twenty-four hours and it'll be a personal best,' I say.

'Do you count everything?' she asks.

28.
A hotel soap

'I'm boy-cutting that new bakery,' says Jackie.

We're waiting outside the bathroom for Dad to finish what Jackie calls 'his necessaries'. He'll bang on the shower screen with his good arm when he's ready for us.

'Which new bakery?' I ask.

'On Beachway.'

'Would we say it's new?' It opened more than a year ago.

'They were rude to my friend,' Jackie continues. 'Said she couldn't buy a half loaf, shouldn't even ask. So I'm boy-cutting them.'

'How will they tell?' I ask.

'What you mean?'

'Well, it's like if I boy-*cott*ed Tampax. How would they tell?'

'There's something wrong with you,' says Jackie.

'Maybe. Do you think he'll be much longer?'

I'm double-booked. The carer agency called and told me I'm needed here as 'family carer' all day and Astrid called and timetabled me for a noon visit there. I tried to explain about Dad but she pointed out that Timo is at hers on weekdays and that meeting outside school hours was 'out of question'.

'*The* question,' I corrected, while agreeing that I'm in no way ready to let Danny's son know I'm sleeping with Danny's not-quite-ex-wife.

I tell Jackie a half-lie. 'I have an appointment. I need to leave in ten if I'm going to make it.'

Seemingly convinced I have a medical need, she agrees I can go once we've got Dad back into his chair.

I stop at the little Tesco before Astrid's and buy sandwiches and crisps. As I long ago predicted, bringing a woman into my life is stretching the spreadsheet's contingencies column beyond repair. But she describes the sandwiches as 'delicious', me as 'romantic' and we seem to both appreciate getting two things done in one short lunch break. As I run back to the bungalow, it strikes me that my particular predicament has not been covered in any of the carer leaflets. I imagine calling the helpline. 'My dad's care needs are virtually round the clock but I've fallen for someone with a demanding libido, what would you advise?' Oh God, what is happening to me?

The second day, Astrid asks to meet in the afternoon. I offer her between 2.30pm and 3.30pm and tell her I will have eaten.

When I arrive, she kills the mood by announcing, 'Timo's back in an hour. And Danny's popping round.'

'Perhaps we shouldn't bother,' I suggest.

'We should always bother,' she says.

My lunchtime cornflakes sit uneasily in my stomach. 'It's all a bit much for me,' I say.

She unzips my coat. 'Oh, come on, Robin. There's something delicious about forbidden love.'

Half an hour later and earlier than expected, Timo arrives. Luckily, we are downstairs in the kitchen, looking for snacks, and both dressed.

'Robin was dropping round some shopping,' Astrid says as Timo stares from the doorway. 'He has Costco membership.'

'OK,' says Timo.

'Much homework?' she asks.

'Science. Started it at lunchtime. Can't finish the last question.'

'Can I help?' I ask. 'Show me.'

Timo drops his rucksack onto a chair, pulls out a ring binder and opens it.

'Ooh,' I say, and do a little jump without meaning to. 'Gravity!'

The teacher has asked them to 'Name six ways we can observe gravity', adding, 'No marks for listing six items sitting on your desk. Hint: Look beyond Earth'.

'Brilliant. Your science teacher's brilliant!' I say.

'OK,' says Timo.

'Have you thought about comets?' I ask.

Astrid holds out her watch. 'You needed to get back to your dad.'

'In a minute.' I reach for the salt and pepper and the pickle jar from the middle of the table and take coins from my pocket. 'Your mum's pickle is the sun,' I begin. 'Everything revolves around it.'

'She thinks so,' says Timo, and Astrid mutters something in German.

I take a teaspoon from the draining board. 'Not to scale. But let's make this the comet. Let's say Halley's Comet. I was born when that was here.' I point to the two-pence coin representing Earth.

Astrid is holding the back of my chair. 'I really don't think he needs this much detail. He just needs to write down six things.'

'Call yourself a professor?' I say to her.

'Lecturer,' says Timo.

More German mumbling from Astrid.

I carry on with my comet explanation. 'So 1986, here. Then this year – ninth of December, to be precise—'

'No way?' Timo interrupts. 'My birthday!'

'What are the chances?' says Astrid. 'But Robin really needs to go.' She takes away our pickle sun, then salt Jupiter and pepper Neptune.

'Yikes, we're losing gravity!' I say. Timo laughs. I resume. 'So yes, the ninth of December, your birthday, is the aphelion, that means furthest from the sun, a turning point, then back this way, getting faster and faster as it nears the sun, and back here in 2061. All thanks to gravity.'

Astrid taps her finger on the worksheet. 'Just write comets. And Robin, you really must go.'

Later that evening she messages: *Believe what you want but don't involve Timo.*

I didn't. Or is the existence of gravity and comets taboo now? I reply.

—*Good word. But no more comets with Timo.*

—*But we're OK to acknowledge gravity?*

I'm booked for a third day running and this time promises to be more leisurely. I have double carers at the bungalow, and it's the morning so no Timo deadline – not that I don't want to see him. I've been thinking about offering my services as a science and maths tutor. Or maybe that's insulting. I could call it 'study buddy'.

Astrid opens the door holding a plate of pastries and we eat them in a patch of sunshine in the garden before going upstairs. When we've finished, instead of getting dressed, she picks up a book. I'm lost. My phone is downstairs in my coat and the only reading material on my side of the bed is in German. I pretend to nap.

As it turns out, I am tired enough to sleep. I'm just going off when she squeezes my arm.

'Anything you don't eat?' she asks.

'What?'

'I want to do a proper meal for us. Friday lunch, I'm working from home. Anything you don't eat?'

'Not much.' I turn over to face her. 'I don't like figs, melon, olives or dill. And I'm allergic to squid. It gives me migraines.'

'Is that possible?' she asks.

'Is it possible? If I'm telling you it's happened on four separate occasions, that makes it possible.'

'Squid. Never heard that one.' She picks up her book and sighs.

'Is this a big blow? Were you planning a squid gratin?'

'Squid and melon salad, actually.' She sticks out her tongue and I take it as an invitation to kiss her. When we pull apart, she says, 'Did you know some squid live forever? Is that why you hate them?'

'That's jellyfish. And I don't hate squid, they hate me.'

Friday comes and Astrid has cooked steaks and sweet potato wedges, served with salad and more pickle.

'You're a hotel soap,' she says as I sit down.

'A what?' I say, still out of breath thanks to a last-minute toilet dash with Dad and the run over here.

'A hotel soap. I realised this morning. Or at least you think you're a hotel soap.'

'Small, free and wrapped in plastic?'

'I brought a soap back from the hotel from that conference. Been using it since, and then this morning, no foam. The middle doesn't foam—'

'Lather.'

'Lather. Anyway, it doesn't. The middle's useless, just there to wrap the outside around, to make the whole thing look big,' she says.

'Ah, I'm big, with a useless middle?'

'The soap's not made for a full life span, because it's hotel soap. Short-stay soap. Like you and your comet.' She leaves the table and returns with three types of mustard.

Dad and Astrid have taken over my faculties and I need to come up for air and admin. I declare Saturday my sorting-out day.

First on my list is Daisy the estate agent. I've been ignoring her calls. Second, and related, is Gemma. To my shame, I have ignored her too. She moved to her sister's the week after our curtailed Italian meal and has asked three times what to do with my keys.

I tackle the two in one email. I write to Daisy and tell her I'll be in touch 'properly' next month, adding: 'In the meantime, I attach my former partner's contact details for you to collect keys from her.'

Then I feel bad and text Gemma: *Thanks for that, and for our pandemic.*

That makes me feel worse. I delete it and write: *Thanks. I wish you well.*

Next on the list is Danny. All week, I've rebuffed his offers of minicab jobs and his pleas to meet ahead of the auction. His messages have become so exacting it's as if he's hired Carol Coombs the social worker to write them. Do I have the deposit ready? Have I read the legal pack? Why haven't I come back about a maximum bid? I reply to all his questions in one email. I keep my answers short and explain that Dad is 'extra needy right now'.

I should sort the bin bags next but I've barely seen Dad all morning. I go through and sit with him for a documentary about tigers. *Ambush – the collective noun for tigers,* I text Astrid.

Aren't they solitary? she replies.

On Sunday, Danny appears at the bungalow as I'm getting ready to leave for Astrid's.

'You smell different,' he says.

'New shower gel,' I lie – it's the aftershave I bought online.

'Sure you rinsed?' says Danny.

'Tea?' I ask in the tone of someone who has no plans.

'Lovely.'

In the kitchen, Danny slaps his free hand on the table, a move as uncharacteristic as his recent telephone manner. 'So,' he begins. 'Auction tomorrow. How are we doing it?'

I fill the kettle.

'It's tomorrow,' he says. 'We need a plan. We need a maximum bid.'

I pour water back out of the kettle.

'Robin! What's going on?'

'Sorry. Overfilled it,' I say. 'What do you think happens if you boil it when it's higher than the line?'

'What? I don't know. Burns your hands.'

'Only if they're near it,' I say.

'Maximum bid. I say we hope for two-two-five but be ready for two-forty.' Danny slides a butter knife under his cast and scratches. 'Yeah?'

'I'm calculating.'

I wash up two mugs. We have Danny's savings and I have twice what we need in my own savings even before selling the flat. But spending that now takes around £20 off each day of retirement.

'It's a lot,' I say. 'And remember what the solicitor said.'

I sent the legal pack to the solicitor I used when I bought my flat. She charged me hundreds of pounds for a written lecture about flooding and planning, and for a phone call about the pitfalls of online auctions and how they bring out people's reckless side. She ended with words that continue to preoccupy me: 'I'm just saying this because it's you.'

Danny is looking at me for more. 'It's too much,' I say.

'You said it wasn't before. And it'll be ours. We'll make it awesome.'

My phone buzzes in my pocket. Astrid will be wondering where I am.

'OK,' I say. 'We aim for two-ten but go to two-forty if we absolutely need to.'

'Yes! God, Robin, I love you.'

The next day, we put the laptop on my desk and sit on the end of my bed, Danny bouncing. I long for a ballroom within seconds of the online auction opening. The anonymity, the automated prompts and the risk of Danny making an unsupervised late-night bid from his phone are all terrifying.

A 'Bidder 1', presumably the music-venue speculator, goes in at £200,000 and an option pops up to bid £201,000. Danny reaches across me to take it. I block his hand. We agree to wait five minutes. 'Stalk like a lion, don't leap like a frog,' I tell him.

'What the...?' Danny laughs.

'This YouTube auctions guy said it. You're being froggish. We have two more days 'til it closes. You need to calm down.'

Danny clicks as soon as the five minutes are up and when the message appears, 'You are the highest bidder', he reads it aloud repeatedly while jumping up and down.

'Ribbit, ribbit,' I say, and pull him back to down to sitting.

Bidder 1 appears to share Danny's impatience and takes the price to £202,000. Danny clicks on £203,000, Bidder 1 goes to £204,000. I let Danny bid £205,000 and the auction site says the reserve has been met. If nothing else changes, we are taking on two decaying Scout huts and their pigeon colony. We'll have twenty-eight days to pay – that's the beauty and the terror of auctions. I breathe through my nose and push down my shaking leg. Next to me, Danny is dancing from foot to foot.

'At this point, we tell it our maximum bid and the computer does the rest,' I say. 'It'll go up in increments as needed,' I add, mainly to myself. It's madness to trust an auction house like this.

'Looking good though,' says Danny. 'Shit. It's happening.'

'Could you stop jiggling?' I pat the bed, and he sits. 'You should go home,' I say. 'And in two days we'll know if we've won.'

'But you'll check back in?' says Danny. 'What if the maximum isn't enough?'

'A maximum is a maximum,' I say.

'But it's not really. What about your flat?'

'The maximum is all we, or I, have for this,' I say. 'And if it's not enough, good luck to the music man.' I stand, open my bedroom door and say to Danny, 'Call Susie or something. Keep busy.'

OBJECT: *Messier Marathon Certificate*
DATE: *March 1997*
NOTES: *How do we find what we're looking for? First, we identify what we're not looking for and cast it aside. That was Charles Messier's approach. It left him with an odd legacy. Still, a legacy's a legacy.*

Messier was a comet hunter. He was one of the first to spot Halley's Comet on its electrifying return in the eighteenth century.

Earlier that century Edmond Halley had made a bold assertion. He believed that sightings of comets recorded every seventy-six years or so throughout history, including one he himself enjoyed in 1682, were in fact sightings of one and the same comet. That same comet would return in or around 1758, he predicted. He did not live to see if he was right – he would have been 102. But others got themselves into a frenzy waiting for the comet's predicted return. Messier began searching for it in 1757. He finally spotted it in January 1759. Halley was vindicated, the comet was named after him and Messier's persistence was rewarded.

Messier went on to discover thirteen comets. His hunting was muddied, however, by other objects in the sky (star clusters, nebulae…) that could easily be mistaken for comets. He started a list of these distractions and it eventually grew to a catalogue of more than a hundred objects. That's what he's remembered for: the things he was trying not to find. I have a chart of them somewhere. And I have this certificate, from my first and only Messier Marathon. Nothing to do with running. It's what astronomers call their attempts to spot all the Messier objects in a single night. Grandad Jim took me to one at his astronomy club. The certificate was rightfully his. He showed me three or four things through binoculars before I disappeared into our tent and the warmth of my sleeping bag. He was there for the star clusters and nebulae, I was there for the camping. He saw sixty. Not bad for an amateur on a hazy night. But all sixty were overshadowed a little before dawn. Grandad woke me, saying there was something I couldn't miss. Still inside my sleeping bag, I wriggled out of the tent like a worm.

The sky had cleared and birds were singing. Someone was cooking bacon on a camping stove. Grandad handed me the binoculars and pointed. 'This one won't be back for thousands of years. Comet Hale-Bopp.'

There it was. As bright as a star and with a perfect tail. Discovered just two years earlier and now blazing in the sky. We saw it again after that night, sometimes without binoculars.

They say it was a thousand times brighter than Halley's had been. Comet Hale-Bopp. Not Halley. Hale-Bopp. People confuse them all the time. They blend the bright comet with the famous name and remember something that never happened.

No chart Messier could ever produce would stop that.

Notes for Dad: *YouTube is full of TV news clips from the nineties, there's a great one with Hale-Bopp.*

29.
A danger

There is a better way to express what the solicitor said about recklessness at auctions: you realise what you truly want when someone else tries to take it.

After Danny's left, I watch as our new bids on the way to our maximum are bettered again and again by Bidder 1.

Bidder 1: a man – it has to be a man – who is taking an extra eighteen pence a day off my retirement with every counterbid. I picture him as an amalgam of the bearded hopefuls on Dad's property shows and the get-rich-quick auction experts on YouTube: suit jacket and large tie knot, jeans on his bottom half.

At £235,000 from us, Bidder 1 goes quiet. I take a picture of my screen and send it to Danny. He replies, *It's happening!* plus several kayak emojis, then another message: *Keep watching.*

I take the laptop into the lounge and sit with Dad. I explain our plans and how close we are to owning the Scout huts.

'What do you think?' I ask him.

Dad makes a whining sound and lifts his better arm. He leans forwards as if he's trying to fling the arm outwards. I follow a line from his arm to the mantelpiece and the laminated alphabet card. We've given up on it the last few weeks but now I reach it down and crouch next to him. His shaky finger taps at the card, then jabs at the air and I understand he needs it higher. I place two cushions on his lap and the card on top. His finger circles the grid as if reacquainting itself with the letters. He stops.

'G, Dad?'

An *mmm* sound. His hand moves again.

'O?' I ask.

'Mmm.' His hand seizes up, relaxes again, edges higher.

'D? Is that a D, Dad?'

'Mmm'

'G-O-D,' I spell out. 'God? You've found God, Dad? Late but understandable.'

Spit hits the alphabet grid as Dad laughs through his frozen jaw. His body shakes.

'You've found God and it's funny?'

He laughs more, and I laugh with him.

'OK. Easy. No choking today.' I squeeze his arm.

The shaking subsides and Dad lifts his finger back to the card. He taps on the O, stops and taps on it again.

'Double O?' I ask and make an *ooh* sound.

Dad splutters with laughter again. Then replies, 'Mmm.'

'Good?'

'Mmmmm.' The longest *mmmmm* he's ever done.

'Oh my God, Dad. You're saying *good*. Good about the Scout huts, about our plan.'

'Mmmmmm.'

I let go of the card and wipe my eyes. We conversed.

On Wednesday, Danny returns to the bungalow for the final ten minutes of the auction. This time, I place the laptop on the coffee table next to Dad. There are no carers due for another half-hour.

Danny and I, known as 'Bidder 2', are still on course to win with our £235,000 – five thousand away from what we've set as our maximum bid.

With seven minutes to go, Bidder 1 comes back with £236,000.

'I hate him,' I shout out.

A Bidder 3 appears.

Now Danny shouts out. 'Oh shit, oh shit. Sorry, Ken. But seriously, Robin, what do we do? Who the hell is Bidder 3?'

I wait for the auction house to automatically place our next bid. 'Look, it's OK. We'll keep outbidding them up to our maximum.'

'And then?' says Danny.

'We're not there yet.'

Dad makes an *mmmm* sound.

'It's alright, Dad.' I put my hand on his. 'We'll get it. I know we will.'

Two minutes to go and Bidder 1 comes back, then Bidder 3. Then Bidder 1 again, then Bidder 3. The screen asks if we want to bid £243,000 – three thousand pounds over our maximum.

'Go for it,' says Danny.

'A maximum is a maximum.'

'You can change it. Quick.'

'It's all I have,' I say.

'You said—'

'It's all I have for this. I need the rest.'

'But we need this. You'll make it back. It's a few thousand. Come on, Robin.' Danny bounces his fist on my thigh and reads out the site's warning not to wait for the final seconds.

With fifty seconds to go, I click.

'Yes! Thank you!' shouts Danny.

The timer jumps back to three minutes.

'What's going on?' he says.

'I read about this. If you bid at the end, they put more time on to give the others a chance.'

'Then it goes on forever,' he says.

'At some point they're out. Or we are.'

We watch the timer count down. The only sound is Dad's breathing. Heavy and fast. He needs this as much as Danny. He needs to leave me with a project. I squeeze his hand. 'A minute to go, Dad. It's ours, it's still ours.'

'Thirty seconds,' says Danny. 'Twenty. Don't do it, Bidder 3. Piss off, piss off, all of you. Ten seconds.'

We count down together. 'Three, two, one…'

'Congratulations', it says on the screen. 'You won the auction.'

I hug Dad in his chair. 'We did it, Dad. We won.'

Danny stares at the screen. 'It's happening,' he says. 'RD Kayaking School. It's happening.'

'R-D?' It's the first mention of a name. 'Like 'Ardy Kayaking School for 'ardy pirates?'

'Like Robin and Danny. OK, DR then,' he says. 'Anyway…' He reaches into the rucksack at his feet and comes back up with a bottle of prosecco. 'Now you can open this.' And he leans to meet Dad's eyes. 'You'll have some, Ken, won't you?'

'He will,' I say. 'We have a special trick.'

In the days that follow the prosecco, things in the bungalow feel almost normal. I chat to Dad with a new energy and even turn Astrid down in favour of watching our lunchtime property show. It helps that I have new material: ideas about the Scout huts, worries about Danny's suitability, favourite models of vending machine. But really, the change stems from one word: Dad's 'good'. That 'good', that moment he spoke to me, is like the emergency phone battery Gemma keeps in her handbag, our little burst of extra life.

I know it will run out. Before it does, I resolve to take us on an outing. I had been planning to go to the graveyard alone, but the day is special to us both. Plus, the forecast is for sunshine.

The rain starts before we're off the estate.

'Such a stupid idea,' I say, turning Dad's wheelchair around to take a kerb backwards. The wind catches the plastic bag tucked over his lap and it lands in an oily puddle. 'Great.'

Nothing from Dad.

I check my watch. I badly misjudged our journey time. I'm going to be late to meet Danny, and he'll gloat. We're supposed to deal with the pigeons today. The farmer's given us the keys but Danny and I have agreed we won't spend any more money on the huts until everything has gone through. Poo removal and pigeon evictions only cost time and courage.

I lean over Dad and shove open the gate to the graveyard. Next comes a stretch of stones and potholes and then deep mud where the path runs out. It's as if the Church and the council have collaborated on a wheelchair assault course.

The rain is turning to hail. I pull Dad's hat down over his ears. At the end of the path, I adopt the voice of a cowboy. 'This is as far as we go.' A shudder of laughter from Dad.

I wipe hailstones off his shoulders, unhook the plastic flower bag from the wheelchair and say in my normal voice, 'Be as quick as I can.'

I pick my way through the mud, thinking another family would have asked for the path to be extended right up to the grave, and then they would feel they had to use it.

I crouch down and trace my fingertip over the fading words.

LINDA MARGARET BLAKE
WIFE • MOTHER • FRIEND
29 NOVEMBER 1956 – 28 NOVEMBER 1998

And I remember how Maddy and her friends had a black nail polish phase in the sixth form. In the spring, I'll come back with my own little bottle and tidy up Mum's letters.

I look around. She's not the only faded one. I've always liked looking at gravestones. I keep notes for my own epitaph. No three-word summaries for me. I'm thinking of using Latin, as on Halley's. I'd like to be able to use the word 'raconteur' too.

I lay the flowers and talk to her stone. 'Twenty-five years, Mum. Nine thousand, one hundred and thirty-two days. Did you know that?' I glance back to the path. Dad has slipped in his chair, his backside about to fall and hit the ground. 'Oh God. I'm coming,' I call. I use the stone to pull myself up. My mouth almost touching it, I whisper, 'It's the disease I hate, Mum. Not him.'

I grip him under the armpits and lift from behind. 'God, Dad,

I should have come on my own,' I say. 'It's not worth it. And this can't be good for you. You're shivering. And I'm late. So late. I told Danny I'd be there an hour ago.' I fumble with the safety belt I should have fastened from the start. 'I'm sorry, Dad. I don't mean to lose it.' We go over a bump and he slumps forwards. I grip his shoulders, pull him back and flick on the brakes. I go around the front of the wheelchair and kick a large stone out of our way, then another, and another. Kicking has to be better than shouting. I work my way along the path, kicking stones, smoothing the ground with my shoe. I pick up a pebble, throw it as far as I can. I grab another, it goes further. The next one hits a gravestone. A child's gravestone. I look around. No witnesses, just Dad. He didn't see, or if he did, he's sparing me.

I have to stop. I have to stop it all getting to me. Swearing at myself, I shake my arms and legs, a self-administered exorcism in a graveyard. It helps. I lean against a tree and breathe in the scent of pine needles. Even rotting they smell better than the bungalow's air fresheners.

I turn back to Dad. 'Right. Path's all clear. Onward!'

Jackie is waiting for us in the drive as we arrive on Sycamore Lane soaked and shivering – Dad with cold, me with latent anger.

She looks like a little football manager with her over-sized umbrella and long black puffer jacket. 'What in evil's name have you been doing?' she says.

'We took some flowers to my mum. It's the anniversary today.'

Jackie's face only hardens, and it occurs to me she spends too much time around dying people. 'In this? Are you trying to kill him?'

'It wasn't forecast for this. And I put a hat on him.' I edge the wheelchair along the narrow space she's left between her car and the empty flowerbed.

She puts her hand inside Dad's scarf as if checking for a pulse. 'He's frozen through.'

'We both are. Actually, now you're here, can you take him in? I'm really late.'

'No way,' she says. 'For a start, we don't have the second carer yet. And you can't get him in a mess and run off.'

I yield and help her take Dad to the toilet and then to his chair.

The second carer is Susie. She arrives late and without apology when there is nothing left to do.

'Finally,' I say to her. 'I was supposed to meet someone two hours ago.'

'Danny?' She bites her bottom lip like a stripper. 'He's running late too.'

'Well ... I still need to get going.' I put on a dry coat and hurry to the door.

Jackie steps in front of me and puts her hand over the latch. 'You shouldn't have done that today.'

'We needed to get out. We needed to go today.'

'You're not up to this,' she says. 'You're a danger to him.'

'I'm all he's got.'

30.
Something I always wanted to try

Astrid and I are finally lying in bed at a conventional time. But nothing else about our Saturday evening has been conventional. She served rice in tomato soup in front of the TV and talked through most of our film. She spent the final ten minutes holding her electric toothbrush against her front teeth. I was uncharacteristically grateful to be watching a film with subtitles.

Now she's propped against her pillow with a sleep mask on her forehead, the elastic puffing up her hair. I reach across and ping it.

'Ouch!' She bats my hand away and our fingers lace together. 'Know what I was thinking...'

'I never do,' I say.

'That you still haven't read me the second list.'

'You'll have to be more specific,' I say.

'The reckless minicab people. The ones who misunderstood. The ones with the crazy final twenty-four hours.'

'Ah.' I untangle my fingers and reach for my phone. 'For you only. Ready?'

Her hair tickles my cheek as she shuffles close. 'Ready.'

'Predictably, you have the one with the giant party, at a venue she'd never pay for,' I begin.

'Don't approve,' says Astrid.

I read on. 'Take out online ads exposing how their boss used company money for his holiday home. Then we have: crash a film set, drink condensed milk until they pass out, hire a private jet and fly back through time zones, also, jump out of a private jet, streak at a football match, hide rotting fish in their neighbour's glovebox, shoot a prime minister – not fussy which one – and finally, rob a bank and give the money to a donkey sanctuary.'

'So much crime and revenge,' says Astrid. 'And then tainting the donkeys with it.'

'Maybe it's the only thing keeping order, that we don't know how long we have to go on living together.'

'I wouldn't have time for any of it,' she says. 'If you gave me twenty-four hours, I'd have to finish all the series, all the podcasts and all the books I have on the go.'

'There's a lesson there,' I say.

'Or not,' she says, and pulls down her sleep mask. It's my cue to get back to Dad.

The money for the Scout huts leaves my account on a Tuesday morning. And because whatever God there is likes to mess with me, a few minutes later, I receive an email from my old colleague Nish. I like to leave emails unread for an hour or so after seeing them; I am beholden to no one (no one who emails) and it's good to emphasise this upside to my situation whenever I can. But in Nish's email the words 'job', 'competitive' and 'remote working' all appear in the first line. He's launched a start-up, he says, and needs a 'numbers man'. He signs off with, 'I'll speak to you later'. Nish is one of the brighter people I have worked with, but he is also imprecise and impulsive.

I file the email in my *WORK?* folder and message Danny: *Scout huts paid. All ours!*

Sending you my chunk now, Danny replies, precisely.

We meet at the huts in the afternoon and Danny brings two small beers to celebrate. Other than that, nothing is any different. The pigeons are still here.

Over several visits, I have managed (with Danny's one-handed help) to clear the faecal Himalayas from the stage but I've yet to cut off the source and a new mountain range is already forming.

'Do you know what they should make?' I say as we sip our beers on the abandoned sofa. 'Pigeon nuggets. An abundant and affordable source of protein. Bet it's greener than chicken.' I shout towards the stage: 'Pigeon nuggets!'

'Shushhhh!' says Danny. 'Don't ever say that in front of Timo. He's mad about animals. He'd kill you.'

'Then he could make robin nuggets,' I say.

'Too fatty,' says Danny.

'Ha! But seriously, this is ours now. We need them out. Today, we reclaim the stage.'

Our beers gone too fast, we go in search of the abandoned stepladder Danny's convinced he saw somewhere. We find it in the other hut.

Danny steadies the ladder with his foot while I climb up and investigate the pigeons' access points at the back of the stage. I find three holes, all seemingly too small for the average-sized pigeon to clear, but how else to explain the mess, some of it still wet?

I rip out the insides of a cushion and fill the first hole.

'You don't think we need a professional?' Danny says from below.

'To shoo them out and block a hole?'

'In a way they'll listen to,' he says.

'Ah, I see. We need a pigeon whisperer? Let me check the Eastgate forum.'

'You know there'll be one,' he says.

'I'd rather not meet them,' I say, and stuff the final hole.

Next, we measure various areas so Danny can firm up his plans.

'I expected to freak out,' I say, holding one end of the tape measure while Danny pulls the other across the hall. 'About the money going through, you know?'

'Oh, Robin, only you would plan a panic.'

'Except, I'm not panicking. Because I've got the lists. If we stick to the lists, we'll be OK.'

'Write down three metres thirty-six,' says Danny.

I type it into my phone. 'You do understand that we need to stick to the lists, don't you?'

'Yep. And two-forty to the first beam.'

Danny has yet to contribute to the lists. There is one for our planning application, another for urgent repairs, another for equipment to research and buy, including boats. We are currently a kayak centre with only four very old kayaks.

Top of the repairs list is reconnecting the electricity. In the meantime, the lack of light makes for short, cold days here.

Today, the darkness arrives faster. One minute Danny is reading out measurements, the next he can't see the numbers. He puts the tape measure in his back pocket and says, 'There's something I always wanted to try.'

'Wearing a tool belt?' I ask. 'I was thinking of getting you one for Christmas.'

'Maybe. Hang on.' Danny climbs onto the stage and drags the

stepladder to the edge, one-armed. 'Open it under the disco ball, will you?'

I carry the ladder to the middle of the room and Danny climbs up.

'Watch this,' he says and grabs hold of the ball with his good hand, spluttering as dust falls onto his face. He turns it until the ribbon is twisted tight and lets go. Then, like a black and white slapstick character, he rushes down the steps, drags the ladder to the wall and climbs again. He points his phone torch at the spinning ball. White stripes race around the walls. I reach out to touch them.

'But...' Danny begins. He moves the ladder closer to the ball. More white stripes, only wider. He holds his torch higher, then lower, then higher.

'Just wait,' I say. 'It's not the angle, nor the distance. It's the speed.'

The ribbon untwists, the ball slows and the stripes split into rectangles. Identical carriages on never-ending trains race along the walls. The carriages shrink until they are fluttering polka dots. Just as they are coming to a stop, the ball twists back on itself and the dots become blocks and the blocks become stripes.

I sit under the ball and shine my own torch upwards. Dots cover the floor. Of course it's the angle too. 'Turn yours off a sec,' I say to Danny. 'See, it works from here.'

He climbs down and we lie side by side on the freezing floor, discs of light dancing all around us.

'I wish it would slow down,' he says. The ball briefly obliges, then turns back on itself and speeds up again.

'Yeah. Slower is better,' I say.

Danny elbows me and the spots jolt in unison as I drop my phone. I pick it up and watch the discs change shape as I move the beam around. 'Fun,' I say. 'That's all we did when we were little, we looked for fun. When did that stop?'

'Fun,' Danny repeats. 'You have to remember to have it.'

'I'll put it on the lists.'

I drive at a maximum speed of twenty on the way home. Danny's bike is in the boot and the lid is ajar. But there's something else: that uneasy feeling that things might be going well.

The feeling bolts as we turn into Danny's road and he says, 'I wanted to ask you something.'

'OK.' I indicate to pull over.

'If you'd come to Timo's birthday thing on Saturday.'

'Will Astrid be there?' My tyre hits the kerb.

'Err, yeah. And Mum. We're going to this buffet on the retail park. Weird place, but it's his favourite. It does pizza, Chinese, Indian. All you can eat. Except Astrid calls it "All you shouldn't eat".'

I finally get the car straight. 'I'd feel like I'm intruding.'

'Don't. Timo asked me to ask you.'

'Why?'

'He likes you,' says Danny.

'Why?'

'He thinks you're funny. And he said you'd love a buffet.'

My hand moves to my belly. 'I do. Please tell Timo I'd be honoured to come.'

'Great. I was thinking you could drive.' He holds up his broken arm. 'Then Astrid and Mum can have a drink.'

'Why didn't you say you were busy?' Astrid scrubs at the same spot on her kitchen worktop. Her kimchi jar exploded after she failed to 'burp' it – her term – and there are neon-orange streaks in all directions.

'You could make a feature of it,' I say. 'Draw some eyes and it'll look like a spider.'

'Spiders in a kitchen?' She makes a *tsss* sound and asks her question again. 'Why didn't you tell Danny you were busy?'

'He said Timo wanted me there. That he likes me.' I tilt my

head. 'From here it's almost an octopus, if you add more orange in the middle.'

Astrid scrubs on.

'It's funny that he likes me,' I say.

'He does. But this is a catastrophe. You have to say you can't come. Call Danny, cancel.'

'It'll look weird. We've been talking about it all week. The buffet has an ice-cream station.'

'And I learn about it now?'

'The ice-cream station?'

'No! You muscling in.' Astrid's buttocks shake as she scrubs faster.

'I didn't. And you're over-reacting. We haven't done anything wrong.'

'Danny won't see it like that,' she says.

'At some point, you need to tell him. And Timo. We have to be more normal about this.' I gesture to the two of us: me at the table in her thin black dressing gown; Astrid at the counter, cream cleaner in one hand, scourer in the other, wearing nothing but an over-sized NASA T-shirt that she bought 'extra' for me. 'Take me to the stars,' she said, answering the door in it. 'Impossible,' I replied.

She throws her scourer in the sink and sits down. 'You agreed we'd keep it secret and now you're forcing me to tell everyone.'

I stroke her arm. 'Fine. We wait. And it's just a dinner. Nothing needs to happen.'

'It will lead to disaster,' she says.

'Not if we don't want it to.'

31.
And so it happens

The day of the buffet, I text Astrid and ask what to wear.

I can't believe you're coming, she replies.

You're not being very nice, I write back, and follow up with: *Guess it will create an illusion of distance. Clever.*

Whatever, she replies.

Thought Timo was the new teenager.

She has no reply to that.

I wait in the car for them outside Bee's. I'm reasonably confident in my choice of jeans, shirt and the thickest jumper I own. Based on reviews online, the buffet is cavernous and shabby.

I'm less confident about the gift. All I know about Timo is that he likes eating, baking and animals.

A light goes off in the upstairs of Bee's house but no one comes out. I wait another minute and lightly beep the horn. Danny comes to the door and waves. Bee appears and helps Danny pull his coat over his cast. Timo follows them out. No Astrid. I climb out and open the front passenger door. 'Birthday boy in the front?'

Danny frowns, but Bee says, 'Excellent plan.'

I breathe deeply as they fasten their seatbelts and say, 'No Astrid then?'

'Mama's coming,' says Timo. 'She's running late. She said to pick her up.'

'Oh,' I say. 'Then I suppose the Round Robin Taxi Service will have to oblige.'

Danny leans forwards. 'She's in one of her moods.'

Bee tuts. 'Needing time to put make-up on is not a mood.'

'I didn't let it make *me* late,' I say, and Timo laughs.

In the two-minute drive to Astrid's, my body turns against me. Sweating and shaky as we pull up, I beep the horn too hard.

'Jesus, Robin. It's a buffet, not tickets to the opera,' says Danny.

Timo makes a loud sucking sound through his teeth.

'What?' I say.

'Mama hates it when Papa beeps the horn.'

'Then your mum should learn to be on time. I thought she was German.'

'Stereotype,' says Timo.

'Fair enough.'

Still no sign of Astrid.

'Anyway, what did you get for your birthday?' I ask Timo.

He slowly lists items that only half make sense. Many are connected to Minecraft, none to baking or animals.

Astrid's front door bangs shut. In the four weeks since that first kiss in the woods, she's looked less than breath-taking on only two occasions. On one, she'd put her hair in two bunches like a toddler. On the other, she'd worn dungarees. If I'm lucky, she'll have been in a similarly regressive frame of mind when dressing this evening. It's too dark to tell.

'Shuffle, shuffle,' she says to Danny as she opens his door. She squeezes Timo's shoulder. 'How's the birthday boy?' she asks and, without waiting for an answer, says something in German that contains the English word 'teenager'.

'God, Mama,' Timo replies.

No lecture about the horn for me, and no hello either.

I'm glad Bee is here. She fills the journey to the restaurant with stories of Timo's previous birthdays and some of Danny's, including the one where we lost Adam from down the road when he wandered out of the McDonald's and into the arcade. 'Then when we dropped him back, his mum said he goes there all the time. Made me seem all neurotic,' says Bee.

'You're not neurotic,' I say. 'Adam's mum was negligent. One minute it's arcades, the next he's selling drugs round the back of the caravan park.'

'Is that what happened?' asks Timo.

'If only he'd had the mental maths for it,' I reply.

Astrid has not regressed; she's evolved. Inside the restaurant, she removes her coat and huge green scarf to reveal a fitted black sweater dress. The high neck is the perfect backdrop for her hair and a pleasing match to her thick black eyelashes.

We've been given what Timo describes as the best table: round and next to the ice-cream machine. No sooner have we sat down than Astrid says she needs to 'find the ladies'.

'We'll order drinks,' says Danny. 'Red?'

'Thanks.' Her knee-high boots clip-clop as she walks away.

I feel under my chair for the gift bag I've brought in from the car. I wrapped the three items separately. I always preferred more parcels as a child. I still do. But Timo's not me. He'll think they're silly. He'd have been happier with a twenty-pound note in a card, just like Jackie suggested when I asked her. My phone buzzes and halts my descent into paranoia. I hold it under the table. A message from Astrid:

Stop being so weird.

I'm not. You are, I type as secretly as I can.

No.

You said nothing about the horn. They noticed.

What? she replies. Then sends a separate confused-face emoji.

When I beeped, you said nothing and acted normal.

Normal is good.

'Robin, Robin. Oi.' Danny is waving in my face. 'Drink?'

I look up. 'Sorry. Carer trouble.'

The waiter doesn't smile back.

'Lemonade, please,' I say. 'No. Hang on, do you have ginger beer?'

'Ginger ale,' says the waiter.

'Is there a difference?' asks Bee.

'Who knows?' says the waiter.

'Ginger ale then, please,' I say.

Astrid has texted again.

Don't stare at me

Why the dress? I write back.

You like it? Forbidden Love! Then too many emojis to interpret. Then another message: *But seriously, it is FORBIDDEN today.*

I put my phone in my coat on the back of my chair and say to the table, 'Sorry. New woman. Lots of questions. Very needy.'

Bee squeezes my hand.

'Can we start?' Timo asks.

I jump up. 'Awesome. I'll come with you.'

As I follow Timo around a badly positioned fake Christmas tree and towards the long counters of food, Astrid returns from the toilets. Based on the number of dishes – twelve starters alone – and the distance to our seats, if Astrid and I time things right and stick to small portions, we can avoid being at the table together for the entire evening.

I take one piece of garlic bread and one onion bhaji and pretend to dither over the salad options. Timo is taking two of everything: two olives, two cherry tomatoes, two mini quiches…

'Won't you fill up on starters?' I ask.

'I don't fill up. I'm growing,' he says.

'Lucky git … Sorry.'

'It's OK. Papa calls me that too.'

We pass Astrid on our way back to our seats. Timo isn't looking so I glance back and forth as obviously as I can between table and buffet to communicate my plan for non-contact to her. She shrugs and pulls a face at the fake tree as if apologising for Timo's choice of restaurant. Then, studying my plate, she says, 'Nice selection. The bhajis are actually not bad.' She pronounces bhaji in what she must imagine to be the Indian way and my face screws up before I can stop it.

I eat as fast as I can. The bhaji and garlic bread are dry but are helped down by the whole pint of ginger ale the waiter has brought.

Danny and Bee are yet to fetch any food. Bee notices me looking at their empty plates. 'I prefer to wait for the main,' she says. Then nodding towards Danny, 'And they have their little system.'

Timo has put his plate of two of everything between him and Danny. Starting with the olives, they eat each item at the same time. 'Size order,' Timo says to me.

'They've done it since he was tiny. Every birthday,' says Bee.

'How does it work with curry?' I ask.

Timo swallows his single tortilla chip and says, 'We come at it from both sides.'

'Ah,' I say. 'Like two ants with a big leaf.'

'Oh my God,' says Danny. 'Timo, we should do that with a poppadom.'

Astrid is back and has heard the ant plan. 'Danny! It may be a buffet, but it's still a restaurant. You two!' It's feigned outrage with a note of sadness. How many times has she had to watch this spectacle of Danny the best-friend parent?

Danny and Timo ignore her and move on to a breadstick, one end in each mouth. They put their hands behind their backs and crunch faster and faster until Danny bursts out laughing. Timo picks a blob of wet breadstick off his ear. 'Gross, Papa. You're so gross.'

'Well,' I say. 'I think I'm ready for my main. Bee?'

As we walk, Bee wiping her plate with a paper napkin, she says, 'You'll always be his first playmate.'

'Playmate?' I say.

'You don't need to be jealous.'

'I'm not. They're funny together.' I can't tell her the word playmate makes me laugh.

We stand at the long table with food purporting to be from every continent. 'So, what do you recommend?' I ask Bee.

'That we keep Danny and Timo away from the spaghetti,' she says.

I take a small portion of something Chinese and seeing Astrid stand up, hurry back to the table.

'They have chopsticks,' says Timo.

'Thanks, but fork is faster,' I say.

'Robin's always in a rush,' says Danny, and winks.

'We don't have forever,' I say.

'Nice birthday talk,' says Timo.

I force down my last mouthful of sticky, battered meat just as Astrid returns.

'Italy next,' I say, standing up. Astrid raises her empty glass to me. When I glance back, she's refilling it.

Back at the buffet, I take one spoonful of the tomato pasta, one spoonful of the creamy pasta and a thin slice of pizza. My plan is working. I'll get Tex-Mex on my next visit, curry after that. Then I just need to get through ice-cream, hand over the gift and drive everyone home. If I drop Astrid last, maybe she'll invite me in to peel off that dress.

I'm on my pizza crust when Astrid and Timo sit down. Timo has gone for dry foods again, two of each.

'Nice,' says Danny, appraising their latest plate.

Astrid has one stick of chicken satay, as if she's understood the portion part of the non-contact plan but is struggling to grasp the timing element. Her second glass of wine is almost empty. Danny tops it up, and his own.

I study my plate: the green bits in the creamy sauce, the two types of pasta shape in one dish.

'Eww!' Timo holds out his tongue and reaches for his lemonade. 'Eww,' he says again. 'That's the grossest onion ring ever.'

'It's calamari,' says Danny, his own ring half-eaten.

'Will you eat it?' Timo says and drops it onto my plate.

'It's just—' I begin, but Astrid lunges across the table, knocking over Danny's wine.

'No! He can't. He's allergic,' she shouts.

'Fucking hell, A,' says Danny. He grabs his glass, rescuing a last sip.

'Danny!' says Bee.

'Napkins,' says Danny, and dabs at the wine with his working arm.

'What's calamari?' asks Timo.

'Squid,' says Astrid. 'Robin's allergic to it. You can't just put things on people's plates.'

'Alright,' says Danny. 'How was he supposed to know?'

'I didn't know you were allergic to seafood,' Bee says to me, her voice gentle and her eyes embarrassed.

'Just squid,' I say. 'Gives me migraines.'

'Is it really a thing?' says Danny.

'If he says it is and he's the one with the migraines, why wouldn't it be?' Astrid takes a large gulp of wine.

'I've always pronounced it "mee-graines",' says Bee.

Danny goes to refill his glass but the bottle is empty. He reaches for Astrid's glass instead and she swipes it away.

Bee leans across me and touches Timo's hand. 'Let's look for the real onion rings.'

'Fuck's sake, A. It's his birthday,' says Danny when they've gone.

'Stop swearing.'

'His fucking birthday.'

'I have his gift here,' I say. 'Completely forgot.'

They ignore me.

'I'm so desperately sorry I knocked over your desperately needed wine,' Astrid says to Danny. 'I'll get you another one.'

'Good,' he says.

'Even though it was an accident,' she says.

'Accident?'

'What then?' she says.

'An accidental dive, to save Robin from an imaginary allergy.'

'I've had four separate incidents with squid,' I say. 'You were there for—'

'Don't bother,' Astrid interrupts.

'Hang on…' says Danny, and I realise that my fifth squid incident has begun.

'Hang on,' he says again. 'How does she know about your squid thing?'

'It just came up. By the sea,' I say, my insides volcanic.

'When by the sea?' Danny waves the empty bottle of wine in the direction of the waiter.

'Let me go to the bar,' I say.

'No!' People look over to us. 'No,' Danny says again, quieter. 'Sit the fuck down. This is about the gnomes, isn't it? You think I'm some fucking idiot.'

Astrid looks at me. 'He knows about the gnomes?'

'Yep,' Danny answers for me. 'Explains why you're dressed as Jessica Fucking Rabbit.'

'I don't get it,' says Astrid.

'Because Jessica Rabbit wears red,' I say. 'But I think it's the tight—'

'Shut up, Robin.' Danny bangs the table.

No one speaks. I arrange my three remaining pasta shapes into a triangle.

'I like him,' Astrid says suddenly. 'We like each other.'

'How fucking wonderful!' Danny stands up so violently his chair tips over. A waiter approaches but I warn him off with my hand.

Danny lowers his voice. 'God, Astrid. I try and I bloody try and you … you do … this.' He looks at me, the 'this' that's been done. I wait for something that never comes. He stoops down and tugs at his coat on the back of the fallen chair. I go to help. 'Get the fuck off!' he shouts and swings his arm back. The cast smacks me in the mouth. I fall back. My lip is bleeding. Danny yanks his coat free and walks out.

As I pull myself up, Astrid sighs. 'And so it happens,' she says.

When Bee and Timo return to the table, Astrid makes up a story about Danny feeling unwell and says he's gone home in a taxi.

'If it's food poisoning, you both ate the same things,' Bee says to Timo. It's an odd way to play along with the lie but Timo doesn't seem to be listening.

'What happened to your lip?' he asks me.

'Banged it on your dad's cast when I was helping him up. So clumsy … And forgetful. Look what's been sitting under my chair all night.' I lift out the gift bag.

'Oh, that's so kind, Robin,' says Astrid.

Timo looks surprised. 'Thank you. Shall I open it now?'

'Yes,' say all three of us together.

Timo unwraps each gift slowly, stopping between the first two to visit the ice-cream station with Bee and me. He goes through every page of the cute-animals calendar, showing Bee each one. Then he opens the animal-shaped cutters I found in the antiques shop and says he can't wait to make cat biscuits. 'Not with real cats, I hope,' I say. Astrid laughs and Timo groans. As Timo comes to the white chocolate, and breaks it up and offers it around, my stomach churns. It churns at the smell of red wine soaked into our table; it churns at the thought of pasta and bhaji in the sea of ice-cream and ginger ale inside me; and it churns at the grotesqueness of what we're doing. It's Timo's thirteenth birthday and we're acting like he's a clueless five-year-old.

To speed up my escape, I offer to pay, and no one argues. We drive home to the sound of Christmas songs on the radio. Bee and Timo are in the back this time. Next to me, Astrid is drifting off to sleep. When Bee and Timo leave, she stirs and says, 'Happy birthday, my baby boy.'

Outside her house, I turn off the engine and wait. She's silent.

'Now what?' I say, louder than I mean to.

She claps her hands together. 'You know Danny.' She kisses her fingertips and blows in my direction.

I turn away from the wine fumes and re-start the engine. 'Drink some water.'

'I can't see you tomorrow,' she slurs.

'OK.'

'Extra choir practice. Christmas.'

'OK.'

'Good,' she says and opens her door. 'Sleep well.'

'How?' I call after her.

As I drive away, I remember a conversation with Gemma. It started with something she read. 'Would you rather be betrayed or get found out for betraying someone else?' she asked me.

'What does your magazine suggest I prefer?' I replied – it was back when Gemma thought I was clever and funny, and I took every chance to prove her right.

'Better to be betrayed,' she said. 'Easier to recover from.'

I creep into the bungalow and check on Dad. The carers have left his radio playing. I turn it off and pull his duvet higher. I watch his chest move up and down with his breaths, steadier at night. His face is almost smiling. Does he find freedom in his sleep? Can he move, laugh and eat like he used to?

'Dream about Sunday roast,' I whisper, and back out.

I try Danny. All four of my calls go unanswered. Around 1.00am, when I'm still reading Wikipedia pages on my phone, he texts me: *You lied to me. I hate that. Fucking hate it.*

It's understandable but inaccurate. I made a point of never lying to him, about this or anything. In the morning I'll explain that, and that it was Astrid's idea to keep it secret and that nothing really happened. It didn't. We've slept together twenty-five times with mixed results; we've shared some meals, many of them disappointing; I bought a multi-pack of toothbrushes; and she bought a NASA T-shirt.

Another message from Danny: *You're not her type.*

Nor were you, I think. *You're probably right,* I reply and turn off my phone. Jackie is arriving in six hours and I've promised to be ready to heave and wipe.

I lie flat on my back and try my old sleep trick: I work back through the comet's dates: *2061 Me, 1986 Me, 1910 Twain, 1835 Twain, 1759 Halley's Proof, 1682 Halley's Observation…* A sound in the dark, then another, something shifting in the bin bags in the corner. I hold my breath, hear it again. I roll onto my side, press my ear into the mattress. They are under there too. I can hear them rummaging in the pots and pans.

No chance of sleep now. I turn on my phone. Danny's seen my message. I hold the phone with two hands as if I might squeeze out a reply. I turn on the torch and point it at the bin bags. More rustling. I roll away from them and check the news. I search for stories about the car arsonist. Then I re-read everything Astrid has ever sent me. She's funny. And she's surprising. No one else is surprising, not positively. 2.00am. I type *Sorry* to Danny and put my phone out of reach. *1607 and 1531 One and the Same, 1456 the pope declares the comet an agent of the Devil.* What did I ever do to the Devil? *1378, 1301…*

More rustling.

32.
A good day for dolphins

'I was a twat.' I wince. 'And so were you,' continues Danny.

We're standing on Bee's front path, Danny having given in to my plea to come outside. He's in Lycra, I'm in a hurry. I've promised Jackie I'll be there for her afternoon call.

'I didn't technically lie,' I say to Danny. 'I didn't betray you.'

He scrunches up his face. 'Betray's a big word.'

'And the wrong one. Because I didn't.'

'But you made me look like a dick.' So much anatomy. 'And you totally ignored everything I told you about her.' He pulls and releases the rim of his cycling shorts as he speaks. Ping. 'I don't get why you didn't just tell me.'

I've come here without a ready defence.

'It was Astrid,' I say at last. 'She said not to tell you. She kept saying "not yet, not yet". And there's not much to tell. I don't even know what it is.' 'Forbidden Love', is what it used to be. What is it now?

'You're the worst match. She's hard and you're … well, you're not hard. She'll squish you into whatever shape she wants. She'll mess you up,' says Danny.

'I'm already messed up. Maybe I want someone to squish me. Look at me. I'm halfway and I've done nothing. I've got nothing. I'm in Eastgate, I live with my dad, I've got no job, no family, my budget's a joke, and now I've got mice.'

Danny's eyes fall to my pockets. 'On you?'

'In my bedroom.'

'Oh.' He sucks in his lips, clearly trying not to laugh. We look into each other's eyes and crack at the same time.

'Mice?' he says.

'Pretty sure.'

'Less poo than pigeons, I'm guessing. Anyway, I'm going out on my bike.'

'I figured. Or that you'd run out of normal clothes.' I nod to his cast. 'A one-armed bike ride?'

'I only need one.' He mimics leaning on the handlebars. 'Come with me if you don't trust me. Thought I'd stop where we saw those dolphins that time. And you can borrow some cycling stuff, so you don't have to wear lady tights again.'

My face burns. 'You saw those?'

'Sadly.'

'Oh God. But it was really cold. It's always so bloody cold down here.'

'You wearing them now?' Danny reaches for my waistband and I jump back.

'Nosey bastard.'

'So you are?' says Danny. 'Ladies' underwear, who'd have guessed?'

I pull at my jeans and prove my tightlessness. 'And tights aren't underwear.'

'Yes, they are. *Ladies'* underwear.'

'Wrong. They're accessories,' I say, and Danny's defeated.

'So will you come?' he asks. 'It'll be fun. Remember remembering to have fun? And it feels like a good day for dolphins.'

I hesitate.

Danny cups his free hand behind his ear. 'Listen – they're calling us.' He takes on the voice of a choking alien. '"Robin, show us your lady tights. Robin, bring us your squid rings!"'

'Oh God, I really want to,' I say. 'Ah … I so want to. But I'm supposed to get back to Dad. It's boring but we're one carer down and—'

'It's fine. It's fine. I get it. Sucks. I mean for you, it does. And for the dolphins.'

'Next time,' I say, and Danny nods.

I'm a couple of houses down when he calls after me. 'You haven't got nothing.'

I mouth *shush*.

'You're right about being messed up,' he continues, and pulls at his own waistband.

'Thank you,' I say.

'But you haven't got nothing. You've got me. We've got the Scout huts. It's going to be amazing. You'll see.'

I want to believe him. More urgently, I want him to shut up. 'Go before it gets dark,' I call back. 'And say hi to the dolphins.'

On the walk home, I count only nine houses on Bee's estate with Christmas decorations. When we lived here, it was the ones who didn't bother who stood out.

I wonder if Dad might like some decorations around the lounge. They'll be in one of the bin bags. Maybe some tinsel and fairy lights would mellow Jackie too. I speed up and I'm at the bungalow twenty minutes before Jackie is due.

I'm picking the knot on the first bin bag when I'm interrupted by a message from Danny: a screengrab from the Marks & Spencer website where a woman is waving fishnet-clad legs in the air. Danny has circled their categorisation as 'lingerie' and written below: *That's French for ladies' underwear.*

I reply with one screengrab from the New Look website and another from asos.com, where tights are categorised as 'accessories'. For comparison, I send a woman in a cobalt blue bra and matching knickers with many straps and write, **This** *is underwear.*

That what you're wearing? replies Danny.

Not for you, I write back, and join Dad in the lounge.

'Here's the plan,' I say, as much to myself as to Dad. 'Don't let on to Jackie but there's a mouse problem in those bags and boxes.' I pause, and when Dad doesn't react, I mute the TV. 'Hear that, Dad? We've got mice.' Dad makes a noise. I continue, 'Good news is, we need to go through them anyway for Christmas decorations. I'll bring them through and sort as we go along. A change from other people's junk on TV.'

Dad makes an *ah* sound in approval.

'Great,' I say.

Then another *ah* and another. I follow his eyes to the remote. I unmute the TV and fetch the first bag.

I use my house key to stab and rip it open. 'Old sheets, Dad. What do you reckon, charity shop or dump?'

Nothing.

The charity shop seems the more generous choice, and it's closer. I start a pile.

Jackie lets herself in as I'm lifting the bags in my room and looking for mouse droppings.

'What in evil's name?' she says to Dad. 'Trip hazards everywhere, Ken. What is he thinking?'

'I was thinking,' I say as I step into the lounge, 'that it's time for a sort-out. And the Christmas decorations are in these bags somewhere. Dad needs a bit of Christmas, don't you, Dad?'

Jackie moves to the corner. 'What's all this?'

'For the charity shop,' I say.

She picks up one of Mum's cookbooks.

'Unless you want any of it,' I add.

'Your castaways?'

'If there's something you want.'

'You can't leave it here. It's not safe for your dad,' she says.

'It's the other side of the room from him.'

'If you're doing a sort-out, do a sort-out. Put it straight in your car and it's ready to drop.'

'Thought I was supposed to help you with Dad.'

Victory. Jackie releases me from care duties on the condition I don't put anything else on the lounge floor.

I work fast, feeling the bags from the outside and taking any that are soft and paperwork-free straight to the car. When the back seats and boot are full, I pile up the passenger seat. I find myself repeating a German phrase Astrid taught me: '*Besitz bindet.*' Possessions tie you down.

Besitz bindet, Besitz bindet, Besitz bindet.

It's true, especially when they're not yours. Each time I return to my room, it feels bigger, and I feel freer.

There are droppings between the final bags but no mice. The website I've been consulting about pigeons also has a mouse section. It confirms they are nocturnal. And 'opportunists', it says. I vacuum then spray the floor with kitchen cleaner.

'You find the Christmas decorations?' Jackie asks as I carry out the final bag.

'Shi——. Must be in the boxes.' Maybe I can check the bags from within the car before I drop them off. I'll make time tomorrow.

Back inside, I start on the boxes. No decorations in the first one.

Just a mix of old papers and rubbish. I place the one item of interest on my desk and push the box against the loose skirting board to thwart the opportunistic mice.

When I turn around, Jackie – a close relation to the opportunistic mice – is standing in my doorway. She nods at the boxes. 'I know a solvents guy selling off filing cabinets.'

'OK.'

'Do you good to file things. Reassure your dad too.'

'Unnecessary.' I point to my laptop, open on my desk. 'There. My whole life mapped out to the last penny and last minute.'

She leans further into my room. 'And the boxes?'

'I don't want a filing cabinet. I'll deal with them when I have time.'

'Does your computer say when that will be?'

'My phone's ringing,' I say and turn away.

Jackie retreats.

There is no call but I do have a message from Astrid, the first since she stumbled out of my car last night:

Are you free later?

Not really, I reply.

What does that mean?

I don't have time for your booty calls. I've wanted an opportunity to write that for a while, ideally in jest.

I'm not interested in your booty, Astrid replies.

Oh. I squeeze the edge of my rejected booty.

Not at this precise moment, she adds.

OK.

I thought we could try normal. Come and have dinner and play cards with Timo and me. Sunday-night tradition

What about your choir?

Just finished. We're terrible. See you later?

I put my phone face down on the bed, turn it over to check the time, place it face down again. Cards and Timo, dinner included.

We do have two carers the rest of today. Or I can get to the out-of-town Tesco before it closes and buy Dad a fake Christmas tree. Except the car is full of bin bags.

I'd like that, I reply to Astrid.

Danny drops Timo at 5. Come at 5.30.

I can come before. Danny and I have resolved things. We always do. After I send it, I realise it's smug. So does Astrid.

Apart from when you didn't speak for years, she replies. Then, *It's not that. I need to talk to Timo first*

This is it. My official introduction, or the introduction of what I officially am. I message again:

What am I?

What? She adds a lopsided face.

What am I to you?

A person with a future of interest

I've never thought of my future as anything but planned.

OBJECT: *Finger guillotine*
DATE: *1995*
NOTES: *Push down and the blade goes right through your finger, or around it, actually. We used to scream for effect. My little finger is the only one that fits in the hole now.*

It's Danny's turn to have it. Has been for twenty-four years.

We were on a school trip to a castle, maybe a museum. I only remember the shop. This was the last guillotine left. We both said we saw it first. Then Danny said, 'Know what? You can have it.'

'Then I'll feel bad forever,' I said.

'And I'll feel good forever!' When Danny grins, he looks like a cat advertising toothpaste.

'Let's share it,' I said. 'Each get it one week at a time. I'll make a chart.'

'I get it on the coach home,' said Danny.

After that, we switched it back and forth every Monday morning. After a while, it mostly stayed in our school bags but the swapping carried on. Then it got forgotten. Until today, when it turned up in a box of junk.

If only it were a real one, I'd behead the mice. My revolution.

Notes for Dad: *N/A. This is Danny's now. I'll take it to show Timo. He can pass it on.*

33.
Not a time for kisses

It's a clear evening and oddly mild. Danny picked a perfect day for a bike ride. He'll have been down on the beach, shouting to the dolphins whether they were there or not.

I walk slowly, avoiding the lines between the paving stones. I've developed a way of sidestepping them so casually that my game would never be apparent to anyone looking out of their window, and in Eastgate they so often do. It's a coastal thing, the legacy of being the nation's supposed defenders against the approaching Nazis. Our hills and cliffs are littered with forts and watchtowers. Dad used to visit them on weekends, nostalgic for more extreme times.

I let out a 'Ha!' when I arrive outside Astrid's not having stepped on a single line. Her path is tiny hexagonal stones. I walk across her lawn, ring the bell and hold out my offering: tortilla chips, little Tesco's last lemon cheesecake and defrosted salsa.

Astrid answers alone.

I step back. 'Oh God. Chat with Timo go badly?'

She looks past me into the dark street. 'Danny hasn't dropped him. He's not picking up. I called Bee and she says he's been gone for hours.'

'Timo?'

'Timo's there. Danny. Danny's gone.'

'He went on a bike ride,' I say.

'With his cast?' She holds up her arm. 'And you knew this?'

'Only sort of. Maybe he didn't go. I didn't see him go.'

'And now he's missing,' she says.

'He's not *missing*. He'll be in a pub somewhere, dead battery.'

Astrid rubs her temples so hard it looks painful. 'He only has one hand.'

'Well, that's not true.' I touch the doorstep with my toe and she moves aside. As I step in, I go to kiss her and she leans away. I didn't expect this hysterical side, or whatever I'm allowed to call it. No wonder Danny was so secretive about the fainting.

In the kitchen, Astrid jabs at her phone.

'What happens when you call him?' I ask. 'Is it *off* off?'

'It rings and rings and then voicemail.'

I sit and watch her try Danny's phone again and again. Eventually, she stops to make tea then returns to her phone, interspersing more calls to Danny with calls to Bee while I scroll through news stories. They've caught the celebrity-car arsonist, a man in his thirties whom police will not name. I message the article to Danny and follow up with, *If you see this, ring Astrid back. She's going mad. Did you see the dolphins?* It remains unread.

'Who goes for a bike ride one-handed in winter?'

I look up and realise Astrid's question is addressed to Danny's voicemail.

When she's hung up, I say, 'He went to this place where we saw dolphins once.'

'So you do know he went on his bike? Where is it? Where's the place?'

'Not that far,' I lie. When we went together it took a whole morning to reach. 'It was just something he mentioned. Who knows if he actually went?'

'Who knows? Who fucking knows?' Astrid drops her phone onto the table.

'How about we walk round to Bee's? Get some fresh air. See Timo. Unless you think you're going to freak Timo out.'

'Why would I?' she spits.

'Because you're losing it over a perfectly healthy grown man going to the pub.'

'He's not at the pub. Why would he be at the fucking pub?'

Putting Astrid and Bee together is foolish.

'I keep calling and he doesn't pick up,' Bee says as she answers the door.

'Same,' says Astrid.

When Danny does finally look at his phone, he'll have more missed calls than a celebrity, or my London plumber. He'll find it hilarious.

'Where's Timo?' I ask as Bee takes us through to the kitchen.

'Upstairs, finishing homework,' Bee replies in a whisper. 'He doesn't know.'

'I'm sure it's nothing,' I whisper back.

Astrid and Bee's nerves are spreading to me. As I sit down, I check again. My message to Danny remains unread. Above it is our exchange of tights and underwear pictures.

Bee nods at my phone. I turn it face down.

'When did you last hear from him?' she asks.

'Ah, maybe just after I popped by. Early afternoon.'

'What did he say?'

'Nothing much.' I'm sweating. 'Silly stuff. You know Danny.' I push my phone into my pocket.

Above us, there are creaking sounds as Timo moves around his bedroom. I picture the wardrobe that won't close, the old bunk beds.

'I do have one idea,' I say over Bee and Astrid's back and forth about one-armed bike rides. 'I just need to call someone.'

'Go on then,' says Astrid.

'Privately,' I say.

I stand at the bay window in the lounge, the furthest point from the kitchen.

'What is it?' Jackie answers.

'Are you with Dad?'

'We're doing his drops,' says Jackie.

'I'll be quick. Susie. Do you have her number?'

Jackie says nothing.

'The younger carer,' I say. 'Blonde. Mainly weekdays.'

'I know who she is. But I can't just disperse girls' numbers to you.'

'I don't want it for me. It's my friend—'

'Or to your friends either,' Jackie snaps.

I take a breath and speak without pausing, 'My friend Danny is missing or not picking up his phone and his family are worrying and he's been seeing Susie and I'm pretty certain he's at her place.'

'That would be weird,' says Jackie.

'Why?'

'Because she's here doing your dad's puree.'

'Oh.' A van speeds past Bee's and in the house opposite someone comes to the window. 'Actually,' I say to Jackie, 'do you mind asking Susie if Danny's at her place?'

'Why would he be?'

'I don't know. To sleep? He doesn't have a proper bed. Just ask her.'

'Is he a grifter?' says Jackie.

'What?' Behind me, a door creaks. Astrid is watching me, eyebrows raised in hope. I turn back to the window and speak quietly into the phone. 'Drifter. No. Ask her, please. It's urgent.'

'OK.'

There are muffled words including 'Danny' and 'his own bed' then Susie comes on the phone. 'Robin?'

'Susie? Yeah, it's Robin. Hi.' I stop. This isn't the time to be weird. I shake my head as if it might reset me.

'What's happened to Danny?' asks Susie.

'Probably just left his phone somewhere. Stopped off in a pub.'

'He's not messaged me back all day,' she says.

'Listen, ask Jackie to give you my number and drop me a text. I'll let you know as soon as he shows up.'

'Cool,' says Susie and I can't tell if she's uncaring or just pretending to be.

'Dead end,' I say as I return to the kitchen.

'What's that supposed to mean?' asks Astrid. She's retreated from her listening post and is at the table scribbling angry notes.

'I thought he might be with a mutual friend and he wasn't. They haven't seen him.'

'Because he's missing,' says Astrid.

'Do you think we should call the police?' asks Bee.

'No!' It comes out too hard. 'I mean, you can't call the police about an adult who hasn't picked up his phone,' I say. 'They won't help us.' Bee starts to cry. I touch her arm. 'I'm just saying, they're overloaded. Did you see how long it took them to catch that car arsonist?'

Astrid's pen hits me in the face. 'You and that bloody arsonist,' she says.

Bee is still crying. Upstairs, Timo is moving around again. If he comes down now it will be a disaster.

I retrieve Astrid's pen from the floor. 'How about this?' I say. 'Astrid and I go out looking in the car, the ways he usually cycles, check some pubs. And you stay here with Timo. We'll find him.'

Bee nods. 'Thank you,' she whispers.

While Astrid goes upstairs to say a hello and goodbye to Timo with whatever excuse she can concoct, I give Bee the food from my bag.

'Timo loves a cheesecake,' she says.

I tap my fingertip on my temple to show I remembered.

Bee sniffs. 'He never just disappears like this.'

'I know. But we'll find him.'

The radio switches itself on as Astrid starts the engine. It's a station dedicated to Christmas songs.

'Really?' I say.

'Timo,' says Astrid.

I switch it off.

'Leave it on,' she says. 'Good distraction.'

Her car is messier than expected and so is her driving. She pulls away without signalling and fails to slow for junctions.

'Are you sure you want this music? It's a bit frantic,' I say.

She turns it down a notch and says, 'So you think the coast road, out towards the point?'

'Yes. And we can check The Stag on the way.'

'It's called The Bootmaker now,' she says. 'New people.'

Driving seems to calm Astrid. But being driven makes me more uneasy – that and what Bee said about Danny never disappearing. My message to him remains unread.

'I'm calling him again,' I say. One, two, three, four rings and then voicemail. I hang up. 'I don't get why he'd not answer or let us know where he is.'

'He forgets his phone sometimes,' says Astrid.

'Oh God. Why didn't you say that before? Give me your phone, I'll ring Bee, ask her to check his room for it.'

Bee picks up immediately. 'You found him?'

'Sorry. Not yet.' I explain why we're calling and stay on while Bee searches for Danny's phone. She finds nothing.

'Never mind,' I say, making my voice sing-songy. 'We're just reaching the pub, bet he's in there.'

'No bikes outside,' says Astrid as she parks. 'You go. I'll wait here.' She keeps both hands on the wheel as if she might slide into the footwell if she lets go.

The pub is quiet. I edge the door open as inconspicuously as I can, but the man behind the bar looks up. I make a show of scanning the room for someone and reverse out.

'Nope,' I say as I climb back into Astrid's car.

'Did you try the room at the back?'

'I didn't see a room at the back.'

'Oh man. Go back and check again,' she says.

'It already looked weird going in and straight out the first time. You go.'

Without a word, Astrid gets out, walks over and flings open the pub door. I bet she'll march right through to the hidden back room and on into the men's toilets. If I'd done that, they'd have asked me to buy something.

Astrid returns to the car alone. The Christmas music resumes as she starts the engine. She reverses without looking and hands me her phone, 'Here, text Bee and tell her he wasn't in the pub.'

'Kisses or no kisses?' I ask when I've typed the message.

'What?'

'To Bee, would you like kisses or no kisses? It seems from your other messages to her that it varies.'

'God, Robin. It's not a time for kisses.'

'Looks cold, but OK.' I hit send and her phone makes a *whoosh* sound.

'Now call Danny again.'

'Yes, Captain.'

I turn off the Christmas station and count the rings to voicemail. One, two, three…

'Hello?' a woman answers.

34.
Like it never happened

'Where's Danny?' I ask.

Astrid lets go of the wheel and reaches for the phone. 'What's happening? Put it on speaker. Hang on, I'm stop—'

I shush her. 'Sorry, not you,' I say to the woman on the phone. 'Did you say you're with Danny?'

'We called an ambulance. They said ten minutes.'

'Ambulance?' I ask.

'What?' says Astrid. 'Put it on speaker. What's…?' She snatches the phone and holds it between us. The woman doesn't reply.

'What ambulance?' Astrid shouts at the phone.

The woman still doesn't reply.

'Oh my God, Astrid, you hung up. You cut her off,' I say.

'I hit speaker, I hit speaker.'

'Just find somewhere to pull over.' I take the phone and call Danny's number again. My mind flashes to the alphabet card and Dad's shaky hand. Gingerly, I press speaker.

'Hello?' says the woman.

'Sorry. We lost you. What's happened?' I ask.

'Why an ambulance?' says Astrid. I gesture to her to be quiet, and to turn into the next side road.

'We didn't hit him.' The woman's voice is young and fearful. 'We almost hit him. He was there and then he was gone. He swerved. We looked back, no one. Like it never happened. But we both saw it. We stopped, went back, it took us ages to find him. He was in a ditch. We called an ambulance, they said ten minutes, maybe twenty, they're talking to us.'

'Oh God,' says Astrid.

'It's coming. I can see the lights,' says the woman.

'Can I talk to him?' I ask.

'It's … He can't talk.'

'What?' says Astrid.

'My boyfriend's doing CPR on him. They're telling him what to do. On his phone. They're here. I have to go.'

'Wait!' I say. 'Where are you?'

'Err. Main road into Greenchurch, past the garage…' There are voices in the background. 'I've got to go,' she says.

'Sorry. Go, go. We'll call this number again in five minutes.'

'OK,' she says.

'I'm Robin, his best friend.' Astrid shoves me. 'And the other voice you heard was Astrid … his wife.'

'I'm Maria.'

'Thank you, Maria. And your boyfriend.'

'It's OK.'

Maria is gone. We stare at the phone, the only light for miles around.

'CPR's just to be safe, right?' says Astrid.

'Yeah. Don't think about it. They're with him. It's OK. It's going to be OK.'

'So where to now?' she asks.

'You OK to drive?'

'Think so.' She does a U-turn back towards the main road. 'Which way?'

'Same direction. I know where they meant. And the ambulance will be taking him to the Blackwell. Either way, same direction.'

We've been driving a while, Astrid almost within the speed limit, when she says, 'Why did you describe me like that? On the phone.'

'You are technically his wife.'

'No, that weird phrase, "the other voice you heard". Like someone in a police show.'

I look away. I was hoping she'd missed that. 'This *is* like a police show. And people say weird stuff when they're stressed.'

'No, no, you were great. Just that bit was weird.'

'Shall I list all the times you've said weird stuff?' The energy I have for this surprises me.

'That's mean,' she says, voice weak.

'Why? Why's it any different?'

'Monolingual prick!' She hits the accelerator into a bend then lets off.

'Childish,' I say.

The road straightens and she shivers loudly. 'It's so fucking cold,' she says.

'Really? It's stuffy in here.' I open my window.

Somehow, she has the power from her side to wind it back up. I open it again. She closes it and says, 'You should call. It's been five minutes.'

'Not on speaker when you're driving,' I say, and wonder where this sudden common sense is coming from. Perhaps somewhere among the window wars and rows about weirdness I've grasped that Danny is in a ditch and having his heart pounded by someone who found him too late. Perhaps I know that whatever is said next will be something Astrid can never bear to hear.

Maria speaks fast. 'They're taking him to the Blackwell. They want the phone. I need to give it to them. They said you should go there.'

There are more voices in the background and the sound of an ambulance door slamming.

'Is he OK?' I say into the phone. 'Did they say he's OK?'

She's gone.

'Hospital,' I say to Astrid. 'Hospital is good.' I go to squeeze her thigh but pull back, the darkness masking my indecision. We haven't touched since the squid incident. We might never touch again.

As we drive, I tell her about my own trip to the Blackwell with Dad. We saw a specialist, who made me feel stupid when I asked if Dad might get better.

Astrid interrupts. 'We need to tell Bee. You need to call her.'

I lie to Bee, beginning with, 'Everything's OK' and finishing with a diversion to Danny's plastered arm. 'I think they need to patch it up.' There's a chance it's true.

'I told him he shouldn't be on his bike with one arm,' she says.

'We all did,' I say, and disgust myself.

The hospital reception is staffed by a woman whose chair is so low we have to peer over the counter to get her attention.

'Daniel Thompson,' says Astrid. 'Daniel Thompson. Broken arm, bike accident.'

The woman seems distracted by something behind us.

'I'm his wife.' Astrid is almost shouting.

The woman holds out a palm. 'Broken arm is A&E.' She points to a sign.

I lean onto the counter. 'What we mean is, he had a broken arm and then he was in a road accident. Paramedics brought him in.'

'Name again?' says the woman.

'Daniel Thompson,' says Astrid.

The woman stretches to reach her phone and gives us a glare that says we should step back. She mumbles into the phone then looks up. 'The doctor's coming.'

The doctor, a woman eerily similar to Gemma's Dr Chloe, speaks only to Astrid. 'You're his wife?'

'Yes. Astrid … Thompson.'

'OK. I'm Doctor Reid. Let's go and find somewhere quieter.'

Dr Reid turns, Astrid follows, and I look at the woman behind the desk for guidance. Her eyes are fixed on her computer.

Astrid and the doctor are speeding away from me. If I was supposed to go with them, the moment has passed. The doctor opens a door far along the corridor and ushers Astrid in.

'There are seats over there,' the receptionist says to me at last.

'Thanks. Should I have…?' I nod to where the doctor has taken Astrid. The door is closed. 'Actually, I'll just…' I walk over to the chairs and sit in the one furthest from a man with a vomit-soaked child on his lap.

In more harmonious times with Gemma, on a drive to Cornwall, a woman on the radio said something shocking yet incontestable. She was talking about her teenage daughter's sudden, but not unexpected, death. I can't remember what from.

'I felt relief,' the mother said. 'When the hospital called with the call I'd always known would come, I felt relief. Relief that the dread was over.'

'It's great for you that I have a date,' I remember saying to Gemma.

'Shush,' Gemma said, turning up the radio. 'Let her talk.'

Now, I watch that closed door where Astrid went in and search for my own release from the dread that set in the day Danny fell off his bike by Mingin' Falls. There is none. There is guilt, and there is a new dread, the dread of being found out.

'Sorry, mate.' A man brushes against my leg as he wheels a bed past me. The patient in the bed is wearing an oxygen mask that barely fits over his thick grey beard.

I tuck my feet out the way. I've always hated the term 'mate'. I am no one's mate, except maybe Astrid's. Probably not anymore.

Down the corridor, the door opens. The doctor comes out, Astrid does not. The doctor catches me staring and she nods towards the room she's just left. Without thinking, I do a thumbs-up. Her eyebrows arch, I hide my thumb and stare at the floor until she's sure to be gone.

It's seventeen steps to the door. I listen to Astrid's sniffs through the gap. She sees me and the sniffs turns into long, painful gasps.

I hold her and she cries. After a while, she shakes herself and says, 'It doesn't make sense.' She presses her face against me, cries more and, like a jack-in-a-box, straightens to say it again: 'It doesn't make sense.' The words become a chant and then, her eyes fixed on mine, they are a plea.

'What if I talk to the doctor?' I ask.

'She said did I want someone.' Astrid sniffs. 'I didn't get it. I said, "just tell me".'

'It's OK.'

'She said he was probably already … When they got here … They tried…'

'Shush,' I say into her hair. 'Shush.'

'That stupid bike.'

'Stupid bike,' I repeat.

The door opens. 'Oops, sorry,' says a man and closes it before we can see him.

It's the circuit-breaker I need.

'I just want to check,' I begin, and Astrid looks up. I whisper, 'Is he ... is he dead?'

'Fucking hell, Robin.'

'You haven't actually said.'

'Fucking hell, Robin.'

Uninstructed on what to do next, we walk out of the room and away from where Danny might be. We follow signs and long corridors to a café. The counter is closed but the lights are on bright. The room has the feel of a cinema lobby desperate to spit out its last customers. Astrid slides onto one of the plastic seats fixed to a table and looks over to a drinks machine. I buy two coffees and scald my hand carrying them to the table. I use my sleeve to brush the remnants of a flapjack onto the floor.

'I know it's not ideal,' I say. 'But I've needed the loo since we got here.'

'Sure,' says Astrid, her gloved hands around the coffee cup.

'Have you been wearing gloves the whole time?' I ask.

'It's a hospital,' she replies.

When I return, Astrid speaks before I can sit down. 'The doctor asked if I wanted to see him.'

'Oh God.'

'I said I didn't know. But I did know. I didn't want to. I was scared he might be ... you know ... grotesque.'

I steady myself on the table. Is this too little English or too much Kafka? 'It's OK,' I say, sitting down. 'No one can make you do anything. Here, I brought you back some toilet paper.'

'Thanks.' She blows her nose. 'If I saw him, I'd know it's really him. Definitely him. Because what if they mixed him up, you know ... with someone else? I said that. She said they had his wallet. They're sure it's him and I just...' She cries, blows her nose again. 'I told her I need to be with Timo. But I should have gone.'

'It's OK. You're right. You need to be with Timo.'

'Timo!' she says, as if she's forgotten her own words from seconds ago. 'How do I tell Timo? And Bee? I can't do this. What do we tell them?'

'Oh God, Astrid. It's not for me to say.' I hide my face in my hands. It's burning at the shame of wishing I could untangle myself. The shame of asking myself how far away I might be from this miserable hospital café if I'd never come back to Eastgate, never found Danny again.

'It is for you to say,' says Astrid and yanks my hands away from my eyes.

'Ow!'

'We did this,' she says.

'What?'

'That's why he went out today. Us.'

'That's bollocks. He just wanted to go on a bike ride. He wanted me to…' No use telling her Danny had asked for company.

'We did this,' Astrid says again.

'No, we didn't. Dolphins did.'

Astrid decides it's best to tell Bee and Timo in person and that I should drive. It seems cruel. Bee has been calling Astrid's phone for the past hour and Astrid hasn't answered.

I jog to keep up with her on the way to the hospital car park. Clearly, people run in corridors in Germany. By the front desk I hesitate. 'Don't we need to tell them we're going?' I ask Astrid.

'Why on earth?' she says, and rushes ahead.

As the night air hits my face, I pause again. She doesn't wait for me.

At the car, she holds out her keys. 'We can talk about what the hell we're supposed to say on the way,' she says.

I take the keys without speaking. The journey will be long enough to make her understand there is no 'we' for this.

I adjust my seat and the mirrors. 'You don't have any sweets, do you? Or gum?'

'No!' says Astrid.

'Alright. I'm not asking for vodka. I just like something in my mouth when I drive.'

At the car-park barrier, we realise we were supposed to pay by the front desk.

'Don't they exempt people for … you know?' I say as I look for reverse.

Astrid mutters 'fuck, fuck, fuck' to herself as she tries all her pockets for the ticket. We find it on the dashboard.

I drive across the car park and let her out near the entrance. 'You should take it to the receptionist, ask her,' I call after her.

Her shoulders shrug in response. She's looking at her phone. She speeds up to a jog. Then, deaf and blind to everything around her, she steps in front of an ambulance. The driver holds down the horn and it judders to a stop. Astrid jumps back and raises a gloved hand. The ambulance drives on and Astrid crosses. Another ambulance follows, but this one stops and obscures her. And it obscures me.

I switch off the engine and leave the keys on her seat.

35.
What else you got?

I follow a path around the edge of the hospital. I'm out of breath. Astrid will be back at the car by now. I feel for my phone in my pocket, check it's on silent. The path rounds another corner. I slow to a walk and breathe out to quell the stitch in my side. Ahead of me are the lights of another entrance.

No reception here but a map on the wall. My finger shakes as I trace along the grey corridors to where I need to be. I walk fast and look straight ahead.

The same woman is on the front desk.

'Danny Thompson,' I say. 'We were just here for Danny Thompson.'

'Yes,' says the woman. 'You disappeared. They need his wife to fill in forms, she'll need them to register—'

I cut her off. 'I want to see him. I have to see him.'

'Oh,' she says. 'Give me a minute.'

'Where is he?' I ask.

'Just give me a minute.'

I grip the edge of the counter. I'm dizzy from running. Alarms and sirens come from every direction. A cold wind blows in as a man – drunk, high or just livid – stands in the automatic doors and shouts that 'no one fucking cares'. This is where we left Danny.

The bed is empty.

'I'm too late,' I say.

Or they've all been wrong.

'Not that one,' says the nurse. 'Over here. Behind the curtain.'

Her shoes squeak as she crosses the room. It's bigger than I imagined, and emptier.

The nurse holds the edge of the curtain, ready to pull it back like a magician.

Danny wanted to be a magician when we were little. He used to do card tricks in the playground. 'Surprised yer,' he'd say. Sometimes, it was a question, 'Surprised yer?' His scruffy blonde head tipped to one side.

The nurse touches my arm. 'You OK?'

I wipe my eyes. 'He was my best friend.'

'I know.' She lets go of the curtain and touches my arm. 'I need to prepare you…' She seems to be waiting for some sign I'm listening. I nod. 'We've tidied him up,' she says, 'But some things might seem a bit odd. He'll have had some tubes in him, and bruising from the CPR. He may look quite different.'

'OK.'

'Ready?' she says.

I blink hard and wish for another empty bed. 'Yeah.'

Danny's mouth is open. There's a sheet up to his chin, his head is on a pillow and his mouth is open. He's a sickly yellow, not cold blue. His eyes are closed. But his mouth is open. They've left him mid-cry.

I look away.

The nurse is watching from the end of the bed.

I put my hands in my pockets. 'Can I touch him?' I ask.

'If you'd like to.'

Scared to feel his coldness, I place my hand where the top of the sheet is folded over and thicker. Without looking, I press until I can make out the curve of his shoulder, the same as before. I slide my fingertips along the outline of his arm, the same as before. Danny is here, solid, strong, almost beautiful, the same as before. Our hands touch through the sheet.

The room is silent. My other hand is in my pocket, holding the finger guillotine.

'I was about to give this back to you,' I whisper. 'It was your turn. God, Danny, I'm sorry.'

The family room, as the nurse called it, is a good hiding place. I don't pick up Astrid's many calls. In the end, she messages me. She's re-parked and will wait in the main entrance, she says. She expresses no surprise at my apparent disappearance.

The nurse comes to check on me. 'Holding up OK?' she says, head round the door, rest of her body poised to retreat.

'Can I show you something?' I ask.

'Sure,' she says.

I scroll through my photos to the Mingin' Falls ride. 'This is what he looked like, before.'

The nurse steps into the room, sits next to me and stares at the picture. She smiles then rubs one eye.

'Sorry,' I say.

'No. It's OK. He was lovely,' she says. 'Looks like a lovely guy.'

'Do you think they can do something about his mouth?' I ask. 'You know, the way it's open. They can't leave him like that. It will scare his wife, his son.'

The nurse folds her arms across her chest. 'I honestly don't know. But I'll ask.'

'Thanks,' I say, and she's gone again.

I leave the photo on my screen. Danny in the late-afternoon light, thermos and coffee mugs aloft, triumphantly happy. God, he was an optimist.

I send the photo to Astrid, and write underneath: *This is how I want to remember him.*

You saw him, she replies.

How does she know?

Another message: *You went back in to see him.*

Yes, I reply.

OK. Can we go now?

Can we go now? As if I've dragged her to work Christmas drinks. *They said you need to fill in some forms*, I write back.

Then I add, *Sorry*, because surely the only way to make this worse is to add form-filling, and that's what they've done.

All done. I'm right by the entrance. Hurry. I need to get to Timo, Astrid replies.

Walking to you, I write and slide off the vinyl sofa.

Keeping to our original agreement, I drive us home to Eastgate.

Astrid called Bee and told her about Danny while she was waiting for me.

'I couldn't leave her hanging on anymore,' she says.

'Sorry,' I say.

'I called Wendy next door, asked her to go and sit with her.'

'Good idea.'

The roads are empty now, late on a Sunday night. I prefer having someone to follow, to pace myself. I ease off and tap the brakes. Soon we'll pass the point where Danny fell. Swerved and fell, the woman said.

'Did they give you his things?' I ask Astrid. 'His phone?'

'It's all still there. Why?'

'Just this silly thought,' I say.

'What?' she snaps.

'Nothing sinister. Just wondered if he saw the dolphins. If he took pictures of them.'

'Would that make it all OK?' she asks.

'You're right.'

When we pass the pub, now in darkness, Astrid speaks again. 'You know we met at the dump?'

'The dump?'

'I was lifting this big armchair up those rickety metal stairs they put on the side of the container things. He grabbed the other side, didn't say a word, just smiled.'

'Charmer,' I say.

'When we'd pushed it into the container thing, he said, "What else you got?" That's the first thing he said to me. I liked that. "What else you got?"'

'And you gave him your number?'

'No. Six bags of garden waste, a cupboard door and then my number.'

Bee's is the only house with its downstairs lights still on. I pull into the kerb a few doors down. 'The thing is,' I say before Astrid can challenge me, 'I really have no place in there. You need to be just family now.'

'Right,' she says. 'You're going? Well, thanks.'

'That's OK.' I hand her the car keys. 'I'll come and check on you in the morning. I can drive you to the hospital if you like.'

She runs her glove along the dashboard.

'It'll all work out,' I say.

'You don't know that.'

'Fair enough. See, I say stupid things. You don't want me in there.'

'Goodnight, Robin.'

'Goodnight, Astrid.'

OBJECT: *Ten-pound note*
DATE: *December 1998*
NOTES: *'About to, about to. You're always about to do something,'*
Dad used to say. About to empty the dishwasher, about to take out the
bins, about to leave forever…

I was about to hand this over. I missed the moment.

It's one of the old ones, with Charles Dickens.

Sandra gave it to me before we left the house to ride in a car behind
the hearse. Why does a hearse call at a person's home? It's not like they're
being picked up from there. Someone should have answered my
questions. Mum would have talked me through the day. All I knew
was that I was riding to the church with Dad, Auntie Sandra (as I
called her then) and Jamie. Mum would have warned me that when
I came out of the house, I'd see her coffin for the first time.

Everyone knows this, but never says it: it's worse to lose your mum
than your dad.

Auntie Sandra told me the ten-pound note was for a collection.

'Of what?' I asked. 'When?'

'You'll know,' she said.

Here's the thing about funerals, you can choose whatever music,
poems and flowers you like, everyone will be fixated on one thing only:
there's a coffin in the aisle and inside the coffin is a dead person. First
Grandad Jim, then Mum.

People came and went, read things out, and I stared at the big metal
handles on the coffin, and sometimes at the Christmas tree up ahead.
We were singing a hymn when Jamie passed a weird velvet bag to me.
Someone behind me tapped me on the shoulder and gestured at it, I
passed it to them, they put money into it and the bag travelled on.

That's my clearest memory from the day. That and the coffin going
into the ground. Less clear but also there is Jamie eating sausage rolls
at the church hall afterwards. And Dad and Bee. They were rowing
in the kitchen. 'What about what Linda would want?' I heard Bee
say. She was unpacking shop-bought cakes.

'Such a bloody fuss,' said Dad, and walked out.

I went home with the ten pounds still in my pocket. Then I moved it to the bottom of the bottom drawer, wrapping it around the new pastry brush I'd bought for her birthday, the day after she died.

Notes for Dad: *Mum would have liked her funeral.*

36.
Old enough to understand

There are carers in the lounge and Christmas songs on the TV. I feel under my pillow for my phone. Messages are stacked up on my screen. I need everyone to disappear. And sleep. I need more sleep. I've had four fitful hours haunted by Danny's open mouth and Dad's heavy breathing.

I unlock my phone.

Susie. Shit. She's messaged three times. It's not like Danny, she says.

I feel wretched. I am wretched.

I lean against my bedroom door. One of the carers is Jackie, the other isn't getting a chance to speak.

I roll deodorant onto my unwashed skin and dress in the clothes from the end of my bed.

Back at the door, I hear the other voice at last.

I step into the lounge. 'Jackie, I need to speak to Susie.' The two of them are either side of Dad, lowering him into his chair.

'Give us a minute,' says Jackie.

'You spoke to him?' Susie asks.

Copying the doctor, I say, 'Let's find somewhere quieter.'

'OK,' she says. Unsurprisingly, she looks and sounds apprehensive, and yet nowhere near as apprehensive as she should be.

I move toward the kitchen but she goes straight past me and sits on my bed. One of my socks is on the floor near her foot. She nudges it away.

'Sorry,' I say.

'Go on then,' says Susie.

I close the door, kick the sock further away and sit on the corner of the bed.

I use other people's words – from TV, from the hospital. The order is wrong and I say it without conviction, because how could it be true?

'There was an accident. I'm afraid it's bad news. About Danny.'

Susie sways on the bed and my stomach aches.

'An accident?' she repeats.

'On his bike. He went looking for dolphins. He was on his way back. Someone found him, they called an ambulance.' I grip the edge of the moving mattress.

'Dolphins?'

'From this lookout point,' I say. 'But that's not—'

'Where is he now?' She's shaking her head.

I say nothing. She doesn't get it. I sigh. That doesn't work either. 'He died.'

'What?'

I've never seen someone change colour before. I lean towards her and touch her thigh by mistake. 'Sorry.' I edge away. 'I didn't know how to say it. He died.'

She lunges and cries into my neck. Our bottom halves are still far apart and I'm losing my balance. She presses her wet face into my skin.

The door opens. 'What on earth's happened?' Jackie's arms are folded but her voice is kind.

Susie sits up, weirdly rigid. I straighten my T-shirt.

'Danny was in an accident,' I say, and then I mouth to Jackie, 'He died.'

'Oh, God,' says Jackie. 'Car?'

'Bike,' I mouth.

'I need to go home,' says Susie.

'Of course,' I say.

Susie stays behind on my bed for a while, cleaning mascara off her cheeks with one hand, typing non-stop with the other. Jackie notices me staring from the lounge. She nods towards Susie's phone, 'All her friends are in there.'

I close the bedroom door. Bloody Danny, going out with an adolescent and now having his death splashed all over Facebook.

When Susie has left, still typing, no longer crying, I tell Dad what he may have already overheard. I keep it short and shallow, on Jackie's orders. 'You have a tenancy to distress him,' she tells me.

I hold Dad's hand as I speak. 'Danny died in a bike accident last night.' I wait for his face to react. 'He was only thirty-seven.' Still nothing. Sadness perhaps, but that's always there. 'It's shit, isn't it, Dad? Thirty-seven.'

Dad grunts, and I see his eyes are wet. My words have filtered through. I lean against him. I want to sob, but Jackie is in the kitchen.

I used to think Dad didn't like Danny. I knew he resented Bee's friendship with Mum, and so it didn't surprise me that he wanted me to branch out to another family for my best friend. He would frame every start to the school year as a chance for me to 'find a new gang' or 'meet a new pal'. One day, a while after the crash, I asked him outright, what was wrong with Danny? 'Nothing,' he said. 'But it's safer to have more than one friend.'

I look up at Dad's face. I wonder if he remembers that now.

Finally, Jackie leaves, and I return to my room, remake the bed and call Astrid.

Bee picks up. 'She's driving,' she says. 'We're going to the hospital.'

'With Timo?' I ask.

'Yes. He's missing school,' Bee replies.

'Oh. I wasn't saying he shouldn't.'

Bee doesn't respond. I wish I could start over. Astrid is saying something in the background.

'She says she'll call you later,' says Bee.

'Only if she has time,' I say, then, 'Bee, I'm so sorry. I don't know what else to say. It's just terrible.'

She starts crying. 'It's OK,' she says, her soft voice now splintered. 'Come round soon. It'll be nice to see you.'

'I'll bring another cheesecake,' I say, which is absurd, but so is everything.

Astrid calls as I'm drifting off to sleep after a late lunch of double beans on toast, half a bottle of wine and eight pancakes with extra syrup. What's the point of a budget now there will be no kayak centre, no vending machines? I went back over Nish's email as I ate. Green airliner fuel isn't a bad idea.

'I need you to come and sit with Bee,' Astrid begins. 'I'm going to take Timo to his favourite pizza place, then the cinema, and I need you to stay with Bee.'

'Can you even believe it?' I say. 'I've had to tell three people and I still don't want to believe it myself. I think this might finish me, if anything could.'

'Maybe,' she says. 'For now, can you come and sit with Bee?'

'Sure.' I sit up, feel sick, lie down. 'When?'

'Now.'

Bee is wearing a bright-pink cardigan. I've changed into my navy-blue jumper, the closest thing I have to black.

'Astrid's just gone – you've missed her by a minute,' she says from the doorway.

Bee clearly hasn't been warned that she is being babysat.

'I came to see you. I said I would, remember?' Hopefully, she's forgotten about the cheesecake.

'Oh, you're lovely,' Bee says, gesturing for me to come in.

As she goes ahead to the kitchen, I untie my trainers slowly, catching my breath and searching for words. I've already made Bee cry once today and I've somehow angered Astrid. And then there's the secret. First, I kept it for Danny, now I need to keep it for my own sake. The safest approach is to be the one asking all the questions.

'How does Timo seem?' I ask, sitting down at Bee's table.

She stares at her hands, completely still, as if someone has pressed a pause button. 'Timo?' she says finally.

'How is he?' I prompt.

She pauses again. 'We waited until the morning to tell him. He…' She stands up. 'I'm sorry. Tea?'

'Do *you* want tea?' I ask. 'Should I make some?'

'I'll make it. Stay there.'

She fills the kettle and takes two matching white mugs from the cupboard. She looks the same as always. Her trousers are ironed, her hair is tidy and her kitchen is tidier still. How is a mother who's lost her only son supposed to look? The dishevelment must come later.

'You'll have a biscuit, won't you?' She opens an unfamiliar orange packet.

'Always,' I say. 'How was the traffic to the hospital? Did you hit rush hour?'

'Not too bad,' she says.

The biscuits are plain shortbread. No hint of orange.

'These are nice. Hospital car park busy?' I ask.

'Took a while to find a space.'

There is something soothing about the noises in her kitchen. The same kettle she's always had, wobbling as it reaches the boil; the same red clock on the wall, its ticks uneven. Not quite quarter past three and the sky is already that winter dark that declares the day as good as over.

'It's inadequate that car park,' I say. 'Did they see you right away?'

'More or less,' says Bee. 'We did a bit of paperwork first, in a funny little office, you know, on the first floor.'

I nod as if I do know. 'Were you able to talk to a doctor?'

'After a wait. They're over-run.'

'Dreadful,' I say.

Bee sighs. 'It's funny,' she begins, and stops. She stares straight ahead as if at something or someone only she can see.

'What's funny?' I ask.

'The doctor. The working theory, she said it was.'

'Yes?' I lift one foot off the freezing tiles and onto my chair.

'It was like your mum.'

'You've lost me,' I say.

'Because he swerved. They need to do tests but they think it was his heart. Not the bike, falling, hitting something … His heart. Like your mum.'

'Like … That's not…' I stop. Bee is looking straight ahead again. I touch her hand. 'Bee, do you think we should get you up to bed? When did you last sleep?'

'His heart gave out, *then* he fell. Like your mum.'

'That's not … you're confused. Mum crashed, remember. It was icy. We hit a tree.'

'But before that her heart stopped.'

'We crashed,' I say.

'It was her heart. She'd been having these … episodes.'

'You're getting mixed up,' I say.

'No. Her heart stopped. It was her heart.'

'Auntie Bee, look at me. We crashed.'

Bee gestures sideways with her hand. 'She drove off the road, away from the cars, saved you.'

My legs shake. 'We hit a tree. By The Anchor. The tree. It's still there.'

She leans back. 'You hit a tree, presh, but that's not what … not what killed her.' She tips her head like she's talking to a toddler. 'She bumped the tree, that's all.' She touches the table at the word 'bumped'.

'We crashed. It was icy. We crashed and hit a tree. But I was lucky.'

It's the line I always use. I was lucky. Sometimes, I explain the luck part, that it wasn't my time.

Bee clasps my hands. 'It's OK. You were so young.'

'We crashed.'

'Oh, presh, it was her heart. They hadn't long found it. I went with her.'

She squeezes my hands harder. She's studying my face, clearly waiting for some sign that I remember this new version of the past that makes no sense.

'No one told me,' I say.

'We didn't want to worry you. Your dad said it was better to wait, until you were older – old enough to understand.'

'He never talked about her.'

'He didn't want to upset you. None of us did,' she says.

'How much more upset could I get? She was dead.'

37.
And now you're stuck

'Have a walk and you'll untangle it.'

Mum used to say that about playground rows when I was little and about maths problems when I was bigger. All life's troubles were balls of string to straighten out, if only you spread them over enough space.

I take the long way back from Bee's, and when I reach the bungalow, I add on an extra loop of Dad's estate.

I've been delusional for twenty-five years. For twenty-five years, I've been reliving something that never happened. I didn't survive a crash. There was no crash.

Or Bee's wrong. She's in shock. Because there was a crash. We hit a tree.

I arrive back to a carer-free bungalow, but it won't be that way for long. I have ten, maybe twenty minutes.

Dad is in front of a new quiz show. I switch it off and take the alphabet card from the mantelpiece.

'Bee said something funny.' I pause for Dad to tune in. 'Bee said

Mum had a heart problem. She had some sort of heart attack. That's how she died. We didn't crash. We rolled off the road. Are you listening, Dad?' His face is fixed in its eternal sulk. My resolve weakens. I'm attacking a man who can't speak. 'Sorry, Dad. I just don't know what to think. She said you were supposed to tell me. When I was old enough to understand. But you never did.' Still, he doesn't react. I crouch lower, look up into his eyes. 'Do you get what this means, Dad? You let me believe we crashed, that I survived a crash. Do you get it? You've made everything ... you've made it ... disputable. It's disputable, Dad. Disputable.'

There has to be a better word, but whatever it is, it means the same shitty thing. 'Indisputable' is a good word. One of my favourites. That and 'cemented'. Now everything is disputable and uncemented. It's flying through the air in a million slippery pieces.

I put my hand on Dad's and hold it over the alphabet card. 'Tell me, Dad. Tell me why you never told me.'

His breathing is loud.

I uncoil his finger, point it at *YES*, then *NO*, then *YES*. 'Please, Dad. I need to know. Were you ever going to tell me? Yes? No?' His hand is resisting. 'Answer, Dad. Was I ever going to be old enough?'

Dad pulls his hand off the card. He lets out a long groan that turns into coughing. Or is it choking? It's quiet yet violent. His hunched body shakes, he gasps. His skin is grey.

I stand behind him, pull from under his arms. 'Don't do this. Sorry, Dad. Let's get your head up.' He slumps again and heaves with every breath. 'Come on, Dad. Sit up.' I move to the front, shift his thighs forwards. I fumble with the chair's buttons until it reclines. He's lying back but his chin drops further, folding his windpipe, cutting off his breathing. I hold down the button but nothing happens. I get behind him again, take hold of the chair and tip the whole thing backwards. With one hand I hold the chair, with the other I clasp his chin and lift his head. 'Come on,

Dad, breathe properly.' The chair's too heavy, I can't hold it. The base shifts. I'm losing my grip. The whole thing slides away from me. Dad's head bounces as he lands. He's on his back, legs draped over the seat. The choking stops. 'Shit, Dad,' I say. 'Let's just get our breath.'

The chair is awkward to lift, and keeping Dad in it makes things harder still. But moving him first would take too long. The carers are about to arrive and one of them is bound to be Jackie. The sudden thought of her calling me a 'health haggard' makes me laugh out loud. I turn it into a cough.

'It's alright, Dad. Almost there. Lean back if you can. There we go.' He's upright, his colour's back. He looks as stunned as I am.

I pick up the alphabet card from the floor – it slid across the lounge when it had the chance. 'I don't know how to do this,' I say.

Dad closes his eyes and opens his lips to make a sound. I wait. I watch his mouth. And I search his face for glimpses of the old him, the Dad who did so little for me, who hid so much. If I could see him, I could find the courage to try again. But all I see is a frightened old man, mute and defenceless.

I put the alphabet card back on the mantelpiece. 'Let's just forget it.'

I retreat to the kitchen, down a glass of wine and stuff the bottle into my coat pocket.

The picnic chair is damp. I pull my coat sleeves over my hands and lift it onto the table.

Something is different. The bottle of wine is unbalancing me. My skin is cold on the outside and hot on the inside, as if something has seeped underneath it. An ache pulses from my head into my shoulders. The roof seems higher, and the table and chair are shakier. I take the wine out of my pocket and place it as far from the edge as I can reach. A car is approaching. It'll be a carer.

I lunge and the chair clatters onto the paving stones. I hang there, jack-knifed: torso on the roof, legs dangling. I wriggle. Gemma would enjoy this. 'You need to work on your core,' she used to say, and it felt like an attack on my soul.

'Let's just get our breath,' I say for the second time this evening and inhale for as long as I can. Then out, then in, and with one giant effort, I writhe until I make it all the way up. 'Ha!' A perfectly suitable core after all.

I roll onto my back. It's a beautiful, clear night. Nothing but space above me. Below me, quite a bit of space too, I realise. Would it have been wiser to go back down, not further up? Too late now.

I unscrew the bottle. 'First, wine,' I say to a particularly bright Jupiter, 'then the matter of being marooned.' The wine is warm and strong. I can't stop. I've fucked up on the climbing apparatus but aced the refreshments.

A car door closes on the other side of the bungalow. Someone lets themself in. Soon after, my phone buzzes. I place it beside me on the roof and let Jackie speak to my voicemail.

Her message is unsurprising. 'Robin, where are you? I've come in to your dad, sat TV off, breathing all hectic…'

I swig. 'Well, there you are,' I say to Jupiter. 'You've got me for another half an hour.' I have half a bottle of wine, a phone battery at seventy-five per cent and a sky full of stars. Fifty, seventy-five, one hundred. A pleasing sequence. Of course, the phone battery will drop any second and, really there is no telling what percentage of the feasibly visible stars are visible at any moment. No such thing as a full picture.

Mum rolled off the road. To save me.

An inquest. That's what I need. I won't get any more from Dad, but Bee can tell me what she knows. And there'll be papers somewhere, hospital letters, the death certificate. When Jackie's gone, I'll make it down somehow, put all the boxes on my bed and empty them out.

I watch messages from Jackie pile up on my screen.

—Robin, you're supposed to be here
—Call me back
—What the hell happened?
—I'm calling social services. He's not safe

'Jackie, don't call them. It's all good.' I keep my voice low and speak away from the kitchen below.

'Where are you? Your dad's in a state. He won't stop shaking.'

'With Danny's mum. She was on her own.' Then in a whisper, 'She's not coping.'

'What about your dad?' says Jackie. 'You can't just drop him and leave him.'

'I didn't drop him.' For a split second, I think she's been watching me with hidden cameras. 'It was an emergency,' I whisper. 'I thought Danny's mum might do something, you know. He was her only child.'

'And you're your dad's, God help him.'

'Anyway, you must be ready to get home,' I say. 'I'll be back really soon to take over. Will you tell Dad for me? Will you make sure the TV's on?'

'I'll stay until you're back.'

'No. Don't do that. I mean, he'll be fine. And you can't go staying on into your own time.'

'It's me on the bedtime call. I'll see you then. I'm not happy about this, Robin,' she says.

Something comes to me. 'I know. But I wanted to tell you, it's not for much longer,' I say. 'I'm looking for a home for him.' I don't mean it, and then I do. Why not a home? This certainly isn't working.

'A home?' she says.

'A home. Better for everyone.'

She has no answer to that.

When Jackie has driven away, I stand, use my phone torch to check for a good landing spot and unzip. The cold is undeniable. I aim.

Despite, or perhaps because of, the full bottle of wine, my jet lacks power. Still, it's something I've always wanted to do and the overall experience is exhilarating, and necessary.

I call Astrid.

'What is it?' she answers.

'I need help,' I say.

'Is it Bee? What happened?'

'I'm not with Bee. But I need help. I'm stuck,' I say.

'I'm going into the cinema with Timo.'

'It'll only take you a minute to help me.'

'Hang on.' She murmurs something in German to Timo, including the word 'popcorn'. 'What do you mean, "stuck"?' she says to me.

'Marooned. I'm on my roof and I can't get down.'

'Is this a breakdown?' she asks.

'What? No. Only in terms of equipment. I need you to come and put the chair on the table. Quite soon. It's very cold.'

'Surely that occurred to you when you went onto your roof.'

'I needed to get away,' I say.

'And now you're stuck.'

'Very clever, Professor. Just come and help me.'

'Our film starts in five minutes. Timo needs this.'

'But you can watch a later showing. And this will make Timo laugh. He needs that too.'

'The film's a comedy.'

'But is it as funny as me stuck on a roof?'

'I hope so.'

'Come on, Astrid. There's no one else I can ask. And I need to get back to Dad.'

'You were supposed to be with Bee,' she says.

'She sent me home. She didn't want me there.' The second part is true.

There's a pause. 'Astrid,' I say, 'I actually think that if I stay up here much longer, I'll lose a finger, toe or other extremity.'

'Fine. I'm coming. I'll leave Timo and he can watch the start without me.'

'Thank you! Thank you!'

I'm getting down. And Astrid cares about my extremities.

'That's the roof?' Astrid looks up and down. 'You're barely two metres off the ground. Can't you just jump?'

'A two-metre fall can be fatal,' I say. 'I Googled it.'

'A jump isn't a fall.'

'You're here now.' I direct her with my phone torch. 'Put that chair on the table and I'll ease myself onto it.'

'Stop waving the light in my face. Have you been drinking?'

'Nope.' I place the bottle on its side and roll it away. It clinks as it hits a tile.

'Right,' says Astrid. 'Anyway, here's your chair. I'm missing the film.'

'Hang on. You need to hold it steady.'

'Fine. Be quick.'

I manoeuvre my legs over the edge and find the chair with my feet. I step from the chair onto the table, sit, then ease myself onto solid ground – no point risking a jump now, however small.

'There you go,' says Astrid. 'And tomorrow, we can talk about this.'

'I had some shocking news,' I say.

'Yeah? We all did. Go and get warm.'

I wait for a hug but she turns and goes. 'Thanks,' I call after her. 'You saved me.'

'You're beyond saving.'

Before Jackie arrives for the bedtime call, I drink three pints of water, brush my teeth and walk to the little Tesco for mince pies. I also buy a Chocolate Orange and I'm waiting with it when she lets herself in.

'An apology for earlier,' I say. 'I shouldn't have left you on your own without warning.'

'You shouldn't,' she says and puts it in her handbag. 'We're at a phase where we always need two of us. It's guidelines.'

'I know. But it's too much even for two.' I gesture for her to follow me into the kitchen. 'You know the industry. Any of these you'd particularly recommend?' I pass her the photocopied sheet that Carol the social worker gave me months ago.

'So, you mean it? You're giving up?' says Jackie.

'I don't think I have a choice. I need to do what's safest for him. And in a home, he'd have more people around. And they have entertainment.'

'He'd hate that,' says Jackie.

'He'd have his TV in his room.'

She hands the list back. 'Won't work. He's too complex.'

'We tried this way and that didn't work either. I don't have any choice. I've been offered a job.'

Arms folded, Jackie looks through to Dad in the lounge. 'It's not what he'd want.'

'He's got what he wants his whole life. Now he can adapt, like the rest of us.'

'Us?' says Jackie and walks out.

Once Dad is tucked in, I take a steak knife and another bottle of wine to my bedroom. I lift the first box of paperwork onto the bed, plunge the knife into the brown tape and slit down the middle. The flaps pop open and a sick feeling fills my stomach.

Where is Danny now? Will there be a post-mortem? Can they scan his heart from the outside?

I drop the knife and text Astrid:

You never told me how the hospital was this morning.

I lie on the bed and drink from the bottle. I'll never get drunk with Danny again.

My message to Astrid remains unread. Maybe she's driving home. I text again:

What film did you see? Speak later.

Nothing back. I delete my message. She isn't driving. Like so many others before, she's had enough of me. And she's right: I killed my mother and now my best friend, and I'm beyond saving.

I write one last message to Astrid: *Good plan. Ignore me.*

I go back to the open box. No death certificate, no doctors' letters. A few school reports. More than one calls me 'reserved', they all say I'm 'able'. My science teacher wrote, 'I suspect he could achieve more than he currently does'. Many bills: gas, water, Dad's magazine subscriptions. And at the very bottom, the menu from the old Chinese place on the High Street.

OBJECT: *Lucky Break takeaway menu*
DATE: *2002*
NOTES: *'Eastgate needs a lucky break,' Dad said when it opened. It was a pet shop before that. It's a betting shop now. They didn't keep the name.*

Danny wrote all over the menu: letter Ds and Rs for when he'd call and order. Ds next to the sesame prawn toasts, the sweet and sour chicken and the banana fritters. Rs next to ribs and the egg-fried rice. Next to the prawn crackers, he wrote 'x2!!' and a smiley face with spiky hair. Always hungry, always excited.

The menu's kept the smell of then: grease, sugar, Danny.

Notes for Dad: *You'd give us money for Chinese if we went on our bikes to pick it up. You had sweet and sour prawns with chips.*

38.
Too many things

The wine and the exhaustion from life being undeniably shit put me to sleep. But because life is undeniably shit, I wake forty minutes later with the Chinese menu stuck to my cheek and a pain inside my head as if someone has trapped my eyeballs in a vice.

I shuffle to the bathroom in search of paracetamol and then to the kitchen for food. Danny's voice is in my head: *You get these pissed wankers wake up hungry in the night and they order microwave macaroni cheese from the corner shop.*

I open the Deliveroo app.

'Sorry for being a macaroni cheese wanker,' I say when I answer the door half an hour later.

'Yeah?' The man hands me a blue plastic bag.

I keep the two-pound coin I'd put ready as a tip.

While waiting for the microwave, I read about the car arsonist. He put a statement up just before he was arrested. Said they all deserved it, that they all had something in common but he wasn't going to 'spell it out'. I'm thinking about how Danny would have loved that, when my phone rings in my hand. I answer without meaning to.

'I wasn't ignoring you. I was asleep,' Astrid says.

'OK,' I say.

'Wasn't sure you'd be up.'

'About to eat. First chance I've had,' I reply. The microwave beeps. I use a tea towel to lift out the macaroni cheese.

'Can you come over?' says Astrid.

'My dinner's only just ready.' I struggle to pull back the film one-handed.

'After you've eaten then?'

'It's late,' I say.

'I dropped everything for you earlier. Saved you.'

I swallow. 'Thought I was beyond saving.'

'Ah, that's why you're sulking,' she says.

'I'm not sulking.'

'Prove it.'

'Fine. Let me eat first.' I scoop up too much and burn the roof of my mouth.

'Don't ring the bell. Text when you're outside.'

I scrape up every last drop of cheese sauce; the delivery charge alone was £9.95. I had to add two bottles of white wine to make the order worthwhile. I take the unopened bottle from the fridge, wedge it into what has become my wine pocket and step out the back door. Halfway down the road, I turn back.

'Emergency. I need to go out,' I tell Dad as I wake him. 'If you need me, red button, not the monitor.' He groans, and I leave feeling reassured that if I'm becoming an alcoholic, it's a highly functioning one.

I remember the command not to ring Astrid's doorbell as my finger comes away from the button. I'm texting to apologise when she opens the door with a scowl, accentuated by one of her huge scarves. Wearing them indoors is a new thing. This one is grey and is over something black that's too long to be a jumper and too short to be a dress. Her skinny jeans wrinkle at the knees.

'Finished?' she says.

I meet her eyes. 'Sorry. You look … warm.'

'I was. But now the door's open.'

I step inside and hand her the bottle of wine. 'Pre-chilled, like me.'

In the lounge, the TV news is playing without sound. In the kitchen the lights are on. 'Where do you want me?' I ask.

Astrid frowns. 'Nowhere. Not tonight.'

'I meant, where are we going? Kitchen, lounge, roof?'

Her face relaxes. 'Lounge. I'll get you a glass.'

Shoes and coat removed, I sit in the corner of her L-shaped sofa, unsure where to put my feet. Up is wrong for what I need to say. Not that I'm sure I'll say it. I was going to wait. But she's summoned me here now. I shuffle away from the corner.

Astrid appears, glass of wine in one hand and a mug of funny-smelling tea in the other. 'Clear head for Timo,' she says.

She hands me the wine and takes the corner spot, stretching out her legs.

'How was the hospital?' I ask, eyes on my glass, unsure when or whether to drink.

'I saw him, if that's what you're asking.'

'I … I wasn't … but good. I mean, if that's what you wanted.' I drink.

'Timo saw him too.' Astrid pauses. 'I read that's better, helps you to believe it happened.'

'They said that with my mum.' Suddenly, it strikes me how the adults in my life so desperately wanted me to grasp some things but never find out about others.

'Bee came in too,' says Astrid, sounding like she's discussing a museum exhibit.

'He looked peaceful when I saw him,' I say, my hand moving to my mouth.

'Yeah.' She's closing the topic.

'How's Timo?'

'Hmm,' she says. 'I have no idea. He won't answer my questions. He wolfed down pizza, said the film was funny. But he doesn't say anything else. It's like he's scared he'll hurt me.'

'Yeah,' I say, and I know that yet again I'm disappointing her. Where's all my wisdom, my first-hand knowledge? I should just tell her I remember barely anything from the first days after Mum. What's to say there is any truth in the few memories I have anyway?

'Something strange happened this afternoon,' I say.

'Besides climbing on your roof and kicking away the chair?' says Astrid.

'You make it sound like it was on purpose.'

'You climbed on your roof by accident?'

'Funny! Before that. Something Bee said about my mum.'

'Oh.' Her face suggests she knows what I'm going to say next.

'She told me something no one had ever bothered to tell me.'

'Oh?'

'You know with … with Danny's heart…' I pause, and Astrid gives me the tiniest of nods. 'Bee said it was the same, that my mum died from a heart problem. Her heart stopped. We didn't crash, not properly. We rolled off the road. Mum was ill. She knew. She just…'

Astrid slides across to me. She clasps my arm. 'It's OK,' she says.

'It's not though. My whole plan, the comet, my life, it's all from that, the crash I survived. And now I'm supposed to believe there was no crash.'

'But surely you remember it? You weren't that young.'

'I was twelve. I don't know what I remember. It was icy. We skidded. There were airbags. You know they go back down again? They … And a tree. It's still there.'

'And the car? The car must have been smashed up,' she says.

'The front was smashed in. You're right. And for a while Dad said the police had it, to check it. Then it was at the garage. And it must have come back because Dad drove it. I remember we had a row – I didn't want to get in.'

'Have you asked your dad?' she says.

'He can't even point to *yes* and *no* anymore. Wouldn't grunt an answer. He had all that time to tell me. All that time I told everyone it was a crash – that I was in a crash.'

'Who cares what you told everyone?' she says.

'I care. For twenty-five years, I've believed total bollocks.'

'Are you sure Bee didn't mix things up? She's had a massive shock. I mean, if your mum was that unwell, she wouldn't have driven, not with you in the car.'

My body stiffens.

'I'm sorry,' says Astrid. 'I wasn't judging. Just thinking out loud.'

'She was driving because Dad wouldn't. She hated driving, especially in the dark. He was supposed to pick me up, but this show was on, his stupid *Gladiators*. It was the semi-finals. I remember that. Mum told me when she picked me up. One of the last things she said. "Your dad's got his *Gladiators*."'

'Wow,' says Astrid.

'Yeah, wow. And now *Gladiators* are everywhere again.'

'I'm so sorry, Robin.' She reaches for my glass. 'More wine?'

As she comes back, with wine for me and a teapot to top up her mug, I say, 'You've never told me anything about your parents.'

'I haven't,' she says.

'So there's nothing to tell?'

'There isn't. They're both academics, so they like what I do. They don't like where I live, that I left and never came back. They rarely visit, but they've got my sister nearby and she's got them tied up looking after her kids. Timo and I try and see them once a year. They're near Berlin. He loves it, Cold War stories, you know, spy crap.'

'Nice.' I wonder what the two German academics made of Danny.

Astrid hops to another topic. 'How's your budget going?'

'Well, I just paid £16.95 to get a microwave macaroni cheese on Deliveroo.'

'Ouch. Next time try the supermarkets. They do half-hour express slots, much cheaper.'

'I couldn't do that to Danny,' I say.

It's Astrid's idea to go upstairs. 'Why don't you sleep here for a bit?' she says.

'Oblique,' I reply, but I'm too tired and drunk to ask questions.

In bed, she initiates things and I feel horrible and comforted all at once. It's over quickly and we fall asleep without speaking.

When I wake, Astrid is reading, sleep mask pushed up onto her forehead. I nudge her until she points her bedside light away from my eyes.

'Can't sleep,' she says, her gaze accusing.

'I was shattered,' I say.

'Find it impossible,' says Astrid.

I check my phone for missed Dad alerts. 'All quiet at the bungalow,' I say. 'Still, need to get back to him.'

'I should take something,' says Astrid.

I face away and linger on a memory of Mum. We were in London. She'd taken me to the Science Museum in the morning, Covent Garden in the afternoon. We stopped between the market stalls to watch a man and a woman in long dark cloaks sing something from an opera. Their faces were angry and their movements fevered. They sang over each other, different tunes and different words. I asked Mum why they were interrupting each other.

'Sometimes people have too many worries, too many things to say,' she replied.

'They should wait their turn,' I said, and Mum laughed.

When we got home, she told Bee, Dad, everyone, what I'd said, the way adults do.

'Maybe I'll never sleep again,' Astrid says now. 'I bet that can happen. After a shock.'

I wait my turn. 'I think you'll reset in a day or so.'

'I'm not a clock,' she says.

'What do I do now?' I say.

'You get up and go home before Timo sees you.'

I sit on the edge of the bed and dress. When I'm done, I say, 'I got a job offer. Sort of remote, sort of London.'

'Oh.'

'I'm looking at homes for Dad.'

Astrid turns on the big light. 'And now is the time to do this?'

'Coming here was an experiment,' I say.

'An experiment. And us?'

I twist to face her. 'Us? Well … I can't stop thinking that it was only when I got here that things got fucked up.'

'Jesus, Robin. Always flattering yourself with magical powers. It's fucked up but it's not you.'

'I know it's me.'

'Oh my God. You're deranged. You've jumped from one idiotic fantasy to another.'

'I killed him,' I say.

'You killed him? Not his heart?' She crosses her arms as if clutching her own heart.

'I knew something was wrong with him,' I say.

'What?'

'I knew. He collapsed before. I knew and I let him go.'

'No.' Astrid is crying. 'No,' she says again.

'Yes. And now I have to leave.'

'Go then. Get out.' She throws a pillow. It misses me. She throws a book and the corner catches the back of my head. 'Get out,' she shouts.

I pick up the pillow and place it on the bed. As I creep down the stairs, Max brushes against my leg in the dark.

Behind me, the landing creaks. 'Mama,' I hear Timo's voice say. 'Mama, you OK?'

39.
In trouble

At some point during the night, Astrid's anger must have given way to sanctimony because I wake up to a message:

You should get your heart checked. Your mum's condition was probably genetic.

I reply, *I understand you're cross. Danny told me not to tell you. Shit excuse, I know.*

She writes straight back. *Check your own heart. No point things getting more fucked up.*

I turn off my phone, and wash and get dressed before Jackie arrives.

Jackie is unusually cheerful and pretending I never mentioned care homes. I pretend too. I'm oddly good at it.

I pretend other things as well: that I didn't find out about Dad's lies, that I didn't tell Astrid I'm leaving, that I didn't see Danny lying dead in a hospital bed. It's as easy as filing away emails without reading them.

Jackie and I work well together. Dad is washed, dressed and breakfasted in record time. We leave him watching a bad morning show while we clean the kitchen.

Jackie washes up and I mop the floor. It's long overdue, and I'm quickly out of breath. My pretending wobbles. I set down my mop and place my hand over my straining heart, suddenly petrified by Astrid's prophecy of doom.

'You've left sods everywhere,' says Jackie.

'Give me a second.' I lean against the worktop and watch her testing the floor for slippiness. I catch my breath and ask her, 'What would you do if you knew you could die any day? You know, suddenly.'

'Is this about you or him?' she nods towards the lounge.

'It's about me. I've had some bad news.'

'And you're about to die?'

'You sound happy. Maybe. I'll need tests.'

'But it could be nothing?' she says.

'Unlikely. Anyway, what would you do?'

She drains her washing-up water, removes her rubber gloves and says, 'I'd get everything in order. My house, money, papers. What money I have. For you, that'll be a lot more to sort out.'

'You don't know that,' I say.

'Yes, I do.'

At any other point in my adult life, my affairs would have been ready for my sudden death. Every penny, asset and item I owned were on a spreadsheet and my solicitor would only have had to open it.

Now my finances are an embarrassment: a flat I've yet to put onto a falling market, pigeon-infested Scout huts I know the auctioneer won't take back, runaway spending on extra carers, and, thanks to Astrid, weeks of ill-documented abuse of the contingencies budget.

In the gap between Jackie's visits I resolve to repair what I can.

First, I email Daisy the estate agent and promise to come up to London after Christmas.

Then I email Nish and tell him his offer sounds enticing and that we should meet – again after Christmas.

Next, I trawl through the remaining boxes of paperwork. Again, no death certificate, no hospital letters, nothing on what was wrong with Mum and what may well be wrong with me. I take it all out to Dad's recycling bin, return to my room and order a watch that will track my heart rate.

My resolve continues into the next day, and I give myself until teatime to clear the charity shop bags from my car. I spread my donations between animal welfare, blindness and heart disease. The man at the heart-disease charity is the most thankful and I wish I'd given the whole lot to him and to the one cause that matters most.

The fourth day without Danny. I don't know how I've made it here.

I keep checking my phone for his silly messages. I look out of the window, expecting him to turn up on his bike. I imagine finding him in the Scout huts, lying under the disco ball.

Determined to keep moving, I drive to the big out-of-town Tesco and use the photo machines to print two sets of pictures from our Mingin' Falls trip. I buy a stack of luxury ready meals, various Christmas snacks, more wine, more toffees, new sheets and new clothes.

Back home, I place the first set of photos in my bottom drawer. Danny's smiling face joins the Lucky Break takeaway menu, Mum's theatre tickets, the cork from my first night with Astrid, my last payslip, the spare key to Dad's Mazda. Nothing good ever lasts and the bottom drawer is my arsenal of proof.

I take the second set of photos to Bee.

'Oh, Robin,' she says as she opens the door.

I hand over the flowers and box of fancy Christmas biscuits I bought for her. 'I went to the big Tesco,' I say.

I follow her in, take off my shoes and pause by the stairs. There's an Amazon parcel for Danny on the bottom step. Bee sees me looking at it.

'Came this morning,' she says. 'I don't know what I'm supposed to do.'

'I don't know either,' I say, and I really don't. I've been punched in the face by a little cardboard box. 'Maybe open it when you're ready,' I suggest.

Bee shrugs. 'Tea?' she asks, and carries on to the kitchen.

'Always. Thank you.' I take the pictures from my coat pocket. 'I brought you something else,' I say, and lay them on the table. Danny, the last of the day's light catching his face, grins up at us. 'I thought you'd like these. It was on our bikes ... our last day out. I love this one, that cheeky smile.'

Bee picks them up and shuffles through them. 'You made him so happy,' she says. She stops on the selfie of us sitting on a log, steam rising from Danny's cup. 'He was so happy you were back. He said he could do anything with you.'

I swallow. 'You'd made us coffee.'

Bee smiles. 'Can't beat a flask.'

I sip my tea in agreement. Where would we be without hot drinks to soften life's corners? 'How have you been? If it's not a stupid question,' I say.

'It's like he's gone away, but on holiday. Like he'll be back.' Her gaze goes to the front door then returns to me. 'Anyway, how have you been? You were so upset when you left the other day.'

'I'm sorry. I was so snappy, so rude. I didn't know about Mum.'

'It's OK.' She touches my hand.

'It's given me a lot to digest. And I wanted to tell you—'

She stops me. 'You're leaving. Astrid told me.'

'Oh.' The words I've prepared clog my mouth. 'It's just, everything's upside down. And with Dad, it's not working. He needs a home. I need a job. I've got this great offer. And I worry about leaving the flat in London empty. And if I sell the Scout huts, Timo can have the money, Danny's chunk. I just can't, on my own...'

She squeezes my hand again. 'I've been wondering if it was just too difficult for your dad.'

'What was?'

'To tell you ... It looks bad for him.'

'It was *her* heart,' I say.

'She wasn't supposed to drive,' Bee whispers.

'What?' I pull at the neck of my jumper.

Bee opens the window a crack and sits down again. 'They told her not to drive,' she says. 'At the hospital. I was there. Because of the fainting. They were going to do more tests, look for ways to treat it. But until then, she wasn't supposed to drive.'

I can't see straight. I squeeze my eyes shut, cover my face. I'm one side of a thick, filthy window, and on the other side is this new past where the adults fucked up and killed Mum.

'We were worried,' says Bee. 'Your dad mainly, but me too. We were worried she'd be in trouble.'

'How could she be in trouble when she was...'

'We just worried what people might say. It seemed better not to mention it.'

'Better for Dad,' I say, and go over to the window, open it wider. The cold air soothes me. 'You know I've never stopped wishing she was here. Every day.'

Bee comes over, touches my shoulder. 'I know.'

We stay there, staring into the garden. A son without his mother, a mother without her son. A sparrow lands on Danny's rope ladder.

'Astrid says I should get my own heart checked. That it could be genetic,' I say.

'Oh, but you did, presh. Remember? Your dad took you. They'd told your mum you needed checking, and I told him too. We had a big row about it at the funeral.' She shakes her head as she speaks. 'He wanted to put it off. Said he had too much to deal with. I wasn't having it. Anyway, he needn't have been so scared. Your heart was all healthy.'

'I don't … Ah.' That trip to the hospital. The same hospital they took Mum to. I imagined she would still be there, waiting for me. I missed the whole day of school because we went to the January sales afterwards. Dad bought me a Tamagotchi. It died.

'He told me that was because of the crash,' I say to Bee now. 'Extra checks.'

'I suppose it was.'

'So, you think I'm OK? I'm safe?' I say.

She nods, eyes closed.

'Oh God, Bee. I'm sorry. I'm so insensitive. Clueless.'

'Don't be silly,' she says. 'You should look after yourself. We all should. Why don't you go and get more checks, to be sure? I'd feel better then too.'

We drink more tea and Bee talks about the funeral directors and venues and food for what she calls the 'reception'. Will people want a full meal, warm drinks, cold?

'People won't want more than a sandwich,' I say. 'Drink's the key thing, no?'

'It's not a party,' says Bee.

'Sorry. You're right.'

'I just wonder: what would Danny want?' she says.

My mug is empty, I sip from it anyway. 'Drink and cake. He'd want drink and cake.' And not to be dead.

'It really doesn't help that it's Christmas. Everywhere's booked up.' She sighs. 'I actually have a bit of a favour to ask.'

'Oh,' I say, panicked. There's no way I can get the Scout huts wake-ready.

'Well, the venue thing, it's such a struggle,' she says.

I watch my reflection in the window.

'And Astrid hasn't got any time in the week,' Bee continues. 'So, I was thinking we could block out Saturday.' She pauses again and I give her a little nod. 'Well, then we could visit a few in one go.'

My shoulders loosen. 'Good idea.'

'It's just Timo would be on his own all day. And so, I wondered if you might do something with him.'

'Wow,' I say, recovering from the Scout-huts scare. 'Do you really think Astrid would want that? That he'd want that?'

'He said he wants to see the Scout huts. He wants to help you with them,' she says.

'But…'

'And you can tell him about the plans. Show him Danny's sketches. It'll be good for him, looking ahead.'

'But I'm not…'

'Just tell him the plans,' says Bee. 'You never know.'

OBJECT: *Oak tree*
DATE: *November 1998*
NOTES: *I went to check on our tree. It's an oak: broad, ancient and set back from the road. I knew it was an oak, but I'm learning it's best to check everything.*

I parked by The Anchor and picked my way through brambles and ice-rimmed puddles. I leaned against it and watched cars come around the bend. That corner's known for being deadly. Flowers marked the spot for weeks after Mum, until the landlord from The Anchor moved them. People said Dad went in and threw a pint glass at him.

No flowers now. Just dead leaves and acorns.

I ran my hand over the trunk, no dents, just ridges. I pushed with all my weight and the oak stood firm. Must have done for hundreds of years. Of all the trees to hit, an oak has to be the worst. They make boats out of oaks. Mum wouldn't drive at an oak. Unless she was unconscious. Shouldn't have been driving. But she was. Too timid to switch off Dad's Gladiators, too timid to ask Simon's parents to drop me home. Simon. I was only at his house because his mum thought we should be friends. Danny said they wanted me for my maths. Always protective.

The trunk's three times my width. I faced it and stepped back. I stooped down, like I was in the car. I looked sideways, like she was next to me. Nothing.

It was dark when it happened. Late. The pub was full. People came out. A man opened my door. Mum was hunched over the wheel, same shape Dad makes now. Don't touch her, the man said, wait for the ambulance. He put a coat around me, called me 'son'. I can remember that. And the ambulance. And Dad waiting for us at the hospital. But what's missing is the part only I could know: how we went from driving along the road to hitting the tree. Did she slump, like Danny on his bike? Did she try to speak? Was she gone before we crashed?

My memory won't play along. We were driving, we hit the oak. There's nothing in between.

Notes for Dad: *Mum wasn't allowed to drive.*

40.
Running

All morning, I think up yes-or-no questions. I run through ways to make him realise what he did. And I push away thoughts of his helplessness. He let her drive with me in the car. Danny was right: I owe him nothing.

Jackie leaves early. I place a chair in front of Dad and turn off his TV. The doorbell goes. I ignore it. It goes again. And again.

'Returning this!' Astrid points a toothbrush at my face like a sword.

I back away. 'I have seven more. But thanks.'

'Didn't want it on my sink. Couldn't throw it away unused.'

'I did use it.' I take the brush and shove it into my back pocket. 'Thanks though.' I need her to go away.

She peers past me. 'I still haven't met your dad.'

'He's not too good today.' I shift to fill the doorway. She cranes her neck like an emu.

'Let's…' I step onto the doormat in my socks and pull the door closed behind me. 'Did Bee tell you she asked me to look after Timo?'

'Yes.'

'Is that OK, given … my move.'

'In times of need, the Devil eats flies,' she says.

'German expression?'

Astrid nods. I suppose I'm a fly and she's the Devil. Sounds about right.

She looks at my feet. 'How about a walk? There are things to be said.'

'Not very inviting.'

'But necessary,' she says.

'Fine. Wait here.'

We make it as far as the bakery on Beachway talking only about inflation and oat milk. We buy coffees and take them to the beachfront, warming our hands around them, and staring out to sea.

'Is it some new sense of urgency? You know, the running away. Because all this has freaked you out,' says Astrid.

'Of course it's freaked me out. I feel so … so angry. Just rage. And I keep thinking, thirty-seven. He was just thirty-seven.'

'Thirty-seven,' Astrid echoes. 'But I was more talking about … I meant the crash that wasn't a crash.'

'It was a crash. We hit a large oak tree.' I gulp, and the coffee scorches my tongue. Astrid ordered it 'extra hot'.

She comes closer. 'OK, but I mean, is what's really bugging you the revelation that the universe doesn't actually have a plan for you?'

'Can we walk? My toes are falling off.'

The beach is colder. A fierce wind blows off the water. Astrid shouts over it. 'That's why you're running away, isn't it?'

The wind is making my eyes water and my ears throb. I speed up.

She jogs after me. 'Now your time's not so predictable. Your body not so invincible.' She pinches my arm and I drop my cup. The remains of my coffee seep into the sand.

'Shit!' I say.

Astrid holds out her cup. 'Have mine.'

'No.'

'So irritable,' she says.

'So irritating.'

'I'm trying to help you,' she says.

'No, you're not. You're enjoying that it's fallen to pieces. The thing you all laughed at.'

'That a comet gets to kill you and nothing else can?'

'See!' I swing my foot and clumps of sand fly in all directions. 'You love that I've lost control.' I kick again, a humiliated and petulant child. I shove the toe of my trainer deeper with every kick. Astrid tugs my arm. I shake her off and keep kicking.

'It's the comet that's lost control.' The wind picks up, and she shouts louder. '*You* have control back. You're free, but you're running scared.'

'You're just pissed off you don't get to watch. You've been waiting for this. I saw what you were ages ago – you're an anxiety tourist. A fun trip to my shitty world and then home to eat your kimchi.'

'Oh my God, more bullshit from your girlfriend's teen magazines. Yeah, I was expecting this,' she says. 'But so were you. *You* were waiting for this. *You* were waiting for *anything* to make you give it up. You've been forcing yourself to believe it and failing for years. God, Robin, someone tells you you're invincible and the best you can make out of it is to become an accountant and live with your dad? You were waiting for this.'

Her mouth's open. Is she finished? I wait a beat. 'Well, don't you just know everything about everyone? Just like Danny warned me.'

I turn to go but she's running at me, hands out, screaming one long sound. I land on my shoulder. Pain shoots up my neck. There's sand in my mouth and in my eyes. I rub them, and I see her circling away then back. I know what's coming, but I'm too slow. Her boot hits my shin. And again, harder. I curl up.

She stands over me. 'And you're even more toxic than he said you'd be.'

Back at the bungalow, Dad is dozing in front of a wildlife show. My chair is where I left it in front of him.

Astrid's attack has weakened me, but I have to do this now. Jackie is due in ten minutes.

I turn off the TV and touch his arm. 'Hey, Dad. I'm back.' His eyes open. 'Dad, we need to talk about what happened, about what happens next. I saw Bee again…' He looks frightened. Of course he's frightened. 'You already know, don't you?' He shrinks away from me. His mouth's agape, his eyes are wider. It's a look of despair. And shame. It's the shame of knowing what he did. It's a shame that's dogged him for twenty-five years. He let her drive. I take his hand, hold it tight. 'Oh God, Dad. It's OK. We all mess up. You could never have known.' One night in front of the TV. One moment of laziness. He sent her out for me and we lost her. 'You couldn't have known.' He groans. I switch from my chair to the sofa next to him. 'Come on, Dad. If she said she was OK to drive, how could you know? And we all bend the rules, we all ignore doctors. God, look at Danny.' He's crying. We both are. He tries to wipe his face with his good hand and misses. I dab at his cheeks with my sleeve. 'It's OK, Dad. Hey, how about this...' I take out my phone and open my notes. 'I've been putting this thing together for us. This woman on the helpline suggested it. Reminiscence. Remembering the nice stuff. There's nice stuff, Dad. Lots of it.' I dry my own eyes and read: 'Maradona's Hand of God, Prince Andrew ... Grandma's dog Dolly ... Well, I need to edit a bit, add a bit of context...' Dad's body jerks as he makes his laughing sound. 'There, you see. And there's how KitKats used to be bigger ... Mum's Christmas dinners ... and how there's no manual for us ... Yeah, well some of them aren't as cheerful. But you know what I mean, no manual for this...' I nod to the wheelchair and I hold up the incontinence pads left on the coffee table. Now he's spluttering with laughter. 'Exactly. But we do alright. And this one, how you said you jumped off the rocks by the dunes and I copied you and you never knew ... And I've been saving these news clips from the nineties for you, from when she was still here...'

His hand grasps at the air in front of him. I catch it. We hold on tight.

'Listen, Dad. All that – I'll come and read it to you properly in the home. It's time for a home. It'll be better there. Cleaner. More carers. And I'll come. I've got a new job. But I'll come. And we'll talk about Maradona and KitKats. And I'll smuggle in the wine.'

He splutters again and his hand loosens. 'It's all OK, Dad. You could never have known.'

41.
There is no absolution

Dad is dead. I'm certain of it. Jackie is banging on my door and shouting my name. My first thought is that I don't want to be in pyjamas for this. I shake myself awake. 'Hang on,' I shout towards the door.

Jackie walks in anyway. 'There's a child here for you.'

I pull the duvet higher and sit up. 'A child?'

'Says you're looking after him.'

'Oh shit. Sorry. I thought he wasn't coming. Can you tell him he wasn't supposed to come?'

'Your dad needs me. You tell him. I'll send him through,' says Jackie.

'Let me put something on.'

'You sleep naked?'

'No!' I pull the duvet higher still. 'Normal clothes. Let me put normal clothes on.'

'I'll tell him to sit on the settee and count to a hundred,' Jackie says, as if we're playing a mix of strip poker and hide-and-seek. 'Chip chop,' she adds and goes back to Dad.

Timo's knock is gentle.

'Come in,' I call, embarrassed at how much I sound like a weary doctor.

Timo does a weird little wave. 'Hi.' He's in a puffy coat, tight jeans and bright-red trainers. His legs look like two extra-long matchsticks.

'Hi.' I wave back from the edge of my bed. 'You're here.'

'Yeah. Mama and Granny Bee are out all day, and I'm supposed to stay with you,' he says.

'Is that what they told you?' I ask. 'Your mum … she changed plans, didn't she?' Surely even Astrid recognises our row was catastrophic. She assaulted me.

'I was supposed to go to my friend's, but Granny Bee said you'd take me to the Scout huts.'

'The Scout huts?' I search for yesterday's socks under my bed. Blood pools in the top of my skull. I straighten, take a deep breath. I'm in no state to care for a child. I cancelled last night's bedtime carer, shared two bottles of wine with Dad then stayed up until 2.00am researching and emailing care homes. How's that for a new sense of urgency? Around 4.00am I woke and remembered Dad's wine-soaked syringe was lying in the kitchen sink, waiting to be discovered by Jackie. Between the washing-up, my unremitting turmoil and the wine, I barely slept.

Now Timo is in my bedroom.

'Does your mum know you're here?' I ask.

'Umm.'

'Oh God, Timo, you've run away? To me?'

'She can track me,' he says.

'Like a parcel?'

Timo smiles a Danny smile. 'On my phone.'

'So she knows you're here?'

'If she checks.' Timo looks down.

'Oh God. She'll go mad. You're going to have to go home.' I pull on my socks. 'Give me two seconds and I'll drive you.'

'I can't. She'll be gone now. She left at the same time,' says Timo.

'And your friend's house? Where you're supposed to be?'

'I texted him and cancelled. His family are out all day. I wanted to see the huts. With you.'

'Right.' I stand. 'Right.' I sit back down. 'OK. You go and watch TV with my dad. I'll call your mum.'

'I have Timo.'

'I saw,' says Astrid.

'It's just … well, I was assuming our row would absolve me of duties.'

She sighs. 'For you, there is no absolution.'

'Funny. But I have plans. I can't have him. And you can't possibly want me to have him.'

'I don't,' she says. 'But it's what he wants, and if he doesn't get it, it's another thing taken away.'

'Oh.'

'He has money on his card. And don't put any more stupid stuff in his head.'

'I di—'

'Just don't. We'll be back by six.' It's her hanging-up voice.

'Astrid, just a sec,' I say. 'There's something I wanted to say about the funeral.'

'Oh God, you're not coming.'

'What? No. It's about Christmas trees.'

'Christmas trees?' she says.

'You shouldn't have any anywhere. The church, the food bit afterwards. Or Timo will always hate Christmas trees.'

'I suppose you're right.' This time she's gone.

On the other side of my bedroom door, a morning news reader announces that it's the coldest day of the year, making it sound like a long-overdue national achievement. I take off my jeans and pull on my tights. *Ladies' underwear*, says Danny's voice in my head. I reach under my T-shirt to roll on deodorant then find my thickest jumper.

In the lounge, Dad is surprisingly upright. 'So, you've met Timo?' I say. 'How's the head?' Dad stares at the TV.

'All sorted with your mum,' I say to Timo.

'Cool,' he mumbles, clearly sharing Dad's inability to communicate while the TV is on.

'Well, I need a coffee before we go,' I say. 'And then I've got big plans.'

Timo stares on at the TV, preoccupied with the prospect of snowfall in Scotland.

'What are we doing then?' Timo asks as we fasten our seatbelts.

'The big Tesco for a Christmas tree. Then lunch. Do you fancy lunch?'

'I usually have lunch,' he says, voice as playful as ever. He's nothing like Astrid described. She said he was 'silent', watching non-stop TV and refusing to go to bed.

'Guess we'll have lunch then,' I say.

We've been driving for a while when Timo says, 'Granny Bee said we were going to the Scout huts. To do some work on them.'

'You don't think it will be too difficult?'

'What work needs doing?' he asks.

None, I think, but I can't tell Timo that. 'Not work difficult. Being where … you know, where your dad was.'

'Ah.'

'Up to you. You can think about it,' I say. 'How about this? First, Tesco, and next to it, there's the nice burger place. Or early lunch then Tesco. And then, if there's time, the Scout huts.'

'Or takeaway burgers and eat at the Scout huts,' he says.

'Possibly.'

'Granny Bee said you've got the plans to show me. The ones Papa drew.'

I can almost hear Danny swearing to himself. The day we collected the keys to the Scout huts, he asked Timo to come with us but Timo said he was busy. And again, every time after that. I told Danny he'd show an interest eventually. It seemed like the right thing to say.

'Fair enough,' I say now. 'There's not much to see. And they're cold. Too cold and dirty to eat in. But yeah, we can go, later.'

I glance across, and see he's smiling at my awkwardness. He has Danny's good looks. There's an air of wisdom to him, too. A sense he understands things that others might wrestle with their whole lives.

'What?' he says.

'Sorry. Eyes on the road.'

'What is it? You're doing a face.'

'Just it's weird, isn't it, how people can merge and make another person.'

'Gross,' he says.

'No, I mean you're a cocktail, bits of your dad, bits of your mum.'

'Grosser,' he says.

I say nothing more. We join the dual carriageway and the tyres make a pleasing *ta-dum, ta-dum* sound on the evenly spaced bumps. Timo breathes onto his window and draws in the condensation.

'What sort of bits?' he says.

'Sorry?'

'What bits of my mum and dad?'

I look at him again. 'You definitely have your dad's cheekbones, especially when you smile, and, apparently, his urge to draw on everything. And then you have your mum's eyes, and the way they go wider when she's surprised, or disappointed. And you have her curiosity.'

He stares in the wing mirror, closing and opening his eyes and touching his cheekbones. 'Was your fight about comets again?' he says.

'Again? What? Oh. The physics homework wasn't a fight.'

'She said you believe crazy stuff.'

'That's unfair,' I say, struggling to multitask. I leave the dual carriageway without indicating and crawl up the ramp to the roundabout.

'I looked up more about Halley's Comet,' says Timo.

A van cuts in front of me, and I hit the brakes. We jolt forwards. 'Sorry,' I say to Timo.

He's oblivious to the Christmas traffic. 'And I saw this stuff about Matt Twain, born with the comet like you and then he died with it. You know he predicted it?'

'*Mark* Twain,' I say.

'And I told my dad about him and he said, "You've been talking to Robin" and I got…'

'Hang on,' I say. The car park is packed and a huge Land Rover is too close behind me. 'Hang on, Timo.'

'And I got Papa to tell me,' he persists – something he has from both parents.

'Hang on.'

'You know when you're going to die.'

'Argh.' I squeeze the steering wheel. 'You've got it all mixed up. It's not…' The Land Rover woman beeps. She points at a tiny space ahead of me.

'I think it's really cool,' Timo is saying. 'In with a comet, out with a comet.'

I hold up a hand: a *stop* to Timo, a *sorry* to the woman. 'Can you just let me park?'

'Sure,' he mumbles.

'Sorry. It's the maniac behind us.'

I drive on, leaving the impossible space for others to fight over. Finally, someone pulls out of an end space.

'Mama says Christmas makes British drivers even bigger bastards,' Timo says as I manoeuvre.

'Is that not a swear word?'

'She actually says "wankers". I toned it down for you.'

'I can handle bad language,' I say.

'Anyway, the comet—'

I hold up my hand again. 'Let's walk and talk. I'm starving.'

42.
Here first

A large neon arrow outside the burger place signals its American aspirations. Inside, the smell of baked beans and vinegar confirms how far it has fallen short. While we wait for someone to seat us, I keep the conversation firmly on fake Christmas trees and away from comets. I scroll through the Tesco website and consult Timo on pre-decorated versus plain.

Eventually, someone notices us and directs us to a counter to order. Timo takes charge, suggesting I choose a 'meal' for better value. I pay and the server gives me a device.

'Wait for the buzz,' he says, as if it's the house slogan.

We head for what Timo calls a 'booth'. My belly rubs against the table as I slide in.

'Can I show you something?' he asks, and takes out his phone. He's distracted by something on his screen. 'Message from Mama,' he says. 'She wants us to swap numbers in case we lose each other.'

'Seriously?'

He places his phone on the table between us.

I take out my own phone, ready to tap in his number. But he isn't showing me his phone number. He's showing me a list. I lean closer, it's periodic comets.

'This one,' he says, zooming in on the screen. 'It was here when I was born, back in August 2047. I get thirty-seven years.'

'But it's—'

'Same as Papa,' he cuts in.

'Yes, but it's all … Look at the next one down, that was almost around in time for you, it was close by. That one gives you, what…?' I pull the phone closer to me. 'Is it eighty-seven years?'

'You can't just fudge it to suit you. It's not horoscopes,' he says.

'It's exactly like horoscopes. It's astrology, not astronomy. It's just stories.'

'What about Matt Twain?'

'*Mark* Twain!' I pause. 'Sorry. He just liked stories. And with this one, he got lucky.'

'What about you? You believe it. But when I do, it's weird,' says Timo.

'No one said it's weird. And I don't believe it anymore. It was just when I was young, everyone kept saying it, and that made me believe it. And then something happened and I kept believing it.'

'Your mum dying? Your car crash?'

'Well…'

'Mama told me you survived a car crash. You were the same age I am.'

'I was twelve, actually,' I say.

'Twelve,' he repeats back. 'A third of my whole life.'

'Argh.'

A woman in the next booth twists round. I hold up my hands. Voice lowered, I say, 'You're not going to die at thirty-seven, Timo!'

'Papa did.'

'Oh for…' I begin, and the woman twists again. I glare back, and she turns away.

I lean closer to Timo, the table cutting into my empty stomach. 'This is madness,' I say. 'So you believe a comet sets your time here? Then what? You're going to have to make that time count. You can't waste a minute. So you plan it out: every day, every penny. And then, guess what, things mess up your plan, people mess up your plan, most of all, *you* mess up your plan, because you're lazy, you're greedy, you're feckless. And it's off course – your plan's so off course you might as well abandon it. But you promised yourself you wouldn't waste a minute. And so every morning you wake up and you hate yourself, and every night you say the next day will be better, but it's worse. And, just like that, you waste it all, *every single minute*. You waste your whole life falling short, all because a comet was in the sky when you were born. A comet!'

He snatches his phone from the table. 'You're worse than Mama.'

'Probably,' I say.

His eyes are fixed on his screen, his fingers fidgeting.

'Sorry, Timo. I didn't mean to scare you. But these things start for fun and before you know it, they mess you up. It's dangerous, like your mum said.'

'I was only joking anyway,' he says, barely loud enough to hear.

'OK then.'

The buzzer goes off and we jump. Timo grabs it. 'I'll go,' he says, and he's up.

I lean back on the bench, lay my hand over my heart and wait for it to slow. I watch Timo take a fistful of ketchup packets from the woman at the counter and thank her. He seems cheerful again. Hopefully, he has his mum's knack for brushing off confrontation. Still, it seems safer to move on from here. Our booth is tainted by my outburst, and the woman with the glare is still on the next table. I pull in my belly and slide out.

'That's all of it?' I ask as I reach the counter.

Timo looks at the ticket stapled to our small paper bag. 'Yep.'

'Great. How about we take it with us and you eat in the car while I run into the Tesco for the tree?'

'Sure.'

A waft of grease and meat escapes from the car as I open the boot to stow my medium artificial tree with baubles. Timo is eating with the windows up, oblivious to the smells and condensation building up around him.

'Left me anything?' I ask as I climb in.

'The chips were all in one thing so I couldn't work out which were yours,' he replies.

I peer into the bag. In the bottom are two lonely chips and a small parcel that hopefully still contains my burger. I suppose it's what I deserve for giving him a lecture on living in the moment.

'I put your drink there.' He nods to the cup holder.

'Oh, that's kind.' I take it and suck up half my lemonade. I wipe the inside of the windscreen with my sleeve. 'Seatbelt on? Lift off!' Grandad Jim used to do a countdown from ten.

Timo isn't listening. He slurps his milkshake and puts the last two chips in his mouth. Still chewing, he says, 'Guess we have lots of time left for the Scout huts now.'

'Guess we do.' Radio on, I take the longest route I can think of – enough for three toffees each.

'This all of it?' Timo asks as we arrive.

'What were you expecting? Disneyland-on-Sea? Eastgate's own Taj Mahal?' I line my wheels up with the car park's two remaining strips of concrete.

'I thought there'd be more buildings. And water.'

'The river's just behind that hedge.' I gesture across the field. It's covered in a thick frost and sparkles in the afternoon sun.

'Are those ours?' Timo points to the abandoned kayaks.

'Came with the huts. There's a ride-on mower too.' I reach back into the car for my burger, now cold.

Timo is still looking at the kayaks. 'Are they any good?'

'Not had a chance to try them.'

'We could take them out now.' He jogs towards the shed.

I swallow and go after him. 'On the coldest day of the year?'

'Just a quick paddle.' He runs his hand over one of the kayaks and pulls it out onto the grass.

'We don't know what we're doing.'

'I do. Been paddling since forever.'

I hold up my keys. 'Come on, let me show you the inside. There's a disco ball.'

'Whoo,' Timo says rudely.

It's astounding how much pigeons can defecate in a week. The stage is splattered black and grey, and on the main floor, new droppings are lined up with the beams.

'They've found a way back in,' I say. 'Your dad and I shooed them away. That stage was pristine last week. It's a bloody resurgence.'

'They were here first,' says Timo. I can't argue with that.

I step around the pigeons' latest work to reach the remains of the cushions Danny and I disembowelled. I open the stepladder and tap it to get Timo's attention. 'First job of the day.'

'Want me to climb up?' he asks.

'You hold the ladder. I'll jam those holes again.'

'You could let them live here.'

'They're unhygienic.'

'Oh my God. You *are* Mama,' he says.

I ignore it and grab a handful of stuffing. 'They'll multiply. If this is what a tiny flock can do, think what an actual shitshow it will be when their kids and grandkids join in.' Timo started it with the swearing.

'So only humans get to have families now?' he says, arms folded.

'Pigeons can have families. Just not here.' I shuffle the ladder around until it's steady. 'They don't need to be indoors. They're wild birds.'

'Because that's what you've decided.' He jumps off the stage with a thud and flops onto the sofa.

His lunch must have worn off. I'll let him calm down for a minute and then we'll use his need for more food as an excuse to leave.

'All done,' I say, when I've finished stuffing the third hole. I tidy the ladder back to the wings. 'You seem hungry.'

'How could I be hungry?'

I look at him, arms folded, head down. It strikes me there's a way to unblock this impasse and deradicalise him at the same time.

'Next job,' I say. 'Mopping the stage. Just got time before it gets dark.'

'What happens when it gets dark?' he asks.

'It's no longer light.'

He flicks the light switches on the wall behind him. 'Oh.'

'Yep. Disconnected. Everything is. Water too. So it's al fresco wee wees, I'm afraid.'

Timo looks disgusted. 'So, we can't mop the stage.'

'Ah … We could take a bucket to the river. There's a gap in the hedge where they used to take the kayaks out. I've been meaning to go and look.'

'Great.' Seemingly revived by the mention of the river, Timo's up. 'Bucket?'

'In here.' I tug on the door to the cupboard by the stage. As it unjams there's a familiar flap of wings. 'Damn you!' I shine my phone torch at the shelves. There's a deflated football, a vase and several large bottles of bleach. Droppings crunch under my feet as I step deeper into the cupboard. There must be more holes, more ways in. 'Oh shit.'

'What?' Timo is behind me. 'Oh my God.'

It's on a shelf at eye level. A nest. I move closer. Among fluff and yet more droppings lies a pale egg. A second egg is cracked open, and next to it cowers an emaciated pink creature covered in bright-yellow stubble. It lifts its head at the light of my torch, opens its long ugly beak and screams a tiny scream.

Timo pushes my arm aside. 'You're scaring it,' he whispers.

'Good.' I shine the light back on the chick.

'Shush. You can see it's terrified.'

'Its brain's too small to be terrified.' I run the torchlight along the shelf, and sure enough, in the deepest corner of the cupboard is a hole in the wall. I grab a bleach bottle. It's the perfect size. I shove it in like a stopper.

'What's wrong with you?' says Timo. 'They can't feed it now.'

'They won't need to.' As I reach for the nest he yanks back my arm. 'Ow!'

'You can't touch it. It's illegal. You can't touch a nest.' His hand tightens around my wrist.

'That's normal birds. Not pigeons.' I wriggle but can't get free.

'How can someone...' His grip loosens and his hand drops down. It's too dark to see but it sounds like he's crying.

'They can't stay here,' I say.

Timo sniffs. 'You're evil. I hate you. I hate this. Papa wouldn't let you. This is Papa's and you can't.'

I start to go after him but stop. I know I'll make things worse, and I know he needs this: to cry about everything cruel and wrong in the world, to rage about his dad being dead, to grieve for all the moments they'll never have. So what if he mixes it up with pigeon rights?

Next to me, the chick is in a frenzy. I shine the torch on its face. Its tiny wings look deformed. There's a lump in the middle of its beak. Its eyes are black and bulging. The hard fact is that people always judge a creature's right to survive on its looks. That's why we eat roast chickens and roast pigeons, but never roast parrots nor roast robins.

Phone between my teeth, I pull my coat sleeves over my hands and press them against either side of the nest. *Illegal*, Timo said. The chick squeaks louder. *Illegal*. It looks around, eyes frantic.

I lower the torch. 'OK. Let's think,' I say out loud. 'Realistically, I won't be selling until the new year.' The squeaks soften. 'All I'm asking is you get your elders to do their business outside. Do you think...' This is absurd. One minute I'm condemning a pigeon chick to death, the next I'm asking it for help. 'Because this...' I turn the torch beam to the stage, 'has to stop.' A soft squeak in reply.

I place an old newspaper on the floor and sit down. 'It's been an odd week. Everyone's been lying to me. I was assaulted. My heart could stop at any moment.' Through the doorway, my torch catches the disco ball. 'And I'm on my own now.' No more squeaks.

I turn off the torch and let my eyes adjust to the dark of the cupboard. In the main hall, an orange light is coming through the windows, taking the chill out of the air. I lift myself off the ground and go to look out. No sign of Timo. He's probably hunched over his phone in one of the sheds. He'll be freezing. 'I'll be right back,' I call over to the chick. 'It's going to be OK.'

'Timo. Timo. Where d'you go?' I shout in the car park.

No answer. Just gulls. Always gulls.

I make my way to the road. Two cars pass and then it's quiet.

'Timo, come on,' I shout. 'I'm sorry. You were right … Timo!'

I circle the larger building, calling out his name. I tell him that I get it, that pigeons have rights. I tell him this isn't funny, that he's scaring me.

I circle the smaller hut. I roar into the darkening sky. 'Timo! For fuck's sake. No one needs this.' I gulp at the icy air. No more gulls. Just the rumble of distant traffic. And another sound, one so constant I stopped hearing it: the faint splashing of the river.

I run to the kayak shed. The boat Timo pulled out is gone.

43.
Life is but

'Timo! Timo!' my throat burns. 'Timo! Timo!' I reach the gap in the hedge. 'Come back!'

Timo is a silhouette down river, heading for the sea. Beyond him, the sun is sinking into the horizon, perversely beautiful.

I shout, and the distance swallows my voice. I fumble for my phone. If I asked Astrid for Timo's number, what would I say? No time for that. The kayak is drifting further. Soon, the tide will catch it and carry Timo away. I have to reach him first. I run to the kayak shed, howling into the sky. 'Fuuuuck…'

I rummage for a paddle. A life jacket hangs off a nail. My hands are shaking too hard. I ball them into fists and thread myself into the jacket. It squeezes my chest and stinks of damp. I tug at the biggest kayak and it thuds onto the ground.

At the water's edge, I call out again, 'Timo, turn back!'

He's barely moved. Perhaps he's paddling back, fighting against the flow of the river. What do I know? Nothing. I know nothing about the river, about boats, about the place that's supposed to be home.

I shout a final plea: 'Timo. Come on. Stop now. Come back.'

I line up the kayak with the edge of the water. Parallel. That I remember. My legs shake and the boat wobbles, but I'm in. The river is gentle. Timo is up ahead.

'Just a paddle,' I say out loud. 'A sunset paddle.'

I force my arms into a rhythm and words come to me, Mum singing as she swirls my bath water. *Merrily, merrily, merrily, merrily; Life is but a dream.* I sing it. And again, louder. '*Merrily, merrily, merrily, merrily; Life is but a dream…*' – a shanty song, a manic prayer. The river is gentle. Timo is up ahead.

And there he remains, chased away by my murderous pigeon rage and taken by the sea. I paddle faster but the gap widens.

The wind drops and there's a shout. I stop paddling. Starlings screech overhead, the rumble of the open sea is getting closer. There's another shout. 'Help!' Timo, shouting, 'Help!' and then more words, but they're just sounds.

I paddle hard, feeling for the water in the fading light. 'I'm coming. It's OK. I'm coming.' I plunge the paddle in deeper and the water splashes up, icy cold. I mustn't go in, Timo can't go in, we mustn't go in. Don't gasp. I remember that too. Never gasp. Never thrash. Float.

My paddle does nothing. I'm not propelling the kayak, the

current is. Just as it caught Timo's boat, now it has me. I drop my arms and let the river's angry mouth spit me out. I'm at sea.

I hear Timo before I see him.

'Rocks,' he shouts. 'Back from the rocks.' A shape and a voice in the darkness. 'I'm holding out my paddle,' he says. 'Grab it.'

'No way!' I shout back. 'It'll pull you in.'

'Push yourself off with your paddle, push against the rocks.'

I slide my paddle through my hands. I'm losing my balance. The sea lifts me and drops me. I feel around for something to push against. The paddle scrapes on something hard. 'Here we go.' I shove and the paddle slips away from me. Into a gap in the rock. I tip and cold water soaks my legs. *Don't gasp.* I press my palm into the hard plastic of the boat and steady myself. I clasp the paddle and feel again for the rock. 'This time.' I push, a wave hits me from the side and my arms fly into the air. 'Shit.'

I reach into the water and grasp around.

'I've lost it,' I call to Timo. 'I've lost the paddle.' I scream, 'Timo!' No reply.

Then a shout. 'It's OK. I'm coming to you.'

'No! Stay back!' Another wave. My kayak shudders as it lands on a shallow rock. I lean from side to side to free myself. I plunge my hand into the water, searching for my paddle, for anything I can grip. The feeling's going in my fingers. I shout to Timo. 'Use your phone. Call for help. 999. Stay back from the rocks. Don't panic. You know what you're doing, Timo. Call for help.'

The waves are fiercer now. They attack me from the side. I find the scrap of rope by my seat and wrap my fingers around it. 'Timo? You still there? … You call them? … It's silly, but you know the song, "Row Your Boat"? I keep singing it. You know, *Merrily, merrily, merrily, merrily; Life is but—*'

OBJECT: *Obit.doc*
DATE: *December 2023*
NOTES: *Thinker, meticulous planner and stargazer, Robin Edmund Blake overcame early tragedy to excel first as an accountant and later as the originator of what may have been this generation's most vital work of non-fiction.*

The only child of lower middle-class parents, Blake was born in the spring of 1986 as Halley's Comet made a return to our skies. He grew up in the small seaside town of Eastgate, 'A place with all the magnetism of a jellied eel, and yet no one leaves,' he once said.

His father was chief engineer at the town's now derelict hosepipe factory, and his mother was a much-loved teaching assistant at its primary school.

A shy and studious child, he showed intellectual promise from an early age. His mental maths was such that he would entertain his fellow pupils in the playground by squaring any number they shouted out. Teachers, however, described him as falling short of his potential.

A central figure in his early childhood was his grandfather Jim Harcourt, a keen amateur astronomer, who first drew Blake's attention to the parallels between his own birth during the passage of Halley's Comet and that of American writer Mark Twain on an earlier appearance of the comet, in 1835. Twain had famously predicted his own death with the return of the comet in 1910. That prophetical feat made a great impression on the young Blake, who concluded his own death would coincide with the comet's next return in 2061. His belief was cemented at the age of twelve when he walked away physically unharmed from the car crash that killed his mother. The accident, on a journey when his mother should not have been driving, left Blake in the sole care of his benign but troubled father.

As a motherless teen, Blake found succour in his unique relationship with his neighbour Danny Thompson. The boys' childhood dream had been to publish their series of comics about a boy who could transform into a dolphin.

Blake mostly stayed out of trouble in his teenage years, with one notable, and unintended, lapse into petty theft. He also admitted to consuming drugs that had been concealed in muffins by an on-off girlfriend.

The comet continued to exert a strong influence as he entered adulthood. Possessed of a natural flair for strategising, Blake organised his future around a predicted death at the age of seventy-five.

After school, he left Eastgate to study maths at University College London and drifted apart from Thompson. London, he said, was the first place he could be 'unashamedly mathematical'. He settled there and pursued a lucrative but dull career in accountancy. He was resented by his peers but tipped for future leadership by his superiors. It wasn't to be.

His father's health had been deteriorating for years and, aged just thirty-seven, Blake returned to Eastgate as a full-time carer.

The move came at a huge financial cost but allowed Blake to rekindle his relationship with Thompson. The childhood friends developed plans for a much-needed outward-bound centre in Eastgate. It also gave Blake the opportunity to dedicate himself to his greatest work: a study on time and how to spend it. Convinced the comet granted him an advantage over others, who 'lived in fear of when death might come', he mapped out his available time and set about cataloguing optimum ways to fill it.

Ranging from the practical, with lists such as 'The Most Cost-Effective Breakfasts', to the more cerebral 'Greatest Questions Raised by Philosophy', his plan represented, he said, a revolutionary method for prioritising our finite time. Others called it 'not stupid'.

Blake's aspirations were cut short by a series of catastrophic events in the winter of 2023, beginning with Thompson's sudden death from an undiagnosed heart condition. Blake is said to have remarked that the loss of his only friend 'might finish me' and, in the days that followed, he was proved right. At the same time, his conviction that he would remain invincible until the comet's return in 2061 *evaporated amid revelations about the true circumstances around his mother's death. She had, it turned out, also died from heart disease, falling unconscious at the wheel. The crash that Blake had supposedly survived was little more than a 'bump', yet his father had perpetuated the lie of a car accident for more than two decades. But Blake remained magnanimous. Later asked if he'd been brainwashed into building his life around the comet, he reflected: 'The belief came from me. I clung to anything that corroborated it. I disregarded anything that challenged it. I thought it was power. In truth, it paralysed me.'*

Blake, who never married but was on the cusp of his most significant relationship, is survived by his father and his cousin Jamie, from whom he was estranged.

At his request, his epitaph will read: 'I was about to do all sorts, but never did.'

44.
The necessary end

I often wondered how my obituaries might read. I set aside time in 2060 to write my own take, scheduled to appear on 30th July 2061. The accident moved things forwards.

Astrid will claim it was her idea.

But all she said was, 'I wonder if he thought about what he was leaving behind?'

She was visiting with Bee. I wasn't supposed to hear, but I did. The obituary was my response. More lament than ode to my old life, it is, above all, a break with it. Now comes my new life. The life in which I take charge. The comet can do whatever it wants, within the laws of physics.

Taking charge begins with a cat.

'You've seen past all expectations this time,' Jackie says as Astrid helps me into the bungalow.

'Surpassed,' I whisper to Astrid. 'Glad to hear it,' I say to Jackie.

'You can't just land an animal on me,' she says.

'What kind of animal?' I'm picturing a rhino. The drive from the hospital drained me, but now I'm unexpectedly buoyed by seeing Jackie.

'That!' She points to my bedroom, where a black-and-white cat is curled into a near-perfect circle on my pillow.

'Oh.' I lean against Astrid. She's still holding me by the elbow, wise not to trust my shaky sense of balance. 'So you're here,' I say to Sal. 'I'm sorry.'

'Sorry to her?' says Jackie.

'Him, actually. Sal.'

'You have a cat?' asks Astrid.

'A woman dropped it,' Jackie says before I can answer. 'Said it was her neighbour's. That you'd left your address for when he passes on. The neighbour, not the cat.'

I settle into the sofa and reach to squeeze Dad's hand. 'Told you I'd solve the mouse problem, Dad.'

'What?' says Jackie.

'Joking,' I say, and feel Dad's hand move. He's smiling.

'You can't just take in a cat,' says Jackie.

'I can and I have,' I say. Then I whisper to Astrid, 'He belonged to my first ever minicab passenger. I picked him up from the hospital. Terminal cancer. I promised I'd take Sal. He liked that.' I twist as best I can towards my room. 'Sal! Come and say "hello". Sal. Sal!'

The cat stretches out one leg then the other, lifts his head and lays it back down.

'Isn't Sal a woman's name?' asks Astrid.

'Something we can bond over,' I say. 'But no. Short for Salvatore.'

'Isn't Salvatore a mob boss name?'

'He's retired.'

'I'd watch out, Ken,' says Astrid, and Dad splutters with laughter.

The moment they met, it was obvious Dad liked Astrid. She sat with him and Jackie when they visited me. Dad let her lift his good hand onto mine. Two invalids stuck together and somehow glad of it.

She knows how to speak to Dad, jokey but slow and clear, looking at him with the same mix of curiosity and kindness she has for everyone. I watched them on their way out of the ward, Astrid pushing the wheelchair as if she's always known how.

'You'll be in charge of the litter tray.' Jackie is behind us.

'Me?' I point to my bruised face, my damaged shoulder.

'He can go outside once he knows where to come back to,' says Astrid. 'Just takes them a while to realise where home is.'

Too tired for metaphors, I reach for the remote. 'Telly?'

We introduce Astrid to daytime TV shows – although the usual schedule is messed up by Christmas, just three days away. In the advert breaks, I tell Astrid and Dad about Sal's owner, Bill, and how he had bulk-ordered a year's worth of cat food. I also share my research into the car arsonist and the minor celebrities.

'Claimed every one of his victims had ignored his requests for signed photos. But it's not as weird as it sounds. He wanted them as prizes for charity auctions.'

'It's more weird,' says Astrid. 'Who would've bid for signed photos of nobodies?'

'Guess that's why they didn't send any. The humiliation.'

'Better than a burnt-out car,' she says, and Dad splutters.

'I don't think they were told that was the alternative,' I say.

At teatime, Bee arrives with Timo and two cakes.

I've only seen Timo once since the accident. If Astrid is to be believed, he insisted on coming to visit me in hospital. We mainly talked about school; Timo had maths homework due the next morning and I simplified equations with him.

'Can't have hit your head that hard,' Timo joked, the only reference to that night in Astrid's presence. But when she went off to the loo, he stared at my black eyes and said softly, 'Does it hurt?'

'So much I can't feel it anymore,' I replied, trying to smile.

'Sorry,' said Timo.

'I'm sorry,' I said. 'And the sea should be too. But you can't be sorry. You called for help. You stayed with me. They told me about it. You did everything right.'

The last part was an inaccurate thing to say to a child who'd taken an untested kayak into icy waters in the dark. But I had orders from Astrid. As I lay there recovering, she'd repeatedly thanked a God she doesn't believe in, and even more times she'd declared that Timo must not be allowed to grow up 'full of guilt'. I blinked in agreement.

'You're looking better and better,' Bee says now as she and Timo stand over me.

I ask Astrid to fetch more chairs from the kitchen.

'And you look well, Ken,' says Bee. It's not true. Dad has deteriorated over the last few weeks, he's thinner and more hunched, his chin always on his chest now. Still, Bee's kindness makes me well up – that's been happening a lot since the accident.

Turning back to me, she says, 'I have something for you. I opened that Amazon parcel.' She hands me a small packet from her handbag. 'He'd want you to have them.'

Men's thermal leggings. Two pairs. 'Yeah, I think he would,' I say.

I wonder how long Danny searched until he found the ones labelled 'specially constructed gusset'. I want to tell Bee I'll treasure them but I'm worried it will come out glib. 'They're perfect,' I say.

Astrid returns with two kitchen chairs.

'Hang on,' I say as Timo sits down. 'First, look through there. On my pillow.'

'Oh my God!' he says.

'That's Sal. He's just moved in.'

Timo goes straight to my bed. He's tickling Sal behind the ears, telling him he's a 'very handsome boy'.

I ease myself off the sofa.

'Look at you!' says Bee in the same voice Jackie uses whenever Dad makes an effort to reach for the toilet paper.

'Full recovery,' I say.

I stop in the doorway to my room. Sal is striking rather than handsome. His face is black and his whiskers are white, as if someone has drawn them on with chalk.

I sit next to Timo on the bed. 'He'll end up with a bald spot,' I say.

'He won't let me stop. Watch this.'

Timo ceases tickling. Sal stretches, stands and nudges Timo's hand, gently at first, then harder. Timo obliges with more tickling, and Sal settles back onto the pillow.

'You try.' Timo stands up for us to swap places.

'Like this?' I ask as Sal pushes his head against my fingertips.

Timo's eyes have wandered from Sal to my hunting horn on the wall.

'I'm not a hunter,' I say. 'I mean, I don't hunt animals. I just found that in the antiques shop. One of the first times I met your mum.'

'OK,' says Timo.

'Seemed it might be useful.'

'OK,' he says again.

'Not for hunting.'

Timo looks at the floor. 'I checked on it,' he says.

'You…?'

'The baby pigeon. Mama had your keys.'

It's my turn to look at the floor.

'It was still there,' says Timo.

'Bigger?'

'Yeah. And hairier, or featherier, you know.'

'Wow,' I say, as much surprised at my relief as I am at the pigeon's resilience.

'Papa and I saved a baby magpie once…' Timo pauses as if trying to remember the details. But instead of saying more, he drops his head and knots his fingers together.

'I'm so sorry, Timo. It's really rubbish, isn't it?' I slide my hand under Sal and tease him upwards. The cat stands and climbs onto my lap.

'Really rubbish,' Timo echoes.

I nudge Sal, and he steps across to Timo's lap and rubs against him.

'We'll get through the funeral next week,' I say. 'And then each day we'll get through that too. And we'll keep remembering him. Always. And I promise it will get less rubbish.'

Timo lifts his head. His voice hesitant, he says, 'Mama got Papa's phone back. She sent me his last video.'

'Oh.'

'No, it's not bad,' says Timo. 'It's good. Look.'

It takes a second to work out what we're looking at. Fuzzy blueish grey over a strip of beige. A beach. Timo turns up the sound. The camera zooms onto the water, and suddenly, with us again, is Danny's voice. 'Pretty sure they're over there,' he says. 'That splashing, the white. Or it's a big log in the waves. But let's say it's them. Because they're there somewhere.'

'Dolphins,' I say.

'Mama's not sure,' says Timo.

'I see them.'

Timo pauses the video, zooms in with his fingers. 'Me too.'

'Can we watch it again from the beginning?' I ask. 'And turn it up a bit?'

We listen to Danny as he draws out the word *pretty* in 'pre-tty sure'. There's the beginning of a chuckle as he admits it might be a log. He's so playful, so alive. And he's right, there are dolphins out there somewhere.

When everyone is gone and Jackie and a new carer have put Dad to bed, I go in to talk to him.

'Fresh pyjamas, lovely,' I say.

Jackie's changed Dad's sheets too, and on his bedside table, she's left tissues folded into triangles, water in a sippy cup and his red button. She's been staying over while I was gone, and now she's on standby if we need her in the night. 'She knows what she's doing, doesn't she, Dad?'

I wait, and he hisses a 'yes'.

I hold the rail along the bed. 'I lost it there for a bit, Dad. You know, Danny, Mum's heart, Jackie nagging me. We're all just doing what we think's best, aren't we? But a home was a stupid idea.'

Dad's hand shifts as if he's trying to pat the duvet. I put mine on top of it. I look into his eyes, a little brighter than usual. 'I'm going to talk to Jackie. See if she'll work just for us. And she can recommend another carer too, and they'll both work just for us. For you.'

Dad hisses again.

My solution is expensive, but for the time we have left it's the best one.

I lean over and kiss Dad's head. 'You get some sleep.'

I return to my room to find Sal kneading the memory-foam pillow.

'If I can't sleep, I'm taking that back,' I tell him. He stretches and kneads on. I go over to the wardrobe and take out the red-and-orange cushions I ordered a lifetime ago for Gemma. I place them next to the pillow and fall asleep to the sound of Sal's purring.

On Christmas Eve, I call Astrid and ask if she'd like to check on the Scout huts with me.

'You mean will I drive you?' she says.

'I could risk driving against doctors' orders,' I reply.

'Are you even up to leaving the house?'

'I feel more alive than ever.'

I do. The biggest benefit of my stay in hospital was the thorough examination of my heart – something I secured with careful answers to all questions about the blackout. Yes, now you ask, my breathing did feel strained. Yes, I'd felt pains in my chest. Yes, there was a family history.

'I've only got an hour,' Astrid says when she arrives to collect me.

'All I can afford,' I reply.

She shakes her head and calls through to Dad, 'Hi, Ken! Happy Christmas Eve.'

Dad makes a sound and moves his good hand.

'I put a mince pie in the blender for him,' I say. 'Improved it, didn't it, Dad?'

No sound for me.

'See you in a bit then, Dad.' I shuffle to Astrid's car, leaving tracks in the frost.

The padlock is stiffer than usual. When I finally wriggle it open, I turn around to see Astrid is gone.

I find her along the side of the hut, looking towards the river and the setting sun.

She nods to the kayak shed. 'You went after him. But you'd stopped with your stupid invincible thing.'

'Of course I went after him,' I say. 'But yes, I'm vincible now, if that's a word.'

She smiles. 'You always were. We all are.'

'But then again, here I am, plucked from the waves, a survivor – and not for the first time.'

'Oh God. You're going back to it,' she says.

'Well…' I lean against her.

She drops her head onto my shoulder. 'Robin?'

We're in the big hall, shining a torch on the disco ball, when Astrid drops the topic of Christmas side dishes and asks, 'Do you imagine how you might die?'

I lean back on the sofa. 'Me? Never think about death.'

'Funny. Or how you might *like* to die?'

'In bed, not alone, could be nice,' I reply.

'During sex?' I flinch, and she continues without letting me answer, 'The ultimate selfish lover. But if that's how you've planned it.'

'No, I just mean, not alone, while in bed. Lots of people die in bed. Mark Twain died in bed.'

'During sex?'

'The opposite. He was reading a history of the French Revolution.'

'Well, that explains it. That and your comet,' she says.

'*His* comet.'

She lays her hand on my thigh. 'You were still born with it.'

I lower my torch from the disco ball and all around us, white dots fall to the ground like snowflakes.

'People make it sound like he had an answer for everything, Mark Twain,' I say. 'I read his autobiography. Not really an autobiography, more thoughts and moans. Anyway, he doesn't have the answer. Not to the biggest question. He tells this story about his daughter Susy. She's seven and pre-occupied with the futility of life: we're born, we work, we grieve, we suffer, we die, and more people are born, and they work, they grieve, they suffer, they die. So Susy asks, "What is it all for?"'

'What is it all for?' Astrid repeats back.

'No idea. I've read the whole book twice and all his stories. What is it all for? Twain has no answer.'

'Would his answer be good enough for you?'

'I doubt it.' I prod Astrid's bag on her lap. 'Bee always sent Danny with a flask. You don't happen to have a flask, do you?'

She peers into her bag. 'Ah, let me check, would you like the tea flask, the coffee flask or the Christmas one-time only offer of *Glühwein*?'

'What's that?'

'Literally, wine that glows. Mulled wine, to you.' She pulls a pretend flask from her bag.

'You know Halley's last act before he died?' I ask her.

'Tell me.'

'He called for a glass of wine and drank it.'

'Good man!' Astrid raises her imaginary flask.

'Next time, bring a real one,' I say and elbow her.

'In case your last act is nigh?' She elbows me back.

We sit in the darkness saying nothing.

Then, she stretches and says, 'Your hour is up.'

'Fair enough.' I hold out a hand for her to help me up.

'Quick, quick,' she says. 'Gnomes to wrap, veg to chop, stockings to stuff.'

'Candy canes to pickle,' I say.

I force the padlock closed, and we stand with our backs against the door, eyes up to the stars.

'Don't get that in London,' says Astrid.

'They don't,' I reply.

Our hands touch and our fingers thread together. I tap my heel against the door. 'I'm keeping them,' I say.

'OK,' says Astrid.

'I can't stop thinking about the vending machines. And Danny. I might hate it. But I need to try. At least for a year.'

'You and your plans.' Her hand pulls away from me and she stamps on the spot, shaking off the cold. 'But I like this one. Let's reconvene next Christmas Eve.'

'Nothing in between?' I ask.

'Oh, Robin.' She reaches up and kisses me on the lips. 'Don't be stupid.'

As Astrid drives me home to the bungalow, I picture her a few moments from now: zigzagging around her kitchen, chopping knife in one hand, roll of Sellotape in the other, a pot of mulled wine on the hob, a pickling podcast playing from her phone. Timo perches on the worktop, doodling in last-minute Christmas cards, and eating slice after slice of reduced-to-clear festive cheesecake. And Bee's in the next room, folding napkins, polishing cutlery and setting the long table for Christmas dinner. There's a place for Dad and a place for me. Tomorrow at that table, I'll give Astrid and Timo my gift: tickets to Goa. A place for us to rule out together, after an all-inclusive stay.

That's what it's all for. Never mind the why and the how long, the how best and how not. It's enough to be here. To love. To be busy. To be curious and hungry. To really live, until the necessary end.

ACKNOWLEDGEMENTS

My thanks go to…

The brilliant team at Orenda Books: Karen Sullivan, West Camel, Cole Sullivan, Danielle Price, Max Okore, Mark Swan and Anne Cater. Thanks for your patience, encouragement and your boundless energy as you put special books out into a crowded world.

Naomi Hilton, for being on the end of the phone, and for being a little bit Astrid.

My sister-in-law, Dr Isobel Wilson, for kayaking details, for lessons in young people's punctuation and for being in our lives. (This full stop is necessary and means no harm.)

My brother, Nic Allen, for eternal kindness, for tolerating my website questions and for letting me look after Tag.

Laura Homer, for accountancy expertise, a lifetime of friendship and a shared obsession with solid chocolate KitKats.

Ville Niiranen, for author photos, cheerleading and cheese.

Everyone at Dulwich Books, for support, recommendations and the fastest ordering in the West.

Professor Sam Mohiddin, for so generously sharing his experience and knowledge of cardiology.

My friend Dr Samiramis Saba, for insights into emergency medicine as well as all-round inspiration.

Professor Steffen Petersen, for cardiology expertise, friendship and for sharing the sticky chilli beef.

All these people answered my questions carefully and thoroughly, and I turned them into Robin's view of things. So any medical inaccuracies are his fault alone – and maybe mine.

The same goes for my use of valuable insights into Halley's Comet from a wonderful book published in 1984 by Sir Patrick Moore and John Mason. If you want to read more about the comet, *The Return of Halley's Comet* (WW Norton & Co) is still available. The lines from William Shakespeare's *Julius Caesar* are taken from Act II, Scene 2. Robin reads the Penguin edition of Franz Kafka's *Metamorphosis and Other Stories*, translated and edited by Malcolm Pasley. He mentions the *Autobiography of Mark Twain* edited by Charles Neider and published by HarperCollins. When Astrid says, 'Happy is the One', she is citing Revelation 1:3 in the Bible (Good News translation).

Special thanks go to the writers and book bloggers who read *Everything Happens for a Reason* and spurred me on to write this book. I'm so grateful for all the online friends I've made in the book world – you make social media enriching and kinder.

There are so many friends I must thank for generally being brilliant and specifically telling me they were waiting to read this book: Sarah Beardsall, Alex Black, Nicole Calo, Megan Ceronsky, Isobel Chin, Jin Chin, Jane Cross, Samantha Curtis, Tamawa Desai, Karen Dowley, Natalie Ganteaume, Sara Green, Shakeh Harikian, Penny Haw, Elsa Humbert, Awais Khan, Clare Leithead, Ellie Marsh, Martin McVeigh, Pam Merifield, Dominic Minghella, Elise Ovanessoff, Payel Patel, Amy Petersen, Leila Robinson, Sue Robinson, Chris Scotland, Eve Smith, Bronwen Tully, Fiona Walsh, Emma White.

And last but never least, massive thanks to Alex, Ella, Ralf, Monkey and Miko. For me, you're what it's all for.